"Have You Forgotten Our Lessons in Lovemaking, Ma Petite?"

Her cheeks a deep scarlet, and her heart pounding with anger and excitement, Isabel, struggling violently, opened her mouth to scream. At that moment, he bent his head and his lips closed over hers. His arms turned to steel, drawing her so close that she could feel the pounding of his heart, as he kissed her over and over again. Caught by her own swiftly ardent response, she was hardly aware of the moment when she ceased fighting him and began to cling to him, answering his kisses with a mounting hunger. . . .

THE LADY ROYAL

Other SIGNET Historical Romances
You'll Enjoy

The
Lady Royal

by Molly Costain Haycraft

A SIGNET BOOK

NEW AMERICAN LIBRARY

TIMES MIRROR

*This, my first Plantagenet romance,
is dedicated, of course, to my father.*

Book I

The late August sun was hot. It had rained, intermittently, all afternoon, but now everything steamed in the humid sunshine. King Edward, as he listened to the scout's report, felt the sweat dripping inside his heavy armor. He sighed. England was never like this; in fact, Philippa and the younger children were probably a little too cool at Woodstock. The old castle had such thick walls. . . .

But it was no time to be dreaming of home. According to this man in the ill-fitting, shabby tunic of a French peasant, kneeling here at his feet, the enemy was less than a half mile away.

"They approach very slowly, Sire," he said. "Their horses look ready to founder and the foot soldiers are straggling all over the countryside."

"Good!" The King smiled at his marshals, standing beside him in the shelter of the royal pavilion, then turned back to the scout. "As we hear that King Philip's army is perhaps three times the size of ours, it is our great hope that their long day's march from Abbeville will even the odds. It's fortunate that we could await them at Crécy after a long night's sleep and a day's quiet preparation for battle."

He rose. "I suggest, sir, that you retire to the baggage square." Pointing to the large palisade erected to protect the great mass of supply wagons, he added a few words of warm thanks for the completion of a dangerous mission. "You have done more than your duty. And now, my lords," he led his marshals out to where their horses were standing, "let us spread the word that the French will soon be in sight."

A true Plantagenet and a brave warrior, even a glimpse of Edward III was enough to set his soldiers cheering. Mounted on a white palfrey, a white baton in his hand, he seemed everything a monarch should be; tall and wide-shouldered, his corn-colored hair and vivid blue eyes unfaded at thirty-four years of age, their royal leader was in the prime of his strength and majesty. Today, wearing brightly polished chain mail and rich surcoat, brilliantly quartered with England's lions and the lilies of France, Edward was Chivalry's true image.

As he rode away from his azure-and-gold silk pavilion he glanced back over his shoulder at the ancient windmill towering over it. The wide wings were motionless in the oppressive air. A dark cloud appeared in the sky.

"More rain!" he announced to his companions, and moved a little more swiftly toward the vast semicircle of green-clad archers, sitting at their ease on the grass. They rose to their feet as he neared them, but he waved them down again.

"Nay, lads," he shouted cheerfully, "rest while you may. The Frenchies are just down the road a piece and you will be busy enough before you know it. Are your stomachs comfortably filled?" When they patted them, laughing, he laughed back. "That's right! Then keep your bows dry." With his baton he indicated the clouds, massing ever more darkly, and looked down approvingly at the longbows in their heavy canvas cases placed carefully beside each archer. "Your task this day," he roared, "will be to prove to King Philip what I know so well—that one English archer equals three Frenchmen."

They were still cheering when he turned his palfrey and rode back to the batallions drawn up behind them. The Prince of Wales, his favorite black armor making him almost too conspicuous in the rows of mounted noblemen, raised his voice, too, when his father called out that the enemy was nearly upon them. His enthusiasm brought a pleased smile to the older Edward's face: a proud smile that remained while the King spoke to the Earls of Warwick and Northampton who, with the young Prince, commanded the first division, and was still visible as he conferred briefly with the Earl of Arundel, responsible, today, for the second line of battle.

Only when he reached his own post on the summit of the hill behind them did he admit to the envy in his heart. This was his firstborn son's maiden battle; his spurs were still to be won. And he, the King, must, for so many good reasons, bring up the rear with the reserves, a position he despised. What wouldn't he give to be sixteen again on this twenty-sixth day of August, in the Year of Our Lord 1346, and be allowed to fight at the head of England's army?

But there was little time for thought of any kind, envious or otherwise. The rain came in a sudden, drenching downpour. There was a shout of "Bowmen!" And Edward had his first glimpse of the drooping, wilting French army, marching slowly around the end of the thick forest.

"Bowmen?" Surprised, he turned to the marshal nearest him. "I thought Philip sneered at bows and bowmen."

A messenger, panting, threw himself at His Majesty's feet. "The advance guard are carrying crossbows, Sire," he said. "From their garb we think they must be Italian soldiers, not French."

Edward, well pleased, sent him back to the front ranks. "So our cousin is using crossbows against us. And Italian mercenaries, by God! I consider this splendid news, my lords. We will teach Philip a lesson or two."

But his last words were lost in a deafening clap of thunder. Before he could repeat them the sky directly over the approaching enemy turned black as night and he heard a curious cawing and flapping noise. As he and the English army watched fascinated, the advancing mercenaries cried out in terror and ran back toward the French knights who were riding close behind them. Some, in their panic, threw down their heavy crossbows and left them on the wet ground for their neighbors to fall over; a few of the more observant kicked them out of the way.

"Ravens!" cried King Edward. "No wonder they run. Birds of ill omen!"

The crows were gone a moment later, as quickly as they had come. The summer shower was over, too, and the hot, late afternoon sun glared full in the faces of the French army. Now the English trumpets sounded and the archers in their green jerkins leaped to their feet, pulling the longbows out of their canvas covers. The French, hearing the trumpets, waited for them to advance, making as they did so a futile effort to restore order in their front ranks.

But Edward's men remained where they were, their bows raised, their arrows in place.

Although reluctant to make the first move, the French nobles gave a great shout and urged the Italians forward. The English stood and waited. Another shout rang out, and an-

*other. The Genoese mercenaries stumbled along, their
clumsy, heavy crossbows clutched in weary arms; they had to
advance, they found, or be ridden down by the knights behind them.*

*Within arrow range at last, the harassed, frightened hire-
lings paused to wind up their awkward weapons. But the
rains had soaked their bowstrings, turning them slack and
useless, and while they tried to twist the complicated little
wheels the air around them was filled again—this time with
sharp, zinging, white-feathered things, a blizzard of death-
dealing snow.*

*The screams of the wounded and dying crossbowmen rose
to a sickening crescendo, but the deadly English arrows sped
thicker and faster than ever, piercing the Genoese breast-
plates as if they had been parchment, not steel. In a futile attempt to survive, those who were still on their feet cried out
in panic and tried to flee.*

*The sight of the wild melee was more than King Philip of
France could endure. His nostrils flaring, he rode out to the
great hedge of French cavalry that was blocking the path of
the frantic crossbowmen. He had planned this battle so carefully, he had hired these Italians to kill Edward's longbow-
men so that the battle could then be fought in the usual dig-
nified manner—a splendid tournament between his knights
and the knights of England. Instead, these mercenaries were
ruining everything!*

*"Kill the cowardly scoundrels!" he shouted, pointing a
shaking finger. "Kill them for me, gentlemen! Cowards, cowards, cowards!"*

*His knights were happy to obey. Unhampered by
squeamishness, the French sprang forward, cutting and slashing at the upstarts their king had hired to be their advance
guard. But while they were busy about this unexpected task,
English arrows began to slaughter them, bringing down ar-
mored men and squealing horses on the blood-soaked slope.*

*Suddenly, for the first time, Philip noticed the lilies of
France on Edward's banners. The hated symbol of England's
claim to the possession of France—a claim all too widely justified in fact if not in right! Aquitaine, Brittany, Gascony....
It drove the last vestige of discretion from his mind. Instead
of withdrawing to fight another day, or pausing to allow his
marshals an interval in which to bring order into their milling*

ranks, he pressed them forward, forward, forward. Sweep the English off the field, drive them out of France, kill, kill, kill. . . .

They did what they could, but in the dreadful hours that followed it was the French who died by the thousands, the English only by tens.

King Edward stood by the windmill, watching his archers speed their hail of death; watching, he realized, too, the French defeat themselves. He was smiling broadly when Sir Thomas Norwich appeared at his side and reined in his mount.

"It goes well, milord," remarked the King contentedly. "A great day for England."

"Aye, Sire," Norwich replied, "but all does not go well with His Highness. He needs your help, Your Majesty, and as swiftly as possible. A band of French have broken through our archers and are harrying him dangerously. I come to ask for some of your reserves."

"Is my son dead, sir?"

"Thank the good God, no!"

"Wounded?" The King's voice was steady.

"Not when I left his side. But he was in the midst of a perilously hot engagement."

"Then return to those who sent you, Sir Thomas, and tell them that the boy must have every opportunity to win his spurs. With God's help, the honor and glory of this day will be his alone."

When the light faded at last the moon rose, making it possible for the carnage to continue long into the night. The English ventured wherever they willed, their relentless swords and knives cutting, slashing, stabbing; blood spurted and dripped and flowed until the battleground was as slippery as an ice-covered pond; horses lost their footing and went down, spilling their riders. Nobles, knights and common soldiers alike fell, too, and although some scrambled up again to face the enemy, most of them were encumbered by heavy armor and as helpless as overturned turtles. They could only lie there, in the rank red muck, waiting for death.

"Mountjoye St. Denis! Mountjoye St. Denis!" King Philip's desperate shouts rang out over and over, to rally his bewil-

*dered and all-but-leaderless army. He called out one order
after another, orders that might, in other circumstances, have
drawn his disorganized men together. But there was no one
around to see that the orders were carried out; most of his
marshals were dead or seriously wounded. Under his very
eyes an English arrow sped toward him and pierced the
throat of his standard-bearer; the lilies of France fell out of
the dead hand to topple in the mud. A moment later a
French knight knelt swiftly and cut it away from the wood,
crumpled it into a great silken bundle, and carried it to
Philip's side.*

*Sir John Hainault rode over and took it in his arms. He
placed it on the saddle in front of him and, before the
French king realized what his intention was, jerked the reins
right out of Philip's fingers.*

*"Come, Sire," he said, paying not the slightest attention to
his royal friend's furious protest. "Come! We have lost this
battle . . . you will win the next."*

*As they sought and found the winding path through the
forest that was the only escape route left, a merciful curtain
of heavy fog dropped over the countryside, enabling all who
could still walk or ride to slip away after their monarch. A
sudden silence, broken only by the groans and moans of the
dead and dying, warned the English that the French had
stopped fighting and must be running away, but the envel-
oping darkness prevented pursuit.*

*With all the speed they could manage, King Edward's men
built great fires and found and lighted hundreds of torches,
but all they saw, in that eerie light, was a handful of loyal
French squires and knights, hunting among the fallen for
their masters, too miserable to care whether they were taken
captive or not.*

*A church bell, far across the valley, pealed once, twice. The
battle of Crécy was over.*

*King Edward, after sending out an order that violence and
looting were strictly forbidden, rode through the fog in
search of his son. Young Edward had been wounded some
time earlier, but not seriously enough to prevent him from
returning into the thick of the fighting. This the King knew
and, for the first time, he allowed himself to feel like a father. All kinds of doubts and fears swept over him, bringing
a clammy sweat with them. Had he been a fool to obey the*

*laws of Chivalry and risk losing his son and heir? Would
Philippa understand why he had refused to send aid to their
Edward? What would she say to him if he carried home a
dead hero when he might have walked toward her beside a
living prince?*

Close to him in the gray mist loomed a tall, ragged, muddy
figure. The King called him to his side.

"Lead me to the Prince of Wales," he ordered, his eyes
blindly flickering over the torn remnants of a crimson-and-
gold surcoat.

"Dear Sir," laughed a familiar voice, "the Prince of Wales
is here, or what is left of him. And a very black prince, I am!
C'est moi, mon père, c'est moi!"

The day that dawned a few hours later was a Sunday, and
while most of the victors rested and prayed, a carefully chosen few were sent back onto the gory battlefield to perform
war's most macabre task—counting and identifying the dead.
It was late when they reported back to the King's silken pavilion, but their mission was only partly completed.

King Edward, with the Prince of Wales beside him, un-
rolled the long, long parchment, the two golden heads bending over the incredible list: one king, ten princes, sixteen
hundred barons, four thousand squires, at least twenty thousand common soldiers. . . .

"I find this hard to believe," Edward sighed. "I must see
some of the dead with my own eyes. Come with me, my
son."

He turned, now, to the Lord d'Albret, a faithful and trusted Gascon noble who had been one of the leaders of the
grim expedition. "Take us onto the field, my friend," the
King said, "and show me . . ." his finger pointed here and
there on the parchment.

The Duc d'Alençon; the Earl of Blois—King Philip's
nephew; Lorraine, his brother-in-law; a hasty glance at their
stiffened bodies was enough. Then. . . .

"The Count of Flanders, Sire," D'Albret lifted aside a satin
banner covering the face of another corpse.

"Ah!" Edward's ejaculation was a groan. "I had so hoped,
my lord, that you were mistaken. I see you were not. And I
had thought him England's friend!" He spoke now to his tall

son, walking just behind him. "Louis of Flanders, Ned, who has been dealing with me to wed his oldest son to our Isabel. His treachery is a sad blow in more ways than one."

He fell silent, but it was apparent that he was shaken, and when their guide indicated a heap of noblemen, all fallen together, and said that one of them was the blind King of Bohemia, he crossed himself and fell to his knees.

When his prayer was finished, he rose.

"Old and blind," he looked down, the tears filling his eyes. "What in God's holy name was he doing in the midst of battle?"

D'Albret showed the King a leather strap that tied his harness to that of two dead knights with him. "One of our prisoners told us that he asked to be led into the fighting, lashed between two of his men. As you see, your Majesty, all three fell together."

Edward crossed himself again and turned away. "Thank you, my lord. And now no more, no more!"

"Well, my son," the King sipped his wine and looked over at the Prince. "What of war now? Is it the game you expected?"

The sixteen-year-old boy shook his head. He had heard so many tales of battles, seiges, forays, all won or lost according to the laws of Chivalry and by noblemen, mostly, and their knights. He had won his own spurs in the great victory here at Crécy but he understood that neither he nor his father nor the other noblemen had won the day. The green-clad archers, yeomen all, had routed the huge French army. Their arrows had done the trick, not the long lances or sharp-edged swords. What, he asked himself, what of Chivalry now?

Chapter 1

Standing high on a wooded knoll, its castellated towers pierced by unusually tall windows, Woodstock Castle was, in September, a chill and drafty royal retreat. And while King Edward, sweating under the French sun, was thinking wistfully of the thick stone walls that made fires there necessary all year round, Queen Philippa, her two oldest daughters, Isabel and Joanna, and the rest of the ladies, listened to the late summer rain beating on the windows and were grateful for their fur-trimmed surcoats.

"My lord complains of the heat," remarked the Queen, looking up from Edward's most recent letter, her blue-black eyes squinting a little as she worked to decipher his scrawl. Having already presented her husband with ten children, eight of them still living, it was not surprising that the Flemish-born queen was growing a bit plump and that her thick braids of black hair, confined today in a sparkling, jeweled net, had lost some of their luster. But the royal marriage had been one of affection even from the beginning, and if Philippa's bloom was fading King Edward had only to look at Isabel, the Princess Royal, to remember how beautiful his wife had been in her youth.

A replica of her mother, the dark-eyed, dark-haired princess was the only one of the large royal family who was not an obvious Plantagenet. Where Joanna and her brothers and little sisters were—or would be, someday—tall, rangy, and handsome, their noses aquiline, their cheekbones high, their blue eyes deepset and their hair the ripe gold of the French flower for which the family was named, Isabel, at nearly fifteen, was small and daintily formed, her nose prettily snubbed, and her unusually white skin satin-smooth.

She moved, now, to her mother's side and peered over her shoulder. "Surely," she said, "this long screed is not solely concerned with the weather! There must be some details in it

17

of our victory at Crécy or word of the army's new campaign.
And what about our brother? Did he win his spurs? Here
. . ." she reached out an impatient hand. "Shall I read it to
you, *ma mère?*"

Philippa gave her a longsuffering glance and held the parchment away from her eager fingers. "No, Isabel, you will
not! And, if you have the slightest desire to please me, you
will try to curb your curiosity and your tongue. Pray return
to your needlework and allow me to finish His Grace's letter
in peace!"

Murmuring an apology not a word of which she meant,
the Princess Royal stepped back to her stool, picked up her
embroidery again, and fell into a whispered conversation with
plain, horse-faced Bess de Burgh, the orphaned Irish heiress
destined to wed young Prince Lionel, and with Joanna, who
was busy trimming one of her wedding robes with gold
thread and pearls. Isabel had helped her sister sketch the daring design of wild stags and wide-winged marsh birds that
would encircle the azure silk skirt, but only the little bride-
to-be was skillful enough with her needle to do the actual
embroidery.

After what seemed to the three girls an interminable time,
the Queen smiled over at them and began to share the contents of her letter. Crécy had indeed been an almost unbelievable victory, a crushing blow to the French forces, and
King Edward was moving on to lay seige to Calais. Prince
Edward, and she read this bit aloud, had "acquitted himself
most loyally. He won his spurs with a bravery that proved
him worthy of being a Sovereign."

"My lord lists many of the French nobles slain at Crécy,"
she added. "One of them was . . . well, never mind that."

Isabel and Joanna, agreeing afterward that their mother at
this particular moment had concealed something interesting
from them, conjectured idly as to what it might have been.
Had someone on the list of those slain been concerned in
some way with Joanna's betrothal to Prince Pedro of Castile?
No, this seemed unlikely to both of them.

Their cousin Joan, the daughter of King Edward's young
brother Edmund and a ward of Queen Philippa now that her
father was dead, joined them while they were still discussing
the matter. "It was probably some scandalous story she was
keeping from your young ears," she said. "But tell me more

of the battle. Did Sir Thomas Holland perform any great feats of valor?"

Exchanging a glance of disapproval with her sister, Isabel said she had heard nothing of him. "And I'm surprised that you ask me about Tom," she went on. "I thought it was your betrothed that you were favoring these days. Or have you changed your mind again, Joan, and decided that you'd rather be Lady Holland than the Countess of Salisbury?"

Having surprised her gilt-headed, early-blooming cousin in embarrassingly intimate embraces with Tom Holland some months ago and then, after Tom's departure for France, in the same position with Will de Montacute, the young Earl of Salisbury to whom she was formally betrothed, Isabel was at a loss as to which of these gallants Joan really favored. *If* she knew herself!

Joan shrugged and gave a small, self-conscious laugh. "When you have two such ardent suitors," she said, "which, of course, you would know nothing about, Isabel, having none," and now there was a sneer in her voice, "it becomes a pleasure to be undecided."

Isabel bit back a sharp retort. It was all too easy to quarrel with Joan and these little interchanges led them nowhere. Still, it *was* aggravating to have her boasting about something of which she should really be ashamed. . . .

But when the royal maidens descended the stairs from their solar to the Great Hall and took their places at the high table they soon had reason to forget King Edward's letter and everything else they had discussed that afternoon. Supper was only half-finished when a lackey ran up to Queen Philippa and fell to his knees on the stone floor in front of her.

"My Lord Percy of Alnwick desires speech with you, Your Grace, on business of the utmost urgency."

As it was no secret that Harry Percy was a Warden of the trouble-ridden Scottish Marches, a hum of excited voices rose over the heavily laden tables. A moment later the Baron of Alnwick strode down the Hall, his red head bare and his disordered, dusty garments telling their own story of a long swift ride. The musicians in the gallery, at a signal from the chamberlain, played more softly.

"Do you bring me worrisome news, my lord?" Queen Philippa, her dark blue eyes anxious, greeted the great border lord and seated him by her side. "But I forget myself. Let me see you drink and eat before I press you with questions. . . ."

"Having been in the saddle these last ten hours, Your Grace, I must confess that I am, indeed, both hungry and thirsty. But there is no reason why I may not tell you why I am here while I down a glass of wine and taste some of that good red beef." He paused, before beginning his story, only long enough to indicate his preference among the dozens of serving dishes.

"You ask me if I bring worrisome news? Well, only the future will really answer that question. News I certainly do bring you . . . The Scots are on the march again and have crossed our borders. King David himself leads them this time, and they are making forays into Cumberland, burning and destroying our towns and villages at will. But we are gathering our own forces near Durham and I am here tonight to warn you that we may, within the next few weeks, meet the Scots on the field of battle."

Queen Philippa tried to keep her face impassive, as a queen must at such a time, but it was obvious that she was stirred.

"I shall always be grateful to you, my friend," she said, "for coming to me so promptly and for not sparing yourself on the way. In my lord's absence I think you and the other leaders will agree that I should set out immediately for the North, to cheer and encourage our soldiers there."

To Isabel's surprise and delight she found that she had no need for the arguments she was rehearsing to herself. The Queen announced that she would take Isabel, Joanna and their cousin Joan of Kent with her and send the younger children, William, Lionel, John, Edmund, Mary and baby Margaret back to the Tower of London to await her there. As a result, old Woodstock was, within a matter of hours, churning in a mad bustle of confusion as the servants loaded up one wagon train for the South and another for the North.

Their royal mistress, who had accompanied the King on several journeys abroad and had, in fact, presented him with Prince Lionel at Antwerp and Prince John at Ghent, thought nothing of traveling from Woodstock to Durham. She even had great hopes, she told her daughters and Joan as they halted for their first day's nooning, of fitting in a visit, before they started south again, to the weavers' colony she had established some fifteen years earlier at Norwich.

Having discovered, soon after she came to England as a bride, that her new country was importing almost all its cloth from either Flanders or France, she had persuaded King Edward to send for a band of the fine Flemish weavers to teach the English this very important skill.

"We settled them in Norwich," she said, "and it soon grew into a flourishing colony. I'm very proud of it and I would like to see it again."

"Norwich," said Isabel thoughtfully, "is in Norfolk. Will you take us to Castle Rising, then, to see our lady grandmother?" This she knew was a provocative question; for some reason, neither the King nor Queen was willing to talk about Isabel, the Queen Mother, for whom the Princess Royal was named. No one except the King had seen her in many years and her grandchildren often speculated idly about her among themselves, wondering why she lived so far away. Perhaps, thought Isabel now, her question would bring her some enlightenment.

"No," replied Queen Philippa shortly. "There would not be time for that, I'm sure." And the swiftness with which she changed the subject left her daughters wondering, again, about the French princess who had been England's queen and was their own father's mother.

But steady September rains slowed their progress and when they reached their destination, a snug little castle a few miles outside Durham, the Queen's complete attention was centered on the great massing of her troops nearby and the imminent possibility of a large battle. Fortunately, even though they were accustomed to such weather, the same drenching downpours had damped the Scots, miring their supply wagons in the bad roads.

As a result, the royal lady and her entourage arrived on the scene first, and it was not until a spell of clear, cool, sunny weather settled in that Queen Philippa was informed that the Scots had encamped on Lord Neville's land, about three miles distant, and that King David had challenged the English forces to meet him in battle on the following morning.

Soon after dawn she rose, donned her most beautiful crimson-velvet and gold-tissue underdress and surcoat lavishly banded with ermine, placed a gemmed coronal on her dark braids, and rode over to the English camp. Now it was England's queen who sat on a white palfrey and urged her men-at-arms and archers to do their duty and defend the honor of their king.

"For the love of God," she exhorted them, very much as Edward had at Crécy, "fight manfully! I recommend you to that same God and to St. George."

It had been thought best for the princesses to remain at the castle although they, too, had left their beds very early. When Philippa returned they plied her with questions about the camp and the men there, and learning that the battle would begin at nine by the clock, they prayed together for the success of their army and then took their needlework to the cheerful little solar, where they did their best to pass the time in casual talk.

Having persuaded themselves that it would undoubtedly be nightfall before the fighting ceased, it was a great surprise when a messenger rushed in shortly after midday with the news that the battle was over, the Scots in full retreat, and that England had won the victory they had prayed for that morning. More than fifteen thousand of the enemy army were slain and many noblemen taken prisoner; King David Bruce himself, the messenger reported, was wounded and a captive.

Again Queen Philippa mounted her palfrey and rode toward the battlefield, this time taking the princesses with her. As they neared it, Lord Percy and the Bishop of Durham came out to meet them, their faces telling the story of the morning's success. After a few moments of happy talk and congratulations, the Queen asked for their royal prisoner.

"Bring him to me, my lords," she said.

A little discomfited, Percy admitted that he had had nothing to do with King David's capture. "A knight from Northumberland, one John Copeland, was the fortunate man," he told her, "and he and eight of his soldiers have taken him, or so I hear, to Ogle Castle, some fifteen miles distant."

Looking astonished, Philippa said angrily that such a thing should never have been allowed. "Send word to this Copeland," she added, "that he must surrender King David to me *at once!*" And, wheeling her mount around, she beckoned imperiously to her daughters and to the others who had followed her to Neville's Cross, and led the way back to the castle.

Nothing more was said of the matter, but when a note arrived from John Copeland the next morning, explaining that his royal prisoner was wounded and needed care and that he, Copeland, would not give him up to anyone but King Edward himself, the two princesses saw the Queen's temper flare. A placid woman as a rule, her days free of the vicious crosscurrents that more often than not plague a queen, she rarely frowned or raised her voice. But Copeland's insolent message struck at the roots of her royal authority, and before she retired that night an indignant letter was on its way to her husband at Calais.

While their mother waited for King Edward's answer, Isabel, Joanna, their cousin Joan, and Alexia de la Mote, a gentle, red-headed girl whom they liked best of their ladies-in-waiting, made the most of this unusually free life. Accustomed as they all were to the formalities of the royal court and to the vast ugly apartments at the Tower of London, Windsor, and Woodstock, they found themselves reveling in the intimacy afforded them in this secluded, small castle. As there was still fear that wandering bands of Scots might be seeking plunder and revenge, they were not, of course, allowed to venture out of its own pleasure grounds but this did not prevent them from enjoying every hour of every pleasant day.

Queen Philippa herself, realizing perhaps that Joanna would soon be wed and lost to her, and that Isabel, too, might leave the nest before long, entered into many of their games and adventures. They had, in fact, just lured her up the steep flight of winding stairs that led to the battlements on top of the tallest tower, and were all admiring the sweep of countryside spread out below with hills to the north, miles of purple heather-covered moors to the east, and rolling blue sea to the west, when a page panted up the steps after them and announced a courier from Calais.

The courier was close behind the tow-haired lad, and the Queen, seeing the parchment in his hand, was immediately all smiles.

"Thank you, sir." She took it eagerly and dismissed him. "But come to me later in the dining hall, if you will. I'm sure you have much to tell us."

This time Isabel had no reason to deplore her mother's slowness either in reading Edward's epistle or in sharing its contents with her daughters. She ripped it open, scattering bits of red wax on the battlement floor, her eyes brightening as she scanned it swiftly.

"Ah!" She looked up and nodded to the maids gathered around her. "So. His Grace has sent for John Copeland and will settle with him himself. Good! Good!"

A moment later she raised her head again, and now her expression was mixed—delight was somehow mingled with an amused exasperation, and she indulged herself in what her daughters, behind her back, called "Our mother's tut-tuttery!"

They exchanged patient glances and waited for her to continue. When she did so they found themselves the prey of even more varied emotions than they had seen cross her face.

"My lord wants me to return to London as speedily as possible," she told them, "and set out for Calais with the first favorable wind. And," now she smiled at Isabel, "you, my dear child, are to accompany me. He does not tell me how we are to ready ourselves so quickly, of course! You, and as many of our ladies as we see fit to bring with us. The siege, he writes, may take many months and we are to be prepared for a long, long stay."

Isabel, who was standing near her cousin Joan, saw an odd, calculating look spread over her face, followed by a heavy frown.

"I suppose," the Princess said maliciously, "that you will be the most eager of us all to reach Calais. Just think, Joan— both your 'ardent suitors' there waiting for you! Which one will receive the first kiss?"

Joan flushed angrily. "I haven't the faintest intention of coming with you," she retorted. "Not the faintest! If there's one thing I despise it's women who run after men. I let my gallants seek *me* out!"

Staring at her incredulously, Isabel gave a derisive laugh. Then a new thought struck her and she hurried to her sister Joanna and whispered in her ear. Joanna listened, nodded, and stepped over to the Queen's side, touching her with an anxious hand. "I am to go, too, Madame, surely? You won't leave me at home when I shall have so little time with you and Isabel? After all, *ma mère,* once I leave England for Castile I may never see ..." her voice faltered and died away, her blue eyes filling with tears.

Philippa, her own eyes misty, leaned down and kissed her thirteen-year-old daughter on the cheek.

"I'm sorry, my darling, but your father thinks you should remain on this side of the water until your wedding plans are more definitely settled. There is still so much to do, you know; your gowns and furnishings are far from being finished."

"Then I shall stay home with Joanna," interrupted Isabel fiercely. "My lord father doesn't need *me* over there! I shall write him and tell him I don't want to go!"

"You will," said her mother firmly, "do exactly as you are told—for once! You are to accompany me to Calais for a very good reason. And you will be told what that reason is when your father decides to tell you, not a moment before. So don't waste your time and mine in questions and arguments."

Chapter 2

Isabel, stepping ashore at Calais, took a deep breath of the fresh air. After the odorous stuffiness of the cabin she had shared with all the other ladies it was delightful to smell only the salty fishiness of the harbor. It had been an unusually smooth crossing, but there were always a few women in every large group who become violently ill the moment they set foot on any deck, sometimes even before the anchor had been raised.

Now, however, everyone looked well and happy, laughing and chatting as they embraced their husbands, fathers or brothers, all the discomforts of the journey apparently forgotten. While Isabel awaited her turn in King Edward's arms—he was very busy kissing her mother at this particular moment—she found herself wondering if men, with a war to be won, really wanted their women underfoot. "If I were a warrior," she decided, "I'd tell my wife to stay at home where she belongs."

But as she watched she saw something in the eyes of the Earl of Northampton that gave her pause. He had just seen his gentle Elizabeth and was hurrying to her, his face alight with love, and the Princess, remembering how kind and helpful Elizabeth had been on board ship, admitted to herself that there could, after all, be some ladies who made themselves welcome wherever they went.

A great noise and bustle and a screaming, parrotlike voice that cut through all the other sounds on the wharf suddenly caught everyone's attention, and Isabel, bristling with dislike, knew instantly who must be causing such a commotion. It was the new Countess of Arundel, pushing and shoving her way through the other lords and ladies in her usual arrogant fashion, because she had been born the Lady Alianor Plantagenet and was King Edward's cousin, she had demanded

26

the second best pallet in the cabin and talked loudly and incessantly when her companions wanted to rest.

After watching her cousin's progress across the quay for a few minutes, Isabel moved to her father's side. When she had been kissed and made welcome by the King and her brother the Prince of Wales, whose bear hug rumpled her veil and pushed her hennin askew, she took her place in the long procession that was beginning to straggle from the harbor to the English encampment.

To her great astonishment, she found herself in a little town made up of rows of wooden huts with straw-thatched roofs on both sides of straight, carefully laid-out streets. A busy market place, set out in the middle, puzzled her even more. "But where," she asked Prince Edward, riding beside her, "are the tents and pavilions? Where are we, Ned? What are we doing in this neat little peasants' village—if that's what it is. I've never seen anything like it before!"

He grinned down at her. "This," he told her, "is Newtown-the-Bold, our camp. And you won't call it a 'peasants' village' when you see how we have furnished your quarters. Nor will you wonder why we aren't all living in tents when winter comes—it's cold enough now, with the November winds whipping across the marshes ..." he shivered in his jagged silk jupon and wished that he had, today, worn something warmer if not so eyecatching. "Just wait for January, chuck, and you'll be glad that our men built these little houses. We'll all be grateful for wooden walls and fires."

"But ..." Isabel was still staring around with bewildered eyes. "It's so peaceful and quiet. Aren't we besieging a city?"

"We're starving it into submission," he told her, his voice grim. "It is not a pleasant way to do it, Bel, but King Philip refuses to meet us in open battle and there is no way to take Calais by direct assault."

He pointed to the city, towering over the little camp, and explained. "There are double walls all around it, you see, and a double ditch that fills with sea water every time the tide comes in. If we could roll our movable towers close to the walls, or place our stone-throwing machines where they would do some good, we might surmount them, eventually, but the ground is too boggy. It's all marshland. So we've blockaded the harbor and our archers are guarding the coast road. The French apparently had their fill of our arrows at

Crécy. Except for an occasional skirmish they're leaving us strictly alone."

He had barely finished his explanation when the procession halted in front of the most elaborate of the huts and the royal family dismounted. Both Queen Philippa and her daughter gasped as they stepped inside. For a long moment, they stared silently at the brilliantly painted arras that covered the crude wooden walls, the handsome furniture, gleaming silver, silken curtains and richly embroidered cushions. A few of these things had traveled with the King from England—Philippa had chosen them herself, thinking of his comfort—but there were scores of luxuries here that she had never seen before.

"A victorious army does not arrive at its destination empty-handed." Edward smiled triumphantly at first his wife and then his daughter; their faces, so much alike, looking inquiringly at him with the same bewildered, black-lashed, dark blue eyes. "Here," he took Philippa by the hand and drew her to a small table which held an intricately carved gold coffer, open, spilling over with glittering gems. "I have a few gauds and baubles for you, my love."

While she was exclaiming over them he reached in and drew out a long necklace of deep-blue sapphires set in unusually heavy gold.

"I thought," he said, "when I first saw this, that the stones were the same blue as our Isabel's eyes." He threw it over her shoulders, then lifted some of its gleaming links nearer her face. "I was right," he announced and bent to kiss her. "A perfect match. Keep it, my child—it's a gift from a proud father to his lovely and obedient daughter."

"Obedient"? There was something in the way he stressed the word that made Isabel feel suddenly uneasy. He had never called her that before, and she examined her beautiful necklace with suspicious eyes. Was it a bribe? Was she going to have to do something unpleasant to earn it?

But when the King began asking questions about Joanna and the other children at home he sounded so much as usual that she soon forgot her instant of misgiving, and threw herself wholeheartedly into settling into her strange but comfortable quarters. And by the time they were all seated for supper, surrounded by the rest of the happily reunited lords and ladies, Isabel was the gayest one at the table, her only regret

that Joanna was not here in Newtown-the-Bold, sharing this
delightful experience.

She was laughing uproariously at something the amusing
Earl of Warwick had said, finding his crooked, quizzical eyebrows and long, elaborately curled mustache almost as funny
as his wit, when Tom Holland, sitting a little farther down
the table, leaned forward.

"But where is the Lady Joan? I thought she would surely
be one of your party? Not ill, I hope?"

His voice was casual but his eyes were not, and Isabel
found herself hesitating over her answer. The picture of Joan
in young Salisbury's arms flashed into her mind and she could
hear her mother, just before they left England, giving Joan
strict orders to behave in her absence. The Queen, Isabel
knew, was not overly fond of her ward, mistrusting her bold
blue eyes, blatantly golden hair, over-full bosom and sensual
red mouth. "Everything about the girl is too much," she had
once said, "and I do not like the way Ned looks at her."

Realizing suddenly that she had hesitated too long and that
her friend Tom was regarding her uneasily, Isabel burst into
explanation.

"No, she's not ill, my lord, but she decided not to make
the voyage. She had just returned from Scotland, you
know. . . ."

It sounded inadequate and it was. Holland nodded and
turned away. Isabel, damning her cousin for a troublemaker,
told herself Sir Thomas was twice the man that Joan's betrothed was, although the young Earl of Salisbury, at
eighteen, was no disgrace to his title. He had fought well and
bravely at Crécy, certainly.

Her brother Ned's first words, when she joined him after
supper, were an echo of Tom Holland's. "Where is our *belle
cousine,* my little Jeannette?" As if already aware that his
mother, who was within earshot, would not approve of his interest, the young Prince spoke softly and drew Isabel aside.

She looked at him in exasperation. No one else ever called
Joan "Jeannette" and he had said it in a caressing sort of way
that justified her mother's suspicions. Well, she decided, she
could certainly tell Ned the plain truth! Perhaps it would
wake him up a little.

"Joan," she said bluntly, "refused to come with us. And if
you really want to know why, I think it's because she's land-

ed herself in a mess. I saw her cuddling—or worse—with
Tom Holland before he went off to Gascony, having apparently forgotten that she is supposed to be betrothed to Salisbury. But she remembered it, certainly, the moment Tom
was gone, when she turned to Will for lovemaking and attention. It's my private opinion, Ned, that she's caught between
them now and was afraid to face the two of them together
here at Calais."

"And if you want *my* private opinion, Bel, you'd better not
talk quite so freely about your own cousin. Anyone as beautiful as Joan draws men to her. She can't help it. You sound a
little jealous to me!"

The court retired early that night, but it was late before
King Edward and Queen Philippa finally fell asleep. There
was so much to talk about—Philippa wanting to hear all the
details of their great victory at Crécy and Edward eager for
more word of the battle at Neville's Cross.

"I sent that Northumberland hothead, that John Copeland,
back home with orders to escort King David to London the
moment his wounds heal," he told her. "My only regret is
that you will not be there to receive him, my love. You were
quite right; he should have been surrendered to you at
Durham. But I couldn't let you remain at home just for that.
I wanted you here with me.

"And," he went on, "as I wrote you then, my lady, I've
been pressing ahead on this extremely delicate matter of our
Isabel's marriage. If the Flemings can make young Louis
agree to it, and he is, I'm sorry to say, proving very difficult,
we should wed them immediately. There would be so many
long delays at home."

"You wrote me, you know, that his father had fallen at
Crécy," the Queen reminded him. "You were afraid that
might ruin your plans."

Edward, lying beside her under the soft feather-filled
cover, sighed. "It may. That and the fact that he has spent
the last few years at the French court where Philip has been
fostering a match between him and Margaret, the daughter
of the Duke of Brabant. It's another contest between England and France, I'm afraid, and I'm trying in every way I
can to prove to the Flemings that our friendship will be more
valuable to them than Philip's."

"Have you any idea as to when the question will be settled?" asked his wife, thinking as usual of the practical side of things. "I brought what I could, but you gave me very little time for anything. And to ready a royal bride *here!*" If there was a trace of conjugal reproof in her voice it was very mild indeed. Philippa, an extremely sensible and resourceful woman, secretly enjoyed a challenge of this kind and her husband knew it.

"No," he replied, "I have not. But I shall go to Ghent myself as soon as we've celebrated Christmas and see if I can't win the burgesses there over to my side. They are more powerful, really, than the nobles."

"Ghent," Philippa smiled in the darkness, her eyes soft. "Dear Ghent! We were happy there, Edward. And the monks of St. Bavon were so kind to me when John was born. I've never forgotten it. I would like very much to go with you, my dear lord."

"You shall, if it can be arranged. And Isabel, too. Does she know why she is here?"

The Queen flushed. "No, she doesn't. I was about to tell her when she angered me. You've spoiled the girl, Edward, although you won't admit it, and she often forgets the deference due me as her mother. I told her you would explain your summons in your own good time."

Laughing, Edward drew her close. "How can I help spoiling the child, my love, when she is so much like you? That's why you draw fire from each other—it's not my fault at all. However, I'm just as glad that she knows nothing of our plans. They may, as you can see, come to nothing."

Although the Princess did wonder occasionally why her father had demanded her presence here in Calais, there was so much activity in the little encampment that she did not have time to brood over the question. There was dancing every night in the hut they called the dining hall and great tournaments were held in the daytime both to amuse the ladies and to keep the knights in fighting trim. They could go hawking, too, when the weather was reasonably fair, and on Wednesdays and Fridays there was the fascinating market to visit. Fresh supplies from England and all the booty brought in from hasty forays around the countryside were set out for sale in the open stalls: bread, cloth, fresh butcher's meat—no wonder that the people from the nearby villages tried to slip in and buy some of these now-scarce supplies.

Never, at home, had it been possible for Isabel to mingle in crowds such as these, and to watch and listen to the bargaining, the chaff and banter, and the occasional quarrels of the buyers and sellers. Here, in this small protected area, it was understood that so long as she wore a simple gown and was accompanied by one lady-in-waiting and a stout man-at-arms she could come and go as she willed.

She and Alexia de la Mote were preparing for this unusual treat one Wednesday morning when a scout rushed in to report the approach of a French supply train, some distance down the road, heading toward Calais.

All work in the market stalls stopped abruptly. Trumpets sounded, horses were saddled, weapons readied, and while Isabel and Alexia, tense with excitement, stood under a scraggy tree near the door of their hut, a large force assembled in front of them and rode off to reinforce the archers who were guarding the road.

An hour passed. Two. Isabel and Alexia settled themselves down over a backgammon board and were soon absorbed in the game.

"Listen!" Alexia, the dice cup in her hand, waited a moment before rattling them. She put it down and rose. "I hear horses, Your Grace."

They rushed outside. Now they could hear the jingle of harness, too, and the rumble of wagons, and after a few minutes, the voices and laughter of the soldiers returning to Newtown-the-Bold, shouting out to the men and women lining the streets that the Frenchies had turned tail and left behind most of their loaded wagons.

As the captured supplies rolled past her, Isabel shouted, too, and clapped her hands. Then Alexia, her small pointed face pale under its dark auburn hair, clutched her arm.

"Oh!" she gasped. "Look, Your Highness, look! How *can* they laugh and cheer!" She was staring at the far end of the long train, where a cartload of wounded was just coming into sight.

"Mother of God!" whispered Isabel, drawing closer to her companion.

While they stood there, sickened as the dreadful sounds and the smell of blood and death drew nearer, a slender young man who had been in a group of spectators gathered some distance away, ran to the rear of the wagon. Without waiting for it to come to a halt, he climbed over the tail-board. The two girls were still too far away to see very clearly, but the shrieks and groans changed, grew less despairing; the stranger, somehow, was helping the wounded and dying men.

"Why," asked the Princess, as they almost ran back to their quarters, "have we ever thought war is romantic?" She shuddered. "Men seem to think nothing of killing and being killed. It's necessary. That's all there is to it." Now, safe again on her own ground, she could remember who she was. The daughter of Edward III lifted her head.

"Wars must be fought," she added. "It's winning them that matters."

The weather turned cold and crisp and, shortly before Christmas, a fleet of English ships arrived in the harbor with a most welcome cargo. In addition to the necessary supplies, they had brought—in response to an order sent home by the King himself—everything that the camp and the court would need to celebrate the holiday. While most of the town's inhabitants watched, they unloaded huge bales of yew and bay, great branches of holly tightly tied together and wrapped in hopsacking, chests of costumes for the mumming, sacks of apples for wassail, casks of mincemeat, sent directly from the royal kitchens in the Tower of London, haunches of venison from the forests at Windsor, boars' heads, marchpane, and even one vast Yule log of English oak, cut for the royal dining hall.

There were letters from Isabel's brothers and sister Joanna and a box of New Year's gifts that they had chosen themselves for her and their parents; some of them made her laugh and some cry but they all spelled home, and, for the first time, she wished she had not come to France.

But except for that bit of homesickness, Isabel and her companions enjoyed their holiday. From the moment that the ships arrived until the day that the garlands of greens and the holly and mistletoe were taken down, my lord of Misrule's tinsel crown thrown into the fire, the bright silks, satins and masks packed away, and the last venison bone tossed out to the camp dogs, Newtown-the-Bold was a noisy, merry place, its inhabitants apparently unaware that behind the double walls of Calais lived thousands of frightened, starving people. There were no carols for them this Yuletide; no gifts, no feasting. They celebrated it with despairing prayers, tightening their girdles as the food dwindled. . . .

The King went to Ghent by himself, after all, and came back looking fairly content. Isabel, who knew nothing of his reason for going there, was relieved when he returned safely, assuming naturally that he had been on some errand concerning the siege of Calais. And as he spent most of his time for the next few days closeted with his council, she had no reason to question that assumption.

"I shall write Joanna," she told Alexia one drowsy afternoon. "And I think I'll wander over to the scribe's hut myself and ask for a sheet of paper. I'm tired of sitting still!" Alexia rose. "No, no, stay here, Alexia. I won't be a moment."

The small room, when she reached it, seemed to be empty. Then she noticed a richly dressed young man who was busy with a fine brush and a row of paint pots, so busy, in fact, that he didn't hear her enter the door. He was bending over the table, completely absorbed in what he was doing, and as she approached, her velvet slippers soundless on the packed mud floor, a ray of late-afternoon sun glinted in through the window opening and lighted his pale gold hair.

She stopped for a moment, amused by the fact that the sun almost made a halo around his head, then came closer and bent down to see what he was painting.

He looked up, startled, and Isabel, feeling as if a hand were clutching at her heart, found herself staring into a pair of strangely luminous gray eyes that met hers and held them. Then his delicate, sensitive mouth broke into a smile and the young stranger dropped his brush and jumped to his feet.

Isabel found her tongue first. "May I see?" she asked, putting out her hand.

"But, of course, your—Your Highness," he stammered. Blushing and bowing a little awkwardly, he snatched his work off the table and handed it to her.

Isabel studied the long piece of vellum, then glanced up at the artist. "It's the most beautiful thing I've ever seen," she told him enthusiastically. "All these animals and birds and flowers—they seem to be living right there on the parchment. I mean it, sir; it's the most beautiful thing I've ever seen!"

As he began to thank her, Isabel was struck by a sudden thought; there was something about him that was vaguely familiar; the way he held his head, or the curve of his shoulders as he had bent over the table. She had seen someone bending, just like that.... Ah! "Aren't you the young man who climbed into the cart of wounded soldiers a few weeks ago?" she asked him. "And helped those poor, pitiful men?"

He nodded. "I did nothing, Your Highness. They were on their way to the sick hut—the physicians were waiting for them."

"May I ask your name?"

"I'm Bernard d'Albret."

"Then I know your father well," Isabel told him. "He's one of *my* father's most valued emissaries. But why, sir, have we seen nothing of you in the dining hall? We dance, you know, and play games." She looked again at his bright hair and handsome face. "I would have remembered you—you cannot have been there with my lord d'Albret!"

"I had only just come up from d'Albret," he replied. "that day of the French foray. And I returned almost immediately. I act as courier for my lord father, Your Grace, bringing and taking messages and letters from home."

"Ah," said Isabel, smiling, "but now that we have met, you must honor us, sir, with your presence! I shall expect to see you with our other dancing partners. You will not be running off again so soon, surely?"

"Not, certainly, until I finish this." Bernard touched the piece of vellum. "His Majesty, hearing how much I love to dabble with paints, asked me to decorate this border for him. 'On a most important document,' he said."

And now Bernard smiled back at the Princess, and in a way that aroused her curiosity. It was as if he thought the King's words would mean something to Isabel. They did not. She tried, but could think of no 'important document' that might concern her in any way.

"I know he will be pleased with it," she said. "Anyone would be. What is its purpose, sir? What fortunate person will receive it when you and the scribes have done their part? Do you know?"

Hesitating for a moment, Bernard looked from Isabel to the document in question. "Why," he replied at last, slowly, "why I suppose you will, Your Highness. His Grace said it was to be your marriage contract."

Chapter 3

Isabel's first impulse was to seek her father out, wherever he was. After a few carefully casual words with Bernard d'Albret, she all but ran from the room. The first guard she saw, however, informed her that the King had ridden off to the farthest corner of the camp.

Her steps slowed, her immediate sense of panic subsided a little, and she began to think more clearly. Why, she asked herself, should she be so horrified—even frightened—to hear that her betrothal was being arranged without her knowledge? Hadn't she been aware, all of her life, that this would almost certainly happen? That her husband would be chosen for her and that she must submit with a good grace, just as Joanna had? Joanna, after all, was a year younger than she, and Joanna had not said a word of protest when her father and mother had informed her that she must go to Castile to wed Prince Pedro, the heir to the throne, and would very likely never see England or her family again.

Joanna had wept, but only at night when she and Isabel were alone.

Facing what might very well be a similar fate, Isabel discovered that she was too deeply disturbed for tears. She admitted to herself, for the first time, that she had always clung to a hope, kept hidden in her heart, that King Edward would allow her to make a marriage of affection, or, if that were impossible, to choose from a list of eligible princes.

When the King returned and granted her a private audience, Isabel had recovered enough of her composure to give him a warm kiss before asking her question. As a small child, Isabel had found out for herself that her father was an extremely affectionate man and that it delighted him to have his dark-eyed daughter run into his arms and kiss him fearlessly; all of his other children tended to hold him in awe, and watched with amazement when Isabel climbed into his

37

lap. What Isabel didn't realize was that although she had inherited her mother's features and coloring, her temperament was so like the King's she knew instinctively how to please him.

So she waited until he was seated in his large chair, then climbed up on the dais and asked him if he thought her too old to sit on a man's knee.

Laughing, he drew her down and kissed her on the cheek.

"Come now, Bel," he said as she settled herself, "tell me what you want. I have only a few minutes to spare you this afternoon."

"Then I won't waste them," she replied swiftly. "It's this, dear lord. I discovered today—purely by chance—that you are drawing up a marriage contract for me. It was foolish of me, I know, but the thought shocked me. It was so—unexpected."

Edward tightened his arms around her and asked her how she had found out. "I was planning to tell you myself, chuck," he assured her, "but the matter is still far from settled."

After she had confessed how she had ventured, unattended, into the scribes' room and described her encounter with Bernard d'Albret, her father laughed ruefully. "It's not easy to keep a secret from you, is it, Bel? Well, I won't scold you! perhaps it *is* time I had a little talk with you. My other pressing business will just have to wait."

Calling a page to his side, he sent a message to the marshals who were waiting in the next room. He would, he said, be occupied with Her Highness a little longer than he had thought.

"I think I need hardly tell you," he began, "that I have always wanted my children to find the happiness in their marriages that I have found in mine. Your mother and I have been so fortunate, so very content together! No king ever had a better queen and I know that no husband ever had a better wife than mine. And because of this, Bel, I keep hoping that you and your brothers and sisters will be happy, too. I hope"—he sighed—"but hoping will not necessarily make it so. Princes and princesses have their duties to perform and furthering the interests of their country by marrying suitably is of the greatest importance. All this you know, Bel. You know, and have always known, that the hand of the Princess Royal can, if properly bestowed, bring added prosperity and perhaps even peace to our England. It is my task, and that of my advisors, to choose a husband for you who can do this."

"And—you have?"

He nodded. "I made up my mind several years ago that if it could be arranged you would wed Louis de Mâle, the Count of Flanders. And it has, ever since I first considered the match, become more and more necessary to strengthen our alliance with Flanders. France is now as eager for their friendship as we are and they have a great deal to offer too; so I must confess that I would rest much easier nights if my Bel were the Countess of Flanders."

"The Count of Flanders," said Isabel slowly. "Is he a recent widower, my lord? When did the Countess die?" Her heart sank; a man as old as her father, with a grown family!

"A widower? What do you mean, child? Louis is only fifteen years old! Oh!" A light broke and Edward hastened to explain. "You haven't heard, of course. No, no, it's young Louis, Bel. The son of the one you are thinking of—young Louis is the Count now, and has been since the battle of Crécy. That, I'm sorry to say, is one of our difficulties! The late Count was our friend for many years but he changed sides, unknown to us, and fought with King Philip at Crécy. We found his body on the battlefield."

"What does this . . . Louis . . . say? Has he agreed to marry me?"

"The lad is in France. I haven't met him yet, but I hope to soon; the burgesses of Ghent are very much in favor of the alliance, I'm glad to say, and they have sent for him."

Isabel, her worst fears eased, grew more cheerful. Even when both parties were in agreement, many things could happen. And the Count had not yet agreed!

Seeing her face soften, King Edward kissed her again. "Promise me one thing, daughter," he said, "and then we won't discuss it any further today."

Isabel stiffened slightly. Why should she promise anything when she had no voice in the matter?

"What?"

"That you will be guided by me and accept what comes to you as England's Princess Royal should—with grace. And that you will try to please your husband—whoever he may be—and make him as good and as loving a wife as you have made me a dear daughter. Being willing to try, chuck, is half the battle."

Suddenly amused, Isabel twinkled up at him and climbed off his lap.

"I promise you this, my lord. I will try to try!"

The King and Queen, after this, took Isabel into their confidence and kept her informed how their plans were progressing. But it was some time before there was any fresh news from Ghent and the Princess began to hope that nothing more would be heard of her father's suggestion.

The rest of January was damp and dull, February increasingly dreary. King Philip continued to say no to every invitation to meet the English in open battle and the days at Newtown dragged by. It was too wet most of the time to hawk or joust and the ladies, with little to occupy them, spent long hours by the fire, yawning over their needlework and wondering when, if ever, the siege would come to an end.

The first hint that the Calaisians might eventually surrender reached them very early on a cold, clear Wednesday morning. The supplies were not yet spread out in the stalls, but many of the men and women were up and preparing for the busy day. To their astonishment they saw a long, straggling procession emerge from around the city walls and begin to pour past their encampment. Thin, shabbily dressed, their faces hopeless and drawn, there seemed to be hundreds and hundreds of men, women, and children in that interminable line, all clutching little bundles in their emaciated arms.

The word spread that something unusual was happening and Isabel, who was only partly dressed, hurried into the rest of her garments, urged Alexia into hers, and rushed outside. Her brother Ned joined them there a few minutes later and they stood and watched as more of the lords and ladies popped out of their huts.

Isabel, seeing Bernard d'Albret's gleaming head nearby, beckoned him over.

"What is it?" she asked him. "Who are they?"

"I've just been over to the gates, Your Grace," he said, bowing to her and the Prince, "and a sentry there, who questioned an old man too weak to keep up with the others, tells me that they are the poor people of Calais, the ones who had no supplies laid in when the siege began. Their friends shared their food with them as long as they could, but the governor ordered them, yesterday, to leave the city and fend for themselves outside the walls."

"Ah," said the Prince of Wales, his eyes brightening. "This is good news for us! We're starving them out at last!"

"I suppose it is, Your Highness," Bernard spoke slowly and sadly as he continued to look at the pathetic people streaming by. "But it's a terrible thing to be suddenly homeless—to face the world without anything—without even food in your stomachs."

He glanced over at Isabel and his face lit up with a new thought. "If we could just give them something to eat! Would it be possible, I wonder? I wouldn't dare suggest such a thing, Your Grace, but do you think that you . . . ?"

Before he had finished, Isabel had run off toward the royal hut and, after a word with the guard, disappeared inside. A few minutes later the Prince, Alexia, and Bernard saw a page speed out and enter the building that housed King Edward's Steward; another page appeared and made his way to the gates, shouting to the sentries to call back the poor people who had already passed the camp.

Isabel, beaming, hurried out again and joined her brother and her friends. "Isn't it wonderful?" she said delightedly. "We're going to feed them! Look," she pointed, "they're bringing it from the kitchens already." Great steaming kettles of thick soup, haunches of cold mutton and beef, whole wheels of cheese, hundreds of loaves of bread appeared almost like magic on the trestles waiting in the market stalls, and the homeless Calaisians, who had been pouring into the square and watching with unbelieving eyes, were now invited to eat.

While they fell on the food like famished animals, Isabel turned to her brother. "And that's not all," she said. "His Grace wants you to come with me, Ned, and put on our velvet mantles and crowns. . . ."

When the first of the two thousand or so townspeople, their stomachs full at last, moved toward the open road again, they saw a strange and wonderful sight. Under a silken canopy stood a beautiful dark-eyed princess and a tall, handsome, golden-haired prince; their hands were full of silver coins, and several fat moneybags waited at their feet.

"A gift from King Edward," they said, giving two sterlings to each man, woman and child. *"Un cadeau du Roi d'Angleterre!"*

A dispatch from Ghent, arriving shortly after that, brought King Edward the news that Count Louis of Flanders had returned there from France, and he sent the Earls of Arundel and Northampton and Lord Cobham off immediately, with orders to interview the lad and to seek his consent to an alliance with Princess Isabel. When they returned and reported that he was unwilling to wed her, Isabel was surprised to discover that she felt alternately relieved and disappointed.

Relief was, of course, uppermost. But the three English noblemen described the young Flemish Count in such glowing terms that Isabel caught herself wondering, occasionally, whether he might not have made her a most acceptable husband. He was extremely handsome, they said; handsome, charming, brave, daring, and with a mind of his own. They had watched him dance and could assure the Princess that he was a most graceful performer; they had jousted with him one day and found him a formidable opponent.

Before they had come to the end of the young man's accomplishments the King announced that he would go to Ghent again and interview Count Louis himself.

"This time," said Philippa firmly, "I shall go with you."

Isabel rose swiftly and knelt before her father. "Take me, too, dear lord," she pleaded. "Don't leave me here to fret and wonder!"

The burgesses led the royal party up the narrow circular stone staircase and into the huge banqueting hall. A blazing fire was burning in the wide hearth built into the side wall and a throne chair had been set on a dais under the steep flight of steps at the far end that led to a musicians' gallery.

"We are ready for you, I see, Your Majesty," said one of the burgesses, surveying the hall with a careful eye. "Now that our Counts live elsewhere here in Ghent, we use the Castle and these rooms only occasionally, and unless we need them for a council meeting, ceremonial visit, or some great entertainment, they stand empty most of the time. A shame, I say, for there isn't a castle in all Flanders that can match our Castle of the Counts for size and magnificence."

While the King, Queen and Princess murmured appreciatively, another of their hosts strode over to a wide doorway in the wall facing the fire, peered inside, and returned to their side. "If you will follow me, Your Grace," he bowed to the Queen, "and you, Your Highness—ladies," he included Isabel and their two ladies-in-awaiting in his second bow, "I will take you into the chapel and see that you are comfortable there. We asked the steward to place a few chairs in it and to find some cushions. . . ."

"You are very kind," said Philippa, smiling warmly, "and we are most grateful. We should, perhaps, have remained quietly out at the Abbey, but Her Highness was eager to see your beautiful city and Castle. And we must set out for Calais again soon after dawn tomorrow. . . ."

As she spoke the other ladies gathered behind her and they moved to the adjoining room. A few minutes saw them settled into the small circle of chairs and the burgess, after another polite speech or two, backed out and closed the doors behind him. Isabel waited until her mother began to chat with her ladies then slipped, very quietly, out of her cushioned seat.

Her one reason for being here today was not to see the "beautiful city and Castle" but to catch a glimpse of Louis de Mâle. The Queen had done her best to keep Isabel in their quarters at St. Bavon, thinking it extremely unwise for either her daughter or herself to venture into the Castle at such a time, but Isabel, using every argument she could think of, had finally persuaded the King to bring them with him. He had agreed, but he had then informed their hosts that the ladies preferred not to meet Count Louis until the question of the betrothal was resolved and suggested that they retire to another room while the meeting was being held.

As she prowled around the small room, Isabel thought at first that her father had outwitted her. The doors into the banqueting hall were thick and tightly closed; she had hoped for screens, or an open alcove. Then, when she was ready to give up and return to her chair, she noticed another door in the wall, a small one at the far end. Opening it quietly, she found herself in a narrow entryway. A few steps took her to the end of it; she paused, found a second door and, pushing it open just enough so she could peer around it, discovered, to her delight, that she was looking directly across the hall to where her father sat upon the dais.

In front of him stood two elderly Flemish noblemen who were bowing to their royal guest. They stepped aside, a moment later, to make way for a younger man just approaching the small platform. This, she was sure, was Louis de Mâle, the Count of Flanders. It could be no one else. She moved a little closer to the crack in the door and watched him marching down the room. She was struck, at first, by the rigid set of his head on his shoulders, which seemed to her to betoken a certain belligerence; then, as she was able to see him more clearly, by his stubborn chin and rather closely set eyes. That he was quite handsome she had to admit, but his was not the kind of good looks that appealed to her. Of rather more than medium height, he was strongly, even stockily built; he had a shock of thick light-brown hair, a large, well-chiseled nose, and a full, sensual mouth. At fifteen he was more man than boy and, she decided, too arrogant, certainly, to be called a "gentil, parfait knight."

She caught herself comparing his face to Bernard d'Albret's, and wishing that she could find in it some of that sensitivity and kindness that were so obviously a part of Bernard's nature. Bernard, of course, was handsomer than Louis; but Bernard was the handsomest young man she had ever seen, and it was ridiculous, she knew, to use his beauty as a measuring stick. It was ridiculous to compare them, in any way for that matter, and she chided herself sharply, pushed the thought of Bernard out of her mind, and turned her attention back to Count Louis.

He was richly clad, as was only fitting, but there was, to Isabel's eyes, something offensively Gallic in the cut of his tightly buttoned côte-hardie and in the exaggerated way that his shoes curled up at the toes. It was a new fashion, she knew, and some of her father's nobles were adopting a more modest version of it at home. But after all, she hastened to remind herself, the young Count had been living in France and would, of course, dress like a Frenchman. What more natural? And she must not drift into prejudice. She must try, for her own sake, to find virtues in Louis, not faults.

She knew she should retreat quietly now and rejoin her mother, who must be wondering where she could be, but the temptation to listen was too great and she remained rooted to the spot where she was standing. The greetings and presentations were said and as her father was wasting no time in coming to the point she all but held her breath in her determination not to miss a word.

"We are here, my lord," he was saying to Louis, "to discuss a marriage between you and the Lady Royal of England, my daughter Isabel, a marriage which was first suggested by your late father when he and I met in Flanders in thirteen thirty-eight. It was his dearest wish then, and I myself have considered it a more or less settled matter ever since, refusing many other offers for her hand."

"That may have been my father's wish eight years ago," was Louis' prompt reply, "but there was no contract between you, Sire, and I know that before his death"—the boy's voice slowed a little, trembling over the word—"he strongly favored my union with Margaret of Brabant."

"You are not, however, betrothed to her?"

Louis hesitated and now Isabel *did* hold her breath, not sure just what she wanted him to say.

"I—consider myself bound to the lady, Your Majesty."

Edward frowned. The two Flemings nearest him bent their heads and whispered in his ear, then the older of the two addressed the young Count in such a firm and definite manner that there could be no doubt as to the truth of his statement.

"I was in your father's confidence, my lord Count, and I can assure you that he had not committed you in any way to the Duke of Brabant. And as you are still an infant in law, any promise of your own need not be considered binding."

Flushing darkly, Louis set his mouth and chin even more grimly in the stubborn lines Isabel had noticed earlier. He took a step forward, drew himself up to his full height, thrust his wide shoulders back, and spoke directly to the King.

"Even if I were to disregard my conscience and my heart and forget my duty to the Lady Margaret, I think you must understand, Sire, that I could never wed the Princess Isabel. You cannot know, or you would not be here today, that I stood beside my dear father ..." again his voice shook and he paused a moment to steady it. "I stood beside my very, *very* dear father on the battlefield of Crécy and watched him die."

The hall was quiet. King Edward, deeply disturbed, dropped his eyes. Isabel, feeling her heart plunge, fought back an impulse to weep. Louis was not pretending; he had loved his father dearly.

His grief had turned to anger when he spoke again, and his voice rang out so loudly that it echoed from the highest point of the vaulted, raftered ceiling.

"I tell you now, King Edward of England, and you, my lords of Flanders, that you are wasting your fair speeches and arguments on me. I am so haunted, day and night, by the horrible picture of my father's death that were I offered half of England I would never wed the daughter of my dear lord's murderer!"

He turned then, and without waiting for permission to retire or for any answer from the others, strode swiftly away.

One of the Flemings, after a short, stunned silence, apologized to King Edward for the young man's behavior. "We will have to be firmer with the lad," he said. "Leave the matter in our hands. He has become too much of a Frenchman, I am afraid, and must be shown where his loyalty lies."

Later that evening, after they had partaken of the wholesome meal provided by the monks of St. Bavon in the huge, vaulted dining hall that reminded Isabel of the hall at Westminster, the King, Queen, and their daughter excused themselves and sought the privacy of the small room set aside for their own use. Now, for the first time, they discussed Count Louis' rebellious attitude. After both Edward and Isabel, who had confessed that she had seen and heard it all, had told Philippa what the boy had said that afternoon, the King urged his wife to speak frankly.

"Should we press the lad further, do you think, or drop the matter?"

The Queen hesitated. Her answer, she knew, must not be given lightly; her opinion had always counted with the King.

"Speaking as our Isabel's mother," she said at last, "I confess that I am reluctant to tie her to an unwilling bridegroom, and one who has a most understandable grievance against us. But as the Queen of England, and a daughter of Flanders, I know that the need to strengthen the bond between our two countries should come before any personal considerations."

"And you, my child?" Edward looked at Isabel, sitting quietly beside her mother. "If he should change his mind will you do your duty and accept him with grace? Will you, as you promised me, 'try to try'?"

"I find myself wondering, father," she said, "whether I could bring myself to marry him if I had watched *you* being killed by *his* people. And then there's his affection, as he called it, for Margaret of Brabant. Is he deeply in love with her? Would you ask me to wed a man who loves someone else?"

Edward frowned and gave his wife an apologetic glance. "I should not have allowed you to accompany me today, Bel," he said. "It was a mistake. A romantic lass of fifteen should not hear the rantings of a romantic boy of fifteen who merely wants his way. No attachment, at his age, can be too lasting. A beautiful young wife would make him forget. . . ."

"You should not have taken Isabel to the Castle," interrupted the Queen firmly, "and I see now that we should not be discussing the matter in this fashion. If Louis agrees to marry our daughter, and you still think the alliance important to England, she will of course obey you. What I feel as her mother, what you feel as her father, and what she feels about Louis' reluctance and scruples have no real bearing on the question. England and the prosperity and welfare of our people—they are what we should think of, not how we feel."

King Edward bent over and kissed her hand. "You are right, as always, my love. To bed then. We will, from now on, await further word from our Flemish friends with open minds and, I hope, the earnest desire to do whatever is necessary."

It was not long before they were put to the test. They returned to Calais and settled down again into the limited life there, and although Isabel found she could not think about her uncertain future without a feeling of dread, she managed, somehow, to pass the days in reasonable content. Her heart sank, however, when she and her mother were summoned to the King's privy chamber and saw him regarding them with an unusually serious face.

"A message arrived from Ghent a short time ago," he said, his eyes on Isabel, "and I have been closeted with my Council ever since. Louis has withdrawn all his objections, it seems, and suggests that we meet him at the monastery of Bergues-St. Vinox on the fourteenth day of this month to celebrate your formal betrothal. Our advisers agree with me, my dear child. We all feel that we must take this opportunity to ally ourselves with Flanders."

Chapter 4

Isabel, mounted on a dainty brown mare elaborately trapped in azure and gold, watched her royal parents riding side by side just a few paces ahead, noticing how easily they sat their horses and how skillfully they kept in step. As they all moved slowly past the ancient ramparts of Bergues-St. Vinox, circled by trees and a deep moat, then proceeded through the town, round-eyed Flemish children clopped alongside them in wooden shoes, cheering, laughing and waving their hands at the gorgeous procession; and in almost every doorway she saw the interested faces of rosy-cheeked women, many of whom were holding up their smaller children so that they, too, could see England's royal family pass by.

Realizing that these might very soon be her own people, Isabel smiled back at them from under her jeweled foliated crown. Perhaps the very next time she rode through this peaceful place Louis de Mâle would be at her side and she would be cheered as their new Countess.

They were approaching the Abbey now and she could see the tall tower supported by huge brick buttresses and decorated with many little pointed tourelles. Inside that unusual-looking building, she told herself, was her rather, reluctant bridegroom, waiting for her arrival. She gave a slight, involuntary shiver.

But when King Edward looked back over his shoulder a moment later to give her an encouraging smile, she was holding her head high and her back straight, and as she sat on the mare with her heavy blue velvet kirtle draped over her feet and a miniver-lined mantle swinging from her shoulders, he decided that this oldest daughter of his made a picture of which he was extremely proud. She answered his smile with one of her own and freed a hand from her reins to salute him gallantly before he faced forward again.

They allowed their horses to move a little faster now and

soon reached their destination. They dismounted just as the
weather-beaten old doors of the Abbey church were flung
open and the young Count stepped out, flanked on both sides
by the two Flemish nobles who had accompanied him at
Ghent. With a courtliness that he had undoubtedly learned in
France he bowed, knelt, kissed the hands of King Edward
and Queen Philippa then rose to greet the Princess Royal.

The King took her cold fingers in his and drew her forward.

"My daughter, my lord Count. The Princess Isabel."

For a long moment the two young people looked at each
other. Isabel, feeling her legs tremble, forced herself to meet
Louis' appraising glance steadily, her blue eyes almost black
as they stared into his. She waited until his wavered slightly,
then she dropped her lids quickly in an assumption of mod-
esty, and extended her hand.

"My lord Count," she said gently. Her voice, her curtsey,
her whole demeanor were perfection, and her father beamed
down on her with silent approval before presenting her to the
Flemish lords. When this was done and they suggested that
the party proceed into the Abbey, he turned back and spoke
to the Count.

"I would like, before the ceremony begins," he said, "to
have a quiet word or two with you, my lord. Over here, perhaps?" Leading the way, he walked a little apart from the
others, just far enough so that he and Louis could talk without being overheard.

"First," he began earnestly, "I want to assure you again
that I was in no way responsible for your father's death. His
presence at Crécy and the discovery that he was among the
slain that day were a great shock and a great sorrow to me,
and to prove that this is so I would like to build a church, a
monastery, or a hospital—whichever you prefer—to his memory."

Louis, his square face impassive under its thatch of brown
hair, murmured a few polite words of acknowledgment and
thanks. "In my grief," he said, "I am afraid I spoke a little
hotly when we met at Ghent. You must forgive me."

"No one could blame you, my son," replied the King. "In
the same circumstance I might very well have said the same
things. Your anger was most natural and quite understandable. However, my second reason for wanting a private inter-

view with you today is to hear from your own lips that you
are now truly willing to wed my daughter."

Instead of answering, the young man beckoned one of his
noblemen to his side. "I would like His Majesty to read the
statement I signed for you at Dunkerque yesterday," he said.
"Give it to him, if you please."

Edward perused it as swiftly as he could, nodding his head
in approval as he did so. "As a treaty of marriage between
him and the Lady Isabel had been previously drawn up by his
late father and the King of England, and had lately been
renewed by the King and his own relatives and good people
of his towns of Flanders, he, Louis de Mâle, Count of Flanders, seeing the evident profit in his land of Flanders and the
love, peace, repose, and tranquility that would result from
this marriage, consented thereto and promised loyally and in
good faith to solemnly betroth himself to the said Lady Isabel and to marry her, in the face of the Holy Church, within
a fortnight after the approaching Easter."

"I am more than satisfied, my lord Count," said Edward.
"You say here everything I wished to hear. Come, we need
not keep the ladies waiting any longer."

When the young couple had sworn their vows and all the
documents were duly signed and sealed—a long, wearying
process—the English party bade Count Louis and his suite
farewell and headed their horses back toward Calais. Isabel,
who had taken her part in the ceremony with dignity and composure, said very little to anyone until they reached Grave-
lines, their halting place for the night. Then she turned to
Alexia, who had attended her that day, and commented bitterly on Louis' manner.

"He was cold," she said. "So cold that he repelled me.
Staring at me with those eyes! They're too close together,
Alexia. I told my father so—but he disagreed. They are.
They make me mistrust him."

"Oh, come," Alexia replied, laughing at her. "That's nonsense, Your Grace! I think he's one of the handsomest young
men I've ever seen. And how could anyone seem anything
but stiff and cold when they are going through that exhaust-
ing betrothal ceremony? You were both like wooden dolls, if
you must know. No, no, Your Highness; I think you are ex-

tremely fortunate. I wish I were as lucky. I'm sure my parents won't find me so young and strong and handsome a husband when my time comes."

Isabel sniffed, but she found Alexia's warm praise of Louis a little reassuring. The girl really envied her, she could see that, and it made her see her betrothed in a more favorable light. He was young, certainly, and if Alexia thought him all that attractive. . . .

"You will make such a beautiful bride and bridegroom," her friend went on wistfully. "What a shame that the wedding has to be at Ghent instead of Westminster Abbey! I can just see you coming down the long aisle there, in a golden gown—or will it be silver?"

The moment they arrived safely back in Newtown-the-Bold the sewing women were summoned and the Princess found herself the center of a whirlpool of activity. With only a few weeks in which to prepare her wedding furniture Isabel had assumed that it would, of necessity, be much simpler than the rich articles ordered for Joanna's nuptials with the heir to the throne of Castile. But this, she soon learned, was not so; the Princess Royal of England would, both her mother and her father assured her, have no reason to be ashamed when her boxes were unpacked in Flanders.

The richest of King Edward's French plunder was to be hers; the shimmering silks, heavy brocades and velvets would make many gorgeous costumes to supplement the wardrobe her mother had brought from England just for this purpose. There were furs and jewels, some French, some English; there were canopies, wall hangings, bed hangings, altar cloths, vestments for her chaplains, gifts for her attendants. . . .

The list was so long that her head swam. She was thinking about it, and fingering a long gold chain, each link of which would keep a family clothed and fed for a year at least, when she found herself longing for Joanna. The strain of the last few weeks was proving greater than she realized, too, and a sudden rush of tears filled her eyes and began running down her cheeks. She threw down the chain and turned away, but her father had already seen her wet face.

"Come, come, chuck," he said. "What now?"

"I don't quite know myself," she admitted, feeling a little

foolish. "I began suddenly missing Joanna, and it occurred to me that I might never see her again."

"I suppose that is true," he answered thoughtfully. "They tell me the child's wedding furniture is all prepared and that she can set out for Castile the moment Pedro's father concludes his part of the contract. I wonder if it might not be a wise move to send for her and keep her here with us until her wedding date is settled? If she is on this side of the water we may be able to hurry matters along."

Isabel's face was radiant now. "Oh father!" She ran and embraced him. "Do. Do send for her!"

"Here you are, chuck," he said, a few days later, and showed her a letter that he was dispatching to the sheriffs of London. They were to load all the ships in their port, it said, with the possessions of the Princess Joanna. When that was done they were to see the Princess and her household settled on board and send the fleet on to him at Calais.

"And now," he added, "I must write the King of Castile."

Having thanked him, Isabel hurried away to tell the good news to Alexia, her eyes bright and her step light. Then, for the first time, she pondered over her father's reason for sending for Joanna. It wasn't just because it would please her to have her sister here in Calais; it was to make the Castilians settle Joanna's wedding date.

What had she done? Joanna, she knew, was dreading the day that she must leave England, never to see it again. She had whispered to Isabel when they parted that she prayed every night for more and more delays. In thinking only of her own pleasure Isabel had, she realized, done her sister a great wrong. Should she seek her father again and beg him to change his mind?

Again the unbidden tears began to slip down her cheeks, but more swiftly this time, and she ran blindly into the chapel that was, fortunately, only a few steps away. Falling on her knees, she buried her face in her hands, fighting for composure as she prayed for help and guidance. The small room was dim and she didn't see a shadowy figure kneeling almost beside her. She did, however, hear his cape rustle when he rose and tried to slip away, and her startled eyes, still brimming with tears, met those of Bernard d'Albret.

"Forgive me for disturbing you, Your Highness," he said

swiftly. Then, seeing her face, he hesitated. "Father John was here a moment ago," he said, his voice concerned. "May I find him and send him to you?"

Isabel was about to shake her head when she changed her mind and nodded instead. But of course, her kind, wise, helpful Father John would both advise and comfort her. "If you will," she whispered. "Please, sir."

In an unbelievably short time the gentle-voiced lad was back, followed by Isabel's confessor. He paused only long enough to see that she was still there, waiting for Father John, then turned and left them alone, closing the door behind her.

Isabel, with a great sigh of relief, welcomed her old friend and poured out her newest trouble. He listened, then reassured her. Joanna, he said, would surely be so happy to be with her family again that she would accept whatever penalty it entailed; if her wedding day was hastened by a few weeks it would not disturb her too much. He, Father John, had discussed her future with the Princess Joanna and knew that she was facing it quietly and calmly. And, in any case, it was nothing that Isabel had done purposely. Besides, there was no way of knowing what the King of Castile would reply; there might be months of delay ahead.

"You *do* comfort me, Father John," said Isabel. "But, then, you *always* do!"

He blessed her and she rose to her feet. She paused, and looked toward the door. "That kind young man who brought you to me, Father—I should never have allowed him to see me weeping. But I didn't see him at first. I thought the chapel was empty."

"Young Bernard?" Father John raised his eyebrows. "You have nothing to fear from him, daughter. He would never gossip or pry, I assure you. And anything that occurs in God's House is as sacred to him as it is to me."

But despite Father John's reassuring words about Joanna and her future, Isabel was secretly relieved when her father told her, some days later, that her sister must remain in England after all. He had, he said, received a most disquieting letter from the Queen of Castile, informing him that her husband was expressing doubts about the wisdom of wedding their son Pedro to the Princess Joanna.

"Before we move further in the matter," said the King, sighing heavily, "we must certainly find out what is in his mind."

The three-hundred-year-old Castle of the Counts of Flanders was the center of more activity than it had seen in a decade. The wedding of Louis and England's Princess Royal would take place there in less than a week and the bride, her attendants, her parents and their suites, and many of the high-ranking guests who were invited to the ceremony had been given apartments in the Castle itself. This had necessitated a great deal of work, expense, and planning on the part of the good people of Ghent. Many furnishings had been brought in for the occasion, and the kitchens had been staffed with the best cooks in that part of Flanders.

It was rather pleasant, Isabel decided, to live in a castle again. After the little huts at Newtown-the-Bold, the spacious chamber high in the keep, with its wonderful view over the town and countryside, was a delightful change. Her ladies were not on top of each other here, getting in each other's way and quarreling over nothing, as they had in the encampment; here they could dress themselves and their royal mistress in comfort; here, with the huge beds set far apart in each corner, they could even snore without annoying everyone in the solar.

They were all, in fact, so cheerful and content that they were not even mildly irritated when Queen Philippa, entering unattended and unannounced a short time before the hour set for the evening's banquet, shook her head over Isabel's costume and insisted on her changing into something quite different.

"You must look your loveliest tonight," she said firmly. "The supper is being given in your honor, Bel, to present Louis' bride to all the lords and ladies of Flanders. That green brocade surcoat and undergown are beautiful, I know, but your new blue velvet and sable—the deep-blue one that matches your sapphire chain—is much more becoming."

By the time the Queen expressed herself satisfied, and before she was through she had made the tiring women sew on a set of sapphire-studded buttons instead of the plain gold ones that fastened the tight surcoat, the Princess was on the verge of tears. As each hour passed, and she saw the time of her wedding drawing closer and closer, she was finding it increasingly difficult to keep her fears of the future in the background, and this hurried, last-minute change, with her mother scolding and fussing, seemed, suddenly, too much to bear.

But as she revolved, finally, before a long sheet of polished steel she admitted a little grudgingly that all her mother's pains were justified; and when the Lady Alianor entered and watched Queen Philippa adjust the gleaming sapphire-and-gold circlet on Isabel's unbound hair, the Princess was confident that her unpleasant aunt would, for once, be unable to find any fault with her appearance. The blue of the velvet made her eyes even more vivid than usual, and her hair, spread over her shoulders in bridal fashion, shone like a black satin cape; the surcoat hugged her slender waist and softly rounded hips, and the bands of sable, framing her white shoulders and bosom, were much more becoming than the ermine of the discarded green gown.

"What a strange shade of blue for a fifteen-year-old girl!" said the Lady Alianor, turning to the Queen. "Wouldn't azure be more suitable, Your Grace?"

Philippa bristled, an angry flush spreading up into her cheeks, and Isabel, equally annoyed, glared at the older woman. What a gift the rusty-haired Lady Alianor had for rubbing everyone the wrong way!

"I think not," was Her Majesty's abrupt answer, her tone making it a rebuke. "Come, ladies. It is time to go to the banqueting hall."

The air, as they climbed in a crablike, wary manner down the dangerously steep and narrow stairs, clutching the wall with one hand and the tails of their gowns with the other, was chilly with her displeasure, and the Queen was still frowning when the trumpets sounded and the usher led them into the dining hall.

The moment they stepped inside, however, Isabel saw her mother's face settle into its usual expression on such occasions, a gracious, warm smile; she made herself forget her own irritation and follow the Queen's example, and long before she had reached her seat of honor on the dais she was beaming in open admiration and pleasure.

Accustomed as she was to elaborate banquets and great dining halls, it was more than obvious that the Flemings had done everything in their power to make the large chamber, so empty and cheerless when Isabel had seen it a few weeks before, beautiful and welcoming for their Count's bride. The vaulted ceiling was thickly hung with brilliantly colored satin banners; the stone walls were covered with bright tapestries, woven, she was told later, in Brussels; a huge fire leaped and blazed on the wide hearth, and a group of musicians sat up in the gallery, their instruments ready.

She noticed, too, that an odd, pungent smell was rising from the rushes under their feet. After Louis de Mâle, a striking figure in a jagged red-and-gold-tissue jupon, advanced to meet her and took her himself to the tall carved chair waiting beside his, she remembered the fragrance and asked him what it could be.

He smiled and whispered an order to the lackey behind his chair. The servant bent down, scrabbled in the rushes for a moment, then handed his master a little cluster of half-opened golden blossoms. Louis, in his turn, gave it to the Princess.

"Why, it looks like our broom," said Isabel, a little puzzled.

"It is—the *plante-a-genet*," and again he smiled at her. "We sent fifty boys out early this morning to strip the countryside of every sprig that they could find. It is still in bud, as you see."

"What a pretty compliment!" Isabel, genuinely pleased, caught her father's eye and sent the bit of broom along the table to him. Recognizing it immediately, the King nodded and passed it on to his wife.

It was easy, now, to talk to the young man beside her. The flower had done its part and given Isabel a pleasant question with which to open their conversation, and they began chatting together almost like old friends. The coldness that had chilled her on the day of their betrothal had disappeared; no one could have been gayer and more responsive than Louis was tonight.

"I am hoping," he said, filling her wine goblet with his own hand, "that the skies will be clear tomorrow. I would like to take you out into the meadows for a little hawking. If, that is, it is a sport you enjoy."

"Very much," she assured him. "My own little merlin always travels with me."

He looked up, his dark eyes surprised. "Then the King brought his falcons to Calais with him too, I suppose?"

"His falcons," Isabel replied, "thirty falconers, sixty pair of hunting hounds, sixty pairs of greyhounds, and a dozen small boats of boiled leather—just in case he tires of hawking and hunting and should suddenly want to fish!"

After a moment of blank astonishment, Louis threw back his head and gave a great roar of laughter; it was so loud that all the other heads at the high table and most of those at the other tables along the walls turned their way.

King Edward whispered to his wife that all seemed to be well with Isabel and her betrothed.

"I hope so," was her answer. "But there's an odd, feverish look in the lad's eyes tonight. His manner makes me uneasy. I don't know why."

Whatever it was that disturbed the Queen did not bother the Princess. And she made a point, when they were retiring, of drawing Alexia aside and confessing to her that she was much happier than she had been. She was beginning to think she and Louis might do very well together, after all.

The skies the next morning were as clear as Louis had hoped they would be, and a large group of lords and ladies accepted his invitation to hawk in the marshy meadows outside the town walls.

The King and Queen decided to stroll around the ramparts instead; they had spent several hours in the saddle the preceding day and welcomed this opportunity to have a quiet morning by themselves, a privilege rarely enjoyed by the royal couple. "You don't need us," they said to the young Count, when he suggested that they join the party, "take Her Highness and have a good day's sport."

Isabel looked up as she rode out of the Castle and over the drawbridge that spanned the moat and saw her parents high up on the walk that circled the castle walls. They were standing close together and she remembered her father's words when he had told her how happy he was in his marriage—that no king had ever had a better queen nor any man a better wife. Would Louis say that someday?

She turned to smile at him and noticed that he was having to hold his mount in check; the horse was a large stallion, and seemed to be doing a great deal of restless curvetting. A good horsewoman herself, she guided her little mare a step or two away, keeping, at the same time, an anxious eye on the stallion's antics. Louis apparently had him under control, but she couldn't be sure.

"He's a bit fresh," said Louis, seeing her concern. "Once we're in the meadows, with the town behind us, I'll let him shake the fidgets out of his legs."

It crossed the Princess' mind that her betrothed's mount was built more for distance and endurance than a morning's hawking, but she forgot all about it when her merlin was placed on her wrist and the first heron was spotted in the sky. At a signal from the chief falconer, she and Lady Kitty, the pretty young Countess of Warwick, unhooded their birds and tossed them free. Up, up they soared, sighting their prey at almost the same moment, and the two ladies rode swiftly after them, followed by the others. It was a spirited contest and everyone cheered lustily as Lady Kitty's merlin soared over the heron, circled once, then pounced.

The Earl of Arundel and Tom Holland were the next to match their birds; then, as the noise and activity in the meadow frightened more and more marshbirds out of their reedy shelters and into the sky the formal pairing was no longer necessary, the lords and ladies choosing their own times to enter the contest.

Her own well-trained merlin having just brought down its second quarry and returned to her wrist, Isabel dropped back to allow it a few minutes' rest, stroking it with a gentle, affectionate finger as she slipped the hood over its feathered head. A little weary herself, she turned and joined the group of ladies who had ridden out just to watch the sport.

Alexia de la Mote was one of them, and she and her royal mistress were chatting quietly together when a large heron rose out of the weeds some distance away. Count Louis and England's Warwick sped their falcons after it at the same instant and, with loud cries, set out at full gallop.

"*Hoye, hoye, hoye!*" shouted the young Fleming, soon out-distancing Warwick. "Hoye, hoye, hoye!"

Isabel and Alexia laughed.

"Your Louis is having a happy day," said Alexia, shading her eyes.

"This is what that great stallion of his has been waiting for ever since we left the Castle," replied Isabel. "My Lord will take a toss if he isn't careful." She watched the wild progress of the horse and rider across the wide meadow, then shaded her eyes too as she raked the sky over their heads for a glimpse of the two falcons and their prey. They dwindled to three little specks before disappearing completely over a strip of woodland, and when she lowered her head she discovered that Louis was already out of sight and Warwick just entering the woods.

Turning her attention to another contest, in which Tom Holland and Arundel, Lady Alianor's husband, again matched their falcons, she found herself smiling as Holland proved the victor for the second time.

"My Lady Alianor will be displeased," she said a little maliciously.

But Alexia wasn't listening. She was watching Warwick emerge from the copse and ride back alone. His falcon was on his wrist and there was no sign of Louis de Mâle. As he neared her, Alexia could see that he had an odd, puzzled expression on his face and that he was guiding his mount over to the two Flemish knights who were always in attendance on the young Count.

"What has happened, I wonder?" she murmured. The Princess, following her eyes, saw the Earl of Warwick talking to the Flemings, his face agitated and his gestures expressive.

"It's that horrible horse!" she told Alexia. "Look! His knights are galloping off into that wood. Louis must be hurt!" Her own face worried now, she rode swiftly to Warwick's side. "Was Count Louis thrown?" she asked breathlessly. "Is he hurt?"

The Earl looked down at her from under his quizzical eyebrows and shook his head. But his face was so carefully impassive that she didn't believe him.

"He is!" she insisted. "Don't lie to me, my lord. If you won't tell me what is wrong I'll go and see for myself."

She wheeled her mare around, ready to carry out her threat.

"No, no, Your Grace!" He caught her bridle in one hand and held her at his side. "I'm telling you the truth. The Count was neither hurt nor thrown; but when I cleared the woods I saw that his falcon had the heron in its talons and that Louis was riding off toward . . ." he hesitated, looked away, gulped, then continued. "Toward the south. I shouted, but he didn't stop or turn back."

Some of the others joined them now, and as Warwick repeated his story Isabel's bewilderment grew. What could he mean? Why would Louis ride south, and why was everyone so disturbed?

It was Isabel's aunt, the Lady Alianor, who answered all her unspoken questions.

"Ho!" She gave her niece a glance that was half pity and half spiteful enjoyment. "My lord Count is heading south, you say? Then I would guess, Isabel, that your bridegroom is running away to France."

Chapter 5

Too young to be comforted by the fact that it was her pride alone that was hurt, Isabel was now faced by days and nights of utter and unbearable unhappiness. Her immediate bewilderment and disbelief, shared by her father (who was sure that Louis had slipped away on some final errand of gallantry and would return for his wedding), were replaced, as the hours dragged by, with anger, misery, and the impulse to run off and hide.

The Flemish knights pursued the young Count until they reached the river bank. Here they questioned a peasant, tilling his field nearby, and were told that a horseman answering their description of Louis had ridden up at full gallop not long before and joined a band of men with a dozen horses awaiting him there.

"They forded the river," he told them, pointing to the spot, "and set out, *ventre à terre,* in the direction of Artois."

When Isabel and her mother heard this they implored King Edward to take them back to Calais immediately. Their situation here in Ghent was intolerable; the castle was already decorated for the wedding, and the guests, some appalled, some secretly amused by Louis' disgraceful behavior, had nothing to do while they waited for more news of him but to gossip and speculate. Queen Philippa, a Fleming herself, felt the blow doubly. To have her daughter betrayed and made a laughingstock by one of her own people. was almost more than she could endure.

Edward, still refusing to abandon all hope of Louis' return, agreed reluctantly that they should, certainly, have all Isabel's wedding furniture and their own belongings packed and made ready for departure. But they must wait, he insisted, until the following morning—the morning of the day set for the wedding—before leaving Ghent.

Shortly after dawn, while the great castle was still locked

for the night, a dusty horseman rode into sight and hailed the sleepy guard. Without identifying himself the stranger thrust a piece of parchment into the guard's hand, asked him to see that it reached King Edward of England. and galloped swiftly away.

Edward was awake. He had, as a matter of fact, slept little since Louis' disappearance. The Queen, too, was awake and dreading the day before them.

As they had long since said everything there was to say and were lying side by side in grim silence, the timid scratch on the door was almost welcome. They looked at each other, in the gray morning light, and the King shouted "Enter!"

It was one of the Queen's ladies, her hair in disarray and her chamber gown only half-fastened. She handed the parchment to Edward, curtsied, and hurried out again.

With a grunt of surprise, the King climbed out of bed and took it to the window. Philippa rose and followed him. They read it together and, when they had finished, they were silent for a moment. Then Edward sighed.

"So," he said wearily, "the lad had his escape planned all the time! I would never have believed it possible! Mother of God, but this is a nasty business. Well, well—I suppose we must send for the child. The sooner she knows about this"— he indicated the parchment, still clutched in his hand—"and we leave Ghent, the more comfortable we will all be."

The same lady-in-waiting, a few minutes later, brought Isabel to the royal bedchamber and, at their request, left her alone with her parents.

Edward kissed her and touched her dark head with an apologetic hand.

"A letter has just reached us," he told her gently, "from Count Louis. I'm sorry to have to tell you, _ma fille,_ that he is in France and has no intention of ever carrying out his part in your marriage contract."

Isabel flinched as if she had been struck across the face. Her father gulped, looked over at the Queen as if for help, then hurried on with his explanation.

"He sends his most abject apologies to you, however, and assures me that had he not been already bound by affection and an early pledge to Margaret of Brabant, he would have considered himself fortunate indeed to win such a charming, gifted, and beautiful bride."

"But I don't understand, sir," said Isabel. "If he was determined not to wed me, why did he agree to everything and take part in the betrothal ceremony?"

"According to this," Edward waved the letter, "he was kept a prisoner here by his guardians, without any comforts, visitors, or exercise. He pretended to give in to their demands so that he could find some way to escape and return to France."

Before the girl could say anything more, Philippa moved to her side and took her in her arms. "I must tell you, my dear daughter, that both my lord and I regret, with all our hearts, the unwitting part we have played in this wretched situation. We had no idea that Louis was being subjected to such treatment. . . ."

"I believed the lad had quite honestly changed his mind," interrupted Edward angrily. "I talked with him, as you know, at Bergues-St. Vinox, and I have his signed statement, attesting to his willingness to enter into the alliance with you. It was all false, false, false! Every word, every action was planned and plotted!"

"I blame his guardians," said Queen Philippa. "Louis is just a boy, after all, and it was both stupid and cruel to force him in such a fashion. But I think that we must now try to forget the whole matter and be grateful that our Isabel's affections were not engaged." As she spoke, she tightened her arm around the Princess and peered anxiously into her face. To her great relief, the girl did not deny that this was so. The price of her freedom had been high, to be sure, but she *was* free, free to return home to England when the siege was over, free and heartwhole. It was pleasant, too, to know that her mother and father were in complete sympathy with her and extremely proud of the way she had behaved in these humiliating circumstances; they made much of her these days, showering her in private and before the whole court with many tokens of their approval and affection.

Her brother Ned did what he could to keep Isabel busy. He and the younger gallants at Newtown saw to it that her days were filled with sport and her evenings with dancing, leaving her little or no time to brood.

All this helped, but it was Bernard d'Albret, she soon discovered, who was the most understanding of everyone at the camp, and with whom she felt most at ease. It was he who appeared at her side when the weather was too cold or wet for hunting and hawking, either bringing her books that exactly fitted her mood, suggesting a quiet hour with his beloved paints and brushes—a privilege he allowed no one else—or finding new songs for her to practice on her lute.

As she said to Alexia one night, she would be an ungrateful girl indeed to continue moping in the face of all this kindness and attention. "I have too many good friends to fret and be doleful!"

King Edward's anger and wounded feelings were being gradually soothed too, but in an entirely different fashion. Fearing that he might show his wrath by cutting off the woolen trade that was bringing prosperity to Flanders, the Flemings who were responsible for the whole thing lost no time in trying to win back his good will. They apologized abjectly and, as a more practical proof of their indignation over Count Louis' defection, immediately raised an army of a hundred thousand men which they sent to Edward at Calais to fight under his banner.

Not long after that the Earl of Lancaster and Sir Walter Manny, with a large band of knights and squires, marched in from Gascony. All this new strength made the King eager to end the siege and he turned his attention to what was, certainly, a most welcome task and diversion.

Realizing that some provisions must be reaching the beleaguered city, Edward gave the Earl of Warwick eighty ships and sent him off to strengthen the blockade with definite orders to pursue any foreign ship that approached the shore of France and either sink it or see that all the food it carried was thrown into the sea.

A tall tower was built on the spit of land that lay between Calais and the harbor and manned with a large force of archers. With the English army encamped on the land side, and the fleet and tower protecting the sea side, Calais was now, after almost a year of semistarvation, completely shut off from the outside world.

Where was the King of France? Why was he not making some attempt to rescue his Calaisians? The hungry people within the city walls asked the question—and so did the English.

It was the end of July when Philip moved at last, and King Edward, hearing of his approach, took immediate steps to protect his position. There were only two roads that led to the city, the shore road along the downs and the inland road over the marshes that was boggy and pitted with ditches. To the forces already posted along these routes, the English king added further precautions: he sent word to his fleet to move in closer to the shore, and he dispatched the Earl of Derby with more archers and a band of men-at-arms to prevent the French from crossing the bridge at Nieullet.

On a hot still night, the French army climbed to the top of a hill at Sangate, a village situated between Calais and Wissant, and came to a halt. The moon was full, and the sentries on the high walls of the beleaguered city suddenly saw, in the bright, white light, the flash of armor, the fluttering silks of the French banners, and the dark shapes of the baggage wagons as the soldiers on the flat hilltop prepared to make camp. "Help is arriving at last!" they shouted to the townspeople waiting below. "Help is arriving at last!"

King Edward's scouts, peering out from the trees on a heavily wooded knoll not far from Sangate, watched King Philip's men pitching their tents. They crept back to Newton-the-Bold with the news.

Confident that Philip would soon find it impossible to move his army any closer, Edward smiled and waited. The fleet waited. The Earl of Derby, at Nieullet Bridge, waited.

They were still waiting, on the morning of the second day, when one of Warwick's men hurried up from the beach and asked for an audience with the King. He was carrying what looked like a small hatchet with a wet piece of parchment tied to the handle.

Edward, the Earl of Arundel at his side, admitted him at once and asked him his business.

"We captured a small vessel last evening, Sire," he said. "It had slipped out from Calais and seemed determined to break through our blockade. Just before the captain surrendered, we saw him throw something overboard—toward the shore. We think this must be it. It was washed up on the beach by the morning tide."

His face alight with curiosity, the King took it in his hand and read the blurred lines on one side of the parchment: "To his Gracious Majesty King Philip of France."

"On my honor, lad!" he said. "Your discovery is most welcome, indeed!" And, breaking the seal with eager fingers, he hastily scanned the contents.

He turned now to Arundel. "It's a desperate plea from Calais' governor," he said. "The city will be ours before much longer! It's splendid news, Arundel. Summon the Council and we'll share it with them."

When the other nobles gathered around him, the King read aloud most of the pitiful missive. "Our city is in great need of corn, wine, and flesh," wrote the Governor; "everything has been eaten up, even the dogs, cats and horses. We can find nothing more to eat but each other and must surrender unless we are immediately supplied with food."

He looked triumphantly around the ring of delighted faces.

"Victory at last, my lords! Another great day for England!" Ripping the damp parchment off the handle of the hatchet, he waved it gaily over his head. "I think we must see to it that this letter reaches its destination. It would be most disgraceful, indeed, to keep it from its rightful owner!"

They were still discussing ways and means of sending it on to King Philip when word came from the sentry at the gate that four French noblemen were riding toward the camp. Edward, more or less expecting such a deputation, gave orders that they be brought directly to his pavilion.

Just before they entered, he tapped the Governor's letter and gave a gleeful laugh. "How extremely opportune! As our Cousin of France would say, 'It arranges itself!'"

The oldest of King Philip's envoys stepped forward and knelt before England's king. "I am Eustace de Ribeaumont," he said, bowing his head.

"And most welcome here," was Edward's instant reply. "Rise, my lord, and present your friends, if you will."

After Lord Geoffrey de Chargny, Sir Guy de Neslé, and the Lord of Beaujou had been greeted in their turn with the same cordiality, Lord Eustace de Ribeaumont delivered his message.

"The King of France," he said, "informs you, Sire, through us, that he is now come to the hill at Sangate in order to give you battle. But as he cannot find any means of approaching you . . ." a rueful look swept over the tall young Frenchman's face as he remembered the archers lining the roads and the

English soldiers gathered around the bridge. None of them had, at Edward's orders, challenged or molested them as they made their way to England's camp, but the four envoys had been allowed to see just how strongly the approaches were guarded. "As he cannot come to you," he repeated, "he requests that your Council confer with his, so that they may choose, between them, a spot where a general combat may take place."

His jeweled crown gleaming in the sunshine, King Edward shook his head.

"I perfectly understand the request of my adversary, my lords," he replied, his voice quiet but firm, "but you will tell him from me, if you please, that I have been on this spot for nearly a twelve-month. This he knew, and he could, had he chosen, have come here much sooner. As he has allowed me to remain so long, and to expend such great amount of money besieging the city of Calais, he will agree, I am sure, that I would be very foolish indeed to risk what I now hope to gain within a very short time. So if, therefore, neither he nor his army can pass this way, he must, I am afraid, seek out some other road."

The disgruntled noblemen bowed and asked permission to return to their master.

"With all my heart," Edward answered. A malicious smile flitted over his face; he turned for a fleeting second and lowered an eyelid at his own noblemen, all watching and listening intently. "But before you go, my lords . . ." Reaching out a hand, he extended the still-damp letter from the Governor of Calais. "I wonder if you would carry this back with you to my cousin Philip? It seems to be meant for him, not me."

At this point Pope Clement decided to interfere in the quarrel and sent two cardinals to try and make peace between France and England. They spent a busy three days arguing futilely with representatives of both countries then threw up their holy hands and rode home.

Not long after their departure, the townspeople of Calais, who often climbed the walls during these despairing times to watch beside their sentries, saw unusual activity on Sangate Hill. Night fell and a great bonfire lighted the sky.

Those who were used to the ways of warfare explained it to the others:

"They're burning their tents and striking camp!"

With the smoke that rose in a dark column went the last hopes of the starving Calaisians. Their king had deserted them. They must surrender.

By the next morning, the only proof that King Philip had made any effort at all to relieve his besieged city of Calais was smoldering campfires and many large piles of refuse being pulled this way and that by a pack of hungry dogs.

Down in Newtown-the-Bold, the King and his nobles waited for some communication from the Calaisians. Today, tomorrow. . . .

Suddenly a great shout went up from the English sentries watching the city walls. The doors of all the little wooden houses were thrown open and everyone poured out into the streets. Even the camp cooks, who were just beginning to prepare the meats for the King's dinner, threw down their knives and rushed away from their worktables to join the others.

There, standing alone on the battlements, was Lord John de Vienne, the Governor of Calais, signaling to those below that he was ready to parley with them.

King Edward, looking around at the exultant faces of his friends, summoned first Sir Walter Manny, the hero of many French campaigns and but recently released from Châtelet, where he had been held prisoner, and, second, Lord Basset of Wycombe.

"Hear what de Vienne has to say," the King told them, "but remember that the stubbornness of those people has cost us much. They must pay in ransom and in lives for our long months at their gates."

When the two Englishmen reached the Governor's side, they were shocked by his appearance. So emaciated that he might have been a hundred years of age, and so weak that he could hardly stand before them, he hastened to make them welcome, then clutched at the wall for support. Sir Walter Manny, a tender-hearted man, took him by the arm and led him to a bench.

"Sir, my lord," he said, "we are old friends, you and I, and if we must meet this day as enemies, we can at least conduct our parley in some comfort. You are not strong enough, de Vienne, to stand."

De Vienne held out a thin hand and let them see how it trembled. "My plight is obvious, Sir Walter. And many of my people are in worse straits than I am, which is why you and I are meeting now." He sat, and smiled feebly at them while he gathered up his strength to begin his painful speech.

"Dear gentlemen," he said at last, "you are both valiant knights. You understand, I am sure, my situation. I came here, at my liege's orders, to defend and guard the town and castle of Calais, and, as its governor, I have done my best. But now, with all hope of rescue gone, I must, on behalf of its people, ask that gallant king, your lord, to have pity on us before we all perish of hunger."

"Entreat him, if you will," he continued, his voice shaking, "to take the town and castle and all the riches of Calais and let those of us who have remained here to defend it depart in safety, to seek refuge elsewhere!"

Manny, sensing the kindest way to phrase his master's hard words, was silent for a moment.

"I am afraid," he replied finally, his face full of compassion, "that King Edward may not be willing to grant your plea. The people of Calais have, by their obstinate defense of the city, cost my lord so much money and so many lives that he is not disposed to allow them to go free. His anger against them, and against you, too, my friend, is very great indeed. He is determined that you must all surrender yourselves to him, to be ransomed or put to death at his will."

"Before God, sir," said de Vienne, turning even paler than before, "your king's terms are too hard for us! We have served our lord and master loyally, suffering much, and would endure more, willingly, if it were possible to protect the lives of those under our care. Return to King Edward, gentlemen, and beg him to have pity on us!"

On reaching the camp again, the two Englishmen found that King Edward had, during their absence, ordered his lackeys to set up his great crimson canopy of state and was seated under it with the Queen at his side. Slightly behind the royal couple, on smaller throne chairs, were Prince Edward and Princess Isabel and, behind them and all around the four sides of the dais, stood the lords and ladies of the court.

Sir Walter Manny advanced, knelt, and related what had passed between him and the Governor of Calais.

Edward shook his head firmly. "No," he replied harshly, "I must have an absolute surrender. Everyone in the city deserves to be put to the sword."

"Sire!" cried Manny, horrified. "Think, I pray you, of the consequences! If you do this the French will retaliate—any Englishmen they capture will be treated with equal cruelty!"

Warwick, distressed, moved forward and added his protest. Arundel joined him; Holland, too, and all the others murmured their support of Manny's opinion.

Isabel held her breath. Surely, she told herself, he was only pretending and would soon relent. Her mother, she noticed, was sitting very quietly beside him, her face impassive.

"Well, gentlemen," said the King, after a few minutes' consideration, "I am not so stubborn as to stand alone against you all. Inform the Governor of Calais, Sir Walter, that if he will send out six of the town's principal citizens, their heads and feet bare, with ropes around their necks and the keys of the city and the castle in their hands, I will pardon the rest of the inhabitants."

Lord John de Vienne listened quietly, grimly. "Remain here, my lords," he said to Manny and Basset. "I must inform my people."

The two envoys watched him crawl feebly down into the market place and heard the bell toll to summon the starving Calaisians. It was impossible, from where they stood, to hear what was being said below, but the wails and cries from the great crowd gathered around de Vienne reached them only too clearly.

A man separated himself from the others and came forward. When he had finished speaking another loud cry went up and many fell on their knees before him. A second thin figure joined him, another—and another. In as many moments there were six men grouped together.

Lord John de Vienne, unable to walk so far, mounted a miserable, scrawny horse—one of the few that had escaped the butcher's knife—and rode with his friends through the town gate and over to the barricade. He turned, then, to Manny:

"As Governor of Calais," he announced formally, "I de-

liver up to you these six citizens, whom I swear to you are
the most wealthy and respectable men of our city. I beg of
you, gentle sir, to beseech the King not to put them to death,
though they declare themselves willing to die to save their
townsmen and women."

"I cannot answer for the King," Manny replied sadly, "but
I will do everything in my power to save them."

The six gaunt Calaisians, a heartbreaking sight, knelt before King Edward and Queen Philippa. Their bare heads
were bent, their feet skeleton-thin, and as they held out the
keys to their city, their arms were not much thicker than the
ropes around their necks.

Walter Manny presented them: Eustace de Pierre, John
Daire, James Wisant, his brother Peter, and two cousins of
the same name.

"Most gallant king," said Eustace de Pierre, "we surrender
ourselves to your absolute will and pleasure in order to save
the lives of our friends, who have, as you know, endured
much distress and misery. Condescend, out of your nobleness
of mind, to have mercy and compassion upon us."

Fighting back her own tears, Isabel heard many of the
lords and ladies around her crying audibly. Prince Edward
gulped. She slipped her hand into his.

"No," said King Edward. "I shall have your heads. Fetch
the headsman."

A groan went up. His face flushed, the king glared around
him.

Manny stepped forward again. "Sire! Sire!" he protested
bravely. "Do not, I pray you, tarnish your noble name with
such a cruel act!"

Aware now that her father was in earnest, Isabel turned
white. The faces surrounding her swam in a mist. She must
not faint, she told herself. A princess must never faint. Besides, scenes like this were expected after a victory; how else
could the vanquished be kept at heel? "Wars must be fought.
It's winning that matters." She had said that herself, to
Alexia. She clenched her teeth and clutched her brother's
hand.

But as she looked away from the stricken, pitiful men on
the ground in front of the dais, her eyes encountered those of
Bernard d'Albret. His lips were moving in prayer. His gray

eyes, however, staring intently at her over the head of a
small page, were pleading with her. There was the same expression on his face that Isabel had seen when he had wanted
to feed the long line of starving Calaisians, the poor people
expelled from their homes. What had he said to her then? "I
wouldn't dare—but if *you* would, Your Grace!" It was as if
he had said it to her again, only more strongly, more inper-
atively this time.

Moving to the edge of her chair, Isabel leaned forward
and whispered frantically in her mother's ear.

"For the love of God, *ma mère,* save them! Save them before it is too late!"

A long, horrible moment went by. Hadn't she heard?

Isabel was about to speak again when Queen Philippa rose
abruptly and threw herself down on the dais at her husband's
feet.

"Gentle sir," she said, in a voice loud enough to reach everyone present, "since the day that I crossed the perilous seas
to come to you here, I have asked not one favor of you.
Now I do. Now I most humbly ask as a gift, as a proof of
your love for me and for the sake of the Son of the Blessed
Mary, that you be merciful to these six brave men."

The King looked down at her and frowned. A solemn hush
fell over the murmuring crowd. He sat still, silent. No one
dared move or speak.

At last, when the situation had become almost unbearably
tense, he rose from his throne and raised the Queen to her
feet.

"Ah, dear lady," he said, with a note of regret in his stern
voice, "I could wish you, in the circumstances, anywhere but
here! But as you have interceded in such a manner, it would
of course be impossible to refuse you. The prisoners are
yours, Your Grace. Do with them as you wish."

Chapter 6

A truce was signed with France, King Edward left Calais in the hands of his beloved and trusted ward Aymery de Pavie, and the English headed for home. By the end of October they had landed, received a conquerors' welcome and had resumed their peaceful lives in their own country.

Having by this time had more than enough war, King Edward now threw himself into the pursuit of personal enjoyment. Hardly a day went by without its tournament or ball at which, as a reward for her obedience and gallant behavior after her bridegroom's defection, Isabel was publicly recognized as the Lady Royal of England and second only to the Queen. And although her mother protested strongly, thinking her too young for such honors and lavishness, the King gave her a large income of her own, twice as many attendants as she had before, and set up a separate household for her under the capable guidance of Lady Throxford, a most delightful young widow. Besides all this, her wardrobe was crammed with the beautiful garment provided for the wedding that failed to take place and she had more jewels than she could wear.

As a result, Isabel almost forgot her bitter experience on the other side of the Channel; remembering, when she *did* think of it, everyone's kindness to her—and particularly that of Bernard d'Albret. Now the only black cloud in her sky was the imminent prospect of saying farewell to the Princess Joanna, for after all the delays, negotiations for Joanna's marriage to the heir to the throne of Castile had finally been concluded. Although the King was aware that the shifty Castilian's might change their minds again, there was nothing to do but assume that they were acting in good faith and send the little bride to her bridegroom.

The two sisters clung to each other all through the Christmas celebrations, and when, shortly before Twelfth-night, it was decided that Joanne and her sister would set out for Plymouth on the ninth day of January, Isabel obtained her father's permission to accompany her at least part of the way. With forty shiploads of wedding furniture and attendants to be carried over England's rough roads there was the certainty of a long, slow journey to the coast and the two princesses rejoiced at the opportunity to be together.

The King and Queen rode with them as far as Mortlake; there they halted, kissed Joanna for the last time, and consigned her to the care of John, the Bishop of Carlisle, and Sir Robert Bourchier, the two men whose responsibility it was to see that she and her entourage reached their destination in safety. It was a tearful farewell. After her parents had turned sadly back toward Westminster, Isabel, for the first time, found it necessary to draw the curtains of her sister's litter until the weeping princess had recovered some of her composure.

Afterwards, they emerged from the jolting shelter and mounted their palfreys; from their position near the head of the long procession, they could look back at the immense cavalcade following them: ladies, gentlemen, chaplains, lackeys, serving women, pageboys, minstrels, sergeants-at-arms, bands of soldiers and archers. It wound, like a glittering snake, along the curving road. And off in the distance, in a cloud of dust, were the baggage wagons, carrying more objects for her future use than Joanna could list or remember; her bed, with its coverlet and hangings of rich Tripoli silk all embroidered in gleaming golden dragons, carpets and cushions, cloth-of-gold vestments for her chaplains, curtains for her confessional, gold and silver articles for her altar, a looking glass, warming pan, bath, tapestries, plate for her table, folding chairs, condiments for her kitchen, scarlet-and-pearl-trimmed saddles for her horses. . . .

Then, of course, there were the dozens of boxes that held her elaborate and numerous changes of costume, many of which Joanna had embroidered with her own hands, but many others that she had not yet seen. There was one she preferred not to think about—a heavy gown of Spanish cloth of gold, opening down the front in the Castilian manner.

To their great delight, the two princesses were not parted for almost a month. The entourage covered only a few miles each day, never traveled on Sundays, and when they reached

a town that could accommodate them in reasonable comfort
they often settled down for a few days' rest. It was the fifth
day of February before they rode into Plympton, a small
town about four miles distant from the port of Plymouth
where the ships were gathering to take Joanna to Bordeaux.
It was at Bordeaux that she would reside until such a time as
she must travel on to Castile, a matter still not settled by
Pedro's father.

Sir Robert Bourchier, after arranging for the royal party
to live at Plympton's abbey until they boarded their ships,
climbed back on his horse and hurried off to Plymouth to as-
certain just when that would be. He returned weary and distressed.

"Less than half the fleet is in the harbor," he told Joanna
and Isabel, and the Bishop of Carlisle, who was with them,
"and even those are not in any condition to sail. I'm afraid
we will have to be here in Plympton for many weeks."

"Good!" said Joanna. "I am in no hurry, my lord. Every
day in England is precious to me."

"And every day with my sister is precious to *me*," added
Isabel.

Bourchier regarded the Princess Royal ruefully and shook
his head.

"I'm sorry, Your Grace," he said, "but my orders are to
send you back to Westminster with the large escort that
brought us here to Plympton. They must, for many reasons,
set out as early as possible on the morrow."

The return journey took only a few days, for which Isabel
was very grateful. She had no desire to dawdle along the
way, and the long, bracing hours in the saddle gave her a
perfect opportunity to regain her spirits. As a result, she was
able to greet her parents cheerfully, to assure them that
Joanna was comfortable and in good health, and even to
make an amusing story of their interminable ride to the
coast. It was sad to think that she might not see Joanna
again, and to hear, as the weeks went by, that she and her
household had not yet sailed for Gascony, and that she might
have had all this extra time with her sister, but instead of
brooding, Isabel forced herself to think of the weeks they *had*
been allowed to share, and entered gaily into the life at court
with the rest of her family.

It was April before Joanna finally set out on her travels

again, and by that time Isabel and the court had moved to Windsor. Spring was early that year, the countryside softly green and the first flowers beginning to open in the unusually warm sun. The perfect weather sent the lords and ladies out into the tilt yard most days, the men to practice for a great tournament soon to be held in the meadow below the Castle, the ladies to watch. It was King Edward's intention to establish a new order of the Knights of the Round Table; he had built a tower for it here at Windsor, enclosing a specially planned round room to hold the round table and the knights' chairs, and he had taken a personal interest in every detail concerning the building itself and the colorful celebration that would begin on St. George's Day.

This exciting contest was, of course, the main topic of conversation at the old castle—among the gentlemen, certainly, although the ladies found it a little more interesting to gossip about Lady Joan of Kent and what most of them described as 'her outrageous behavior.' Whether or not it was outrageous, it was, Isabel thought, unwise. Ever since Tom Holland and the young Earl of Salisbury had returned from Calais she had divided her attention between them, playing one against the other until neither man knew which one she preferred.

The Queen told Isabel that she did not care how the contest ended; both Tom and Salisbury were too good for the brassy-haired Joan. "As long as she keeps her paws off our Ned," she added, "I will be content. And the sooner she is wed the safer I will feel."

Isabel, sitting beside her mother as the lackeys finished clearing out the long tables and the musicians struck up the music for the first dance of the evening, saw Salisbury lead Joan onto the floor. She watched them idly for a few moments, then realized that she was not the only one whose eyes were on the bright-haired girl in the scarlet gown. Standing alone, with a tense, angry look on his face, was Tom Holland, his intent gaze following every nimble step of her velvet shoes; his head was slightly bent to one side also, making it only too apparent to Isabel that he was trying to hear what Joan was saying to her partner.

Glancing around, Isabel noticed that the Queen was watching. So were the King and the Prince of Wales. In fact, it seemed to her that the attention of everyone in the Hall was caught by the one pair of dancers who, unaware of the

stir they were causing, talked and laughed together until the
music stopped. They were so absorbed in each other, in fact,
that they stood alone in the center of the great room, not realizing for a moment or two that everyone else had left the
floor.

A smothered laugh reached Joan's ears. As she turned
hastily and moved toward her seat, her blue eyes met those
of Holland, still fixed angrily on her face. She paused involuntarily, and a hush fell over the entire room.

There was a gasp and another smothered jeering laugh;
then another, and another and another. On the spot where
Joan had been standing, just a second before, lay a bright
blue silk garter.

She looked down and flamed as scarlet as her gown. The
laughter, rising in waves around her, sounded so malicious
that she flinched and put up one hand in a small gesture of
protest. The Earl of Salisbury, oblivious to what had happened, was hailing a friend nearby. Tom Holland, his face
red, too, took an indecisive step toward her and then halted.

Prince Edward rose from his chair on the dais but the
King, already on his feet, strode past him and leaned over
the dainty piece of blue ribbon. He picked it up, then held it
high over his head so everyone could see it.

"Honi soit qui mal y pense!" he announced loudly, tying it
snugly around his sleeve. Pausing in front of his blushing
niece, he took her hand in his and raised it to his lips.

Now he returned to the dais and sat down again beside the
Queen. "It's a pretty trifle," he said, touching the ribbon with
a long finger, "and I've had a sudden thought: my new order
of the Round Table—I think I shall name it The Order of
the Garter!"

This was not the first time a garter had been used as a dec-
orative device, nor did King Edward have any way of
knowing his Order of the Garter would continue on through
the centuries. Although the order was, on the surface, a re-
vival of King Arthur's Round Table and dedicated to the
deeds of Chivalry, it was, initially, a military organization,
formed so that England's military leaders could meet and become friends; and as it would inevitably be held a great
honor to be among those chosen, the King selected his
bravest soldiers, the ones who had well earned such a reward.

Most of these twenty-six noblemen who were the first Knights of the Garter had proved their valor at Crécy; a few were seasoned warriors—the King, the Duke of Lancaster, the Earls of Warwick and Stafford, Sir Walter Manny, Sir Thomas Holland. Many, however, were young friends of the Prince of Wales and had, like His Highness, just won their spurs; the Earl of Salisbury, Sir Hugh Courtenay (the Earl of Devon), and Roger, the Earl of March, were among them.

Gascony's brave Captal de Buch, Sir Henry Eam, a gallant Fleming, and Sir Sanchet d'Aubrèchicourt, a knight of Hainault, were included; Sir Nigel Loring, Sir John Chandos, and Sir James Audeley, three of England's most daring and adventurous knights, added a hint of spice to the short list.

Their ladies, as the Dames de la Fraternité de St. George, rode beside them in the great procession before the opening tournament, the Queen with the King, of course, and the Lady Royal with her brother Edward. It was a magnificent spectacle and, as everyone agreed afterward, surpassed anything of the kind ever seen in England, as did the Garter ceremony itself and the colorful exciting days of the tournament.

Jean de Grailly, the darkly handsome, rather hawknosed Captal de Buch, told Isabel, as they sat side by side at the banquet which marked the end of the celebration, that he would remember it all his life.

"When I return to my little castle at Teste," he said, "I shall look over the blue Gulf of Arachon and listen to the wild sea birds screaming in the lonely dunes and marshes of Les Landes and think of your green England and your great Windsor Castle and the pleasures of these days. And the beautiful ladies"—leaning a little closer, he gave her the kind of smile that made it clear to Isabel why he was known at home as *la fleur de la chevalrie de Gascogne, gallant avec une pointe de gaillardise.* . . .

Slightly uncomfortable, for the Princess was as yet too young to accept exaggerated gallantries with ease, she returned to his description of his home. Just where was La Teste?

"In my Captalet," he told her. "Hidden away in a bit of rough, wild country that lies between the sea and the Gironde. Many of my friends find it too lonely there, but I never have, not even when the soft mists roll in and there's nothing to see but the long sea grass below the windows, all silver and beaded with the damp." He took a sip of wine, and grinned. "Fortunately for them, La Teste is not too far from Bordeaux. I send them there when they tire of my solitude."

Bordeaux—Joanna. Isabel looked down at the table and indicated Lord and Lady d'Albret, sitting with some of the other guests who had come to Windsor to watch the great event. "Tell me more of Bordeaux," she said to the Captal. "My Lord d'Albret has just informed me that my sister must remain there all summer, and I have been wondering how she will pass the time. Her wedding will not take place until November and that is so many months away. . . ."

De Buch nodded. "But the months will not seem long to Her Highness," he reassured her. "She will enjoy Bordeaux, I am sure, and the old Castle is comfortable. It does grow a bit oppressive in July and August, but perhaps we can persuade her people to bring Her Grace to La Teste for the hottest weeks."

"Oh!" Isabel gave an envious sigh. "How delightful it sounds, my lord."

"Some day I may even have the privilege of *your* company there, Your Highness. Who knows?"

His words meant little at the time, but they returned to her mind later that evening when she heard that the D'Albrets would sail home in a fleet of her father's ships; supplies and messages for Joanna's household would go with them, and they would spend a few days with her in Bordeaux before traveling south to their château at Dax. Why should she not accompany them to Bordeaux and spend the summer with her sister? And, if Joanna agreed, accept the Captal's invitation to visit his little retreat by the sea?

It was such an enchanting thought that she sought out Lord d'Albret and asked him if he and his lady would have any objections to her joining the party.

"Objection! Your Highness! We would be only too honored, of course."

"Then will you help me persuade my father and mother?" Isabel, growing more and more excited as her sudden idea turned into an actual possibility, smiled earnestly up into his kind, pleasant face.

"I shall tell His Majesty what is true, Your Highness," he

said, "that the Princess Joanna is very sad and lonely. She had tears in her eyes when we bade her farewell."

After she had thanked him and was about to join the younger guests, she turned back. "I have been wondering," she said, "why your son did not come with you and Lady d'Albret? We would have made him very welcome here at Windsor, my lord, very welcome!"

"Bernard?"

Isabel nodded. "We became good friends in Calais," she said. "I hoped he would accompany you and take part in the tournament."

"I'm afraid he prefers his paintbrush to the lance, Your Highness." Lord d'Albret's voice was grim. "I could wish ... however, I must not bother you with my worries. You are extremely kind to remember the lad and I know that my lady will be most grateful for your interest."

"Take me to her ladyship now," said Isabel impulsively. "If we are, perhaps, to travel together, there are many questions that only she can answer. I know so little about the life in Bordeaux and what my ladies and I would need to take with us."

Book II

Chapter 7

It was the middle of May before the little fleet of ships, with the Princess Royal and Lady Throxford on board, finally sailed up the yellow Garonne and into the harbor at Bordeaux. Isabel, during the long uneventful days of the voyage, had found herself growing fonder than ever of her lady-in-waiting and much less taken with Lady d'Albret than she had been when they first met.

The Gasconne, a short, rather squat woman with the suggestion of a mustache on her upper lip, was so unlike her son Bernard that Isabel wondered how she could be his mother. Not only in appearance (which Isabel, the one dark Plantagenet, found easy to understand) but also in everything she said, did, and, apparently, even thought. No matter how the conversation began, it would end up, when Lady d'Albret was talking, in a discussion of her own lineage, her two handsome sons, and the importance of the vast d'Albret holdings south of Bordeaux.

Where both Bernard and Lord d'Albret were slightly reserved and quietly deferential, my lady alternated irritatingly between overfamiliarity with the Princess and occasional spasms of servility. She tended to paint her face too brightly for Isabel's taste, too, and bedecked herself in such a glittering array of jewels that all the other ladies, laughing at the garish display, began to leave most of theirs in their jewel caskets; and Lady Throxford had to scold them more than once for speaking too critically among themselves of the Gasconne and her ways. And Isabel, when she saw Lord d'Albret flush and turn away in distress as his lady received an openly scornful glance or ill-concealed sneer, added her voice to Lady Throxford's and curbed her own desire to join in the malicious talk.

It was aggravating, however, to be delayed on the busy, hot quay at Bordeaux by Lady d'Albret's insistence on taking

charge of the little group. She led them with annoying
slowness, through the piles of bales and boxes, past the clam-
oring vendors and noisy, brightly clad women of the town,
all eager to stare at these strange English ladies and gentlemen, and halted them abruptly in front of a long line of city
officials, drawn up to greet them.

Isabel was, of course, expecting such a deputation, and
bowed, smiled, and pretended to listen to the interminable
speeches. But when Lady d'Albret, after they had finished at
last, began to question them about her Bordeaux friends, rolling their titles on her tongue and preening herself as she did
so, the Princess had a difficult time concealing her impatience.

All this was forgotten, however, the moment they left the
quay, for there, beaming at her from between the silken curtains of a handsome double litter, was Joanna. No one could
hold Isabel back now; she ran ahead of the others, her one
thought to be in her sister's arms.

When the Lady d'Albret and Lady Throxford were helped
into a second litter and the cortege began to move, the two
young princesses were sitting side by side on the soft cushions, so deep in conversation that it was some minutes before
they realized that they were on their way to the Castle.

"What fools we are," said Joanna, leaning across her sister
to jerk open the curtains on the other side of the litter. "Gab-
bling together when I should be showing you this enchanting
city! We have all summer to talk. Quick! See that odd head-
dress on that woman—and those purple and scarlet blossoms
on that wall!"

Isabel, entranced, exclaimed over everything in sight; the
red-and-white houses lining the narrow, cobbled streets, the
picturesquely clad Gascons, and the small brown donkeys
struggling along under burdens of every description. "I must
have one of those donkeys," she said to Joanna. "I shall take
it home and keep it as a pet."

"I know," Joanna laughed. "I said the same thing when I
first arrived here in Bordeaux. But I'm not so sure—they can
be stubborn little fellows, you know."

Lord and Lady d'Albret, eager now to be with their own
family, saw Isabel settled into Bordeaux's old Castle and
turned toward the south. They would be returning to Bor-

deaux long before the summer was over, they promised, and they assured Sir Robert Bourchier that there would always be a warm welcome awaiting the whole English party at their château in Dax.

The reunited sisters, more than content to be alone, sped them on their way, then threw themselves wholeheartedly into the delightful task of enjoying their summer together. Except for one hour a day which must be spent with Joanna's Spanish teacher, their time was their own, and their only cause for complaint the swiftness with which it passed.

The ancient Castle, with its thick old walls lapped by the broad river and its tall turrets providing a wide view of the wooded hills beyond the city, was actually part abbey. Its Grande Salle opened into a pretty garden that was encircled by cool, shaded cloisters, and here, under a clear turquoise sky, the ladies took their exercise. The King of Spain had, some weeks earlier, sent his very best minstrel to amuse his son's little English bride-to-be. His name was García de Gyvell, and as he had a gift for storytelling that almost equaled his charming voice and his way with a lute, the evenings slipped by as happily as did the daytime hours.

But Bordeaux in May and June and Bordeaux in July and August were two different cities. The glorious, beneficent sun turned hot and angry, glaring brassily down on the browning garden, and the princesses, as the weeks dragged away, understood for the first time why everyone in the city retreated into their bedrooms for most of the afternoon. They tried, at first, to sit in the cloisters when the sun was high, taking their needlework into the deep shadows under the arcades, but the deadly heat followed them even there. The soft evening breezes disappeared, too, leaving the nights so sticky and breathless that sound sleep was a thing of the past, and all those whose apartments opened over the river were forced by the unpleasant smells that arose from the sluggish water either to close their windows or move.

Remembering her conversation with the hawk-nosed black-bearded Captal de Buch, Isabel began to hope that he would appear and spirit them off to his hidden castle by the sea. The more she thought of it, in fact, the more inviting the vague prospect became, and she set a few discreet inquiries afoot concerning his whereabouts. No one in Bordeaux seemed to know where he was or what he was doing, and the d'Albrets, returning as they had promised, told Isabel that they had seen him last at Windsor.

Their only suggestion was that the English party should come home with them to Dax, but Joanna and Isabel, after discussing their invitation with the older members of their suite, declined it with thanks. To venture so much farther south would, they were sure, be a mistake. And again, as each day grew hotter, Isabel thought wistfully of De Buch's La Teste where, according to the Captal, the cool sea mists wreathed the castle towers and the sea grasses turned silver. . . .

Then, just as the d'Albrets were on the point of setting out again for home, a terrible rumor reached Bordeaux Castle. A great and deadly plague which had broken out first in China in 1347, spread over the plains of Tartary and moved on to Greece and Italy within the last few months was not, as everyone had assumed, being prevented by the mountains and seas from spreading farther. At this very moment, according to the courier who brought the news to the ancient city, there were several cases of it in Avignon.

"Avignon!" Lady d'Albret turned an ashy white and began to shake. She looked first at Sir Robert Bourchier, who had given them the horrible report, then rushed over to her husband, just entering the room behind him.

"The plague at Avignon!" Clutching Lord d'Albret's arm, she pulled him into a far corner, but her voice was so shrill that Isabel could hear everything she said. "We must start for home *this moment!* I'm ready—come, my lord! Let us leave immediately!"

"Now, now," Lord d'Albret's reply was obviously intended to quiet her but the two princesses saw that his face was drawn and almost as white as hers. "Try to be calm, my love. We must think of their Highnesses, you know, and see what is best to be done for them before we set out."

"Their Highnesses have enough people to look after them! Take me home!"

"Hush! Try to control yourself. And lower your voice, please."

"I wish he would take her home," whispered Joanna to Isabel. "Poor man!"

Sir Robert, who had been talking quietly with the Bishop

of Carlisle, now interrupted Lady d'Albret's frantic whispering. "We think, d'Albret," he said, moving over to join the two Gascons, "that our first step is to seek out the Governor of the city and confer with him. My first impulse is to flee Bordeaux, but we might be safer right here. Avignon is, after all, a good many miles away."

When the three men were gone, the others sat in frightened silence. Lady Throxford, rousing herself at last, tried to cheer them by talking of other matters; but it was no use. After a sentence or two every subject failed.

The cathedral bells rang out but no one counted the strokes. They rang out again before the door opened. Sir Robert and Lord d'Albret were accompanied now by both the Bishop and the Governor of Bordeaux, and Isabel, watching their faces as they entered the salon, was relieved to see that no one looked very worried.

"Well?" Lady d'Albret again rushed to her husband's side.

He patted her shoulder with a reassuring hand and smiled over at the other ladies. "Our good friend the Governor here," he said, "is quite sure that the disease will not reach Bordeaux and that their Highnesses will be just as safe here as at Dax. But if you, my love, would be happier at home, we will set out immediately."

Joanna, standing under a window in the Grande Salle that opened into the cloisters, felt a wave of fresher air.

"A breeze!" she exclaimed. "A breeze! Bring your lute, García—hurry, everyone! Let's not waste a moment of it."

Isabel, who was nearer the door, led the way into the long stone cloister, then stopped abruptly and gave a little cry of delight. The late July moon, now nearing its full, was casting an enchanted spell on the scorched garden, and it seemed as beautiful tonight, in the soft silvery light, as it had in glorious May. There was, as Joanna had thought, a gentle, cooling breeze; enough, at any rate, to stir the leaves on the olive trees and to turn the splashing, sparkling waters of the fountain into a soft spray.

At Lady Throxford's suggestion, a page brought an armful of silken cushions and the ladies settled themselves in a little circle near the moonlit fountain.

García de Gyvill struck a soft chord or two and began to sing. His tune, a haunting, slow melody, was new to his lis-

teners but the words were familiar and well loved by them
all. It was *The Romance of the Rose* that he had set to music
and he sang the poet's own description of the God of Love,
beautiful as an angel of the Lord, his head crowned with
flowers, as he listened in a magic garden to the dove, night-
ingale and skylark. It seemed to Isabel, dreaming tonight a
dream of her own, that she could actually see Love in the
shadow of the stunted olive trees. His hair shone silver-gilt in
the moonlight, and his strangely luminous gray eyes were
seeking hers. . . .

A quick footstep on the stone floor of the arcade startled
her back to reality; a dark figure moved swiftly over the
lawn to where the ladies were sitting. The minstrel, recognizing Sir Robert, stopped singing and dropped his lute on the
grass. Something, he was sure, was wrong.

Something was indeed very wrong.

"We must leave Bordeaux immediately," announced Bourchier grimly. "The plague has reached the city after all."

The brilliant moon was gone and the first rays of the sun
beginning to light up the sky when the English party, after a
night of fear and panic and confusion, neared their destination. Loremo was a small, peaceful village set on a wooded
hill and surrounded on all sides by miles of open country. Sir
Robert had two good reasons for choosing it as their retreat:
its healthy situation, and the fact that the only house of any
size there was owned by a prosperous wine dealer, Vidal
Buzet, who sold countless tons of good red wine each year to
John Chaucer, King Edward's Butler.

Sir Robert was sure that he would be willing to shelter the
two princesses, and the warmth of Buzet's welcome, after
they had explained why they were rousing him at such an
early hour, proved him quite right. His château, he said immediately, was theirs for as long as they needed it. He must,
himself, set out in a few hours, on a tour around the
vineyards to inspect the fast-ripening grapes and would be
absent from Loremo for several weeks. And as he was a widower whose only daughter had married and moved some distance away, the château stood empty so much of the time
that he was delighted to have them occupy it.

His repeated use of the word *château* made Isabel smile.
At home, she would have called it a manor house. It had,

they soon discovered, only one large salon and one reasonably comfortable solar, but the ladies, too weary to care,
climbed the stairs and settled themselves down on the beds
and pallets for a few hours' rest. The gentlemen did not complain, either, although the only accommodations available for
them were in the outbuildings that surrounded the cobbled
courtyard.

As Joanna said, awaking later from a refreshing sleep, "we
are *safe!*" She stretched, climbed down from the high bed,
and wandered over to an open window.

"How beautiful the countryside is, Isabel," she said cheerfully. "Come and see. And I do think it is much, much cooler
here than it was in Bordeaux."

Isabel glanced around, saw that the other ladies were
asleep, yawned, and joined her sister. Together they studied
the pretty scene that would become so familiar to them in
the weeks ahead—Monsieur Buzet's own vineyard, planted in
tidy rows on the sunny hillside, a shady grove of trees that
seemed dwarflike to their English eyes but were, at least,
green; a patch of meadow bordered by a narrow, shallow
stream; and, off in the distance, the white walls of the city
from which they had fled, topped by the gilded spire of the
cathedral.

They moved quietly over to the windows on the other side
of the long chamber and found that they were staring down
into the courtyard, its only inhabitants at this hour a cackling
hen wandering aimlessly about and one fuzzy brown dog curled
up on the warm stones.

Thus began an odd, unreal interval in which time seemed,
often, to stand still. Each new day was so like the last that
the two sisters soon lost track of them; had they been at
Loremo for ten days, they asked each other, or was it only a
se'ennight?

Sir Robert, after the first crowded night, had made everyone more comfortable by moving most of the household to
Creon, the village nearby, keeping only Lady Throxford, two
chamber-women, one cook, three lackeys, one squire, two
men-at-arms, and a page to attend the two royal ladies. The
chaplains were sent away with the rest of the suite as John,
the Bishop of Carlisle had, with the royal physician, accepted
the invitation of Loremo's priest to share his small quarters

beside the church. He would take care of the princesses' spiritual needs himself.

The one who had protested most at leaving Loremo and the royal party was García de Gyvill, and when he was reluctantly bidding his ladies farewell he gave his best lute to Lady Throxford.

"Her Grace will need music," he insisted, almost indignantly. "And I know that you left all her own instruments in Bordeaux."

This was true. There had been no time, nor had it been thought wise, to pack and move to Loremo anything but the most necessary things and lutes did not seem, in that hour of wild and frightened bustle, necessary. Lady Throxford had tucked in a few books, and now, with empty days to fill, they found these books and García's lute their only source of amusement.

Confined as the three women were, to two chambers, all formality was set aside. Lady Throxford might well have been an affectionate and charming aunt, entertaining her two young nieces in her small country home, so simply and easily did she accept the unusual situation.

"I think we are most fortunate," said Isabel to Joanna one hot August day when they happened to be alone. "Think of being shut up here with some of our other ladies!"

"I wish she belonged to *my* household," answered Joanna wistfully. "I love her, Bel. I do! I'm still a little frightened at the thought of living in Spain—and—and everything, but I wouldn't mind it quite as much if I had her with me. Why didn't our parents give *me* Lady Throxford?"

"Take her," said Isabel immediately. "You need her more than I do. We'll speak to Sir Robert first, and then ask Lady Throxford herself whether or not she is willing."

But Sir Robert, when they finally caught him in a corner of the courtyard, had too many pressing worries to be of much help. The plague, after that first warning, had proved to be an isolated case or two; but suddenly, and this message had just reached Loremo, the people of Bordeaux were falling ill of it and dying at a horrifying rate. Conditions there were growing more ghastly every hour; corpses were piling up in the streets; victims were being deserted by their families; in a few cases to survive but more often to die alone; and every ship in the harbor had sailed away, crammed with panic-stricken men, women and children.

"I'm afraid I made the wrong decision," he told Lady Throxford, who joined the little group at this moment. "We should all have sailed home to England—or perhaps down to Bayonne. It is too late now. No ship will venture into the harbor at Bordeaux and we have no way to send messages back to His Majesty."

"Perhaps our friends at Dax could help," suggested Lady Throxford. "The d'Albrets might find us a ship, my lord."

"I'll set out immediately," Bourchier looked almost cheerful at the thought. "And if there is no sign of the plague down there I will make all the necessary arrangements for our whole party to follow me. I'm sure d'Albret will be happy to supply litters, horses, everything that you will want to make your journey comfortable."

"Don't waste a minute," was Lady Throxford's swift response. "I will take care of their Highnesses and inform the Bishop. Between us we'll see that everyone is prepared for whatever you and Lord d'Albret think best."

The following evening, the last day of August, was even hotter than usual and the two princesses and their lady were disrobing for bed before a cooling breeze began at last to stir the leaves on the mulberry tree below their windows.

Joanna, her face flushed and her eyes a little inflamed, thrust aside the chamber gown in her tiring woman's outstretched hands.

"Let me sit in my shift for a little while," she said. "And do bring me a cold drink. I'm parched tonight! My throat is so dry I can hardly swallow."

Lady Throxford, just donning her own chamber robe, stood, for a moment, quite still. Then she moved quickly to Joanna's side and touched her forehead with a gentle hand.

"You do feel warm," she said quietly. But although her voice sounded perfectly natural, it seemed to Isabel that her face, in the dim room, was paler than it had been a minute earlier.

"Fetch me a basin of water from the spring house," Lady Throxford said now, turning to the tiring woman. "Quickly, please."

After the door had closed behind her, Isabel finished put-

ting her jewels in their casket and moved toward her sister.
Lady Throxford, standing between them, halted her with a
gesture of her hand.

"How stupid of me," she smiled at Isabel. "I should have
told the woman to send a lackey for our good physician. Forgive me for dispatching you on an errand, Your Grace, but I
do think we should ask him to come. Will you carry the message for me, please, while I make the Princess Joanna more
comfortable?"

When Isabel just stood there and stared at her with frightened eyes, Lady Throxford gave her a little push.

"Run along, please . . ."

"But, Joanna?"

"Has a little fever, perhaps. That goose at dinner was very
rich and we sat out in the sun longer than we should have
this morning."

"I'm just hot and thirsty," protested Joanna. "Please don't
fuss!" But her voice was thick and Isabel hurried off to send
for their doctor.

She sped back up the stairs after delivering her message
and found, to her astonishment, that the door into the solar
wouldn't open. She turned the handle again and pushed hard.
It seemed to be locked.

"Who is it?"

"It's me, Lady Throxford. Let me in."

The key turned and the door opened a narrow crack.
"Your sister may be a little restless tonight," said Lady
Throxford softly, standing just inside. "And the physician will
be arriving soon, too. So ask one of the house servants to
make up a pallet for you, Your Grace, in the salon. We will
all be more comfortable that way."

"No!" protested Isabel fiercely. "I want to come in, Lady
Throxford. I want to be with Joanna. Open the door wider."

"Isabel! Be quiet and do what I say!" The older woman's
voice dropped to a low commanding whisper and all titles
were forgotten. "Now go below, please, and stay there. If the
doctor says you may, I will let you come back. But not until
he has seen your sister."

Chapter 8

One of Sieur Buzet's housemaids brought in a straw pallet, gathered together all the cushions she could find, and made a very cosy-seeming nest for the Princess in one corner of the salon. But Isabel, thanking her, continued to pace the floor.

After what might well have been an eternity, Joanna's physician, Master Philip Harton, hurried into the château and ran up the stairs. Just behind him was the elderly Bishop of Carlisle who turned, instead, into the salon and met the frightened Isabel with outstretched hands.

They said little; the word *plague* was not mentioned, and after a short prayer, in which Isabel joined, the two gave up any attempt at conversation and sat together in tense silence.

"I cannot bear this!" said the Princess suddenly, springing to her feet. "I must find out what is happening up there." And without waiting for the Bishop's protest she ran out of the room and up the staircase. The door to the solar was still locked, but by putting her ear to the large keyhole she could hear Joanna moaning and Lady Throxford talking to Master Philip.

"There's a swelling under her armpit," she said, "and she began spitting blood just before you arrived."

"If you look here—and here—you will see the black spots appearing. Her throat and tongue are very dark already. I'm afraid there is little hope."

The doctor's terrifying words were the last that Isabel heard: swirling mists gathered around her and there was a queer humming in her head. She reached for the door handle to keep from falling, but it was too late.

When she opened her eyes she was down in the salon again and resting on the pallet. Bending over her and holding something pungent under her nose was the Bishop. Behind him, their faces anxious, stood the two squires, Thomas Went-

93

worth and Stephen de Cusynton, and Marthe, one of Sieur
Buzet's women.

At first she was confused, wondering what had happened.
Then the memory of what she had overheard in the solar returned to her and she sank back, covering her eyes with her
hands.

The Bishop, with a quick gesture, dismissed the others and
knelt by her side.

"You must be brave, Your Grace," he said. "We will pray
together and hope. There is nothing else for us to do."

"But—Joanna!" Isabel wailed, sitting up and clutching his
hand. "I must be with her! She must be wanting me, wondering why I am not by her side. . . ."

"She is too ill to recognize anyone now, my child. The
good Lady Throxford and our own Master Philip are doing
all that can be done for her and we cannot allow you to risk
your precious life, too."

When the long night ended at last, the Bishop tried to persuade his royal charge to leave the château and join the other
lords and ladies at Creon. But this she refused to do. "You
have locked me out of my sister's chamber," she said, "but
you cannot force me to leave this house."

They remained together in the salon, praying and waiting,
praying and waiting. The sun, outside the windows, climbed
high in the sky. It set, and a lopsided moon appeared, lighting the vineyard that covered the hill.

Isabel was staring out with unseeing eyes when a knock on
the door brought the Bishop to his feet. He had apparently
been waiting for it, for he snatched up his vestments, his
crucifix, and several other articles that were resting on one of
the tables and rushed out of the room. Isabel, close behind
him, saw the solar door open to admit him, then close again.
She shook the door handle and called but there was no answer.

All she could hear, at first, was a soft murmur. Then the
Bishop's voice was raised in prayers and a long ritual, and Isabel, falling to her knees, tried to pray too.

She was still kneeling when the door opened. Lady Throxford was standing inside, the Bishop behind her. Isabel rose
and moved toward them but Lady Throxford stopped her.

"Remain where you are, Your Grace!"

The Princess paused, her legs trembling, her eyes asking the question her lips refused to frame.

The Bishop answered it. "Her Highness has gone to God," he said gently. "God rest her pure white soul!"

Seeing Isabel sway, Lady Throxford spoke again, even more sharply this time. "Sit down on the floor and bend your head between your knees. Let the faintness pass and then listen to us! Hurry, Your Highness. Do exactly as I say!"

Isabel, dazed, obeyed her.

"Now," said Lady Throxford, watching the color return to her face, "we will tell you what you must do. No one in this room dare approach you until we know that we are not carrying the seeds of this disease. You must now take care of yourself. Summon one of our squires immediately and ride with him to the village. Seek out Father Anselmo, the priest, and ask him to accompany you and Wentworth—or de Cusynton—to Creon, where you will remain with the rest of our suite until you hear what Sir Robert wishes you to do. I will join you the moment I think it safe to do so."

Too shocked to protest or think for herself, Isabel rose and stumbled down the stairs. Within a few minutes she and Wentworth were riding into the village and had reached the little house by the church where the priest lived. A word from the squire was enough; he led the Princess inside and made her sit down while he hurried off to fetch her a glass of wine.

As she sipped it she managed to tell him what Lady Throxford had said, and to ask him, in a trembling voice, whether he would see her safely to Creon.

"Gladly, Your Highness," he replied, "but I'm afraid it is too late. I heard, only an hour ago, that the plague has broken out there, too, and that everyone in your suite is gone. They fled toward the south, apparently."

Turning to Isabel's squire, Father Anselmo gave an expressive shrug of his lean shoulders. "Very few people do not panic," he said. "Our village is empty and has been ever since we heard of the Princess Joanna's illness. I can only suggest that Her Highness remain here with me until you make some other arrangement for her safety."

"If you will rest, Your Highness," said Thomas Wentworth, "I will ride back to the château and fetch horses, our men-at-arms, and one or two of the chamberwomen. I think the sooner we set out from here the better and we should, with luck, meet Sir Robert or his messenger on the road."

While Isabel cried herself to sleep on the priest's narrow bed, Wentworth galloped into the courtyard of the château. Except for de Cusynton and one stout English soldier, it was deserted. They were nailing together what was obviously a rough coffin, and an empty farm wagon stood nearby.

The Bishop, de Cusynton told Wentworth, had decided to take Princess Joanna's body to Bordeaux for burial. He indicated his helper, hammering away at the narrow box. "John and I are the only ones left here," he said grimly, "except for the Lady Throxford, His Grace, and Master Philip. All the others have disappeared."

The Bishop suddenly appeared at a window and called Wentworth over. When he heard why the squire was not on his way to Creon, he gave a great groan. "We have no one here to send to Her Highness," he said. "The women and lackeys—everyone has run away. But she must not remain in this neighborhood an hour longer than necessary. Take John and leave me de Cusynton—one of us will see the Princess Joanna laid to rest. I dare not set out alone and perhaps fall ill on the way!"

"But Your Grace, the Princess Royal cannot travel without at least one woman in attendance!"

"In times like these she could even travel alone! But perhaps you can find a woman in one of the villages or towns nearby who will be willing to accompany you. Offer any sum, any inducement."

Isabel, after sleeping most of the morning, was in the village church praying for her sister when she heard a great clip-clop of horses' hoofs and the sound of wheels in the narrow street just outside the door. The deserted village had been so quiet that day that she rose from her knees and hurried out to see who it could be, her heart lightening at the thought that it might be Sir Robert de Bourchier come to take her to Dax.

As she emerged into the sunlight she saw a gaily painted *charette*, a baggage wagon, and a small group of men on horseback all coming to a halt in front of Father Anselmo's house. One was Thomas Wentworth and another, she realized a moment later, was young Bernard d'Albret. They were talking very earnestly together; then, when they had dismounted, Wentworth caught sight of her in the church doorway and the two men walked swiftly over.

"I bring you a friend, Your Grace," said Thomas, nodding at Bernard. "We met on the road about five miles from here and rode back to Loremo together. As Father Anselmo may have told you, I was scouring the countryside for some woman to attend you, a hopeless errand, I'm sorry to say. I was returning to report my failure and to urge our immediate departure when I saw Sieur d'Albret and his most welcome little cavalcade approaching."

"I am deeply shocked by the sad news of Her Highness's death," said Bernard, bending over Isabel's hand, "and by the way your lords and ladies have behaved. If we had had any fear of such a thing happening I would have brought a woman or two with me. As it is, I have here only a few lackeys and, as you see, my mother's *charette* and a wagon for some of your boxes. Sir Robert and my father are riding up and down the coast in search of a ship or two to take you home and I came to act as courier and guide."

"It has been a nightmare," said Isabel slowly. "A nightmare."

"It has indeed," Wentworth spoke again, his face set in lines of anxiety. "And now, Your Highness, if you will forgive me for interrupting, I think we must not waste another moment. How soon will you be ready to set out on our travels?"

Isabel, riding along beside Bernard, turned and waved a last farewell to Father Anselmo, a lonely figure in the deserted street of Loremo. Her thoughts, however, were with Lady Throxford, whom they must leave behind. Lady Throxford herself had said so, Thomas Wentworth had said so, and Father Anselmo had said so but Isabel, now that they were actually on their way, found she could not obey their peremptory orders. They were asking too much of her. . . .

Just ahead of them, on her right, was the lane that led into Sieur Buzet's château; Wentworth was already some distance past it, leading the caravan, and she and Bernard were far enough in the rear to be almost out of his sight.

"Don't follow me," she said to her young companion in as commanding a tone as she could manage. "Ride on, sir. I will join you in a few minutes."

Then, without giving him an opportunity to protest, she wheeled and galloped up the tree-lined avenue and into the cobbled courtyard. Bernard, startled into a moment's immobility, jerked his horse's head around and spurted after her, shouting to Wentworth to halt. When he pounded into the little enclosure he saw that Isabel had dismounted and was peering in one of the château's windows.

She gave him a stubborn look as he jumped off his horse, too, and ran to her side; then she pushed at the casement with impatient fingers.

"The door is locked," she said breathlessly, "and so is this window. The whole place seems deserted. Something is wrong. I know it is!" She banged on the window and began to shout.

"Lady Throxford! Lady Throxford!" over and over. There was no answer, but suddenly the window burst open under the violent barrage of Isabel's fists and she, without a word to Bernard, climbed swiftly over the low sill and disappeared inside.

A cry of horror took him through the window, too, and into the salon. Isabel, her face contorted, was staring down at a woman lying on a cushioned pallet. The woman, Bernard saw instantly, was very, very ill.

"Your Highness!" he strode to Isabel and jerked her away toward the open casement. "Do you want to die, too? Is that Lady Throxford?"

Isabel choked and nodded. Then she glared at Bernard, her eyes flashing blue fire. "And I can see that she has the plague, sir. But don't tell me I must run away and leave her alone to die because I will not do it! She risked her life to nurse Joanna and *I* shall look after *her!*"

A moan from Lady Throxford took her back to the side of the pallet. "But what must I do? Where is our physician?" She leaned over and began wringing her hands.

"Water!" muttered the poor lady, her blackened, swollen tongue protruding. "Water!"

Bernard, pushing Isabel aside, snatched up a pitcher of water from the floor near her feet and pulled a soft linen kerchief out of his jupon sleeve. Dipping the cloth carefully in the water, he knelt beside the pallet and squeezed a few drops directly into Lady Throxford's mouth, then a few more, and a few more. . . .

He waited until she was quiet again then he rose and faced the Princess.

"Please, Your Highness," he said, "ride back and join the others. Leave me here with the poor lady and I will do what I can to ease her. There is very little that even a physician could do, I'm afraid, but the brothers of St. Vincent have taught me how to use herbs and simples and I may be able to make her more comfortable."

Isabel was opening her mouth to protest when her eye caught sight of a grubby piece of paper lying near the window. She picked it up and read it. "At least," she said, "I know now why Master Philip, our doctor, is not here with Lady Throxford. This is a message from Creon, asking him to come and help with the plague victims there."

She threw it down and turned back to Bernard. "If you will help my dear lady," she said, "I will be grateful to you as long as I live. But don't ask me to leave you! Tell me what to do. I'll do anything!"

A horse's hoofs sounded in the courtyard. She ran to the window and waved frantically to Thomas Wentworth, who was just riding in and was staring in bewilderment at the other two horses.

"Here!" she called. "Over here, sir!"

She knelt on the wide sill and leaned out. "Lady Throxford is very ill," she told him. "There's no one here, no one at all. Fetch us a doctor, quickly, and a priest."

Bernard appeared at her side. "It is too late, Wentworth," he said. "The lady has only another hour at most."

Wentworth, a rugged, sensible man with a shock of bright red hair and a pair of steady blue eyes, stared at the two young people. Consternation and sorrow were written all over his face, for he, like everyone else in the royal household, admired and respected Lady Throxford.

"There is not another priest within twenty miles," he said slowly, "and as we know, sir, Father Anselmo was leaving for Creon the moment we were out of sight. He said they needed him there."

A faint moan from Lady Throxford gave Bernard an ex-

cuse to send Isabel out of the room. He had been wondering
how he could manage a word alone with Wentworth.

"Could you fetch us some fresh water, Your Highness?" he
asked. Isabel, only too happy to be given something to do,
picked up the pitcher and disappeared.

"Now, sir," Bernard spoke swiftly, "we must arrange matters, you and I. Both Her Highness and I may very well fall
ill, after this day's work, and someone must keep our party
together. She and I were riding in the rear. Go back to the
men and move ahead slowly. Don't tell them anything, however, or you'll lose them. The moment Lady Throxford dies
we will follow and fall in behind you again, keeping as far
away from all of you as we can. This disease strikes swiftly
or not at all. A few days and we will know."

"Leave everything in my hands," was Wentworth's immediate response. "I understand, sir. One of us must live to see
Her Highness to safety. And as for poor Lady Throxford—
well, the dead must give way to the living in these terrible
times." He looked up at the sky. "I should think all the an-
gels in Heaven would be waiting to welcome her," he said.

Bernard had done what he could with water and vinegar
and herb poultices, but it was obvious now from Lady Throxford's labored breathing that the end was near. As he knelt
beside her and recited the prayers for the dying, Isabel,
kneeling too, listened to this surprising young man with a
heart full of gratitude, wonder, and something that was almost awe. She thought of her brother Ned and several of
their other friends and tried to picture any one of them here
in Bernard's place. They, she was sure, would have been as
helpless as she was.

When they had finished their last, macabre tasks, which included nailing a note on the door to warn anyone who might
come there that there was a dead plague victim inside, the
Princess tried to thank Bernard; he merely shook his head.
"There was no hope," he said sadly. "No hope."

He waited until they had mounted their horses and galloped within sight of the slowly moving cavalcade ahead of
them before he slowed their steeds and told her what he and
Wentworth had arranged.

"For the next few days and nights," he said, "we will be
well advised to keep away from the few towns and villages

that would, in ordinary circumstances, be our stopping places."
He avoided telling her his fear that he and she might
spread the plague; actually, he did not know, nor did anyone
else, just how the disease was passed from one person to another. Instead, he said that the plague could already have
reached these little settlements, and they would make camp
at night until they were well out of the neighborhood.

"I wonder," he said, "what you will think of our Les
Landes. It is strange, wild, marshy country and much of it is
under water part of the year. Many people find it bleak but not
I; I think it's beautiful. Perhaps because I know it so well—or
perhaps because it has belonged to the d'Albrets for so many
centuries. Some day, I suppose, it will be mine." And for
some reason he sighed, fell silent, and stared ahead.

They had halted for the night and had shared a supper of
cold meat, bread, cheese, and wine set out for them on the
still-green grass before Isabel fully realized how extraordinary her situation had become. Never in her sixteen years
had she been alone with a man for more than a few minutes;
here she was, now, some miles south of Bordeaux, traveling
into the wildest part of France, the only woman in a small
group of men, which consisted of one squire, the young son
of a Gascon nobleman, and a handful of lackeys and men-
at-arms. And when, shortly, she would retire for the night,
her only shelter was to be the curtained *charette*, waiting for
her on the sandy ground under a stunted olive tree. She
looked over at the spot, a little distance away, where the rest
of the party were already bedded down and asleep. She shivered.

"Are you cold, Your Highness?" Bernard asked, putting
down the wooden tankard he had just emptied. "Let me
bring you a robe or coverlet from the *charette*."

"No, no, it's very warm tonight. I was—thinking about animals," she confessed. "In the night. Bears."

"Bears?" He laughed. "Perhaps a hare or a fox, but I don't
believe even they would venture very close to our camp.
However, I shall be sleeping not far from your coach, Your
Grace. Just call out if anything worries you."

He rose. "Come, let's see if Thomas Wentworth has
remembered everything you will need to make you reasonably comfortable." Helping her up from cushions on which

she had been sitting, he led her over and opened the leather curtains. They peered inside. It looked very snug in the failing light. A heap of pillows had been shaped into a pallet and covered with several of her warm mantles; and a small pewter basin of water, two soft linen towels, the box that held her combs and brushes and the cochineal paste she sometimes rubbed into her cheeks were waiting for her in one corner.

Suddenly so weary that she decided not even to wash her face, Isabel bade Bernard good night, climbed in, and curled up among the cushions. She would, of course, sleep fully clothed.

She wakened only once, heard the soft patter of light rain on the roof, hoped that Bernard had some kind of shelter, and fell asleep again.

The sound of masculine voices calling to each other and the stamping and snorting of horses nearby roused her soon after dawn. Stiff, and still drowned in sleep, she pushed open the curtains and crawled out. Bernard, looking as rumpled as she felt, was setting out another meal for the two of them. Catching sight of her and noticing, instantly, that her eyes were clear and her color natural, he smiled and pointed toward a small stand of trees.

"There's a little brook over there," he told her. "Just beyond those trees. I washed my face in it and found it most refreshing. Try it."

By the time she returned, feeling quite comfortable, she realized that she was, for the first time since Joanna had been taken ill, really hungry. Starving, in fact. And as she plumped herself down on her cushion and reached eagerly for more of the bread and meat that she and Bernard had shared the evening before, she was almost cheerful. Here, away from the rest of the world, with the early-morning September sun sparkling on the damp grass around them, she found she could shut away the grim pictures haunting her and control the tears that were still dangerously near the surface.

"The hour of Prime," announced Bernard, his gray eyes blinking up at the sun. "Fair weather again, thank the good God above us. With this brisk start we should be well down into Les Landes by nightfall." He cut her another hunk of bread and pointed to the place where her *charette* had stood.

It was gone and their two horses, already saddled, were waiting there instead, quietly cropping the grass.

"Here comes Wentworth," he said, looking over Isabel's head.

Standing a short distance away, the squire called to them that he and the others were ready to lead the way. "But tell me, Your Highness, is there anything you need in the baggage wagon? No? Then we will be off. If it should rain again we will send the *charette* back to you."

But the skies remained clear and the country, after a few hours in the saddle, began, as Bernard had said, to change. They were traveling fairly close to the coast, the center of Les Landes being too soft for safety, and except for the irregular outlines of the dunes between them and the sea, all that Isabel could see around them was miles and miles of marshland, deeply and dangerously green where the marsh grass hid bottomless bogs.

Their halting place that second night was completely unlike the pretty country in which they had camped the previous evening. There was no little wood and rippling stream to which Isabel could retire for a few minutes' privacy. The wooden *charette*, standing apart from the spot Wentworth had chosen for himself and the serving men, was her only refuge and shelter.

Again, when she settled down among her cushions, she fell almost instantly into a deep sleep, too drugged by a day in the saddle and the wonderfully fresh, salty air to think about her troubles. This time she never roused once and it was bright daylight when she finally awoke. For a moment or two she looked bewilderedly around the narrow wooden enclosure, wondering where she was; then it all came back with a rush and she struggled up on the pile of cushions.

As she prepared to climb out, doing what she could to straighten her disordered kirtle and surcoat, it struck her, suddenly, that everything was amazingly quiet. There was no rumble of male voices, no stamping or neighing of horses, no jingling of harness. . . .

A seagull screamed. Off in the distance the surf boomed softly. A little frightened but not sure why, Isabel clambered hastily down onto the ground and stared at the little encampment. The baggage wagon was there where it had been when she retired, some hours before, and off to her right, about a hundred feet distant, were a few of their horses, unsaddled and quietly eating the moist marsh grasses. But where were the others? Where was Thomas Wentworth? Where were their men? Where was Bernard?

Her wonder, as she looked all around the empty landscape, turned to panic. She was apparently alone, miles from anywhere, in this strange, eerie land. Turning first this way, then that, she made aimless little dashes from place to place, her heart pounding with fright. Her dark hair came unbound and blew into her face; she pushed it back with trembling fingers and stumbled on the dusty hem of her gown.

What she didn't realize was that the shocks, agonies and anxieties of the last few weeks had all added their stress to this particular moment. The flight from Bordeaux, the underlying fear of the plague that haunted everyone during the seemingly peaceful days at Loremo, the ghastly hours when the disease struck, then struck again. . . .

Until now the Princess Royal had borne Fate's blows fairly well. She had wept when she was alone, but she had managed, for the most part, to present a brave face to those around her. This apparent desertion, this strange, mysterious disappearance of her whole escort, however, was too much for the girl. Her careful composure cracked into a thousand pieces.

Distraught, and shaking violently from head to foot, she began to scream. A hand touched her shoulder. She spun around, her eyes wild with fright.

It was Bernard. Before he could say a word, she flung herself into his arms, clutching him frantically and sobbing wildly. She burrowed her head into his shoulder and he held her there, soothing her as he might have soothed a terrified child or animal, stroking her bent head with a gentle hand and murmuring comforting, quieting things into her ear.

A long minute passed in the circle of his arms before Isabel came to her senses. She was about to pull away when she felt her heart flutter and her body tingle; the touch of Bernard's fingers on her rumpled hair set her pulses jumping. Obeying an impulse stronger than herself, she moved closer to him and raised her lips.

But as she moved, he moved, too, first holding her tighter, then quickly freeing himself from her embrace.

"I—was frightened," she explained shyly, after an awkward pause. "I—couldn't find anyone!"

He nodded and she saw that his face was strained and white. "You had good reason to be frightened," he told her, taking one of her hands in his and holding it firmly. "Something sad and terrible happened while we were sleeping, something that frightened me, too. Everything was—as it is now—when I awoke. I looked for the others and found only one. Our squire, my lady, Thomas Wentworth. Dead. This was beside his body."

He drew a ragged, dirty piece of paper out of the pouch at his waist. Written on it were a few roughly printed words:

WE DO NOT WANT TO DY TO.

Chapter 9

Isabel looked at Bernard as if she couldn't believe her ears. She took the message out of his hand and read it again for herself.

"What does it mean?" she asked. "Did they kill him?"

"No, no! Of course not! It was the plague again. That's why our men ran away. It can kill in hours, you know; sometimes almost instantly." He shuddered and glanced, involuntarily, toward the solitary baggage wagon.

"Is he . . . over there?" Isabel's eyes had followed his.

He nodded. "I didn't move him, or touch him. I had just finished heaping sand over his body when you screamed. I suppose that's why you didn't see me. I must have been bent over behind the wagon."

She forced her eyes away from the spot where poor Wentworth lay. She saw again the horses tethered near the edge of the marsh and began to realize what this new tragedy meant to her. She, the Princess Royal of England, was now completely alone with a young man. Alone, cut off by the plague from the rest of the world, with Bernard d'Albret. Then a disturbing—a dangerous—question sent the blood sweeping up into her face. Was she falling in love, perhaps? No, she told herself firmly. No!

Bernard, feeling her hand tremble in his and thinking it due to fright, clasped it more firmly. "You must trust me," he said, "to bring you safely out of this terrifying situation. If I do not fall ill too, I mean. In that case, Your Highness, I want you to promise me that you will leave me wherever I am immediately—*immediately*—and ride swiftly on to the nearest village or town. Take your money and jewels and pay someone there either to escort you to Dax or to send for Sir Robert. You must not think of me at all."

"I won't promise you that, Bernard." She smiled warmly into his face and his name slipped out, for the first time, quite naturally. "But I do promise to behave as sensibly as possible and not run around in a blind panic as I did this morning. And what if I fall ill, sir? Will you promise to leave me immediately—*immediately?*"

She imitated his voice so perfectly that he couldn't help laughing. "Never mind that," he replied. "That's my business."

"Because you are a man, I suppose," she said impudently, "and I am a woman! Well, we could waste half a day arguing that question. Let's decide what we should do now while we are well and strong. For instance"—she pointed to the cumbersome wagon—"why not leave that great thing here? And the *charette*, too. If you can sleep in the open, so can I."

"So?" he gave her a questioning look, his gray eyes full of laughter. "But what about the bears?" He waited for her answering chuckle, then shook his head. "No, I think we'll take the *charette*. Until, at least, we feel we may spend our nights under someone's roof."

After that the young couple began working together in fairly cheerful harmony, gathering up whatever they thought essential for the remainder of their journey. And when Bernard would have carried and packed and tied the collection of food and other gear himself, Isabel refused to allow such a thing; from now on, she said firmly, she wanted to help him prepare their meals and even look after the horses. "Four hands are better than two," she told him. "These tasks are as new to you as they are to me, and I must confess that I'm tired of sitting around helplessly while you think of ways to make me comfortable."

Although at first she hindered more than she actually helped, Bernard accepted her assistance in the spirit in which it was offered, and by the end of the day they were more at ease with each other than Isabel had ever been with any man but her brother Ned. So much at ease, in fact, that much of the time they rode along in companionable silence and once exchanged sharp words over the best place to stow away some of the clumsy objects in the *charette*.

When Bernard finally agreed to try Isabel's suggestion and smiled over its obvious failure, she glared at him and gave the offending box a vicious kick.

"Kicking won't make it go in, Your Highness!"

"No," she agreed, "but it makes me feel better!" Then, while he began stacking the gear all over again, she leaned on the front of the *charette* and burst into delighted laughter.

His questioning glance brought a fresh burst.

"It was the way you said 'Kicking won't make it go in, *Your Highness!*'" she finally told him. "The *Your Highness* sounded so ridiculous when you were practically gritting your teeth at me. And when I look so grubby, too." She pointed first at her dusty creased gown, its short train filthy from dagging around the ground, and second, at his own soiled and travel-worn jupon. "Until we are clean and tidy again and surrounded by people who would disapprove of such informal manners, let us forget *sirs* and *highnesses* and call each other Isabel and Bernard."

The weather having turned a bit cooler their second evening alone, Bernard suggested, after they had finished their supper, that they build themselves a fire. It was not an easy matter to find firewood, but after setting out in opposite directions they finally returned to their little camp with an armload each of small sticks and branches; and when Bernard reported that he had almost fallen over a large, dry log, Isabel walked with him to where it lay and they dragged it back in triumph.

At first they sat quietly, enjoying the leaping flames and cheerful comfort. Then Isabel caught sight of a large hare, resting on its haunches just outside the circle of light. It was cleaning its whiskers with one busy, furry paw. She nudged Bernard.

"Look!" she whispered. "Have you ever seen anything so droll? Could you draw him for me, Bernard?"

Without a word Bernard picked up a charred stick from their fire and, reaching for a piece of parchment that had been wrapped around the last of the bacon, turned it over on its cleaner side and began to sketch. Isabel, fascinated, leaned closer and closer, watching the swift, skillful strokes of his slender fingers. As the rabbit grew rapidly under her admiring eyes, she became suddenly aware of the fact that her head was almost resting on Bernard's shoulder. Again she felt her heart flutter. A delicious, disturbing thrill ran up and down her spine.

Surely, she thought, Bernard must be feeling it too. But as

she studied his face in the firelight she realized that he was completely absorbed in his work; his gray eyes, following the lines on the parchment, had that luminous shine that she had noticed the first time they met, and his lips were curved in a small, contented smile.

Isabel drew away. She sat very still, watching him, until the hare, catching sight of them at last, hopped quickly out of view; then she rose, walked to the *charette*, plunged her arm inside and pulled out García's lute. It was one of the odd-shaped things that were cluttering up her curtained sleeping quarters but she was glad, now, that she had insisted on bringing it along.

Bernard was still bent over his drawing. Isabel, sitting down beside him again, ran her fingers over the lute strings. He looked up, smiled, then poked around in the embers in front of him for another piece of charcoal; a moment later his silver-gilt head was intent on the parchment, everything else forgotten.

At first Isabel played very softly and hummed to herself. She was trying to recapture the tune with which García de Gyville had entertained them that last moonlit night in Bordeaux, and as it came back to her she strummed a little louder, singing the words in a small, clear, sweet voice. She remembered the vivid fancy she had had in the castle garden, when the God of Love had seemed to be there with her, resembling in some strange way her companion of tonight. It had been a trick of the moonlight, of course, but she could see, even now, that if Bernard were crowned with flowers and had a bow in his fingers instead of a piece of charcoal, he would be any maid's image of the God of Love.

The fire died down and Isabel finished her song. Bernard threw away the crumbled stick and, after studying the parchment with a critical eye, handed it to her. There sat the hare, so alive that his whiskers, as he washed them with his paw, seemed to twitch.

Isabel gave a cry of delight and tried to tell Bernard how much it pleased her.

"I'll keep it always," she said. "I do thank you, Bernard!"

"And I will have the memory of your song," he told her. "I will keep it always, too." Rising, he reached for her hand and helped her to her feet.

Long after they had parted for the night, and Isabel was shut snugly inside her leather curtains, the touch of his fingers remained on hers. She peeped out, once or twice, and saw him, wrapped in two thick cloaks, curled up on the sand near the graying coals of their fire.

A parfit gentil knight, she decided, telling herself over and over how fortunate she was that Bernard *was* so gallant and thoughtful, that he had never, by word or deed, taken advantage of the fact that they were a man and woman alone, miles from anyone. What if he had taken her in his arms tonight and carried her into the *charette*. . . .

Isabel's heart beat faster in the darkness and it was some time before she fell asleep. But when she did there was a smile on her lips and the hand Bernard had held in his own was tucked carefully under her cheek.

The fear of the plague, of course, rode with them most of the way. Their first thought, on awakening each morning, was to discover whether the other one had fallen ill during the long night and Bernard, even during the day, kept an anxious eye on Isabel's eyes and cheeks. But neither sickened and, as they neared the end of their journey, he told her at last that he was sure they were safe from the dread disease.

"We may now," he said, "stop avoiding other people. I shall find us a comfortable inn for tonight and hire a woman to accompany us the rest of the way."

"When," asked Isabel, "will we reach your château?"

"In two more days."

"We have enough food, Bernard, I know that, and it would make so much fuss and talk if we try to explain our situation to anyone but your people and mine. Let us continue on as we are."

Sir Robert Bourchier and the d'Albrets were waiting in a small salon that looked down the long tree-shaded avenue leading to their château. Lady d'Albret's red and swollen eyes told the tale of recent, violent weeping but she had, for a little while at least, regained her composure.

Sir Robert, noticeably less plump than he had been when he arrived in Bordeaux, alternated between pacing the floor and sitting restlessly near one of the long windows. Ever since Joanna's attendants had ridden into Dax with the story of the plague breaking out in Creon and their instant flight south, he had acquired a new and irritating habit of drumming loudly with his fingers on the arm of his chair, a habit that Lady d'Albret, in her own distressed state, found almost unbearable. Even his jerky pacing was better than hearing that constant noise and she had to control the impulse to tell him so.

The last few days had been so full of shocks and horrors. Everyone, including the lords and ladies from Creon, had assumed that the two princesses were on their way here to Dax in the care of the Bishop of Carlisle and in the vehicles that the d'Albrets had sent to Loremo. They were actually making plans to send an escort to meet them when the little group of d'Albret lackeys and men-at-arms galloped in with the frightening news that the Princess Joanna was dead and with the garbled story of their own desertion of their young master and England's Princess Royal.

Since their arrival, soon after dawn that morning, both Lord d'Albret and Sir Robert had suffered agonies of remorse and anxiety. Why, they asked themselves and each other, as they tried to decide what must now be done, had they listened to the Governor of Bordeaux? And why had they sent Bernard for the Princesses? He could have attended to the business of finding a ship while they themselves rode back to Loremo with the little caravan.

What, though neither of the two men said this aloud, would King Edward say to them? One royal daughter dead and the other either dead, too, or alone in the marshes of Les Landes with a young man. . . .

Sir Robert drummed louder than ever, then sprang to his feet.

"If they don't find that physician soon," he said, "I shall set out alone. This waiting is unbearable! First those cowardly lords and ladies running away from Creon without making sure that their Highnesses were safely on their way here, then your lackeys wasting more time for us!"

"I suppose we should consider ourselves fortunate that the men finally found the courage to come to us with their story," replied d'Albret as patiently as he could. "Michel tells me that they were too frightened at first, both by the plague itself and then by the thought of what I might do to them when I discovered that they had abandoned the Princess and our Bernard. They had actually ridden halfway to Roquefort, where Michel has a sister, when he regained his senses and persuaded the others to turn back."

His eyes, as he mentioned the name of his son, sought his wife's swollen face. She, of course, cared for nothing but Bernard's safety and was haunted by the fear that he had died, too, somewhere in the wilderness. He tried to smile comfortingly at her, failed, and turned back to Sir Robert.

"One source of mild reassurance," he told him, "lies in the fact that Bernard knows much about healing the sick. He's ... greatly interested in such things. If Her Grace should fall ill while she is in his care, he will make every effort, I know, to save her life."

The door into the salon opened and the chamberlain entered, his long thin face almost as worried as his master's.

"Everything will soon be in readiness for your departure, my lord. Sieur Vibert the physician has not yet been found but Brother Jacques from the Abbey is preparing to accompany you and Sir Robert. The horses are saddled, the supplies packed, the litter. . . ."

An exclamation from Sir Robert, who had moved closer to the window, interrupted the end of the chamberlain's speech.

"Come here, d'Albret," he said in a voice trembling with hope, "and look at the two people riding up the avenue. One seems to have very light hair and the other is certainly a woman!"

Isabel stretched out comfortably on the deep cushioned divan and told herself that the English could learn a great deal from the Gascons in the matter of making large drafty chambers livable. The thick rugs underfoot, instead of rushes, the vividly colored hangings that Lord d'Albret had brought home from Castile, the lacy carved screens, so much more delicate than any she had ever seen—everything had a delightful exotic flavor that appealed to her strongly. As did the incomparable view from the large windows that faced south; what could be more beautiful than the towering Pyrenees, their jagged peaks melting away in an unbelievable purple haze?

A question from one of Joanna's ladies-in-waiting brought her wandering thoughts back to the dreary business of packing her few remaining boxes for the journey home. Her possessions were, she realized, scattered all over Gascony; boxes had been left in Bordeaux and Loremo or abandoned along the way in Les Landes, and many of her garments were, today, being discarded as too dirty and worn for any further use.

Ever since Isabel had been reunited with the little group of English ladies here at the d'Albret château she had had to listen to innumerable apologies and explanations. Inclined, at first, to blame them for their flight from Creon, she grew more sympathetic as they told their stories. Everyone had run away from Loremo, too, she reminded herself, as had the d'Albret lackeys when they found Thomas Wentworth dead of the plague. And she herself had fallen into a panic more than once.

But she smiled, thinking of how eagerly they had worked to make her comfortable in that first hour after she and Bernard had ridden into the courtyard, the swiftness with which they had stripped her of her filthy garments, the tenderness with which they had bathed her with their own hands, sending the chamberwomen to find fresh clothing for her from their boxes.

It was amusing to compare that interval of attentive bustle with the days she and Bernard had spent alone together on the way, sharing menial tasks that these ladies would certainly consider beneath their dignity. Amusing, and sad, for she discovered that the strange little interlude was already fading from reality and assuming the shadowy outlines of a dream. Had she really helped tether horses, fetch water, build fires, pack and unpack the dry loaves of bread and lumps of stale meat and cheese that made up their meals? Was it possible that she, the Princess Royal, had crept wearily at night into a small leather-curtained enclosure and curled up to sleep among such things as a lute, washbasin, and Bernard's other pair of pointed shoes?

Bernard.... Suddenly restless, Isabel rose from the soft divan and walked to the window. She looked out at the bold line of mountains but she didn't see them. Where was Bernard and why had he changed toward her? They had, of course, resumed more formal manners in the company of others, but he had arranged one delightful expedition for her, soon after their arrival, during which they had talked and

laughed as easily together as they had on their long ride
down through Les Landes. At his invitation, Isabel, several of
the younger ladies, he, and Sir Robert Bourchier had ridden
to the southeast border of the d'Albret holdings, where they
reveled in a landscape made up of mountains, patches of
deep green forest, wild chasms, and occasional frothing
waterfalls.

Lackeys followed with delicious food and wine, carried on
the donkeys that Isabel found so enchanting, and she and
Bernard chuckled over the contrast between the luxurious
meal, spread on an elaborately embroidered linen cloth and
served by a band of servingmen that outnumbered the guests,
and the crude suppers they had prepared for themselves.

They were still discussing it when he led her away from
the rest of the party to see a huge cork tree which, he said,
often held the nests of some unusually large birds with extremely vivid plumage.

But they had both fallen silent. Standing close together,
their heads bent back as they stared upward, Isabel felt her
pulses quicken. Here she was, alone with Bernard again, in
the cool and silent wood. Would this be the last time? And
was he, too, aware that it might be? Was his heart beating a
little faster, perhaps, as hers certainly was?

"There!" He spoke suddenly and pointed. Isabel, startled
out of her wistful thoughts, saw a flash of flame and bright
sapphire disappear into the glorious sky above them.

As she exclaimed at its beauty, Bernard, after peering into
the foliage again, announced that he could see nothing more
and suggested that they return to the others.

"I wish we need not," said Isabel shyly. "It's peaceful
here."

"Yes," he replied, smiling at her. "It is. And the air is so
clear. Different from the atmosphere at home. I knew you
would like it, Your Grace."

"Your Grace?" Stretching out a tentative hand, Isabel
touched the sleeve of his silk jupon. "Here—alone—must I
be Your Grace again, Bernard?"

Under her questioning eyes, Bernard flushed and moved
closer. He took her trembling fingers in his and Isabel felt
them tremble, too. While she said nothing, holding her
breath, he lifted her hand to his lips and held it there. Time
stood still. . . .

Then Bernard released her hand. He gave her a sad little nod. "Yes," he said, turning away, "I'm afraid that it has to be Your Grace. Again—and always."

After that, had he really resisted all her attempts to arrange a few minutes alone together before her departure? Was it possible that her hints and suggestions had been unmaidenly? Had she been behaving like her cousin Joan of Kent?

The very thought brought the blood up into her face; she felt a little sick.

One of the ladies chose this moment to bring her a creased and greasy piece of parchment.

"I found this with your lute, Your Highness. Shall I throw it away?"

A saucy rabbit washing its whiskers stared up at Isabel. With a smothered exclamation that was almost a sob, she snatched it out of the woman's hand.

"No, no!" she said. "I want it. Give it to me!"

She was looking at it with a wistful smile on her lips when Lady d'Albret entered and came to her side.

"Ah," she said brightly, peering over Isabel's shoulder, "that must be some of Bernard's work. He makes his little animals seem so very alive, doesn't he?"

Startled, Isabel merely nodded and dropped the parchment on the nearest table. Lady d'Albret, after a shrewd glance at the girl's flushed face and drooping head, made a swift decision.

"My son has given me many of his finest paintings," she said. "I have them all in my own small retreat. Would you like to see them? I would be very honored. . . ." She turned, gesturing toward the door.

Isabel followed her, saying little until she had viewed and admired the enchanting pictures spread out before her. She had been waiting for a private moment with her hostess to thank her properly for all the d'Albrets had done for her and this seemed the perfect time.

"You have been so very, very kind to me, my lady," she began. "You and Lord d'Albret, and, of course, Sieur Bernard. Will you thank you brave son for me, please, and tell him I will remember his kindness and his courage as long as I live? I feel that I owe my life to him and that there are no words strong enough to express my gratitude."

"Why not tell him yourself, Your Highness?" was Lady d'Albret's immediate reply. "Shall I send someone for him?"

An hour earlier Isabel would have agreed delightedly. Now doubts about her own behavior made her hesitate.

"Poor Bernard!" said Lady d'Albret, not waiting for Isabel to answer. "My poor, poor son! I was thinking just this morning what a fortunate thing it is that he likes to spend much of his time with the good brothers at the Abbey. They will comfort him in ways that I cannot, and help him to bear his great unhappiness."

"Unhappiness?" Isabel, looking up, caught Lady d'Albret watching her with a strange intensity.

"Bernard—Bernard is unhappy?"

"Could he be anything else?" Lady d'Albret's tone suggested that Isabel knew the answer to her question even better than she did. "But you must not be distressed on his account, Your Highness. It is not your fault that you are beautiful and lovely and that my son was not born a prince." She sighed heavily and shrugged her shoulders. "Ah, if he had been! With what delight would my husband now approach the King, your father! But it is impossible—the disparity in rank is too great. It would be presumptuous."

Isabel had listened to Lady d'Albret's disjointed words first with honest bewilderment and then with a dawning excitement.

"Do you mean that Bernard is unhappy because of me?" There was such rapture in her voice that the older woman only just succeeded in hiding a triumphant smile.

"Can you doubt it?" she said sadly. "He assures me that you traveled as brother and sister, but it is not as a brother that he looks at you. If he thinks of you as a sister would he be breaking his heart in silence?"

"But," Isabel spoke slowly and she clutched Lady d'Albret's arm with trembling fingers, "but perhaps the disparity is not so great, my lady. Bernard is nobly born, he will be Lord d'Albret some day. And he saved my life! My father should be grateful and willing to grant him anything he asks. . . ."

Lady d'Albret looked doubtful. "I'm afraid you make too much of Bernard's assistance," she said. She sat for a moment in thoughtful silence, then she took Isabel's clutching fingers in her own and began to muse aloud.

"No," she murmured softly, "Bernard would never dare plead his own cause. He's too shy, too modest. Nor would my lord speak for him in this unusual situation. And he is right; the disparity *is* great!"

"I think," interrupted Isabel warmly, "that you are *all* too modest! The Lord d'Albret is one of England's very best friends! And my lord father loves me and wants me to be happy. I know that; he has proved it in the past. I shall speak to him myself, my lady, and tell him everything that is in my heart."

And now for the first time Isabel admitted to herself what *was* in her heart. .

"Oh," replied Lady d'Albret, "that of course makes everything possible! If you are willing to do *that*, Your Highness. . . ."

Chapter 10

That summer of 1348 had brought constant rain to England. Not merely the ordinary showers that, over the centuries, keep her grass green and velvety and her flower gardens the loveliest in the world but rain, rain, rain, descending, day after day, in drenching sheets. There were floods, and even hailstorms, which frightened the people; some parts of the country were plagued by earthquakes and, as if all this were not more than enough, terrifying stories of whirlwinds and showers of serpents falling in the east spread among the peasants, causing them to shut themselves into their hovels and neglect their work.

Despite this strange and ominous weather, however, the King and his court had enjoyed a summer of pleasure, taking advantage of the rare hours when the skies cleared to hold their tournaments and, when they clouded over again, making merry indoors. For as King Edward often said, there seemed no reason why, after their long months abroad, he and his warriors should not spend these damp months amusing themselves; the truce with France still held, and all was quiet here at home.

But the older and more superstitious of his nobles muttered together of dire and dreadful things to come, and the waning of the summer proved them right. On a dark wet day in late September the news of Princess Joanna's death reached her parents and early in October the plague jumped from Calais to Dover.

When, not long afterward, the Lady Royal and Sir Robert Bourchier stepped ashore there, after enduring a stormy crossing, the first thing they saw, in the early morning light, was the familiar scarlet cross, painted on the door of a fisherman's hut near the quay. Knowing only too well what this meant, they ventured no further into the town; instead, they waited for the horses to be unloaded from their ship and set

118

out, weary and travel-worn, for the royal palace at Guildford.

For the first time in all these troubled months good fortune smiled on Sir Robert and his choice of a stopping place proved to be the right one. When the plague threatened London the royal family had taken up their residence in Guildford and, long before she had any hopes of such a blessing, Isabel was in her parents' arms, weeping and being wept over.

Joy and relief over her safety was tempered by grief over Joanna's death and after the first loving greetings, Edward and Philippa settled down to the sad task of listening to her tragic story. When she had described how the dread disease had driven them from Bordeaux, followed them to Loremo and taken the lives of Joanna and her dear Lady Throxford, Isabel related her further adventures, making as much as she could of young Bernard d'Albret's courageous and chivalrous behavior. Although she had been marshaling and rehearsing her arguments in favor of a possible marriage with him, arguments which seemed convincing while she crossed the Channel and galloped up to Guildford, she began, as she talked to the King and Queen, to have a few doubts. Would their gratitude for Bernard's help be so great that they would think him a suitable husband for her? Was a future Lord d'Albret of high enough rank to aspire to her hand?

She saw that this, in any case, was not the time to present her plea. Even if Bernard had been born to the purple, the King was in no state of mind, or so it seemed to Isabel, to consider another foreign marriage for one of his daughters. Feeling that he had, all unwittingly, sent Joanna to her death and risked losing Isabel too, by allowing her to venture across the water, he announced that until the plague had run its course no member of his family should travel anywhere except with the court.

As a result, Isabel determined to hold her tongue for a while. The right moment would come, she was sure, and she would take immediate advantage of it; a few weeks could make no difference.

When she heard that her father and the King of France had extended their truce until the following October because the plague made communication between the two countries almost impossible, she comforted herself with the thought that the d'Albrets, in these circumstances, would not be expecting any messages either from her or from the King. Nor, she knew, could she hope for any letters from them.

In January the plague raged so fiercely in London that Parliament, which had been called, was prorogued. People were dying by the thousands and there was not enough hallowed ground in which to bury them; there were not enough priests to perform the funerals, and the city was full of rotting corpses. The disease was spreading to the animals wandering around the deserted streets, and as the terrified Londoners fled to distant towns the plague leaped ahead of them and met them there.

More than fifty thousand were dead in Norwich; two thirds of the inhabitants of Yarmouth had succumbed; and in Bristol, too, where the grass was growing high in the streets, the plague victims outnumbered the survivors.

As the reports worsened the royal family and the court moved from place to place in the hope of escaping infection; Woodstock, King's Langley, Clarendon. Travel in the winter was difficult at best and now, with fear driving everyone, it became a nightmare. Queen Philippa, heavy with her eleventh child, was exhausted by the continuous changing of residence. Her temper, usually so even, grew short, and Isabel, her heart heavy over the long, long delay in settling the question always foremost in her thoughts, resigned herself to waiting a little longer.

The terrible winter ended at last. Spring came to England and, by June, when the court was established at Windsor, the dread disease had almost run its course; ships began to cross the Channel again, the Queen was delivered of another boy, and the King announced that the court should celebrate the little prince's birth with the customary festivities.

Isabel, determined to waste not another moment, asked for a private audience with her father. He kissed her affectionately, after the usher left them alone, and drew her down into a chair beside his.

"This is most opportune, my child," he said cheerfully. "I was about to send for you myself. I have something to discuss with you, too. Now what do you want to do first—talk or listen?"

"Listen," replied Isabel. She was feeling a little less brave than when she had planned this meeting with the King.

He smiled at her again and poked around in the mass of papers in front of him. Finding, after a moment's search, an unusually long document, he put it aside and turned back to his daughter.

"Now, my love," he said, "you may have thought, because of these dreadful times, that I was not thinking of you and your future. This was not true; it has been in mind since the day that Louis de Mâle betrayed our trust. But, as you know, I want, above all things, for you to be happy, and it was not until I received this report"—he indicated the paper on his desk—"that I felt I had found you a suitable husband."

Shocked and horrified, Isabel opened her mouth to protest.

"But—Father!"

"No, let me tell you, chuck! It's Charles, the new King of Bohemia. His father fell at Crécy, if you remember—blind old King John—and in the short time since he came to the throne, Charles has, according to this letter, proved himself a fine man and a good king. He is already improving his cities, establishing universities, and insisting on fairer laws for his people. He is thirty-one years of age—not a young and unformed prince—and a widower who was, they say, a generous and affectionate husband. In fact, Isabel, the very man to whom I feel I could trust my dearest daughter. And here," he pointed to a half-finished letter on top of the other papers, "is a letter I am writing to him, telling him so. Needless to say I did not want to approach him until I had received the report on his qualifications."

"But Father!" Isabel said again, her heart pounding and her hands beginning to tremble as she felt the full impact of the blow he had just dealt her. "I came to you today to ask your permission to wed someone else!"

"Someone else?" the King sounded more startled than angry. Isabel forced herself to go on. "Someone whom I love with all my heart. Someone who saved my life and risked his to do it. Someone who holds my every hope of happiness in his two hands. Someone whose father has been a good friend to you and to England. . . ."

When he still looked puzzled she named him.

"Bernard d'Albret, my lord. Lord d'Albret's oldest son."

"Oh!" Relief flooded over the King's face. "Young Bernard! And so you fancy yourself in love with him, do you?

Well, what more natural, in the circumstances? He's a brave
lad and an unusually handsome one, too."

Then his eyes darkened and he leaned toward her, speaking softly so that the guard at the door could not hear him.
"I must have the truth, daughter. Did young d'Albret take
advantage of those days and nights alone with you? Are you
a maid still, or not?"

Isabel flushed hotly. "Bernard never so much as kissed me!
He behaved in the most chivalrous fashion possible!"

"Thank God for that! And did you exchange any vows?"

She shook her head reluctantly. "We had no opportunity,
Sir. He was too shy, too aware of the disparity in our situa-
tions, to speak of his love to me. It was Lady d'Albret who
told me how unhappy he was. . . ."

"I see." King Edward turned his face away and was silent
for a moment. "Well, my dear child, I must confess to you
that he was right in being aware of that disparity. It is too
great, much too great. I'm sorry, Bel, but I could not let you
wed so much beneath you." He sighed and fiddled with the
papers in front of him, then went on, his voice gentle. "And
your love for him will pass, whether you believe that or not.
Propinquity leads us into mistakes, often, and you might find,
even now, if you met again, that you had nothing in common
but the memory of your adventure together.

"However," he continued, not giving her an opportunity to
interrupt, "I am relieved about one thing. I could not offer
Charles of Bohemia a deflowered bride. The plague excuses
many things these days, but not that. Now be a good lass, Isabel, and put all this nonsense out of your head. It's nothing
but a romantic dream and one you must put behind you."

A scratch on the door and the entrance of his chamberlain
made it possible for the King to dismiss her without hearing
the wild protests that rose to her lips and Isabel retired to
her own apartments shaking with frustrated indignation.

Finding Alexia de la Mote there alone, she allowed herself
the luxury of confiding in her, something she had not done
before. Now she poured out her heart to her young friend,
telling her the whole story of her love for Bernard and her
father's unfeeling and peremptory treatment of her.

"I am not a child!" she raged. "How could he say it was
nothing but a romantic dream—and that I must put it behind
me? How does he know? And asking me if I were a maid

still! I wish I'd lied and said no! I was a fool, Alexia. If I'd
had the sense to say that Bernard and I lived as man and
wife all the way from Loremo to Dax he would have been
forced to let us wed." She paused and a look of truimph
came over her face. "It's not too late, perhaps, If he tries to
make me marry that Charles of Bohemia I shall say I lied—
that I am not a virgin, after all!"

At a signal from Sir Hugh the men-at-arms, having raised
the portcullis, let down the drawbridge and the three young
people pounded over it toward the wide spread of Dartmoor
just ahead of them. Isabel, Prince Edward and Edward's
friend Sir Hugh Courtenay, heir to the castle here at
Oakhampton and, indeed, to all the vast Courtenay estates
that the Earls of Devon had acquired over the centuries, were
eager to be out in the glorious September air and away from
the fug of the Great Hall.

Their horses were fresh, too, and with Sir Hugh leading
the way, they gave them their heads, galloping swiftly
through the sea of heather. The sky overhead was a vivid
blue, the purple carpet under their horses' hoofs alive with
small animals that scuttered out of their path, and the wide
moor, often a somber sight, was, today, warmly welcoming.
It was, Isabel decided, wonderful to be alive. Her eyes shining and a delighted smile on her lips, she threw back her
dark head and made a loud, happy sound, half laugh, half
hunting call.

Sir Hugh, just ahead, looked back and echoed both the
smile and the call, his round face beaming with joy. When
they were well away from the castle walls, he suddenly
slowed his mount and fell back.

"Fool that I am," he said to Edward, "I forgot to arrange
for that special music we want this evening. Ride on slowly
and I'll go back and see to it. You can't lose yourselves here
on the moor."

He was off, leaving the brother and sister alone. Edward
pointed to a lonely stunted tree, the only landmark on the flat
countryside that surrounded them.

"Race you!" he said, touching his spurs lightly on his
horse's flank.

Almost before the words were out of his mouth, Isabel
shot forward, her dainty mare passing the heavier stallion; a

moment later they were neck and neck, then the Prince's steed, rolling an indignant brown eye at the little satiny mare, spurted past, leaving her far behind.

Quite openly shouting with excitement, her headgear gone and her black hair blowing in her face, Isabel tore after them, reaching the tree soon after her brother, both of them laughing and a little breathless. Edward suggested that they dismount, tie their horses to the tree, and wait for Hugh in its shade. He spread his cloak on the heather and they sat down, the Princess busy with her disordered locks. As he watched her smooth them into place with skillful fingers, he was struck by the glow of happiness on her face.

Was she over the shock of Joanna's death at last, he wondered, or was she just sharing his relief that the plague had run its course? Not that life here in England would be quite the same, with half their people dead. . . .

"It's good to see you looking your old self again, Bel," he told her. "I like to hear you laugh!"

"It's wonderful to feel like laughing," she confessed. "I haven't for a long time. Not since the day I heard that I might have to wed the King of Bohemia."

"I wonder why he didn't agree to the match? Did our father tell you his reasons?"

Isabel shook her head. "No, I didn't care enough to ask him. I was so happy to hear the news—and," she hesitated, wondering whether or not to confide in him, "and—and about something else—that I just thanked him and ran away."

" 'Something else'?" Edward, his face alive with curiosity, stared at her. "Come, Bel," he said, "you may as well tell me. You're bursting with it."

Isabel touched the front of her woolen riding costume and felt a piece of parchment hidden there. She smiled a secretive little smile. "If you must know," she replied, "It's a message from the man I love."

"Good lass!" said her brother, beaming at her. "I was hoping you would wake up and discover what a splendid fellow Hugh is! By God, I wish you could have seen him fighting at Crécy! He's been my choice for you ever since. Has he spoken to His Grace yet? Not that there could be any problem there—Hugh's a great-grandson of the first Edward, after all, and richer than Croesus."

In his enthusiasm, he didn't notice that Isabel was shaking her head at him and trying to halt the flow of his disjointed words. His question finally gave her an opportunity to set him right.

"Don't be ridiculous, Ned," she told him sharply, "of course it's not Hugh! It's Bernard d'Albret."

"D'Albret?" He looked at her with astonishment. "Young d'Albret? But he hasn't even won his spurs, has he?"

"What difference does that make?" Isabel asked hotly. "Is that all you think of, Ned? He risked his life to save me from the plague, didn't he? I can assure you that that took more courage than dashing around a tilt yard or riding into battle!" Her eyes flashed blue fire.

Edward laughed. "All right. All right. I apologize to your hero. But what does our lord say to this, Bel? Sieur Bernard d'Albret is hardly a fitting husband for our Lady Royal."

"He wasn't very encouraging, I must admit, but he was hoping to wed me to the King of Bohemia when I first asked him. Now that I am free of that fear, I shall try again. I have a letter here from Lady d'Albret—the plague never reached Dax, she says, and Bernard is so unhappy that he is threatening to go into a monastery."

"And you think that will influence the King?" Edward pursed his lips and frowned thoughtfully. "I doubt it. But I'll give you one piece of advice, girl, and that is to wait until little Jeannette's problem is settled before you bother him again with yours. I heard today that he's put it in the Pope's hands and that she, Salisbury, and Holland have all agreed to accept his decision. Poor little thing, being tugged this way by one man and that way by another, and afraid to ask our mother for advice or help! She told me that she is sure Her Grace dislikes her and that without anyone to turn to she became terribly confused. . . ."

"Confused?" Isabel sounded scornful. "I should think you would have to be more than 'terribly confused' to contract yourself in marriage to two men at the same time."

"God," said the Prince, flushing angrily, "how spiteful women can be about each other! I forget from time to time!" Then, just as they might have quarreled further, they saw Sir Hugh riding toward them across the moor; without another word they rose, mounted their horses, and cantered off to meet him. Another brisk hour in the saddle blew away the small cloud that hovered between brother and sister, however, and by the time they returned to the ancient castle they were friends again.

Very soon after this the court, having finished its Progress, moved back to Westminster. As the Palace had, in the long months of its absence, been well cleansed, as the weather had turned cool and crisp, and as there had not been a plague death reported anywhere in the city for some weeks, it was considered safe, at last, to take up residence there.

Foreign trade was brisk again, too, and with dozens of ships leaving and sailing into the port of London daily the King was no longer cut off from his friends—and his enemies—across the Channel. It was possible, now, to send letters directly to the Vatican; and the Pope, in answer to King Edward's plea for a swift settlement of the Holland–Salisbury question, began demanding information as to what physical acts, if any, had taken place between the parties involved.

To Isabel's surprise, her cousin Joan discussed the whole matter as freely with her and the other ladies as she apparently did with her uncle the King, admitting frankly that she and Tom Holland had lived together as man and wife long before he went off to fight in France, adding that she herself had no idea as to how the problem should be solved. The young Earl of Salisbury had, according to her, taken her off more or less by force one day and, using the fact of their childhood betrothal, persuaded her that she must go through a marriage ceremony with *him*. It would, as she put it, "take a wiser head than mine to decide whether Tom or Will is my husband."

Greatly relieved that Joan had not involved Prince Edward in her tangled affairs, Queen Philippa and Isabel told each other that perhaps the revelations of his "little Jeanette's" amorous activities would put an end to his boyish passion for her. However, he merely observed, when the Pope decided in favor of Holland and tidied up the loose strings by granting Joan a divorce from Salisbury, that he thought His Holiness had made the proper decision.

Thinking it time to reopen the question of her own future, Isabel asked for another private audience with her royal father. It was arranged for early the following morning, and still uncertain as to what she should say and how she should say it, she sent her ladies off to walk in the garden so that their chatter would not disturb her thoughts.

Having reread Lady d'Albret's letter, and having found in it several passages that she wanted to quote to her father, she was busy underlining them with good black ink when the door opened and her brother walked in, unannounced and unheralded.

"Good!" he said. "You *are* alone here. Alexia thought you would be." He sounded a little out of breath and Isabel, dropping her letter on the table, told him to sit down.

"What brings you here in such haste?" she asked him. "And why are you so glad to find me alone?"

"The most extraordinary thing, Bel," he replied. "I still find it hard to believe my eyes! But I thought you would like to know that I just saw Lord d'Albret, muffled to the ears in a long cloak, being shown through that private door into our lord father's privy chamber."

Isabel was sure that such a coincidence was unlikely and when there was no sign of Lord d'Albret at the supper table that night she told Ned that he must have been mistaken. He agreed, but insisted that the man had looked enough like the Gascon nobleman to be his double.

The King, the next morning, was in as extremely affectionate mood, kissing his daughter warmly and apparently more than willing to listen to anything she wished to tell him. Encouraged by this, Isabel, after beginning her plea a little hesitantly, warmed to her subject and poured out her hopes and her desires in a flood of passionate words. When she paused for a moment, she saw him watching her with an odd expression on his face.

"I thought all this was to be forgotten," he said. "Why are you bringing up the matter again?"

"It will never be forgotten," she replied fiercely. "Never! And Bernard has not forgotten, either. Here, my lord, read this letter from Lady d'Albret ..." she held it out and pointed to one of the bits she had underlined. "If we don't wed, he wants to retire to a monastery."

Instead of reading it, King Edward rose and opened the door that led into a small retiring room. "Please join us, my lord," he said, poking his head inside. "The Lady Royal is with me and will, I know, be very happy to see you."

He had his arm around his daughter and was laughing into her surprised eyes when Lord d'Albret entered and made his bow.

"Now before we talk of anything else, Isabel," the King said, "I must impress on you that my lord d'Albret came here to bring me news of an extremely confidential nature, and we have decided to keep his visit a secret between us and a few of my advisers. So do not mention it to anyone."

He resumed his seat and gave the others permission to be seated, too. "I may also say," he went on, "that I am very glad to have this opportunity to thank his lordship for his kindness to you, my dear child, and for his son's courageous rescue. And I must tell you that my good friend here," he smiled warmly at d'Albret, "has now added to that great obligation by performing a service for me that can never be repaid—never!"

Reaching across the table, he took Isabel's hand in his, then turned back to Lord d'Albret who, as yet, had said nothing. "It is possible, however, that this self-willed daughter of mine may have shown me a way in which to discharge, in part, my overwhelming debt to you."

Lord d'Albret flushed and put out a protesting hand. "Please, Sire," he said uneasily, "you owe me nothing. And I cannot have you thinking that I am here to plead Bernard's cause. I have warned him, and my lady, that they must not set their hearts on something far above our reach. Young people are romantic and they forget that a king must think first of his country's needs."

"I thank you, my lord," answered the King warmly. "You are most understanding. But Her Highness has just assured me that if she and Bernard are not allowed to wed her life will be ruined and your son will enter a monastery. What should we do, do you think, in the face of these grave threats?" Edward's face was serious, but his eyes twinkled as he looked from one to the other.

Shrugging, Lord d'Albret spread his hands wide. "As I have said, Sire, young people are romantic."

"They are. And my first answer, when the Princess confided in me some time ago, was that she and your son must forget their little dream and marry more suitable partners. However, as their affection seems undiminished and as they were thrown together in such an unusual fashion. I wonder if perhaps we should not test their love a bit further before dismissing their union as an impossibility."

"I'm not sure I follow you, Your Majesty." D'Albret looked bewildered, as indeed he might, by the King's long and involved speech. Isabel, on the other hand, was watching her father's face with shining, suddenly hopeful eyes.

"I'll make it very simple, then. The Princess and your son must promise not to write or see each other for another year; but if, at the end of that time, they have not changed their minds, and if no alliance has been proposed for Her Highness that I feel she must accept, I shall then, in recognition of the invaluable services rendered to me and my country by you, Lord d'Albret, agree to their marriage."

What Lord d'Albret replied, if, indeed, he did, Isabel never knew. She was on her feet, and at her father's side almost before he finished speaking, reaching out her arms to embrace him and shower him with grateful kisses.

Chapter 11

On sober reflection Isabel was, perhaps, not quite so happy about her father's proposal; a year with no communication between them seemed to stretch endlessly into the future, particularly as she had already suffered through a twelve-month without seeing of hearing directly from Bernard. In fact, when she began facing the situation squarely, she realized that she had none of the assurances and memories so dear to lovers. She and Bernard had never kissed, exchanged words of love, or promised themselves to each other.

But, as she hastened to remind herself, she was England's Princess Royal and her courtship must, inevitably, differ from that of other maidens. And if she was to wed the man of her choice, a rare and wonderful thing to happen to a king's daughter, it was obvious she must accept with grace whatever conditions her father imposed on her. The kisses would come later.

While she brooded over these matters the King, closeted with Lord d'Albret, summoned the Prince of Wales. After young Edward had greeted their Gascon friend and been warned, as Isabel had been, that no mention must be made of his presence in England, his Majesty asked Lord d'Albret to tell the Prince of the reason for his secret visit.

"It's an almost unbelievable story," he said, "and a most unpleasant one, Your Highness. But I'm afraid it is true; in fact, I learned it in a manner that proves it true. It is just this: Aymery de Pavie has promised to sell Calais back to the French for twenty thousand crowns."

The Prince looked at him in horror then turned to his father.

"It's impossible, Sire," he said at last, his voice shrill with disbelief. "Completely impossible. Aymery grew up with me here at court. You treated him as one of us—one of your own sons. How could he be capable of such treachery? How could he?"

130

"A question I have been asking myself ever since d'Albret here first told me what he had heard. Had I had the slightest doubt of de Pavie's love and loyalty I would certainly not have trusted him with Calais, which I need not tell either of you is one of my most precious possessions. If it *is* true, and my lord d'Albret has convinced me that it is, we have no time to waste. De Pavie, fortunately, has no reason to suspect that we have discovered his treason; I have sent for him, Edward, and when he arrives we will give him an opportunity to prove his innocence."

Thinking that he had merely been invited to Westminster to take part in the Yuletide festivities, the Lombard wasted no time in obeying the King's summons. He crossed the Channel immediately and rode swiftly up to the Palace, where he was ushered into the privy chamber; Prince Edward, his father's only companion for the interview, watched him approach the throne and was more certain than ever that d'Albret had made a mistake. There was not, he decided, the faintest shadow of guilt on de Pavie's face or the slightest sign of restraint in his voice.

He was now so sure of his friend Aymery's innocence that he almost protested when his father, with chilling abruptness, made his accusation.

"I entrusted you, Aymery, with the thing which, after my wife and children, I hold most dear. Calais—the town of Calais and its castle! And now, my friend—my foster son—I learn that you have sold them to the French. Prepare yourself to die, de Pavie, for die you will!"

Prince Edward gulped and waited for the Lombard to defend himself. There was a moment of stricken silence, then, while the Prince watched with shocked and incredulous eyes, de Pavie fell to his knees and groveled in front of the King.

"It was the money," he wailed, "the money! I deserve to die, but have mercy, gentle King, for God's sake have mercy! Let me break the bargain—I have not yet received one penny from de Chargny."

Young Edward, who had not heard the details of the plot, was startled to dear de Chargny's name. He remembered him well as one of the envoys sent by King Philip of France to Newtown-the-Bold.

"The plan is de Chargny's," de Pavie continued, his voice a pleading whine. "Because of the truce he has not informed

King Philip. He and Ribeaumont have not yet settled the day
or made the arrangements for me to surrender the city."

King Edward rose from his throne and gave the man at his
feet such a look of contempt that the Prince shivered and de
Pavie hid his black-bearded face in his long bony fingers. The
tall Plantagenet monarch moved one foot as if to kick the
cringing figure, then turned away and began striding up and
down the chamber.

A ray of sunlight reached the hourglass standing on a
small table nearby, and while the King, deep in thought,
walked slowly back and forth, his son stared, fascinated, at
the grains slipping down through the narrow neck.

He was almost startled when the King spoke suddenly,
swung around, and returned to his throne chair.

"I should hang you as high as Haman, Aymery," he said,
sighing heavily, "but I'm a weak fool. I find I cannot do it.
Go back to Calais and continue to play your treacherous part
in this filthy bargain. Inform me immediately when the date
is set and then obey implicitly the orders that will come from
me. If all goes as I hope you will receive my pardon. Now
go, before I change my mind. I never want to see your trai-
torous face again."

The wind was favorable, and the fleet of ships that had set
out from Dover carrying King Edward, the Prince of Wales,
and a force of three hundred men-at-arms and six hundred
archers, reached the harbor at Calais an hour before dawn
on the last day of the year. The whole party crept ashore and
proceeded quietly through the sleeping town and on to the
dark Castle. Sir Walter Manny, who had remained at Calais
ever since its surrender, was waiting at the gate with two of
his strongest men-at-arms; the great chains that raised and
lowered the drawbridge had been well oiled the day before,
and the moment he saw the long file of men approaching
silently in the shadowy early-morning light, he gave the signal
to let it down. With hardly a creak it moved slowly into
place and the King, the Prince, and their small army marched
swiftly into the Castle. Almost on tip-toe, and without making
a sound or uttering a word, Sir Walter Manny led the way
across the inner bailey, through the heavy door of the tallest
tower and into several vast, sparsely furnished chambers.

Only then did he kneel and welcome his King.

"All is in readiness here, Sire," he said. "Sir Aymery assures me that this tower is seldom occupied and that the only members of the castle staff who will need to know of your presence are completely trustworthy and have already been sworn to silence."

"Each man carries his own food," Edward told him, "and I expect that we will all sleep through most of the day ahead. Don't forget, my lord, that from this moment on you are the leader of this enterprise and His Highness and I will be fighting under your banner. Are there any changes in the plans?"

"None. Pavie expects Chargny at midnight."

"Splendid!" replied the King, yawning. "A superb way to welcome in a new year! Well, we'll be ready for him, Manny. We will be ready!"

Sir Geoffrey de Chargny and Sir Eustace de Ribeaumont, riding together across the Bridge of Neiullet as they had on that futile, earlier mission, looked ahead at the city walls and the tall castle towers and discussed, for the last time, their carefully plotted strategy. Behind them, in full battle array, marched a large force of excited men, their banners fluttering in the chill night breeze, their weapons clutched in numb fingers. This, despite the weather, was a great adventure, and there was not one among them who had not responded eagerly when, a few weeks ealier, de Chargny and de Ribeaumont had ridden through the country mustering men.

Once over the bridge and within a short distance of the castle, the two young leaders halted and waited for their rear to come up, sending at the same time a pair of their squires on ahead to one of the castle gates. Sir Aymery, as they had expected, was standing there in the shadows.

"Is it time to advance?" they asked him.

"It is."

They galloped back with his answer and de Chargny gave his final orders to the twelve knights and hundred men-at-arms who had been chosen to go on ahead.

"Here is the money, de Renty," said de Chargny, handing Sir Odoart a large, heavy canvas bag. "When you have given it to Sir Aymery he will admit you and your men to the Castle. Take it, disarm the guards, post our men in their places, then unlock the Boulogne gate for the rest of us. Go, and God be with you!"

All seemed in readiness. Sir Aymery, the drawbridge already down, was waiting beside the open gate that led to the Castle itself. Without saying a word he took the bag from de Renty and strode ahead into the inner bailey; while the Frenchmen followed he unlocked a small door in the nearest building, threw the money inside, and locked it again. Then he swung around and faced Sir Odoart.

"I presume the twenty thousand crowns are all there? As it is almost midnight I will not take time to count them now. Yes? Then come with me to the Great Tower and my duty will be done. Once inside you should find it a simple matter to master the Castle."

As he marched over the cobblestones his head was bent so low that his curly black beard rested on his chest. After him came the twelve knights and, after them, the hundred men-at-arms. A moment later they reached the heavy old door that opened into the Tower; Aymery, moving a little to one side, reached over and pushed back the huge bolt. The door flew open and out poured a mass of armed men, waving their swords and battleaxes and shouting, "Manny, Manny, to the rescue!"

In less time than it takes to relate it, the startled French were surrounded by a force that was double theirs, and, seeing that defense was impossible, surrendered. They were disarmed instantly by the jeering, wildly triumphant Englishmen, herded inside the same tower where their captors had lain in wait, and again the great bolt was tugged into place.

Sir Geoffrey de Chargny, shivering inside his chilled armor, looked impatiently from the town gate to his friend, Pepin de Werre, who was gentling his restless mount. The breath of man and horse hung in small white clouds and de Chargny heard de Werre's teeth chattering.

"By God," he said, "if this Lombard delays much longer in opening that gate we'll all die of the cold!"

"They're a suspicious folk," answered de Werre. "He's probably biting each coin to test its metal." And he, too, peered into the darkness, hoping to see a surreptitious figure approaching from the castle. Instead, there came from behind the walls the jingle of harness and the unmistakable sound of horses' hoofs clopping along on frozen ground.

While they were still straining their ears and wondering

what this could mean, the gate was flung wide and out rode the English forces shouting, again, "Manny, Manny to the rescue!"

In the confusion of the next few minutes, de Chargny, realizing that he had been betrayed, shouted desperately to his followers:

"Gentlemen! Gentlemen! If we run now we will lose everything! *A moi! A moi!* Fight, fight—we may yet win the day!"

"By St. George," answered an English voice, "you are right, sir. The devil takes the man who thinks of running away!"

Both sides cheered, eager to do battle. The French dismounted, sent their horses on to one side, and drew up in fighting formation; Sir Walter Manny, after a word with the King, ordered his knights to do likewise.

The contest began, and Sir Eustace de Ribeaumont, Chargny's strongest warrior, found himself challenged by a tall, broad-shouldered knight in plain armor. Almost equally matched, they began hand-to-hand combat that brought admiring shouts from those around them who were less busy; for a long time, as the rest of the battle seethed on all sides, the large Englishman had the advantage, forcing Ribeaumont farther and farther back from the gates. Suddenly, with a skillful, slashing stroke of his broadsword, the French knight brought his opponent to his knees. He was up again, and the struggle continued; he was down again, and Ribeaumont moved forward to disarm him. But before he could claim his prisoner, a younger man appeared out of the darkness and took the fallen knight's place, fighting with a ferocity that soon proved too much for the now-tiring Ribeaumont.

Meanwhile more and more of Manny's men had been making their way through the gates, until the French were helplessly outnumbered. De Chargny, seeing at last that any further resistance would lead to slaughter, ordered his men to surrender and gave his own sword to Sir Walter. De Ribeaumont, when informed that the French had lost the battle, handed his to the tall knight with whom he had so vigorously fought.

"Sir knight," he said, "I yield myself your prisoner. The honor of the day belongs to the English."

The prisoners, a few hours later, were astonished when a page entered their quarters at the castle and announced that

all the knights were invited to sup with Sir Walter Manny.
While they were discussing the evening ahead of them, regarding their battlestained garments with rueful eyes, a pair
of castle servants hurried into the room, each carrying an
armload of fresh robes.

Rested and suitably attired, they followed the usher up the
stairs. The dining hall, a vaulted chamber with arras-covered
stone walls and boldly carved massive rafters overhead, was
arranged as for a great banquet. A long high table was set on
a dais, the other tables were ranged along the side walls, and
a large group of musicians were gathered in the gallery, their
instruments tuned and ready.

Sir Walter Manny, as their host, met the French knights at
the entrance, bade them welcome, and led them down the
center of the hall to the high table. There was, they could
see, a taller chair than the others, placed in the middle, under
a brilliantly embroidered canopy. It was already occupied by
a large man whose bright golden head was encircled by a
chaplet of pearls; on either side of him, behind the empty
chairs, stood a group of richly dressed English knights. On his
right, one obviously much younger than the others, bore him
an amazingly close resemblance.

Too startled and horrified to say anything, the Frenchmen
followed Manny in solemn silence. When they reached the
dais, de Chargny and de Ribeaumont knew that their worst
fears were, indeed, true; they were in the presence of the
King of England and his son, the Prince of Wales, both of
whom they had met face-to-face at Newtown-the-Bold.
What, they wondered, would happen now? A grim meal at
which the victors would gloat openly over the vanquished;
then, perhaps, the rope?

But they soon discovered that, whatever might be in store
for them later, they were, at supper, the guests of the King
and his son, and, as such, entitled to the greatest courtesy.
After they had made their obeisance to the King, the two
leaders of the French party were placed on either side of
him. The musicians struck up a gay lifting tune and the
Prince, followed by the other knights, left the dais. They met
the castle lackeys, now hurrying in from the kitchens with
steaming platters of meat, poultry and fish, and, taking the
platters into their own hands, returned to the high table to
wait on the guests themselves.

When the trenchers were filled the Prince and his companions retired to another table nearby, leaving the servants to serve the other courses. De Ribeaumont looked with awed, speculative eyes from the King, on whose left he was sitting, to Prince Edward, in the place of honor at the second table. He had been struck by a sudden, private fear of his own. And when King Edward, talking only on such safe subjects as the effects of the recent plague on their two countries, the cold weather, and the excellence of the French wine in their goblets tonight, turned and asked him whether he thought the wine of Burgundy superior to that of Guienne, it seemed to Ribeaumont that the bright-blue eyes twinkled with secret amusement and the voice had a familiar ring. Beyond any doubt he had heard it earlier that day.

The meal finished at last, the King rose and ordered the tables removed. Prince Edward and the other English knights joined him and the talk became general as they formed little groups in the center of the hall. Then when the room was cleared and the servants bowed themselves away, the King, his face now serious and stern, mounted the dais again and raised his hand for silence.

Sir Walter Manny, who had been waiting for this moment, led de Chargny to the foot of the small platform. He fell to his knees and Manny moved away.

"You will not," said the King, speaking directly to the man on the floor in front of him, "be surprised, Sir Geoffrey, when I say that I have little reason to like you. You attempted, last night, to steal from me for a mere twenty thousand crowns something that cost me many English lives, vast sums of money, and long months of labor. Had you succeeded, you would indeed have struck a fine bargain! With God's help, however, we were able to disappoint you. But in the face of the truce between our two countries, I must confess that I find it impossible to reconcile your act. Have you anything, my lord, to say to me?"

De Chargny, his head bent, was silent. Edward looked down on him for a long tense moment, then, when he made no answer, signaled Sir Walter to take him away.

This done, Manny now brought de Ribeaumont to the dais. To the Frenchman's relief and astonishment, he saw that the King was smiling pleasantly at him.

"Sir Eustace," he said, in a tone completely unlike that in

which he had addressed Chargny, "you are the most valiant
knight that I have ever seen! I have never encountered anyone who, man to man, gave me so much to do as you did today. So, above all my own knights who engaged in our recent battle, I award you all the prize of valor. It is justly
your due." And reaching up, the King removed the handsome
chaplet from his own head and placed it firmly on de Ribeaumont's dark locks.

"As the best fighter this day," he went on, "and I should
know, for twice you forced me to my knees, I beg you, for
the love of me, to wear this chaplet all this new year. I have
heard from a good authority that you do not dislike the company of ladies and damsels; go and tell them I gave it to you.
I quit you of prison and ransom. You are free, my lord, to
go in safety, when and where you will."

The two Edwards, completely content with the success of
their adventure, and with the promise of the large ransoms
that would be paid for the French knights being held at
Calais, now returned home. Nothing, they told the Queen and
the Princess Isabel, could have been better planned and ex-
ecuted, and the English had certainly performed their parts
in the whole affair in strict accordance with the laws of
Chivalry.

It was, in fact, a great triumph. The tale lost nothing
in the telling, and if Philippa and Isabel shuddered at the
thought of King Edward risking his precious life for the dubious pleasure of taking part in the hand-to-hand combat that
preceded the inevitable surrender of the enemy, they could,
of course, say nothing. Chivalry demanded that ladies send
their knights off to do deeds of valor, smiling bravely and
wishing them well, and to welcome them home with enthusiastic admiration for their success.

When the King had finished his story, making much of the
banquet and his gracious treatment of de Ribeaumont, who,
he told his listeners, had given him the finest fight of his life,
he turned to Isabel.

"And now you know, my dear child, why I am so exceed-
ingly grateful to our good friend Lord d'Albret. It was he
who brought me the word that de Pavie had turned traitor.
But for him we would, today, be mourning the loss of
Calais."

Chapter 12

King Edward threw down his pen, stretched a little wearily and turned to his secretary. "Send for the Lady Royal. I think she will be pleased with the document."

He was standing at one of the windows when, a few minutes later, Isabel entered; he called her to his side. "Come here, daughter," he said, "and feast your eyes and ears on all this peace and loveliness. Our England at its very best."

Smiling affectionately down on her dark head, he drew her into the circle of his arm and pointed to the sweep of garden below. April had been ususually warm here at Windsor and the flowers were bursting into bloom, making bright patches of gold, white and purple in the carefully tended beds; the trees had leafed out in every soft shade of green, the hedges were snowy with the May; as they stared down in appreciative silence, a blackbird called to its mate in a long, liquid trill and from a dovecote someplace out of sight came a muted, continous cooing.

"May Day," said Isabel's father. "May Day—the day for lovers. Doves, blackbirds, and perhaps even princesses. But how can you look at this beautiful scene and be willing to leave it, chuck? You've been to Gascony; you've seen it with your own eyes—all hot sun and bare landscape, a few olive trees! Will young Bernard make you so happy that you won't hunger for our gentle skies and sweet countryside?"

Isabel laughed, and nodded. "I think so, my lord. And Gascony is not so far away, after all. With your permission, we will come home to you from time to time, and later, when Bernard is Lord d'Albret, you shall make him your royal lieutenant, as his father is now, and then his duties will bring us here quite often."

"So they will," replied the King, dropping a kiss on her glowing cheek. "So they will! Well, as you do not seem to have changed your mind in this matter, and as we hear that

Bernard's heart is still yours, I think I will let you read a proc-
lamation that I have been sweating over all this long, warm
morning."

Leading her back to his worktable, he settled her in a
chair beside his own, handed her a long roll of parchment,
then sat down himself and watched her face as she deci-
phered the inky scrawl.

THE KING TO ALL, ETC., GREETING.
Know that we, considering in grateful memory the sincere
love and solid fidelity which we have ever found in our
faithful and dearest friend, the potent nobleman, Bernard,
Lord of Albret, and with what constancy he has ever exposed himself for us, not avoiding either personal danger
or the expenditure of his goods; and desiring to kindle in
him and his posterity a closer attachment to our royal
house, and to bind them more intimately to us; and considering the elegance of our beloved Bernard, eldest son and
heir of the said Lord of Albret, and drawing from the laud-
able auspices of his youth a good presage of future
things, and hoping that the paternal excellence, happily
propagated in him, will advance with pleasant increase, we
have treated with this said Lord of Albret, his father, and
have agreed with him, with mutually glad hearts, concerning a marriage between the said Bernard, son of said Lord
of Albret, and Isabel, our very dearest eldest daughter,
whom we have loved with special affection; to be contract-
ed by the grace of God, under a star of happy omen.

Having read thus far, and seen that the rest of the contract
was concerned with such dull matters as her dowry, Isabel
looked over at her father and tried to thank him. It was difficult, for the document was such a strong proof of his love
for her, his kindness, and his generous understanding, that it
brought tears to her dark blue eyes and a lump into her
throat. Finally, after a stammered sentence or two, she rose,
threw her arms around his neck, and whispered the rest of it
in his ear.

"There, there," he whispered back, "there, there, my love.
I just want you to be happy, that's all. Be happy and I will be
content."

From that moment on Isabel, except for two small worries, was the happiest damsel in England. One of the things that distressed her was that her mother, for some reasons of her own, was not too pleased with the match, making it clear that she considered the part that King Edward had played in it another evidence of the way he insisted on spoiling their eldest daughter.

The other cloud in her sky, and this one Isabel argued away every time it bothered her, was that now that she and Bernard were allowed to correspond with each other she found his letters disappointing. Although they were full of earnest promises to try and make her happy, they were not the ardent love letters for which she yearned, the letters that she was only too ready to answer in kind. But, as she continued to remind herself, Bernard was shy and undoubtedly still in awe of her royal rank; once they were together, all, she was sure, would be as she wished.

In the meantime, the arrangements for the wedding kept her almost too occupied. It was to take place in the royal chapel at Windsor, which would be hung with cloth of gold for the occasion, and the d'Albrets had promised to bring Bernard to England in early October for the weeks of celebration that would both precede and follow the actual ceremony. Dozens of sewing women were at work on Isabel's robes of velvet, cloth of gold, Tripoli silk, and a rich brocade called Baudekin; others were busy embroidering more than a hundred circles of silk and velvet with gold and pearls, the wedding favors which would be worn by the honored guests.

Of all the garments being prepared for her, the one dearest to her heart had been designed by the Princess herself; it was a mantle of Tripoli silk, banded with ermine, to wear over her wedding robe. Having chosen the fabric and the little snowy pelts, and having decided that it should be embroidered all over in gold and silver thread, she dispatched a courier to Bernard asking him to draw her a design for it that would include some of his enchanting animals and birds. When the messenger returned with the sealed roll of parchment she opened it, spread it out on a table and gave a gasp of sheer delight. Alexia de la Mote ran to her side and peered over her shoulder.

She gasped, too. "I've never seen anything more beautiful," she told Isabel.

Bernard had sketched a forest glade, a delicately lovely leafy scene; doves, in romantic pairs, leaned on each other among the leafy branches of the trees, and down beneath them, in the waving grass, gamboled a whole family of amusing hares. The very sight of them brought a glow to Isabel's cheeks, for one of them was washing his face with his paw, an almost exact copy of the drawing she still treasured. Bernard, she told herself, was using this device to prove to her that he remembered the magic hours that they had spend alone together so many, many months ago.

She and Alexia were both smiling over his delicious fantasy when she suddenly burst out laughing. There, peering from behind a tree trunk, was a large furry bear. As she pointed it out to her lady-in-waiting and confessed to her foolish fears back there on the road from Loremo, she could actually hear Bernard's joyous laugh and reassuring voice.

"I shall stich that bear myself," she announced. "The seam-stresses must leave that little bit for me to finish."

By late September Isabel began to count the days. Then, when the date of the d'Albret's arrival was only two weeks away, she was summoned to the Queen's privy chamber.

"I have a letter here from Lady d'Albret," she told her daughter with more than a hint of annoyance in her voice. "She is ill, apparently, and as she cannot make the journey to England at this time she is asking us to send you to d'Albret instead. If you will permit it, she would like the wedding to be solemnized in the cathedral at Dax."

Isabel's heart sank. All her father's wonderful plans—the tournaments, the feasts, the gold-hung chapel. . . .

"We will refuse, of course," went on her mother firmly. "There is no need for Lady d'Albret to be present and I, for one, will be extremely relieved by her absence. A most ambitious, officious, scheming woman, I have always considered her, with a mistaken idea of her own importance."

Isabel, stung by the Queen's scathing words, sprang to Lady d'Albret's defence, convincing herself, as she did so, that she was quite willing to be married in Gascony. And when the King entered, a few minutes later, to find his wife and daughter still wrangling over the matter, she even went so far as to say that she would prefer it.

At this, after a bewildered glance at her earnest face, King

Edward shook his head. "Well," he said at last, "I find it very hard to understand, daughter. If you really mean it, however, I suppose we must agree. But you will have to go alone, you know; I cannot leave England until we have ransomed King David and settled this new unrest in Ireland. Are you serious, Isabel? Are you quite, quite sure that this is what you want?"

Isabel swallowed, then nodded. "Quite sure, sir."

Edward smile ruefully at his wife. "This should please your thrifty heart, my love. Our child is saving us a pretty penny! Shall I answer the Lady d'Albret for you?"

Philippa shrugged. "As you please, my lord."

The two sewing women brought the mantle and spread it over Isabel's lap. She examined it with delighted eyes, complimenting them on their beautiful handiwork. One of them pointed to the bear, outlined in chalk on the rich Indian silk, and handed her two needles, one threaded with gold and one with silver.

"When you have finished, Your Grace," she said, "we will add the ermine border and the lining."

As she plunged the needle in and out, Isabel smiled contentedly, and, when she had finished and cut off the thread, Bess de Burgh, now married to Prince Lionel, left her own needlework and crossed the room to admire the now-completed design.

As they bent over it, studying the glinting gold and silver pattern which Bess prounced perfection itself, one of King Edward's ushers entered the sunny solar and announced that his Majesty requested the immediate presence of the Princess Royal in his privy chamber.

"I think I'll take this mantle with me and show it to His Grace," said Isabel to Bess.

"Let Geoffrey carry it for you," suggested Bess, beckoning to her little page. "I don't give him nearly enough to do."

The boy hurried over, uttering an involuntary cry of admiration as he saw the lovely garment he was to take into his arms.

"Do you like it?" asked Isabel, pleased.

"It's as beautiful as a poem," he replied, folding it carefully.

The Princess, on her way to the door, looked back over

her shoulder in surprise. "A poem, Geoffry? Are you so fond of poems, then?"

He blushed. "Indeed I am, Your Highness," he said shyly. "They come into my head and won't go away."

King Edward was waiting at the door of his privy chamber with such a grave expression on his face that Isabel, who had assumed that he wanted her there to discuss some detail of her imminent departure for Gascony, felt suddenly chilled. But despite his forbidding aspect, she asked young Master Chaucer to spread out the mantle on a table before she sent the lad back to his mistress.

"Look, my lord," she said to her father, "my wedding mantle. Isn't it handsome? Bernard sent me the drawing for the embroidery . . ."

Before she could finish what she was going to say, the King snatched up the piece of heavy silk and flung it aside so angrily that Isabel stared at him in shocked surprise.

"My lord!" she said, running to him and taking his hand. "What have I said? What have I done? Why are you so angry with me?"

"Angry with you? Good God, Isabel, of course I'm not angry with you! Sit down. Sit down."

Something was terribly wrong. He was going to tell her that Bernard was dead. . . .

"I have something to tell you," he began abruptly, his voice strange and harsh. "And, by God, I would rather cut off my right hand than do it. I don't even know how to begin!" He groaned aloud and spread his long fingers wide on his knees, a gesture Isabel had never seen before. "I had an unexpected visitor this morning, child—a priest named Father Michel. He is, he says, young Bernard d'Albret's confessor."

Isabel raised her head and tried to speak. Bernard was not dead, then.

"He came here secretly on a most distasteful and distressing mission. He came, my child, to tell me that you and Bernard must not wed."

Not knowing what to think, completely stunned, Isabel did not move. Her face was drained of color, her frightened eyes were fixed on his.

"According to him, Isabel, and I have no reason to doubt the man, Bernard has always wanted to be a monk—he has a genuine vocation, the strongest that Father Michel has ever encountered in any young man, and he has spent most of the last few years at the Abbey, studying with the other monks. His every thought, until he met you, was of and for the Church, and your betrothal has made him increasingly unhappy. But I think, my poor child, that you should hear all this from Father Michel yourself. He is waiting for you in my chapel. Come back here to me when you have listened to his story."

"But—but I don't understand, Father!" Isabel raised her white, bewildered face to the priest standing in front of her. "If Bernard has always wanted to be a monk, why did he become betrothed to me? How could such a thing happen, if he was unwilling?"

"I'm afraid, Your Grace, that he had very little to do with it. I do not pretend that the lad was indifferent to you; he was not—and as he had never been drawn to any woman before, this feeling of love and desire was a new and, for him, a frightening thing. It threatened everything he had always believed and dreamed of. He was torn, first one way and then another. But if it hadn't been for Lady d'Albret's interference, he would have fought his battle alone and you would neither of you be in this terrible situation today."

"Lady d'Albret?" Even as Isabel asked the question she knew the answer. She could see Lady d'Albret's face when she hinted of Bernard's love and realized, instantly, how the Gasconne had laid her clever snares. She, Isabel, had fallen into the lady's trap, but surely all Bernard need have done was refuse?

"He tried, Your Grace, but it was not as easy as you would think. My lady didn't tell him that you were going to approach your father until shortly after you left Dax, and then, if you remember, there were long months when our two countries were cut off by the plague. It was then that he began to realize what a mistake it would be for him to wed you, or any woman. The Church's call was stronger. Much, much stronger." Father Michel sighed heavily and spoke slowly and reluctantly. This task he had set himself was a painful one, and the agony on Isabel's lovely young face was making it even worse. "But by the time the plague passed his mother was determined to see him married to you. She wrote you at the first possible moment and pretended that he was eager for the match. When he protested, when Lord d'Albret expressed *his* doubts and fears, she screamed them both down, fainted, fell ill. . . . Before long they were all caught in the web she had woven—poor Lord d'Albret, torn between her strong will and violent scenes and the knowledge that he must, if he interfered, offend and distress you and the King; and Bernard, hearing from my lady's physician that if he opposed her wishes she might even die!"

"Surely Bernard didn't believe that?"

"No, not really. But that was when he came to me and sought my help."

Almost against her will Isabel was beginning to see the answers to so many things that had puzzled and worried her in the past: Bernard's avoidance of any lovemaking at moments when she knew he was drawn to her, his unsatisfactory letters, Lord d'Albret's reluctance when her father first broached the possibility that she and Bernard might wed.

But what should she do? How could their marriage be stopped now, when all the world knew that it was to take place in a few weeks? Was she to face everyone as a girl who had been twice jilted? Practically at the altar? Was she so repulsive that no man could bear the thought of marrying her? Bernard had loved her enough to be greatly torn—perhaps she could win him away from the Church?

A little shyly, and not sure just how to frame her thought, she suggested this to Father Michel. "If we did wed, Father, surely Bernard's—feelings—for me would return and grow? How can we turn back, now? Might we not be as happy as most couples?"

Father Michel looked at her sadly. "Bernard would be living against his conscience, Your Grace. Have you any idea what that means, would mean, to anyone as sensitive and deeply religious as Bernard? I wish I could tell you—let you see the misery it would bring you both, the years of heartache, the sense of guilt. Gentle as he is, he might—he might blame you for his betrayal of his faith, of God's command." He laid his hand on her head, his touch a small gesture that seemed to her to be pleading for Bernard.

Then he said it. "Let the boy go, Your Highness. If you love him, if you care for your own future peace of mind—let him go. He realizes, I realize, Lord d'Albret realizes, that this decision must be yours. If you insist, Bernard will keep his troth. But I warn you, daughter, if you do, you too will be living against *your* conscience!"

Isabel shuddered and turned even whiter.

Father Michel struck again swiftly. "Let the boy go and his father will withdraw all his objections to his entering the Church. I am sure of that."

So it was, truly, a decision she must make herself, alone. Isabel buried her face in her hands and tried to think. But how could she think when she was suffering such pain, when her heart was threatening to burst? What had she done to deserve this unbearable burden?

A gentle hand rested on her bent head again. "Come, daughter," he said gently, "we will pray together. For help and guidance."

King Edward knew when he saw his daughter's tortured eyes what they must do between them. He took her in his arms for a long moment, then he led her to a chair and brought her a glass of wine. "Drink this, my love," he said. "You need it."

As he saw some color return to her cheeks, he gave a little sigh of relief. "That's better," he said. "That's better."

"I—have promised Father Michel that Bernard and I will not wed." She swallowed convulsively and tried to go on but it was impossible. Another word and she would break down.

"Yes," said her father. "I know, chuck, I know. You were right, you *are* right, although I would have allowed you to go ahead with the marriage, if you had insisted."

"Don't you mind," asked Isabel, bursting into tears at last, "being the father of a girl who has been jilted twice?"

King Edward let her cry for a few minutes, patting her comfortingly on the shoulder. Then, as the first violence of her grief subsided a little, he answered her. "I think, my love, that I feel it almost as deeply as you do. But this time, Isabel, it will be you that does the jilting."

She raised startled eyes. "I? But it is Bernard. . . ."

"You will change your mind. You *have* changed your mind! You are here at this moment telling me that doubts have been worrying you—that you are unhappy at the thought of wedding someone you have not seen for many,

many months and that you wish to break your betrothal and remain here in England with your parents."

"No one will believe it."

"You must make them, Isabel. It won't be easy, but you must pretend. For your sake, for my sake, and for Bernard's sake. If I understand the situation at Dax, Lady d'Albret must not be given a weapon of any kind whatsoever or she will keep that lad from entering the Church. And that, I'm sure, would make none of us happy."

"No," Isabel agreed. "No."

"After a while," he went on, pouring out a little more wine, "we will try again. But we will choose more wisely next time, you and I. . . ."

"No, no, no!" protested Isabel violently. "No, father. Never, never, never! I will do what you say now, hard as it will be. I will do the very best I can. . . . But, if you love me, you must promise me faithfully that I need never think of marrying anyone else—ever! Please, if you love me at all— promise me!"

Tipping up her face, the King kissed her. "Of course I love you, Isabel. And although I'm sure you will change your mind one day I now promise what you ask. If you wish to remain single, my love, you shall."

Book III

Chapter 13

The sudden termination of the Princess Royal's wedding plans, when everything was prepared for her departure and a fleet of ships was already anchored at Plymouth to take her and her possessions to Gascony, was the subject of much speculation not only in England but all over Europe. The unequal match itself had been widely discussed and criticized; Isabel's change of mind was even more surprising. And when it became generally known that Bernard d'Albret had renounced his inheritance in favor of his younger brother Arnaud Ameneus to take the vows of a Cordelier monk, the Princess was generally condemned as a heartless jilt. What, people asked each other, was King Edward doing to allow such behavior?

So while the nobles gossiped, Princess Isabel played the part assigned her by her father, hiding her aching heart and doubly wounded pride behind a mask of gaiety. She had wanted to run away into the country but the King had refused to allow it. No, he had said firmly, if she wanted the world to believe that she was the jilt and not the jilted she must remain and present a smiling face to the court.

This she did by plunging herself into a giddy round of activity that never stopped; hunting, hawking, dancing, singing, visiting; anything that kept her too busy to think. Her needlework remained in its basket, and reading, she soon discovered, was impossible; every book she picked up seemed to be about love and lovers, a subject she must avoid.

Bed time she postponed just as long as she could, for the moment that her tiring women extinguished the candles and bowed themselves out of her chamber she was at the mercy of the agony she had striven all day to conceal. Only by tiring herself physically during the daytime and evening hours could she hope to find oblivion, and prevent the yearning for Bernard that too often set her weeping into her pillows

151

through the long black nights and wondering, now that it was too late, whether she had been right to let him go.

At eighteen, of course, such violent unhappiness cannot last forever. But when the pain eased and the weeping stopped, she found that she had no interest in any kind of flirtation or romantic overture. She shied away from the gallantries of the young noblemen around her and, after a while, even those who were considered eligible enough to aspire to her hand learned to leave her alone. There were not many of these, of course, and the most likely of the lot, Hugh Courtenay, the young heir to the Earldom of Devon, had recently died, thereby putting an end to Prince Edward's hopes that his good friend might be the one to change his sister's mind.

She had, certainly, many compensations for her single state. Recognized everywhere now as England's second lady, and the mistress of great manors in York, Lincoln, and the Isle of Wight, she had Carisbrooke Castle for her own use as well as many other smaller castles and country houses. And as if this were not enough, King Edward continued to spoil her, or so said Queen Philippa, encouraging her to do anything she wished and showering her with lavish gifts of money and jewels. Now, as always, he made his great love for her the reason for his generosity: "his beloved Isabel, his eldest daughter" he described her in one letter patent, and later, when he was bestowing on her five additional grants of farms, manors and priory revenues, he wrote, in the preamble to the deed of gift, "on account of the kind of love and especial affection which we bear to our dearest daughter, Isabel, and that she may be able better and more decently to support her state."

There was no question but what it all came in very handily, for while her mother frowned and her father indulged her, Isabel whirled faster and faster, moving from one place to another, ordering fresh gowns, giving sumptuous feasts and entertainments for her friends and neighbors; spending, without a thought, the money that flowed into her hands. When she ran into debt she merely laughed, at first, and turned to her father for more. Then, when she was, after several such applications, a little ashamed, she let her servants wait for their wages for many long months. Thinking, finally, to make all right, she pledged part of her jewels to the royal chamberlain and treasurer, who, naturally, wasted no time before informing the King of his daughter's transaction.

He summoned her to Windsor immediately and there, behind closed doors and without even a page in attendance, they had a talk that Isabel never forgot, and when she emerged, alone, and joined her ladies again, more than one of them noticed that she was unusually subdued. She and her father continued, however, to be on their customary affectionate terms, and the only thing that she told Alexia de la Mote about their interview was that she had promised to repay the money he had already advanced to redeem her jewels.

Although she did not now actually change her way of life or completely curb her extravagant habits, she did begin, after that day at Windsor, to spend more of her time with the other members of the royal family. Her brother Edward had his own household, and had for many years. In his gay, bachelor establishments she was always welcome and always enjoyed herself. The only other royal children who lived away from the court was Prince Lionel; his wealthy bride, a niece of the Duke of Lancaster, plain sensible Bess, was six years older than her jolly, rather stupid boy husband, but as she had been well trained by her foster mother, Queen Philippa, she ran both her sport-loving Prince and their new home so skillfully that Isabel was very happy there and visited it more and more often.

Isabel had, after all, grown up with Bess. But it was only now that she discovered how much wit, intelligence and understanding was hidden under Bess' shy awkwardness; and, as there was a great deal of room for friendship in Isabel's empty life at this time, she and Bess grew closer than they had ever been before, so close that she told Bess the true story of her broken betrothal and thereby eased a little her still aching heart.

The Princess Royal was not, however, Bess' only frequent guest. Her little cousin Blanche, the Duke's daughter and heiress, who was generally understood to be the future bride of Prince John of Gaunt, often visited her kinswoman. The two Lancaster cousins could not have been more unlike; Bess, tall, rangy, and horse-faced, was a sad contrast to dainty, delicate Blanche, with her flyaway pale-gold hair, her light-blue eyes, her natural grace, and her pretty tinkling laugh.

But although Blanche had all the elements of beauty, both Isabel and Bess agreed that something was missing. She was, perhaps, too serene, too placid—she lacked the animation that would make her irresistible.

"All that pale color of hers never changes," Isabel said, as they watched her dance.

"Nothing seems to touch her," agreed Bess. "I suppose she will drift through life much more easily that we will, Bel."

"Certainly more easily than I *have*," agreed Isabel, remembering the dreadful hours when she faced the truth about Bernard. Then she saw, as she so often did, his eyes looking into hers, and it was if someone had stabbed her suddenly with a sharp knife.

Time, which had dragged for Isabel for so long, now moved more swiftly. Days turned into weeks, weeks into months, months into years with a rapidity that almost frightened her, driving her occasionally into a fresh whirl of pleasure-seeking activity. There were still the moments when her heart cried out for her lost love, but she was, for the most part, fairly content to be England's Lady Royal, secure in the knowledge that she need never leave her own country or change her single status unless she so wished. And, although she did not realize this, she had, over the years, grown a thick protective shell between herself and the rest of the world, a shell that made her a mere spectator while around her those she loved were playing their active roles in the game of life.

These same years were extremely difficult ones for the King, occupied as he was in the frustrating task of trying to arrange a permanent peace treaty with France that would be acceptable to both countries. King Philip, who had lost the battle of Crécy, was dead; his son John was now King of France and although one of his first acts in coming to the throne had been to ratify the truce with England, neither he nor King Edward could agree on the answer to the all-important questions which must be settled between them.

Documents were written, rewritten, torn up; intermediaries stepped in, suggesting this and that in the way of compromise; the truce was extended, renewed, extended again. It was all a waste of time. John's terms angered Edward, and Edward's demands were so impossible that the French king listened to them in grim silence and refused to answer.

By the beginning of 1355 it was apparent to the English that they must again invade France. The Captal de Buch came to London with the news that the French were raiding the border towns of Guienne, and that one of King John's lieutenants was doing his best to take the towns and castles in Gascony that were within easy reach of his own holdings. With this as provocation, King Edward and his advisers made a plan; the King would invade from the North, his ally the King of Navarre would meet him in Normandy, and the Prince of Wales would sail directly to Bordeaux and do his bit by harrying all Southern France.

With this strategy in mind the King asked for and received from Parliament the necessary grants; men were mustered, ships requisitioned and readied, sheaves of orders for all the needed supplies were issued, and the Prince of Wales, having been appointed Lieutenant in Aquitaine, was given full authority to make treaties, purchase horses and supplies there, and to receive them. Then, when all this was done, young Edward set his armorers to work on a new suit of the black armor that was to send him down in history as The Black Prince.

It was September before Prince Edward and his thousands of soldiers set sail for Bordeaux, and it was the end of October before the King and his younger sons, John and Lionel, crossed to Calais. Some time later news of them began reaching home and both Isabel and Lionel's wife Bess moved into Westminster Palace, wanting to pass the period of inevitable anxiety with the Queen and to be at hand when letters arrived from France.

Joan of Kent, now for some years the Lady Holland, came to Westminster, too. Her husband Thomas, after a twelve-month away from her, pursuing the King's business in Bretagne and Poitou, was, even now, riding south to join the Prince of Wales at Bordeaux; Joan was bored down in the country and glad to have a good excuse to join the court again where she could enjoy herself, or so she thought, while her two boys were cared for in the royal nurseries.

As it turned out, she found that there was little to do at Westminster, these days, and she amused herself by bickering with the Queen. That good lady succeeded fairly well in holding her temper but her deep-seated dislike of Joan and the fact that her nerves were not too steady in these worrying times often led her to the brink of an open quarrel with her young tormenter.

Isabel did what she could to pour oil on the troubled waters, and she was, actually, interrupting a most promising verbal battle one afternoon when a courier entered and made her intervention unnecessary.

The Scots, despite the fact that their King David had never been ransomed and was still a prisoner in the Tower of London, had marched over the border and were besieging Berwick.

This time the Queen did not ride north herself; instead, she informed her husband of the serious news and awaited his orders. The King immediately announced that Prince Edward was old enough now and sufficiently experienced to lead the French campaign in his absence and returned to defend his own borders.

By the middle of January King Edward had relieved Berwick, but it was March before he and the two princes reached Westminster and the anxious Queen. There had been little opportunity to keep Philippa informed of their progress. So, when they rode into the palace courtyard, weary and travel-stained, and then sought her out in her private apartments, she and her daughter Isabel greeted them with a flurry of tears, kisses, scoldings and exclamations of relief.

While his father and the two younger princes had been fighting the Scots, the Prince of Wales was sending back glowing reports of his progress in France. It had been, for him, a glorious winter. He and the Gascons, equally greedy for booty and plunder, had taken five hundred villages and towns, stripping each one of every beautiful and valuable object they could find before moving on to the next. The people in this part of France were prosperous, and the châteaux and castles were full of rich silk hangings, elaborate furniture and floor carpets, chests of handsome clothing and caskets of priceless jewels. So many of these things went back to Bordeaux with Prince Edward and his friends that their horses could barely put one foot in front of another, and, as a result, he left behind him a grimly embittered foe, determined to avenge this cruel pillaging at the first possible opportunity.

Early in July, after a few weeks' rest, he wrote his father that he was setting out on a new expedition; he was planning to raid the North, this time, with a force that consisted of two thousand men-at-arms and six thousand archers. The King and his wife, spending their summer quietly at Windsor, waited eagerly for more news; it was slow in coming. Edward, after another period of relentless ravaging, was encamped at Vierzon, which he had taken, when he was shocked to hear from his scouts that King John had marched down from Paris with an army at least six times larger than his and was already at Chartres. This was too close for comfort, so the Prince, after killing most of his prisoners, moved over to the little town of Romorantin; there he took three days to consider the situation, then set out in the direction of Poitiers.

The French, in those three days, outmaneuvered the English prince by riding swiftly across the country and reaching the same destination some time before he did, thus making it impossible for the English forces, who had been hoping for reinforcements that did not arrive, to delay much longer in meeting them on the battlefield.

Outnumbered and aware that the enemy was occupying the most advantageous situation available, the Prince of Wales, facing almost certain defeat, halted his men and encamped six miles away.

At Windsor, the royal family was gathered in the garden, enjoying an unusually fine warm September day. They were watching John, Edmund and young Jack de Montfort wrestling on the grass in front of them when a servant, carrying a thick packet of letters, approached the King. Isabel, seeing that he was wearing her brother Edward's livery, touched her mother's arm.

"Look!" she said.

Philippa, following her eyes, and noticing, too, the intent expression on the King's face, rose and moved to his side. Isabel followed, standing a little apart.

Edward raised his head, then beckoned them closer.

"Good news?" asked the Queen.

"No ... very bad, I'm afraid," he replied soberly. "Ned, when he wrote this, was about to suffer a crushing defeat at the hands of the French. He promises to send further word the moment the battle is over, but God knows what has happened in the meantime! They were at Poitiers, King John's army is four to six times larger than ours, all attempts at mediation had failed, and they were to engage in battle the following morning." He turned to the Prince's messenger. "That would be the morning of the nineteenth day of this month?" he asked him.

The man bowed. "Yes, Sire. I set out on the evening of the eighteenth and it is now the twenty-fourth, is it not? I reached the coast in a few hours but the winds were not too favorable."

When he had been dismissed and had returned to the castle, Philippa, her face white, clutched the King's sleeve. "I told you that Edward was too young, my lord. He's too hotheaded, too eager to fight! I *asked* you not to let him. . . ."

"No, no," King Edward interrupted her hurriedly, "you are quite wrong, my love. Read it for yourself!" He handed the letter to her. "You will find that Ned was quite willing to surrender, had King John been reasonable. He offered to free all the prisoners he had taken, give back the towns and castles, and promise not to make war against France for seven years. What more could he say?"

Isabel saw her mother thrust the letter away with a shaking hand. "I can't read it now, my lord. I'm too frightened. What was King John's answer?"

"He demanded the impossible. The surrender of our son and one hundred of his knights."

The young princes, realizing that something had happened, stopped their sport and ran over. The King outlined the situation briefly, but cautioned them not to discuss the news with anyone until further word arrived from France. Then he called over a page, handed him letters from the packet that were addressed to the wives of several of the noblemen fighting at the Prince's side, and hurried into the castle to confer with his advisers.

The Queen and Princess Isabel watched him go in stricken silence.

"Come," said Philippa at last, "let us retire to my closet and pray."

"It's too late," said Isabel grimly. "But there's nothing else for us to do."

Despite their determination to remain reasonably calm, that night and the day that followed it were long and harrowing. Warwick's wife Kitty, whose husband had written her, too, on the eve of the battle, moved from her house farther up the Thames into the Palace itself and added her prayers to the Queen's. Warwick had written her a few details that Prince Edward had omitted, and these she shared with the royal family. When mediation failed, Geoffrey de Chargny, Warwick wrote, had suggested that the issue be fought out by a hundred knights chosen by each side; but that he, Warwick, advised the Prince to refuse that proposal, too. "The French cannot be trusted," his letter added, "Each man must fight his best and let God uphold the right."

"Let God uphold the right. Let God uphold the right!" The words kept running through Isabel's head, but when she prayed it was for Edward's life.

They were seated at the supper table, making a brave effort to eat, talk, and look as usual, when there was a bustle at the far end of the Hall. A royal usher, his face alight with excitement, ran to the high table and announced to the King that Roger de Cottesford, the Prince of Wales' squire, had just ridden into the castle.

Isabel's heart leaped into her throat. Now they would know. . . .

"Bring him to me." Her father's voice was strained and his hand, gripping a goblet of wine, shook.

The long chamber fell silent and everyone watched Prince Edward's favorite squire stride past the narrow tables. He was smiling, and he carried a knobby, rounded bundle under his arm. It seemed to be wrapped in a piece of silk that was edged with golden fringe.

Marching up to the high table he placed the object on the board in front of the King, stepped back and fell on his knees.

"For you, Sire," he said, in a loud, quavering voice. "From my beloved master, His Royal Highness, Edward, the Prince of Wales."

King Edward looked first at his wife sitting beside him. Their eyes clung, then she smiled and nodded at the package.

He reached out with trembling fingers and pulled away the

silk wrapping. Isabel, from her chair on the Queen's right, could see now that the piece of silk was a banner and that it was embroidered in gold *fleurs de lys*. Edward tossed it aside and stared incredulously at the gleaming object resting on the table.

He rose so suddenly that his goblet of wine upset. He turned and snatched a flaming torch from the wall behind his throne chair, then, holding it high in one hand, he picked up the Prince's gift in the other and raised it over his head, so that everyone in the Hall could see it. It was a helmet, and there, encircling it and sparkling in the light of the torch, was the royal coronet of France.

Chapter 14

The miracle of Poitiers, a victory even more crushing to the French than the battle of Crécy and in which, incidentally, both de Chargny and de Ribeaumont had been slain, was not eight months in the past. Prince Edward and his highest-ranking prisoners, who included King John himself, little Prince Philip, the King's youngest and favorite son, James de Bourbon, John d'Artois, the Earls of Estampes and Graville, Lord Enguerrand de Coucy, and Lord de Partenay, had spent a gay and often riotous winter in Bordeaux, waiting, at first, for a fresh truce to be arranged; then, with that accomplished, for good weather and the fleet of English ships to bring them all back to England.

It was late April before they finally set sail, leaving Lord d'Albret, assisted by three other Gascon lords, in charge of England's newly conquered territories. They landed at Sandwich on the fourth day of May and proceeded slowly up to London, resting here and there on the way; for most of the French prisoners this was their first glimpse of the English countryside, and the Prince leading them through the beautiful lanes, admitted to himself that they could not have seen it at a better time.

As the word spread that the Prince was home and was bringing his royal prisoners to London, the people left their fields and houses to line the roads and cheer him with wild enthusiasm. The closer the long train came to its destination the thicker the crowds grew, and by the time it had crossed London Bridge the shouting, singing, laughing, exulting onlookers jammed the narrow streets, slowing the procession to a snail's pace.

Side by side at its head rode the young conqueror and the French king. John, his dark eyes grim in his long, narrow, unhappy face, was mounted on his own huge white charger; the Prince of Wales, either as a chivalrous gesture or because

161

he had an innate sense of the dramatic, had chosen a small, unpretentious black palfrey to carry him on this triumphant day. Whatever his reason, the two men presented a picture that was never to be forgotten by those who saw them ride by—the black-haired, black-bearded king on the large snowy horse, and the golden-haired, clean-shaven prince on the small black gelding.

Immediately behind them was King John's fourteen-year-old son, sitting stiffly in his handsome saddle, his back a ramrod as he stared straight ahead at his father. His lips trembled from time to time, but he never turned to look at the loud, enthusiastic throngs on his right and left, nor did he see the bright banners, tapestries, rich silks and gleaming bits of silver and brass.

Only once did he move his head, and that was when a pretty damsel, hanging over the cobbled street in a gilded cage, tossed a shower of gold-and-silver filigree blossoms down on the Prince of Wales and his royal captive with such a wild and lavish gesture that a golden rose hit the young lad squarely on the cheek. Catching it neatly in one hand, Philip rose in his stirrups, threw it back inside the glittering cage, then settled back in his place, apparently still oblivious to all the curious faces around him and even to the charming English maid, now smiling down on his proud head.

Princess Isabel, sitting beside the little Prince that night at the great banquet given at Westminster Palace by the King Edward and Queen Philippa for King John and the other noble prisoners, thought Philip arrogant rather than merely proud. Every attempt she made to engage him in conversation ended abruptly; there was no subject, it seemed, that the boy was willing to discuss with her, no question that he would answer with more than a monosyllable, no pleasantry at which he would smile. It was such an uphill task that she abandoned it, after a few minutes, and turned to her old acquaintance, the hawk-nosed Captal de Buch, seated on her other side.

Here she had better fortune. He was only too ready to talk, telling her in detail of their amazing victory at Poitiers, when defeat appeared to be inevitable, and of the gay winter at Bordeaux that followed the battle.

Isabel, in her turn, described some of her own adventures in that same fascinating city, avoiding as much as possible the tragedy of her sister's death and her subsequent flight from Loremo.

"Those were dreadful days," he agreed, "although the plague did not touch my remote little castle at La Teste."

"There was a time," said Isabel, "when Bordeaux was so blazing hot that I remembered wistfully all that you had told me of your hideaway."

"But where was I, Your Grace?" he asked her. "I invited you to visit me, you know. Why didn't you send me a message and remind me of my invitation?"

She was about to answer him when she heard Prince Philip give an angry, stifled exclamation. He was staring furiously at her father's cupbearer, kneeling with a flagon of wine at King Edward's feet. While she looked at the boy and wondered what could be wrong with him now, he sprang up so abruptly that he almost upset his tall-back chair. Striding over, he boxed the man sharply on the ears.

"My father is unfortunate," he announced loudly, "but he is, at least, the sovereign of the King of England. Serve him first, varlet!"

A shocked hush fell over the entire banquet hall. To Isabel's great relief, King Edward laughed, reached out a friendly hand, and ruffled the indignant Prince's hair.

"*Vous êtes Philip le Hardi!*" he said. "But you must remember, my boy, that you are in my kingdom now, not your father's."

King John, who had been sitting in gloomy silence and eating little, leaned forward and whispered something in his son's ear. The lad flushed, bit his lip; then, after bowing to each of the kings in turn, moved slowly back to his seat.

"If those are French manners," murmured the Princess Royal to the Captal, "I think I prefer ours!"

"Don't be too hard on the poor little princeling," the Captal replied. "He worships his father and this is a bitter business for him, you know. I am told that he insisted on following King John onto the field at Poitiers and stood right behind him, holding a battleax, all ready to defend him. He never budged an inch, even through the most furious of the fighting, and saved his Father's life several times by shouting 'Father, look to the left! Father, look to the right!' when the King was too occupied with one assailant to see another approaching. He's a brave boy, Your Grace, under that touchy, belligerent manner."

Needless to say, this incident did not ease the already strained atmosphere at the high table, especially as King John grew more gloomy and more silent. Finally, feeling that something must be done, King Edward slapped him on the back. "Come, come, Cousin!" he suggested in a much too hearty voice, "Sing and be merry with us!"

The French king raised his dark eyes and gave Edward a scornful glance.

"In the words of the Israelites," he answered slowly and grimly, "how shall we sing the songs of the Lord in a strange land?"

After that depressing speech there seemed little that anyone could say, and it was a great relief when the tables were cleared away and the dancing began; and although the French monarch refused to take part and continued to sit aloof in his place of honor on the dais with his young son crouching at his feet, the other noble prisoners responded gaily and gallantly to the sound of the music.

Isabel was claimed first by King John's cousin, James de Bourbon, then by John d'Artois and, after that, by the young Lord de Coucy. De Coucy was much the best dancer of the three, strikingly handsome in a dark, almost sinister fashion, and bubbled with a wit that Isabel discovered was delightfully contagious. After her frustrated attempts to chat with Prince Philip, she found herself laughing and talking so easily and merrily with de Coucy that she was sorry when the music stopped and they returned to their places.

Isabel strolled slowly back toward the Hall, her thoughts far away. Her conversation with the Captal de Buch earlier in the evening had set her dreaming, during the few minutes she had spent alone in one of the retiring rooms, of the past and of her sister Joanna; and now, as she walked through the quiet, almost deserted corridor, she actually passed several of her friends without seeing them.

She was, as a result, extremely startled when a young man stepped out of one of the window embrasures and spoke to her. In the light of a flambeau, set high in the stone wall over his head, he looked, at first glance, vaguely familiar. He had very fair hair and eyes, as he straightened up from his deep bow and raised them to hers, were a light gray that made her heart jump into her throat.

Even more startled, she moved toward him, then, seeing his face clearly, she stopped. No, it was not Bernard. For a moment she had thought. . . .

"Forgive me for not waiting to be presented to you, Your Highness," said the young man quickly. "I did not mean to frighten you. But I wanted a moment or two with you to speak privately and that, as you know, is very difficult to arrange. I am Arnaud d'Albret, Bernard's brother."

"Bernard's brother! But no one told me that you were here at Westminster, sir. Is my Lord d'Albret with you?"

He shook his head. "No, he remained in France as Prince Edward's Governor. We were both at Poitiers, however. What a victory, Your Grace! What a day for all of us!"

"And Lady d'Albret? Are she and—your brother well?"

"My lady is, yes. But Bernard. . . ." He hesitated. "That is why I wished to speak to you alone, Your Highness. He fell ill shortly after Christmas, and although the good brothers of his order did everything in their power to save him, it was impossible."

All the color left Isabel's face. She tried to speak, but there seemed nothing to say; her only feeling, for the moment, was a vast emptiness, a queer paralyzing numbness.

"Come," said Arnaud gently, taking her by the arm. "Sit here in the window, my lady. I've been trying for days to think of the right way to tell you my sad news and here I am, making the worst possible botch of it!"

"No, no," Isabel protested. "I know . . . I could see it in your face. And I am grateful, sir, for your thoughtfulness. His goodness, his kindness to me . . . how could I ever forget?" Words failed her again as it suddenly occurred to her that Arnaud must think, with the rest of the world, that she was responsible for the broken betrothal, that she had been the faithless one. But if he considered her a jilt, why had he sought her out, why was he apologizing for distressing her?

"I was with Bernard when he died," went on the young man, answering the questions in Isabel's stunned and bewildered heart, "and he told me, for the first time, that it was you who had made it possible for him to obey God's command and withdraw from the world. He knew only too well the burden you were taking on your shoulders for his sake, but he was powerless. Caught. He felt, in fact, that anything he might have done then would merely have made matters worse for you both."

"I know," said Isabel, almost inaudibly. "I know. And I know that Bernard was not to blame for our—misunderstanding. I was greatly responsible myself, for much of it, and I wonder now how I could have been so blind! I closed my eyes to so many doubts and questions. . . ."

"Well, all that matters tonight," Arnaud answered gently, "is that my brother had his heart's desire. 'If you ever see Her Grace,' he said to me, 'give her my grateful blessing and tell her I died a happy man.' "

It was almost impossible, after that, to return to the banqueting hall, but Isabel knew she must. For the Lady Royal to disappear on such an evening without first excusing herself would disturb her parents and set too many tongues wagging. So she sent Arnaud on ahead and, with a heavy heart and a reluctant step, she followed him.

As she entered the Hall, pausing a moment just inside the doorway, she saw that the rest of the royal family were doing their best to entertain their guests: the King and Queen, sitting one on each side of King John, seemed to have discovered, finally, a subject that interested him; Prince Edward was deep in a game with the difficult Prince Philip; John of Gaunt was listening intently to the Captal de Buch, the thirteen-year-old Princess Mary was spinning around the floor with young James de Bourbon, whose father had fallen at Poitiers, and pretty Blanche of Lancaster was smiling sedately up at John d'Artois, the Earl d'Eu.

She hesitated; perhaps, after all, she wasn't needed here. Why not join her mother and father on the dais for a few minutes, then plead a headache and retire?

But before she had quite made up her mind, some of the figures in the pleasant tableau changed. The Queen, who had been chatting so easily with King John, swung around in her throne and stared across the Hall, her heavy brows drawn together in a frown of disapproval. On the dance floor nearby Isabel saw Tom Holland lose his place in the intricate figure and tread on the tail of a lady's gown. At the chess table her brother Ned suddenly leaning forward, a pawn gripped in one hand, and glared over her head.

She turned. There, behind her, so close that she could smell the stale wine on her breath, stood her cousin Joan, her gold hair rumpled; she was laughing foolishly and swaying as she clung amorously to the attentive gallant at her side. It was Lord de Coucy, the handsome young Frenchman whose company the Princess had so well enjoyed earlier that evening.

He saw her now, sketched an amused and exaggerated little bow, and lowered one eyelid for a split second; but Isabel saw a smear of Joan's red lip paste near his rakish brown moustache.

She knew instantly what she must do, realizing too, that it would provide the perfect reason for leaving the Hall. Moving swiftly toward Joan, she stepped in front of her, blocking her from view. "Thank you, my lord," she said to de Coucy, "it was very kind of you to look after her ladyship. You may join your friends now, if you will, and leave her with me. I see that she is far from well and should retire to her own apartments."

Then, dismissing him with a stiff nod, and disregarding Joan's tipsy insistence that she was perfectly well and was going to dance the next dance, the Princess gripped her cousin's arm, turned her around, and marched her firmly out into the corridor.

After Isabel had scolded Joan into taking off her disheveled gown and seen her settled down to sleep, she slipped away to the peace and quiet of her own bed.

But by the time she had disrobed, dismissed her chamber women, and crawled between the welcoming covers, she discovered, to her surprise, that instead of the heavy storm of weeping that she assumed would overpower her as soon as she was alone, she experienced nothing but a weary lassitude; now that the first shock of Bernard's death was past she felt only a dull, gentle ache and a sense of greater loneliness than before. It was almost as if a burden had been lifted from her heart, leaving that small ache in its place.

Before falling asleep she allowed herself the luxury of reliving those strange, wonderful days when she and Bernard had been entirely alone. This was something she had not done since she had been forced to face the fact that he had never loved her as much as she loved him.

But tonight, comforted by his message of thanks and his blessing, and healed, too, more than she was willing to admit by the passing of time, she was able to remember Bernard not as a man who had rejected her but as a brave, beloved companion with whom she had shared a rare and dreamlike adventure.

Chapter 15

Having now received the King of France and the other prisoners in a suitably festive and elaborate manner, the English were faced with the problem of where and how to house them until the peace terms were settled and their ransoms paid. That the negotiations would take a long time seemed inevitable; the Dauphin, who had escaped at Poitiers and was ruling the kingdom in his father's absence, was not a man to make things easy for his enemies. And France itself, after the disasters of Crécy and Poitiers, and the constant looting and foraging, was so impoverished and that the peasants, already taxed to the verge of rebellion, were not going to be much help when it came to raising ransom money.

The Tower of London, the obvious place for a royal prisoner, was not sufficiently comfortable or luxurious for a lengthy incarceration; and King Edward certainly did not want King John and his nobles living under his own roof; they might visit at Windsor or Westminster from time to time, but they must be quartered elsewhere.

After much deliberation it was decided that they should be moved to the Savoy Palace, the Duke of Lancaster's white, many-turreted dwelling situated a short distance along the Thames from Westminster. Lancaster himself was off in France again, this time in Bretagne, where, with young Jack de Montfort, he was trying to reclaim the boy's lost inheritance; but when he heard what was needed, he wrote the King that he would be happy to accommodate their royal captives.

It was very old, and without exception the loveliest of all the palaces in the city; King John might well consider himself very fortunate. Accustomed as he was to Paris' dank Louvre, a rabbitwarren of odorous staircases and small, crowded chambers, the Savoy, with its spacious light-filled halls and solars, overlooking the Thames on one side and, on the other, the Red Rose Court, deliciously fragrant during the summer months with the scent of hundreds of roses that had been brought over many years earlier from Provence, should have seemed a haven of peace and pleasure to the unfortunate monarch.

King John was, at this time, only about forty years old, and as he was free to go to Windsor to hunt, hawk, or compete in the royal tournaments held there, and as several of England's most charming ladies were only too willing to provide him with any other kind of sport he might be missing, his spirits soon rose and he did not seem to mind that his exile was stretching into months. His son Philip, still with him, now remained in the background, studying his books and practicing in the castle's tilt yard.

His nobles, equally welcome at Westminster and Windsor, discovered too that they need not sit and sigh for their wives and sweethearts. The story that all Frenchmen were ardent and skilled in the arts of love had spread over England and there were women of both high and low degree who wished to find out for themselves if this were true.

Princess Isabel, still living inside her shell, took little part in the salacious talk around her and watched with open disgust her cousin Joan's pursuit of the two young French noblemen, James de Bourbon and Enguerrand de Coucy. What the other ladies did was their business, but Joan's behavior, she knew only too well, reflected on the whole royal family.

Isabel was apparently not the only one thinking this, for early in July Tom Holland, who had good reason to know his wife's ways, took her and their children off to Kent for the rest of the summer. The court moved to Woodstock at about this time, and Isabel retired to the coolness of her estates on the Isle of Wight.

But her life there, for some reason, was not so satisfying as it had been; the days dragged and the evenings seemed endless. Her minstrels, sensing her growing ennui, tried to interest her in new songs and dances; her jester wearied himself and everyone else with frantic bursts of strained humor; and her lords and ladies scoured the small island for any wandering troupe of players or mummers who might provide a few hours' amusement.

As a result, it was a definite relief to the little household at Carisbrooke Castle when, late in November, a messenger arrived with a letter from Prince Lionel's wife Bess, urging the Princess to join their party at Hatfield for the Christmas festivities. Blanche, she wrote, was already with them, and both Prince John and Princess Mary had promised to ride up from Westminster, bringing with them one or two of the younger French gallants. And, she added, "You must see my infant, Bel. She grows more delightful every day."

Hatfield Palace, built some two hundred years before as a manor house for the bishops of Ely, was a pleasant if drafty dwelling standing halfway up a wooded hillside and overlooking the picturesque little river Lea. The bishops had, in that two hundred years, improved the original structure, glazing most of the windows and building chimneys in the principal chambers. They also made themselves a walled vineyard, a rare thing in England; they had encouraged the great oak trees that were Hatfield's pride, and they had kept the ten miles of parkland filled with fat deer.

Hatfield still belonged to the Church, but the bishops used it seldom and were quite content to lend it to the King's second son and his rich young wife. Located an easy seventeen miles from Westminster and perhaps twenty from Windsor, it was comfortably accessible even in the winter months, and Isabel, making the journey from the Isle of Wight, was able to spend her final night on the way with her parents and still reach Hatfield in time to change for supper.

She found the old palace filled with familiar, welcoming faces and noisy with the sounds of loud laughter and Christmas music. The halls were garlanded with bay and ivy, huge branches of evergreen scented the smoky air, and sprays of red-berried holly and white-berried mistletoe hung from the rafters and over each arched doorway.

The first person to greet the Princess Royal was the young host himself, her tall, jolly, foolish, handsome brother Lionel; he gave her a bearhug that almost cracked her ribs, kissed her loudly on both cheeks, then turned her over to his smiling wife.

"Well, well, well!" he shouted as the two women beamed into each other's faces and exchanged more gentle salutes, "Our company grows—our company grows! John and Mary arrived yesterday, Bel, bringing de Bourbon and de Coucy, and we expect our Uncle Lancaster and Jack de Montfort almost anytime now."

Isabel looked at him in astonishment. "I thought Jack and your uncle were in Bretagne!"

"So they were. But the campaign was not very successful, apparently, so they signed a four-year's truce and set sail for home."

After sipping the cup of hot spiced wine that Lionel thrust into her chilled fingers, Isabel climbed the stairs and found both Blanche and Mary awaiting her in the solar.

Blanche, she soon saw, had changed a great deal in the months since they had last met; she had been a thin child, with arms and legs like dandelion stems. Now she was slender rather than thin, and there was a mature, almost wise, look in the calm, pale turquoise eyes that met Isabel's darker ones. Mary, on the other hand, was still, at about thirteen, an angular lass and as awkward as a young filly. But she was growing so much like Joanna that Isabel saw her beloved lost sister in the line of Mary's brows and the sweetness of her smile.

They chatted for a few minutes, then turned to the important business of readying themselves for supper. Isabel chose a new crimson velvet surcoat, bordered in marten almost as dark and glossy as her hair, that opened over a matching undergown, cut daringly low, and wore around her neck a massive gold-and-ruby necklace, a gift from the King, that picked up the glowing color of the velvet, as did the large ruby buttons that marched down the front of the snug bodice.

She was quite pleased with her own appearance, but when she saw the Lady Blanche all in frosty white brocade and snowy ermine, her only jewels a shimmering rope of pearls, she wondered if her costume were not, perhaps, a little flamboyant.

They descended to the dining hall and Prince John, now seventeen and as tall as the Prince of Wales, stepped forward with a proud look that indicated that he considered the beautiful Blanche his special property. He hardly left her side all evening, and when he maneuvered her under a bit of mistletoe and snatched a kiss it was obvious that he, at least, was eagerly awaiting the day when he would claim her as his bride.

A smothered sound from someplace behind her made Isabel turn. There in a shadowy corner stood Bess' young page, Geoffrey Chaucer, clad in a new jagged paltok and a pair of gay red-and-black particolored breeches. His face, however, was far from gay; as he watched Prince John kiss the little snow maiden, there was such a hungry look in Geoffrey's eyes that Isabel, seeing it, felt quite sorry for the boy. The serene, golden-haired Blanche, who was not a bit stirred by John's lovemaking, would, of course, appeal to the romantic heart of the peotry-loving page; she was, most certainly, a perfect "Lady Fair."

But although Blanche had merely submitted gracefully to John's caress and freed herself gently at the first possible moment, the sight of the young couple in each other's arms awoke something in Isabel's heart, too. Again, as she had often done in the past, she fought back a sudden dread of the lonely years to come by counting her blessings. The fact that she had recently heard shocking tales of the cruelty of both the Count of Flanders, whom she might have married, and of Joanna's betrothed, Pedro of Spain, to the women they had finally wed, made this quite easy. She was fortunate indeed, she told herself sternly and firmly, that she was unmarried and could remain so.

And when, a little later in the evening, Enguerrand de Coucy managed to catch her under the mistletoe, she repulsed him almost angrily. If anyone had asked her why, she would have said it was because he had played the fool with Lady Joan.

She pushed him away, her cheeks as red as her gown, and moved swiftly across the room to where some of the others were choosing partners for a romping country dance. Lionel, who was arranging the couples, stopped suddenly and held up his hand for silence.

"Just a moment," he said, beaming. "I think I hear a familiar voice in the corridor!"

In the bustle of greetings and embraces that followed, Isabel found herself wondering what could be wrong with Jack de Montfort. A merry, affectionate and demonstrative lad as a rule, he seemed unusually quiet and oddly withdrawn; his rather homely but likable square face was shadowed, his brown eyes somber, and instead of joining enthusiatically in the laughter and babble of talk he answered questions as briefly as he could, then with a haste that was almost rude, he excused himself and retired for the night.

Seeing that her sister was distressed and a little hurt, Isabel moved to Mary's side and whispered in her ear that she must not worry. Jack, she assured her, was undoubtedly unhappy over the failure to win back his duchy of Bretagne and was probably also extremely weary from his journey.

But although Jack was more himself the next day, he continued to pay so little attention to Princess Mary that Isabel was not surprised when, at the end of it, she found the girl in tears. She was reluctant to talk at first, then she confessed to Isabel that she had missed Jack terribly all summer and had been dreaming happy dreams of his return.

"I thought he would realize that I'm not a child any longer," she said, "and see that I love him. I'm as old as Blanche and you must have noticed how John kisses her and follows her around!"

"Well," replied Isabel reasonably, "You may be as old as Blanche, Mary, but you do look younger. Try to be patient—and don't forget that Jack may have been advised to wait until nearer you wedding day before showing his feelings."

While she talked she suddenly remembered making the same excuses to herself for Bernard's lack of ardor. The very thought was disheartening; was Mary to suffer from unrequited love, too? And John, who seemed strongly attracted to beautiful Blanche—would he discover before long that there was no fire under that layer of ice?

On Christmas night, when the wild and outrageous demands of Lord de Coucy, their Lord of Misrule, had everyone in gales of laughter except Jack, Isabel drew her uncle Lancaster off to one of the small retiring rooms and asked him outright what was wrong with the lad.

Looking vague, he made the same excuses that Isabel had made to Mary. Jack was travel-weary, he said, and unhappy over the failure of their campaign.

"Nonsense!" retorted Isabel, shaking her head at him. "Jack has always been as merry as a cricket! Besides, I've seen him unhorsed a dozen times in the tilt yard and still

laugh and try again. So do tell me, my lord, for his odd behavior is making our Mary miserable."

His Grace sighed and stroked his silvery beard, pulling it
into a point under his chin, something he always did when he
was disturbed. "I hesitate to reveal the reason for his distress
to you, my child," he admitted finally, "because it makes
Lady de Montfort seem cruel and unfeeling, which she is
not—she's a brave and gallant lady, as you know. But you
know too how mothers can be when they think their children
need protection—and, actually, she was completely wrong;
the Demoiselle de Ponteallen was deeply in love with Sir
Taneguy de Chatel and hadn't the slightest interest in young
Jack!"

Isabel, confused, tried to sort out his story. "I'm afraid I
don't understand, my lord," she said to her uncle. "Has Jack
fallen in love with his mother's lady-in-waiting? I've seen her
and she *is* most lovely."

"It was nothing but a boy's infatuation, Isabel. These
things happen. No, it was his mother's treatment of the girl
that had made him so unhappy. Instead of wedding her immediately to de Chatel—the handsomest and most gallant
knight in the Montfort household, by the way—Lady de
Montfort sent that charming lass into a nunnery! It was a
stupid and unnecessary thing to do. If she'd been reasonable
about the situation our Jack would have mooned around for
a while, sworn to kill de Chatel or himself, and been all over
it by now."

"Poor Jack!" said Isabel. "Poor Mary! No wonder he
avoids her. How can she hope for a happy union after this?"

"Now that, my dear Isabel, is exactly why I was so reluctant to tell you the boy's secret. You romantic ladies always
make too much of these early attachments; they are as much
a part of growing up as the adding of pounds and inches to
the body. Just tell yourself that Jack and Mary have the best
possible foundation for a good marriage; they have equality
of rank, the same interests, and they have always been the
best of friends and companions. When Jack forgets his
charming lady-in-waiting and when Mary is less of a child
and more of a woman, and looks at him, some moonlit night,
with love in those blue eyes of hers—why, who knows?" We
may even have to hurry up the wedding!"

Isabel laughed and admitted that His Grace might very well be right.

He drew her closer to his side, now, and smiled down into her face. "But what about you, my dear child? Isn't it time you called a halt to all this foolishness of yours and allowed us to find you a suitable husband?"

"No, no," she said. "I think not, my lord. I'm much better as I am."

By Twelfth-night the weather had turned so cold and snowy that Isabel decided to spend the rest of the winter at court. The Isle of Wight would offer little in the way of amusement at this time of year and when her visit at Hatfield drew to a close she was glad to ride back to Westminster with John, Blanche, Mary and their entourage, and to settle into her old apartments there.

The weeks passed swiftly. With Prince Edward at home, and with the King of France and his nobles established in the Savoy Palace, just a stone's throw from King Edward's own gardens, there was always sport of some kind during the day and feasting and entertainment at night. Isabel threw herself into it all wholeheartedly, and no lady, young or old, was gayer that winter that England's Lady Royal. Not even Joan of Kent, who seemed equally determined to enjoy every hour. But while Joan, as usual, found most of her pleasure in flirtation, Isabel continued to discourage anyone who wanted to cross the line between gallantry and serious lovemaking. She was willing to hunt, hawk, ride, dance, play games, sing, talk, and laugh with her handsome friends, but that was all. And when James de Bourbon hinted that an alliance between them might help to bring about the peace they were hoping for, she shook her head and told him to forget the thought; single she was, and single she would remain.

The weather continued cold until late March when it decided to go out like a lamb, and by St. George's Day, when the court moved to Windsor as usual to celebrate the occasion with a great tournament at which the Knights of the Garter challenged all comers, it was beautifully clear and sunny. Isabel, sitting with her parents on the canopied part of the scaffold erected for the spectators, decided she had rarely known a more perfect day for jousting.

The townspeople were still streaming into the meadows in the hope of finding room to sit or stand, and the horses, already caparisoned for the tournament, stamped, tossed their heads and whinnied in impatience. One, even fresher than the others, succeeded in jerking himself free from the groom holding his bridle and to the great delight of everyone on the scaffolds galloped madly around the field. His efforts to elude his pursuers were cheered to the echo; his inevitable capture some minutes later was loudly jeered by the shouting crowds. Even King Edward, who was suffering from a sprained wrist and could not take part in the events of the day, laughed and added his voice to the noise.

But at last everything seemed in order. The knights were mounted, the barrier in place, the king-at-arms was ready to announce the opening of the tournament, and the pages' brass trumpets, gleaming in the sun, were raised high.

They pealed out together, a joyous sound, and the king-at-arms stepped forward. Having heard his long, formal speech so many times that she could have made it herself, Isabel turned her attention to the helmeted knights, lined up behind him. Her brother Edward and King John of France were the first pair, Edward wearing his familiar black armor and King John mounted on the handsome white stallion on which he had first ridden into London. Behind them she recognized the slightly stooped shoulders of her Uncle Henry, the Duke of Lancaster, paired, she assumed, with James de Bourbon. Lionel was next, riding beside a knight who must be the Comte d'Artois, then Prince John of Gaunt, paired with the Lord de Coucy, the only other French knight who was to take part in the competition. After them came the rest of the contestants, some English, some from abroad, all arranged in the order of their rank.

They circled the field, bowing from right to left, then guided their horses over to the royal dais where they dismounted and made their obeisance to the King and Queen. That done, many of them stepped forward, their eyes on the lovely ladies facing them.

A ripple ran around the crowded, cushioned benches, and it was obvious that most of the ladies were fumbling in their laps for something. Isabel sat still; if anyone requested a favor to wear in his helmet from *her*, he would have to be satisfied with the small cluster of wood violets tucked in the front of her surcoat.

As was correct and proper, King John of France, taking precedence, bowed, smiled, and asked Queen Philippa if he might be her champion this day. Smiling back, the royal lady tossed him a bright blue bowknot which had been sewn very lightly to her sleeve. When he had caught it and fastened it to his helmet, a trio of other knights moved forward at once and Isabel, almost sure that they were all looking up at Joan of Kent, drew in her breath and glanced over at her parents. The Queen was frowning and so was the King; there was a split second in which Tom Holland and the Lord de Coucy hesitated and then the third knight, Prince Edward, pushed past them, called out to his "little Jeanette."

But before she could answer her cousin, the scene shifted so rapidly that Joan, afterwards, could not claim that she had actually been approached by three of the jousters; as she reached in her lap for the bit of veiling she had ready, Enguerrand de Coucy smiled over her bright head directly at the Lady Royal.

"A guerdon, oh damsel fair?" he shouted, in such a gay exaggeration of the formal language used on the fields of Chivalry that a little gust of laughter swept over the other ladies, and Isabel, annoyed at both his tone and her suspicion that she was his second choice, found it difficult to respond graciously. She could not refuse, of course, but, on impulse, she quickly divided her flowers before passing them down to him, returning the others to their place in her bosom.

The next suppliants were already standing below their ladies—Prince John beaming up at his Blanche, and Jack de Montfort was holding out his hand for Princess Mary's favor.

While the rest of the knights crowded forward and a shower of ribbons and blossoms filled the air, Isabel turned back to her parents who were still talking in low tones about Joan.

"Send her away!" she heard her mother say angrily. "Tom Holland is a good man—you can certainly use him to advantage in some position across the Channel. Make it appear to be an honor. He's earned some recognition for his bravery, after all. And tell him he must take his wife and family with him."

The King grumbled something, but although Isabel strained her ears she missed it.

"I don't care what she thinks or says! I will not have my son making such a fool of himself. Mother of God, it's disgraceful no matter how you look at it. Married, a family in the nursery, and still rolling her eyes at every gallant who glances her way—and you may as well face it, my lord, Ned will never wed anyone else as long as Joan is here, waggling those overgrown breasts and buttocks at him!"

In the exciting hours that followed, Isabel should have taken great satisfaction in the fact that the Lord de Coucy was proving himself the undisputed champion of the day. But while he unhorsed one knight after another, she found herself remembering the arrogant motto of his family: *Je ne suis roi, ne duc, prince, ne comte aussi. Je suis le Sire de Coucy!* And when he rode over, his head bare, to claim his prize, and Queen Philippa handed the laurel wreath to Isabel, she climbed down off the dais almost reluctantly, her dark brows drawn together in a faint frown.

However, the moment she faced him, and a hush fell over the laughing crowds around the field, she forced herself to smile and to make her accolade in a voice that was at least polite and gracious. To her surprise, she saw that he was answering her smile with one of his own that held, for once, no hint of sly amusement or mockery; there was something new and very warm in his eyes, something she had never seen in them before.

Suddenly confused, she blushed and, as she was stretching out her hand to place the victor's wreath on his head, she dropped it at his feet. Without thinking, she bent over; he did, too, and their hands touched. An odd little thrill ran through her and she discovered, to her horror, that her fingers were actually trembling.

She took the wreath from him, however, and settled it carefully on his handsome brow, avoiding his eyes as she did so.

"Thank you, Your Highness," he said, and then added, in a lower voice, "and now I claim my right!" And before she could move away, he reached forward and pulled the rest of the violets out of her bodice, touched them to his lips, and placed them, with the others, in the helmet under his arm.

Chapter 16

Noticing that the music was about to begin, the Prince of Wales walked swiftly over to where Lord and Lady Holland were standing and smiled at them both.

"May I steal Jeanette away from you, Tom, for this one dance?"

"Certainly, Your Grace." Tom Holland returned Prince Edward's smile as he replied, but his voice was strained and, after giving the stiffest of little bows, he moved away and left them together. Ned, feeling uneasy, watched him go, and when he turned to lead Joan onto the floor he saw that she also was looking disturbed and was staring after her husband with smoldering eyes.

"Is something wrong, Jeanette?" he asked, dropping his voice. "Did I disturb you two in the middle of a quarrel?"

Her color high, Joan shook her head. "Not a quarrel, although it would have been one very soon. A scolding, sir! My lord was annoyed, it seems, by the fact that he was not the only knight who wished to wear my favor at the tournament this afternoon."

Edward gave a small, guilty whistle. "And then I, the worst offender, chose that moment to rush over and ask you to dance! I'm sorry, Jeanette, but I never thought. Shall I take you back to him?" He glanced around. "But I don't see him anywhere."

"Nonsense! Don't be ridiculous, Ned. Tom must learn to control his stupid jealousy, as I've told him over and over. I'm his wife—what more can he want? And plain Lady Holland, when I might have been the Countess of Salisbury! If I'm not even allowed to enjoy myself, I shall certainly begin to wish that the Pope had made a different decision."

The music started then and they said nothing more, but Joan's face was still stormy and flushed when the dance ended and the Prince knew that her anger had not yet subsided.

He glanced around the room again, trying to see her husband in the crowd.

"Apparently Tom hasn't returned yet," he said. "You look hot, Jeanette. Shall we stroll out into the corridor?"

"Thank you, no," she replied, with a small, bitter laugh. "When Tom has gone off somewhere in a huff, and Her Grace is glaring at us from the dais? I think not, Cousin. No," she went on, furiously, "I'd rather give them something else to talk about." And she beckoned to Enguerrand de Coucy, who had been dancing with the Princess Isabel and had just taken her back to her seat beside the Queen.

"I'm a little faint from the heat," she said when he joined them. "We can't find my husband and His Grace is needed elsewhere. Will you see me safely out of this hot room, my lord?"

"I shall consider it a privilege, my lady," he answered, bowing and taking her on his arm. As they moved toward the doorway, however, he looked back over his shoulder, almost as if he were reluctant to leave the Hall, and when they reached the corridor outside, he led her to the nearest embrasure and settled her immediately on the deep seat.

"There," he said, smiling politely down on her. "It is much cooler here. May I find one of your women for you, or has the faintness passed?"

"Oh come, Enguerrand!" Joan gave him a glance that was half invitation and half impatience. "You know better than that!" She rose and placed her hand back on his arm. "Take me farther away from all these people."

He hesitated, then matched his step to hers.

"I was sorry that I could not give you my favor today," she said, as they left the other strolling couples behind, "but His Highness, as you saw, reached me first. It was clever of you, I thought, to move so swiftly to the Princess Isabel. She may not realize that she was not your first choice."

Enguerrand opened his mouth to protest. But how can you tell a lady that she is mistaken about such a thing? And perhaps it had looked as if he were approaching her first. He had, he remembered now, moved forward with the Prince and Tom Holland. He hoped that Princess Isabel wasn't under the same misapprehension. No, she wouldn't have been so sweet to him when they were dancing, a few minutes ago.

She had never been as friendly before, and she had never been more beautiful, either. . . .

"The Lady Royal, of course," said Joan loudly, "has made it quite well known here at court that she has little interest in gallantry of any kind. And most of our young noblemen are perfectly content to have it that way. I cannot say I blame them!"

Lord de Coucy's attention was all hers now. He stared at her in astonishment.

"I don't believe I understand," he said. "Why are they content to have it that way?"

"Because they fear that she might treat them as she treated poor Bernard d'Albret. But you know that story, of course. Everyone does."

"I know there was a broken betrothal," he replied stiffly, "but that's all. I'm afraid I don't enjoy gossip very much, my lady. Perhaps we should. . . ."

"This is not gossip," Joan said, her color mounting. "After wheedling the King into letting her wed the lad, who was madly in love with her, our Isabel decided at the last moment that she would rather not marry so much beneath her. And Bernard, with nothing to live for, gave up his inheritance and became a monk. He died, I hear, not long ago; of a broken heart, according to a friend of his mother's—the Lady d'Albret should know, if anyone does."

Lord de Coucy was silent for a moment. "Her Highness must have been very young at the time," he said.

"Eighteen, at least. I don't remember exactly. Not what I would call very young."

"No. Well, it's not a pleasant story, and I suppose I should thank you for putting me on my guard. Although I do not think there is much danger of my dying of a broken heart! Do you? And will you tell me, my lady, why we are wasting all these precious minutes when we might be making the most of this dark corner?"

A throaty chuckle was his only answer and when they returned to the Great Hall some time later, Prince Edward was relieved to see that the Lady Joan was her usual gay self.

Isabel was having a pleasant evening too, and although her thoughts were very much with Enguerrand and had been ever since earlier that day on the tilting field, she somehow missed seeing him leave and return to the Hall in Joan's company. She had enjoyed their dance together, and she was surprised and even a little hurt that he did not ask her again.

She was still puzzling over this when she retired for the night, but after a few minutes she stopped wondering why he hadn't returned to her and began to question herself about her own interest in this charming young Frenchman. Never, before tonight, had she lain awake in the dark and thought of any man in this way except Bernard. Never since those days with Bernard had a man's touch set her pulses racing. But how, she asked herself, was this possible when Enguerrand was so unlike Bernard? No two men, certainly, could be more different. How, after loving that gentle lad, could she be drawn to a gallant who was probably as skilled in the Courts of Love as he had shown himself to be in the tilt yard? How, after adoring someone who looked and behaved like a young saint, could she turn on her pillows now and yearn for my Lord de Coucy, whose dark handsomeness resembled a picture she had once seen of Satan?

She settled back, shut her eyes, and willed herself to think of Bernard only, to recapture the joy of their hours alone, to grieve, to wish that he were here, in her arms. To suffer, again, and to drive away these new, tantalizing thoughts. Bernard. . . .

But it was no use. She could not do it. Bernard was a dream, long lost in the past; the dream of a very young and romantic girl. A woman wants a man, she admitted, not a boy. And she, Isabel, was a woman.

Was that the answer? Was this unusual interest in Enguerrand proof that she should change her way of life, that she should ask her father to find her a suitable husband? Not my Lord de Coucy, certainly. That, she reminded herself, would be madness! To ask the King again for permission to wed beneath her was unthinkable. She had had her way once; it could never happen a second time.

No, even if she loved Enguerrand—which, of course, she did not—they could never marry. And she would be a fool to consider an alliance with some foreign prince when it was not required of her. She sighed, and turned again on her pillows. It was hot and stifling in the vast, curtained bed; would sleep never come?

As she tossed, she remembered the soft breezes at Carisbrooke Castle and wished herself there, free from her dis-

turbing thoughts. Why not go there and be peaceful again?
She yawned, and smiled in the dark. That was it: Of course!
She would go home. . . .

Isabel looked regretfully back over the blue Solent at the
green, curving hills that encircled Carisbrooke Castle and
wished her mysterious grandmother, for whom she was
named, had chosen some other season in which to die. It
seemed too bad to leave the Isle of Wight in such lovely October weather and travel to Westminster swaddled in those
heavy sable garments and annoying long veils.

But then, she told herself, her father's French-born mother
had always made difficulties and problems. She knew very little about the Queen Mother's history, for as a child Isabel
had been hushed and sent away every time she asked about
it; and no one since that time had been willing to tell her
anything but the barest outline. She had heard that Queen Isabel, with the help of Roger Mortimer, the Earl of March,
had forced her husband the King to abdicate in favor of her
son; and she had heard too, that the Queen and Mortimer
had then ruled England as Edward III's regents until after
Edward II's death at Berkeley Castle.

But just why the nobles of England had then risen against
Mortimer, accused him of treason, and hanged him at
Tyburn Hill without a fair trial, she was not sure. She tried
to remember whether her grandmother had, in past years,
ever appeared at court, but although she had a dim recollec-
tion of seeing her, long, long ago, very briefly at Windsor
Castle, it was all so vague that it might not really have happened.

What Isabel did know was that the elderly lady had lived
for many years in complete seclusion at Castle Rising in Norfolk, where the King, who never allowed anyone to speak of
her with disrespect, visited her from time to time. He never
took his wife or children with him on these journeys, nor was
there the fanfare and panoply that usually marked all royal
travel; accompanied by a few gentlemen and a small escort,
he would ride swiftly to his destination, then disappear into
the old Norman fortress, sending his suite off to Royal King's
Lynn, a few miles away, to await him. He was always a little
sad when he returned to his home and family, and they soon
learned not to ask him any questions.

But the Queen Mother alive and the Queen Mother dead were, apparently, two different matters; there was to be nothing quiet or surreptitious about the way she was to be laid to rest. Her choice of a burial place was, however, causing a great deal of comment. No Queen had ever been known to select such a place as the Church of the Grey Friars within Newgate.

When the Princess Royal and her suite arrived at Westminster after what had been, as it turned out, a very pleasant journey up from Southampton, it was to find that she might, had she wished, have remained some weeks longer in her own castle. There had been many delays in bringing the dead Queen down from Norfolk and the funeral would not take place until some time in November. The city was busy already, however, for King Edward had given orders that the streets over which the grim cortege would proceed must be cleansed of all dirt and impurities and that Bishopsgate Street and Aldgate he graveled against, as he put it, "the coming of the body of his dearest mother, Queen Isabel."

As the court was in mourning, Isabel spent the intervening time quietly with her mother, father, younger brothers and sisters and the other members of the royal household. She discovered that the King had obeyed the Queen's wish and sent Sir Thomas Holland with his wife and children off to Normandy, where he was now the Governor and Keeper of the Castle at St. Saveur. The Prince of Wales, since their departure, had been at court very little, seeming to prefer his house on Candlewick Street, the Manor of the Rose.

She learned, too, that although the King of France and his nobles were still living at the Palace of the Savoy, there would be, during these weeks before the funeral, no exchange of visits. This made her both glad and sorry; she had not seen Lord de Coucy since the festivities at Windsor in April and she was torn between the desire to encounter him again and the knowledge that it would be much better if she did not. She realized, of course, that she would eventually meet him again, for the Queen Mother had been a Princess of France, the daughter of King Philip le Bel and a cousin of King John's father, Philip IV; this meant that the French king and the other French prisoners were in deep mourning for their kinswoman, also, and would be given places of honor in the funeral procession.

It was the twentieth day of November when the cortege finally wended its way to the little church in Newgate, a day so cold that the mourners had a difficult time holding their mounts down to the slow pace required of them. Isabel, riding behind her mother and father and King John, and beside her brother, the Prince of Wales, told Ned that she was in sympathy with the restless horses in the long, sable-draped line.

"I feel rather like pawing the ground and snorting myself," she said softly, tightening the reins in her gauntleted hands. "I've been actually longing for a good gallop or a day's hawking."

"Why not bring Mary and one of the other ladies to dine with me tomorrow?" he suggested. "I'll ask Jack de Montfort and a few other friends and we'll have some sport in the afternoon. There's no reason why we shouldn't ride out for a bit of hawking once this gloomy business is over."

Isabel looked ahead at her mother and the two kings and agreed that if Her Grace had no objection she would be delighted to join his party. "By the way," she said, "how much longer will King John be here in England? Is France really so poverty-stricken that they can't ransom their ruler?"

Edward shrugged. "I wonder sometimes," he confessed, "whether the Dauphin wants him back. But I do know that the country is in all kinds of trouble right now; there are bands of professional soldiers, some French and some English, who call themselves Free Companies, going around looting and pillaging, and, to make matters worse, groups of peasants are doing even more ghastly things, burning châteaux, raping noblewomen, torturing and killing their lords and masters! They call themselves 'the Jacquerie.' "

"Do you mean to tell me," asked Isabel incredulously, "that King John and the other French nobles are content to remain over here in peace and comfort while such outrages are happening in France?"

"Of course they are not! King John has no alternative, of course. But those who refused to be ransomed because they preferred to stay with their King are making arrangements to return almost immediately. And as the truce ends in the spring, no one knows just what will happen. We may have to invade France again to make them give us our rights there, and this would mean another long campaign for me. So why not spend your winter at Westminster, Bel? It's been distinctly dull without you and little Jeannette."

She was about to tell him that he was himself largely responsible for Joan's absence when a signal brought the procession to a halt. The Grey Friar's Church was just ahead, the cortege bringing the Queen's body from the North was approaching and was about to turn the corner of Aldgate. They heard the dirges; then with bowed heads everyone waited until the elaborately draped bier was carried inside the church; the mourners from both processions dismounted, entered, and the somber services began.

Princess Mary was delighted to accept the Prince's invitation, Queen Philippa saw no reason why her daughters should not spend a few quiet hours in their brother's company and Lady de Montfort, who was still extremely active and a superb horsewoman, suggested that she be the one to accompany them to the Manor of the Rose.

When, however, they arrived at the handsome house situated beyond Chelsea on the bank of the Thames, they were told that dinner was not nearly ready for them. The other guests (and Isabel was a little startled to see that Enguerrand de Coucy was one of them) were already there, having a glass of wine with the young host. Edward, after drawing the ladies into the comfortable circle around the fire, apologized for his tardy staff.

"Some trouble in the kitchens," he said, laughing ruefully. "A chimney caught fire or some such thing. A bachelor is at a disadvantage in these matters, you know. I must just believe what they tell me!"

"We might take advantage of the noonday sun," said Jack de Montfort, smiling down on Princess Mary, "and see those famous swans of yours, Ned."

"Has he been boasting about his birds again?" asked the young princess. "What fresh tricks have they learned this season?"

"None," was the answer. "But the new cygnets copy the older swans now and ring the bell for bread. We have some rousing fights, I can tell you. They're strong you know; they'll break your arm if you aren't careful."

He beckoned to a page, dispatched him for several loaves of stale bread, then asked whether everyone wanted to stroll with him down to the riverside. Lady de Montfort, thinking this an excellent opportunity to send her son off with his young betrothed, replied that she would remain by the fire. "I've seen your swans before," she said, "and I will have enough exercise this afternoon when we go hawking."

Even in November, with the trees bare and the flower beds brown, it was pleasant to walk through the gardens of Prince Edward's home. There was a maze, into which no one ventured today, and a pretty water garden which had been made by cutting a channel in from the bank of the river. Here the Prince had hung a bell from an overhanging branch, and his swans, swimming in and out of the Thames, soon discovered that if they tugged at the bellcord dangling just above their heads, someone would usually run down from the kitchens nearby and throw them scraps of bread.

They had been rather neglected lately and as a result were very hungry. They performed nobly, delighting everyone by ringing the bell loudly, snatching hurriedly at the crusts of bread tossed them and hissing furiously at each other as the stronger and greedier gobbled down the lion's share of the food.

Princess Mary was the first to tire of the sport, and Jack, seeing her shiver, announced that he, too, was ready to return to the house. Most of the others agreed that it was growing chilly, but Enguerrand de Coucy protested.

"I must see that that small cygnet has a meal first," he insisted. "The poor little runt has lost every battle. Stay and help me, Your Grace," and before Isabel could answer, he had thrust a loaf into her hands, and was pointing to a scrawny cygnet, still feathered in brown.

The others were already strolling away, and Lord de Coucy was watching her with an odd, quizzical look, very different from the one he had given her when he was putting the wreath on his head at Windsor. She felt quite at ease with him, shrugged slightly and set about the task he had given her.

It was not easy. No matter how they tried, the larger swans continued to outwit them, and it was not until Isabel had lured them off to one side that Enguerrand was able to surround their tiny friend with a circle of crusts, most of which she gulped down before the others reached her again.

It was much warmer now, for the breeze which had driven the rest of the party away had died down; they chatted idly for a minute or two while they threw what was left of the bread into the water. When Isabel made a casual reference to her grandmother's funeral, he answered it with a remark that startled her.

"Your father's tolerance," he said, "surprised us very much. Not many Englishmen would forgive their mothers as he did, and then allow her to lie in the same church with the body of her lover. And, at the same time, to have her husband's heart in her coffin! Even in France we would consider that a most unusual arrangement."

"Her lover?" Isabel stared at him. "Are you telling me, my lord, that the Earl of March was the Queen's lover?"

Now de Coucy stared. "But of course. Everyone knows that. It was no secret, certainly. They were lovers from the time she took your father to France, while Edward II was still King of England, until the day Mortimer was hanged."

"I think you must be mistaken," Isabel said slowly. "If they were lovers they would have wed, surely, when my grandfather died."

"Not when so many of her people thought them responsible for his death—and, if what I have heard is true, a brutal, horrible death it must have been!" He shuddered. "They stopped calling her Isabel the Fair after that, both here and in France. Isabel the Wolf was her new name."

Completely shocked, Isabel said nothing. Her grandmother had been born a French princess, after all; de Coucy would have no reason to blacken her name, invent wild stories about her. And there had certainly always been a mystery about the Queen Mother and her past history.

"Don't blame Her Majesty too much," he continued. "It must have been most difficult for a woman with such a passionate nature to be tied to a man who cared little for her or, for that matter, any other lady."

"They had children," Isabel retorted. "He cannot have despised women altogether!"

"My best bitch has pups, fathered by the dog I choose for her. The business is arranged for them and quickly accomplished, but that is not what a hot-blooded Frenchwoman craves, believe me!"

And without a word of warning he reached out and drew her into his arms, bending his lips to hers. Isabel struggled for a moment, but he held her tighter. Then his kisses grew more and more demanding, and he began to caress her with skillful fingers.

Her body, new to the raptures of lovemaking, turned into a flame and her lips opened under his. She was so oblivious to everything else that it was a physical shock when he pulled himself away and laughed.

"That," he said, "will perhaps show you what I mean. But the sun is very high, my lady, and kissing always makes me hungry. Let us join the others and continue the lesson another time."

A slap in the face would not have been so insulting. Isabel, her face scarlet, stood as if rooted to the ground, while he smiled at her mockingly. With a sob that was half fury, half shame, the Princess turned away and gathered up the tail of her gown in a trembling hand. She fled, then, up the walk and through the garden, not glancing back to see if he was following her.

Chapter 17

As the royal barges moved slowly along the Thames toward the Tower of London, the crowds on the riverbanks thickened. Isabel, sitting as usual with her parents in one of the gilded, brightly canopied vessels, looked ahead at the one in front which, today, had been turned into a bower of roses for Prince John of Gaunt and his bride.

Blanche, she told herself, was truly a storybook princess, and it was no wonder that the people of London had flocked to the water's edge to cheer themselves hoarse at the sight of her and their tall Plantagenet prince. Clad, on this third day after her wedding, in a shimmering surcoat and kirtle of the same pale gold as the hair that hung down to her waist, and with a faint smile on her delicately chiseled face, John's little wife looked more like a carved and gilded saint in a niche than a flesh-and-blood woman. Or—Isabel, smiling a little guiltily, resolved not to repeat this comparison to anyone—a marble effigy on a tomb.

Just so had Blanche of Lancaster appeared on her wedding day, just so had she smiled while she watched her husband jousting in her honor at the tournaments held at Reading to celebrate their nuptials; just so, without a doubt, had she welcomed John when he turned to her in the privacy of their marriage bed.

Isabel flushed and tried to think of something else. Blanche's response to John's lovemaking was none of her business and these days the thought of love reminded her much too vividly of those shaming moments at the Manor of the Rose when she had played the wanton and Enguerrand de Coucy, for some reason completely beyond her comprehension, had treated her like one. Her only comfort was that she need never encounter him again and need never see that mocking look in his eyes that had shown how he was enjoying her discomfiture; the people of Coucy, to whom she

191

would be everlastingly grateful, had raised his ransom at
last and he was, she had heard, now back home doing everything in his power to wipe out the terrible Jacquerie.

The barges, nearing old London Bridge and the treacherous currents that swirled under its high arches, crept along
slowly. The bridge, like the riverbanks, was a mass of roaring
spectators, hanging out of the windows of the hundred or
more shops and houses that were crammed together in a long
line from end to end of the twenty-foot-wide span, all waving
and calling out to the royal family on the barges that passed
beneath them.

A royal chariot and a long line of saddled horses awaited
them when they disembarked at the Tower wharf, and without entering the huge, rambling fortress, they turned back
toward Westminster, the ladies riding in the jolting old
eight-wheeled vehicle and the men on horseback. They were
covering the same distance twice as a part of Prince John's
wedding celebration; in this way at least double the number of
townspeople could view the gay procession.

Queen Philippa, Isabel, Blanche and Mary perched on the
narrow cushioned benches inside the coach, the Queen and
Blanche waving out the windows on one side, and Isabel and
her sister Mary out the others. John and the King rode
ahead, leading the way; the Prince of Wales and Blanche's
father, the Duke of Lancaster, followed right behind them;
and the other two princes, Lionel and Edmund, brought up
the rear.

As the whole family had risen at dawn and had been on
the river since the hour of Prime, everyone was so tired and
stiff that they said little to each other. Their smiles, as they
jolted over the cobbles, became a painful effort. Wave, smile,
wave, smile, wave.

The chariot gave another lurch. Isabel, keeping her seat
with difficulty, felt her head throb and saw that her mother,
clinging to the sill on the other side, was fighting back an attack of nausea. Mary, who looked green too, was muttering
that she'd never ride in the horrible thing again, but Blanche,
showing no signs of discomfort, sat serenely at her window
and obeyed the instructions the Queen had given her before
they left the Tower—smile, wave, smile, wave.

The sound of trumpets and loud shouting finally broke the

deadly pattern and Edward, riding up closer to the open tail of the chariot, called to them that it was a messenger sent out by the Lord Mayor and the sheriffs and aldermen of London. He was announcing, Edward said, a great three-day tournament to be held in honor of the young bride and groom.

The trumpeter's voice drifted back and the ladies heard him say "His Lordship and their Honors will challenge all knights from home or across the water. Come one, come all!"

The tournament turned out to be unusually exciting, and to everyone's surprise the band of twenty-four knights who were wearing the heraldic arms of the City of London carried away the honors, defeating all the English noblemen who had responded to the challenge and even such skilled and gallant warriors as the Captal de Buch, his cousin Gaston de Foix, Denis de Morbec of Artois, and James de Bourbon—all, except the Captal, still waiting to be ransomed. But much as the spectators and the combatants themselves enjoyed the three days of well-matched jousting, there was one thing that disappointed everyone. The Queen and the princesses and Lady Blanche sat, day after day, on the stands, but the King and his royal sons never appeared; and although it was generally known that they were occupied at this particular time in preparing for another invasion of France, the feeling was that they might have spared three days for the Lord Mayor's celebration. John certainly should have been there; the bridegroom's absence was almost an insult. And the vanquished noblemen and foreign knights agreed among themselves that the Mayor's men would not have won so easily had they been tilting with England's five tall, golden-headed Plantagenets.

Despite this disappointment, the crowds cheered lustily when the victors, who had kept their visors closed throughout, lined up in front of the royal dais to claim their prizes.

The Queen, after thanking them on behalf of her son and his new wife, leaned forward and raised her voice until it could be heard the length and breadth of the field.

"Remove your helmets, if you please! We are all eager to see the faces of such skillful warriors!"

As one man the band of knights obeyed her, and a wild roar swept over the scaffolds. Hats were thrown in the air,

feet stamped on the boards under them, the women waved
scarves, ribbons, kerchiefs, anything that came to hand.
There in the center of the group, wearing the arms of the
City of London, stood five tall knights, their corn-colored
hair gleaming in the June sunshine—King Edward of England and his four royal sons, Edward, Lionel, John and
Edmund.

Nothing could have endeared the King more to his people
than this, and at the banquet he gave that night for the Lord
Mayor and everyone who had taken part in the tournament,
his guests continued to laugh over the way he had deceived
them.

The Captal de Buch, Isabel's partner again, confessed that
he was much happier when he saw who it was that had de-
feated him so ignominiously. "My cousin Gaston and I," he
told her, "would have returned home with very low heads
had it been otherwise."

"But do you plan to leave us soon?" Isabel asked.

"The moment Gaston's ransom arrives, and I hear it is on
its way. We are both eager to offer our swords to the valiant
noblemen who are struggling to subdue the Jacquerie."

Isabel looked puzzled. "But I thought that the Jacquerie
was threatening the country north of Paris—Soissons, Coucy,
Noyon? That's King John's land, surely, and no concern of
yours. You fight under England's banner, my lord."

"I do," answered the Captal, his long-nosed face grim, "but
this is a different matter altogether. I cannot sit back and see
these peasants commit such atrocities on our neighbors, enemies or not. And it might spread, you know. Our own wives
and children could be raped and killed."

He did not think, of course, of the reason the French peasants had risen against the nobles: the land laid waste by the
roving companies, the unpaid soldiery, the impossible heavy
taxes levied on them to pay for the long years of warfare and
the ransoms of their masters. Nor did Isabel think of these
things when he began to relate the horrors they were com-
mitting.

She did, however, ask if some of the stories might not be
exaggerated. Tales so often grew in the telling. . . .

"Whatever you have heard," he replied, "is probably far
short of the truth. The more horrible the deed, the greater

the applause for the Jack who is responsible. When I tell you
that they tied one lord to a stake, after taking his castle,
raped his wife and daughter in front of his eyes and then
killed them, all while he was watching, you will know what I
mean. Oh, they murdered him, too, before they were done,
and burned the château to the ground."

Isabel stared at him.

"Mother of God!" she said finally. "What a tale!"

"I could tell you another," de Buch replied, "but you will
not want the rest of your supper."

"Go on, my lord. I think I should hear the truth about all
this."

"At another château, Your Grace, they first murdered the
owner, then spitted his body and roasted it; and this time it
was the lady and the children who had to watch. Then a
dozen Jacks violated the poor wife, forced her to eat some of
her husband's flesh when it was cooked, and ended the
outrage by knocking her brains out on the stone floor."

A wave of nausea swept over her; she reached for her
wineglass and took a hasty sip.

"You are right to fight the monsters," she said. "If I were
a man I would go with you. Have you ..." she hesitated,
flushed, then decided to ask the question. "Have you heard
any word of Lord de Coucy? His château is in the thick of
these attacks, is it not?"

"It is, and I believe he's fighting day and night to wipe out
the scourge. So far as I know, he and his home are still safe.
So far as I know."

When de Foix was ransomed, soon after this, he and the
Captal sailed to La Teste, rounded up sixty skilled lancers,
and marched north. The truce with France was worn thin
and drawing to a close but it still protected them as they
crossed over what was enemy territory for de Buch. Their
reason for coming there would in any case have accorded
them a warm welcome; for the Jacks, they learned, were
growing more rapacious every day, and the Duke and Duchess
of Orléans had fled to Meaux, hoping to escape, taking with
them three hundred frightened ladies and children. But the
Jacquerie, adding to their mobs as they swept around the
country, now numbered seven or eight thousand, and it was
doubtful that Meaux, despite its high walls and ancient forti-

fied castle, could withstand an attack by so many desperate men.

As this seemed to be the spot where their assistance was needed most, the two knights rode swiftly in that direction, reaching the city just in time. Only a few hours before their arrival, a scout had reported to the Duke, King John's brother, that the Jacks, having heard that Meaux was crowded with ladies for raping and much loot for the taking, to say nothing of a royal duke to be caught, tortured, and killed, were marching toward the city, gathering strength from every village and town through which they passed.

"They will undoubtedly reach here by morning," the scout had said. "At least nine thousand of them: badly armed, and without the slightest kind of discipline, but a pack of wild wolves can be more vicious than a trained army."

As a result of this terrifying news, the sight of de Buch and his cousin and their sixty lancers brought a loud cheer from the men guarding the ramparts of Meaux. And when they rode into the castle courtyard, their weapons shining and their gay pennons fluttering in the breeze, the King's brother was standing there himself, waiting to embrace them.

The ladies streamed out to greet them, too, weeping with joy. The Duchess, drawing the Captal aside for a private word or two, whispered in his ear that if they were to be saved he must make some kind of plan for their defense.

"His Grace," she told him, "thinks that all we need to do is lock the city gates and barricade the castle. And having heard what had happened to other nobles recently, I am truly frightened. Anyone," she went on, her voice trembling, "can die with dignity—but to see one's husband mutilated, tortured, burned alive—and to watch your daughters being ravished. . . ."

The men were deep in consultation and had already weighed and discarded several plans for defending the city. A plan of Meaux, drawn roughly on a large sheet of parchment, lay before them on a long trestle table. Arrows and crosses were inked in here and there, and a lot of little blocks of wood, cut to represent barricades, were scattered on the map, the table, and the floor.

Raising his head suddenly, the Captal held up his hand for silence.

"What was that?" he asked, jumping to his feet. "I'm sure I heard a trumpet!"

"Not the Jacks," was the Duke's swift reply. "They shout and yell. You can hear them for miles. It's a sound you never forget!"

A scratch on the door, a few minutes later, answered their question. A lackey, given permission to enter, announced the arrival of Lord de Coucy.

"The very man we need, by God!" swore Orléans, his face lighting up. He was small, almost dainty, and had little courage in such a situation. "He's been dealing with the vermin in his own territory and knows all their tricks."

De Coucy was not the gay graceful gallant who had charmed the ladies at King Edward's court and caught the Princess Royal herself off guard. Gone were the laughing glance and the mocking smile; in their place were a pair of grimly set lips, and two cold eyes intent on the pressing business at hand.

"Well, my lords," he said to Foix and de Buch, after the Duke had made him welcome, "I am equally happy to find you two here! We've swept most of my part of the country clean at last, and left it under a strong guard, but we were never faced with a pack as large as the one that is on its way here today. We shall need every man we can find, trained and untrained, and we must not waste a moment in readying the defenses."

"Are you alone, de Coucy?"

He shook his head. "I have a hundred of my finest men-at-arms with me. All I could spare, I'm afraid, after manning my own castles."

Orléans clapped him on the back and led him to the table.

"You put new heart in us," he said. "De Buch and de Foix here marched in a few hours ago bringing sixty lancers. With them and with your good men, I have some hope, for the first time, that we may win the day. Sit down, my lord, and give us the benefit of everything you have learned in these last ghastly months. Here is the plan of the city; we thought that if we set up barricades at these points. . . ."

Once they had agreed on what must be done to defend the city and had given their orders, there was little left to do but wait for the Jacquerie to reach the city gates. Scouts slipped out and returned with word of their progress, and the three young noblemen, after snatching a few hours' sleep, took turns watching with the sentries high up on the castle ramparts.

Dawn broke, the sky lightened, and it was possible now to see a dark mass moving along the road below.

"It will be an hour, at least," surmised de Buch, standing beside Enguerrand de Coucy.

"It will. And in less than half that time we must climb down from here and join our men. In the meantime," and de Coucy turned to sit on a crenellation in the stone battlement, "tell me what you can of my Liege. Was he at Westminster when you were last there and what are the chances of his returning home? I've heard nothing since I left England."

The Capital, after assuring him that John was in fairly good health, first described the tournament in London and its dramatic denouement, then admitted that there seemed little prospect of John's release. And, as it was no secret from the French, he added that King Edward was planning another invasion of France.

"You and I will be enemies again," he said, smiling ruefully at de Coucy. "Tomorrow—or is it today?—we fight side by side. After that, who knows?"

De Coucy looked off into space and shrugged his shoulders. "Who knows, indeed. But it will be a sorry moment for me if I meet you face to face, de Buch. In a tilt yard, yes. But not, please God, in battle!"

"Amen." Silence fell for a minute or two, then the Capital spoke again.

"The Princess Isabel asked me for news of you," he said, "but I had little or nothing to tell her. I had been spoiling her supper with tales of the Jacks."

"Oh?" A cold gleam came into de Coucy's face for a second. Then he laughed. "So Her High and Mightiness deigned to mention my name? And not in anger? I must confess, for your ears alone, de Buch, that I rather enjoyed myself at the great lady's expense just before leaving England."

De Buch, bristling, stared at his companion.

"I've always found the Lady Royal charming, delightful in every way," he replied coldly. "But I am not, of course, *de Coucy!* I know your family motto—I am neither king, duke, prince nor count. *I* am the Lord de Coucy—and I suppose you feel that even she should bend the knee to you. It is an attitude I find hard to understand, however."

"No, no, no," de Coucy interposed hastily. "Don't misunderstand me, my lord! My resentment against the lady and my determination to humble her stem entirely from her brutal jilting of young Bernard d'Albret, who became a monk, for love of her, and died of a broken heart. I was told the story only recently—quite a while after I arrived in England, as a matter of fact. And I may tell you that I heard it just in time! I was on the verge of falling in love with the girl myself."

"You heard the wrong story," said de Buch shortly. "She allowed that tale to be spread abroad so that Bernard, who had a strong vocation, could do what he wished. His brother Arnaud himself told me that Bernard had taken a vow of chastity, and that Princess Isabel was the one with the broken heart. Lady d'Albret brought about the whole miserable business and the two young people suffered equally." He paused, saw that Enguerrand was distressed, and added, "I think you should know, de Coucy, that, according to Arnaud, his brother died blessing the Princess for freeing him from their contract."

Enguerrand raised his eyebrows. "If that is true," he said, "I played an extremely ugly part. I regret it deeply and if I see the lady again I shall try to make my peace with her."

Hearing footsteps, he rose. "And I suspect that Her Grace will not make it very easy for me! Well, she should not. I deserve whatever punishment she heaps on my damned impulsive head. But here comes Gaston. We must go to our stations."

The noise of the approaching Jacquerie began to reach the castle. At first it sounded like thunder. When the ladies were able to distinguish some of the jeers, howls and screaming insults pouring out of nine thousand throats, many of them succumbed to panic and locked themselves and their children in the remotest part of the tallest tower.

Below, in the town itself, there was as yet no sign of fear or disorder. Most of the townspeople had already fled to safety and those who remained were gathered together in a quiet group with orders to keep as far away as possible from the area where the fighting would take place.

There was a great hammering on the gates. The shouting rose louder than before. Inside the castle the ladies clutched one another and trembled, while the more valiant peered down from the narrow slits in the turret to see what was happening.

"They've broken down the gates," one lady reported. "The filthy rabble are surging in. It's as if a wave of black beetles was filling the streets! They approach the market place and the barricades. . . . Ah! here come our knights to meet them! And a brave sight they make with their banners and pennants and their armor glinting in the sun! Stand fast, sirs, stand fast—for the love of God, stand fast!"

The Duchess pushed her aside and leaned far out of the window opening. "They are standing fast," she said. "I can see the Captal lining up his men-at-arms and the Count de Foix close behind him with his soldiers. They've formed a solid phalanx. They're moving up to the barricades . . . now they've halted! Oh, Mother of God, the Jacks are tearing up the barricades, they're charging at our men with those crude staves. Hear them howl! Wolves, they sound like a pack of wolves!"

The scene below the castle was all confusion and even the bravest of the ladies began to panic. How could their knights survive the onslaught of those screeching madmen? How could those small bands of trained men stand fast in the face of the seething mass that crammed the streets from city gates to where the barricades had stood? It was moving relentlessly forward, some of their own will, some shoved ahead by the shouting mob behind them.

If it was frightening to watch, it was even worse to hear—the crash and clang as the Jacks' metal-tipped staves met the soldiers' lances and broadswords; the loud snorting of the knights' horses, caught in the heart of the frantic melee; and the exultant screams as the Jacquerie leaders urged their followers on, on, on. . . .

Then suddenly another sound reached the ladies: the clear war cry of de Buch, answered immediately by Enguerrand de Coucy, marching in with his men from another part of town. Hearing it, the ladies cheered and hugged and kissed the children, and everyone, the worst of their fears forgotten, crowded to the windows.

Louder and more horrible screams could be heard now—

but these were the screams of the Jacks. Trapped in the narrow streets by their own unruly pack, unable to retreat and with no room to form any kind of orderly battle line, they were being slaughtered like cattle.

One thousand, two thousand, three—five—seven. . . .

The bodies were tossed into the Marne, flowing serenely around the castle. It ran red over the heaps of the dead and dying, and the knights, their arms weary, paused at last.

"Form a guard around the survivors," shouted de Coucy. "March them to those wooden out buildings and lock them in! Come, de Buch, we must bring out the ladies and children!"

The few townspeople still in Meaux left by one gate, the Duke of Orléans and his friends by another. There was no one in the city now but the last of the Jacquerie, unaware of the punishment planned for them.

De Buch, as he rode away, looked back over his shoulder and saw what he had been expecting to see—a jet of flame shooting up in the darkening sky and a cloud of black smoke rising over the city walls. And again, even more hideous than before, the screaming began.

Chapter 18

Once the festivities for Prince John's marriage were over, the King concentrated completely on the preparations for invading France. Realizing that they would find very little in way of comfort or even sustenance in the impoverished country, he and his Council arranged to take with them most of what everyone would need, and this, for an army of upwards of a hundred thousand men, was no small undertaking. The mere necessities of life would not, of course, suffice for the King and his sons and their nobles; they must have with them all the luxuries to which they were accustomed as well as their hawks, greyhounds, and hunting dogs; mills for grinding corn, ovens in which to bake bread, and forges to repair weapons and armor and to shoe their horses.

Another serious problem which must be settled was England's security while they were absent. Most of the able-bodied men would go to France with the King, which meant that someone must be appointed in each county who would, in the event of an attack, raise, train, and arm what extra men could be found to augment the Queen's forces. Beacon fires were laid along the coast, to be lighted if the enemy approached and landed, and King John and the remaining French prisoners were moved to Somerton Castle, where they were placed under close guard.

Isabel, who actually had no desire to leave the scene of such intense activity, promised her father that she would remain at court until his return; she was at the Queen's side when the King and the princes set out early in October.

The journey was made more swiftly than usual and a courier brought home a letter saying that the English forces had reached the other side of the Channel on the twenty-eighth day of that same month. But after that the word of their progress reached the Queen with the customary maddening slowness. When it came, it was dispiriting: King Edward's own army, which was so numerous as to be a problem itself, was being added to daily by the large bands of Free Companies who, were, by now, more than willing to pledge their swords to England for their keep and a share in the loot. Unfortunately, the countryside over which they were traveling at the rate of about three leagues a day was already picked clean.

Another discouraging factor was the weather. It rained, he wrote his wife and daughters, every day. And not just showers. This, like the rain that fell in England just before the plague, descended from the heavens in sheets, hour after hour, day after day, soaking everything—the men, their horses, their tents, their food, their supply wagons.

"There is never a long enough interval to dry anything," Philippa read in one of her husband's letters. "We splash along, over muddy roads, through what seems to be a deserted, nay, an abandoned, countryside. In a day or so we will reach Rheims, and if no one offers us battle there I shall make camp and remain until the skies clear."

That was in late November. In January they were still at Rheims, and Edward, growing more impatient every minute, finally decided to march on Paris. Again their progress was unquestioned and unimpeded, but when they encamped at Châtillon, perhaps five kilometers from the city walls, the Dauphin hastily ordered the burning of St. Germain, St. Marcel, and Notre-Dame-des-Champs.

But, although King Edward sent his heralds to the Dauphin with a formal challenge, he refused to meet the English in open battle. And so the weeks passed, and the winter was at last over. It was April, and Sir Walter Manny, in the fore of the army as always, grew tired of inaction and led his men up to the gates of Paris itself, only to find that the French prince had forbidden his knights, now as eager to fight as were the English, to pass the barriers.

Sir Walter returned to his monarch at Châtillon and reported that the streets in the areas just outside the once rich and prosperous city were deserted and overgrown with grass and weeds; the houses were in ruins, many of them having been put to the torch, and the people had fled, leaving nothing of value behind them.

King Edward listened and called in his marshals.

"We might settle in for a long siege," he said when they,

too, had heard Sir Walter's news, "but I think we might be better advised to take our weary and hungry army to Brétagne for a few months, to rest and refresh them and ourselves. If we replenish our supplies there we can return and force the Dauphin to fight or accept our terms."

As everyone wanted to see the last of damp and dreary Châtillon, they agreed. And, after informing the French that they would be back later to take the city, they turned south. When they reached Chartres, on Easter Sunday, they were overtaken by a small band of negotiators who brought to King Edward the Dauphin's peace terms. The Pope, it seemed, had been urging him to make peace and he was also thoroughly alarmed by now at the size and power of the English forces.

Edward, enraged by the Dauphin's delaying tactics, made his answer.

"I will agree to nothing," he told the heralds, "but the unconditional acknowledgement that I am the rightful King of France."

The Duke of Lancaster leaned forward and whispered in his cousin's ear, suggesting that it might be wise to be a little more moderate in his demands.

"You have heard me!" Edward shouted, after glaring angrily at Lancaster. "Go!" The heralds bowed, shrugged slightly, and obeyed.

The weather was fair on that Easter Sunday, and while the King was occupied with the French negotiators, his men enjoyed a rest in the warm sun. But they awakened the following morning to find a heavy mist settling down and the temperature falling rapidly. This, however, did not daunt His Majesty, who had roused early and was giving his orders shortly after dawn: strike camp! And so again the tents were folded, again the horses were hitched to the baggage wagons, again the King, the noblemen and the thousands of soldiers set out on their travels, leaving Chartres behind.

Their progress was even slower than usual; the fog, instead of lifting, grew steadily worse. Still they plodded on, seeing little but their own feet, and the hours dragged away. One league was behind them at last, two leagues. . . .

The sky, which they glimpsed for a moment through a patch in the mist, had turned an ominous black; it began to

hail, small stones at first, then larger and larger until it
seemed as if the heavens were falling on them in huge, icy
pieces. The temperature suddenly dropped away below freez-
ing and a knight rode to the King's side with the word that
their men were dying in their saddles.

A great clap of thunder rent the air, lightning flashed and
crackled. Horses screamed and dropped in their tracks as the
thunderbolts fell, turning the dark sky so bright that King
Edward was able to see for himself that hundreds of his
most loyal knights and thousands of his finest destriers were
being struck down.

Shaking with horror, the King, surrounded by the dead
and the dying, dismounted. He fell to his knees and as another
streak of lightning outlined the towers of Notre Dame de
Chartres, now about three leagues away, he raised his arms
toward that great cathedral and prayed aloud.

"Let this storm cease," he shouted to his God, "and I will
make reasonable terms with France!"

The French had made only one successful raid on the
coast of England during all this time, but it was enough to
frighten Queen Philippa into moving King John into the
Tower of London again and to garrison the castles of Old
Sarum, Marlborough and Pevensey.

For the first time King John was discontented and miserably unhappy; life in the White Tower, where his apartments
were, was dull and uncomfortable, completely unlike the gay
and pleasant days at the Palace of the Savoy. He was tortured, too, by the thought that King Edward might, by now,
have conquered all of France and been acclaimed its rightful
sovereign, and by the realization that he might never return
home again.

May is no month in which to be shut up, especially in
England, when the country is always at its loveliest, and John,
one morning, after pacing restlessly up and down the long
bleak chamber, climbed the steps that led to the unusually
deep window embrasure and stared out of the high window.
The square of green grass below called the Constable's garden, and the only place for a bit of fresh air and exercise,
was much too small to be very tempting, and when he turned
his head and looked the other way it only made matters

worse; he found himself watching the busy water craft plying up and down the Thames and wishing he was on one of them, however small, setting out for France.

Hearing a footstep behind him he turned and saw Nicholas de Beche, the Constable of the Tower, kneeling below the embrasure on which he stood. "Ah, de Beche," John greeted him, waggling his little black beard, "I have been thinking I might ask to walk in your garden this morning. This is no day to remain inside these damp walls."

"I have come to offer you a better change than that, Sire," said de Beche. "Her Majesty wishes me to bring you to Westminster for a private interview. Not even your gentlemen are to know where you are going," and he glanced back at the group of nobles lounging around the card and chess tables set up at the other end of the apartment.

"With pleasure," was King John's answer as he walked briskly down the shallow steps. "Has she news from France for me?"

"I don't know, Sire. Her orders were merely to bring you to the Palace as secretly as possible. May I suggest, Your Grace, that we announce simply that I am inviting you to accompany me on a short expedition up the river?"

As the two men left the White Tower a few minutes later and began strolling toward the wharf, a lackey ran ahead and blew the conch to summon the Constable's barge. They heard the boatman whistle in answer and, by the time they reached the water steps, the barge was ready and waiting. It was a perfect day for a ride on the Thames and the French king enjoyed sitting at ease in the soft spring sunshine, free of the pomp and ceremony that were an inescapable part of his life, even during his imprisonment. He was under guard, there were a half-dozen men-at-arms on the barge with them, but he was, except for them and the bargemen, alone with the Constable; and when they landed at Westminster he and de Beche climbed ashore and strode swiftly past all the sentries and guards there with nothing more than a nod and a wave of the hand.

A page, who was waiting for them in one of the doorways, led them along corridors new to King John and into King Edward's private chapel. "I leave you here, Sire," said de Beche, and turned back.

A little bewildered, John walked farther into the room and heard the door close behind him. He saw, in the dimness, a small group of ladies and gentlemen gathered at the far end of the chapel. As he paused, not sure what was expected of him, the tallest of the men moved away from the others and advanced to meet him.

"Sire!"

"Sire!" They spoke simultaneously, then laughed together.

"My dear Cousin," said John, "what a surprise! I had no idea that you were back in England. De Beche said Her Grace wished to see me—and we were all but smuggled into the Palace. I was beginning to suspect all kinds of dark schemes."

"No, no," replied Edward. "Nothing, I can assure you. The truth of the matter is that the Prince of Wales and I landed at Rye at dawn this very morning, jumped on our fastest horses, and were here with the Queen by three hours after Prime. And as the Dauphin and I seem to have come to terms, at last, I wanted you to hear the news from my own lips, before it is known to anyone else. But come, Sire, and join the others; Ned and I saved our tale for your arrival."

A good storyteller at any time, the English monarch made the most of the events leading up to Black Monday, as the day of the storm was now known, and of the tragic and terrifying holocaust itself. He described the fog, the hail, and the cold and the thunderbolts that between them had killed a thousand of his knights and six thousand of his finest destriers; nor did he spare himself in the telling. He admitted that in his anger and impatience he had made impossible demands, and that God Himself had taken this means to show him how wrong he was.

"I no longer insist on being recognized as King of France," he said. "Instead, I have agreed to accept the full sovereignty of Aquitaine, which means, of course, Guienne, Ponthieu, Calais, and much of the territory surrounding it. Neither you nor I, Cousin," he added, speaking directly to King John, "shall consider ourselves the sovereign of Flanders or of Bretagne. Their fate will be settled later in another discussion."

"And what of me? Am I to be ransomed?"

King Edward nodded. "You are. The sum set was three million golden crowns."

John sighed and waggled his tufty beard. "Will my people

pay such a vast sum for me, I wonder? I have been away from them for so long; many will have forgotten a King called John."

"If your brother and some of your sons will agree to act as hostages—and a reasonable number of noblemen and wealthy citizens of France, too, of course," said Edward, "you shall go home and raise it yourself."

He turned and spoke to Prince Edward, who was standing beside his sister Isabel. "We'll escort His Majesty to Calais, Ned," he said. "You and I and your brothers. And you, too, my love." Smiling, he took the Queen's hand in his. "I have missed you sadly all these long months."

But Philippa shook her head. "No, no, my lord. My travelling days are over. Allow me to remain here at home, if you will, to keep watch over our kingdom." She pressed his hand warmly, however, and smiled back at him. "Take the Princess Royal," she said. "Take Isabel instead."

Chapter 19

The sailing master, his face anxious, bowed low before the King. "I am very sorry, Sire," he said in a quavering voice (he had never actually spoken to Edward before and was greatly in awe of him) "but these squally winds are making it impossible for us to put in at Calais. We have been blown some miles up the coast already and every minute takes us farther off our course."

Isabel, leaning on the ship's rail nearby, looked out over the surging whitecaps and up at the dark clouds scudding across the September sky. The sails over her head were taut and straining at their stays, and the rigging creaked like wild music as the vessel cut through the water. You never knew what the Channel weather would be; some weeks earlier, when her brother Ned and the Duke of Lancaster had escorted King John to Calais, they had made the crossing from Dover in a few hours.

"If the wind remains constant," said her father, "you feel, sir, that we would be wise to put in at Sluys?"

"It's dead ahead, Your Majesty."

"Then take us there. We will spend a night or two at Bruges, and sail back to Calais when the weather is more favorable."

"Bruges," said Isabel thoughtfully as the master bowed off the deck. "I've never been to Bruges."

"No," answered the King, "you have not. When you were a little maid and I took you to your mother at Ghent, we anchored in Sluys harbor and rode there by way of Ardenburgh."

"I remember it very well," said Isabel, smiling. "How could I forget? That sea battle with the French fleet at Helvoetsluys. . . . The other ladies were terrified, but I was only eight and I thought it all fine sport."

"I should never have risked bringing you with me." King

Edward looked rueful, merely thinking of it; he had won a great victory, to be sure, but it was no joke to find the whole French fleet waiting for you when you have only two hundred ships of your own.

"There were so many of them!" Isabel was still picturing her first glimpse of the French ships, drawn up across the mouth of the harbor. "Their masts looked to me like a thick forest. And you sailed right into them, Father."

Edward laughed. "So I did! Well, I was young then."

Isabel was on deck with two of her attendants when the ship tacked up the Reie and sailed under the wooden Minnebrugghe bridge that guarded the entrance into the Minnewater, the busy harbor of Bruges. Once safely inside, she was fascinated by the number of trading ships that crowded Flanders' most important commercial port, and she was quite content to stand and watch as their own craft moved slowly toward a vacant quay. England's royal pennant was attracting a good bit of attention; sailors hung over rails as they passed, calling greetings in many languages, and a loud cheer reached the Princess' ears from an English trader that slipped swiftly by them on its way out.

By the time they were tied up, the news of their arrival had apparently reached the city itself, for a richly garbed group of its most influential citizens was just setting foot on the wharf below them and came hurrying toward the ship. They were on board a few minutes later, making their royal visitors welcome with a great waving of hands and clattering of tongues; but Isabel before long realized that there was a note of apology in the long, flowery speeches. King Edward and the Princess Royal, it seemed, had chosen an awkward moment to surprise and honor Bruges with their presence. The only dwellings suitable for their accommodation were in the midst of an annual cleansing that was the delight of every Flemish housewife and the despair of every man—noble, burgomaster or plain merchant.

Edward, listening sympathetically to their voluble explanations and watching their plump, crimson faces, laughed. Was not his own wife a Fleming? he asked them. Had he not been forced, many and many a time, to vacate castles and palaces while Her Grace turned them upside down? In any case, he assured them, his stay at Bruges would be short; a day or two at the most, while they awaited a fair wind for Calais.

And although he planned to conduct some business with his countrymen who lived here, he would actually find it simpler all around to spend his nights on the ship.

"But is there, perhaps," he went on, drawing Isabel forward, "some religious house nearby where Her Highness and her ladies could rest quietly while I am occupied with my merchants? They are all a little weary of life on board, and Queen Philippa," he added warmly, "has never forgotten the comfort and courtesy shown her by the good brothers of St. Bavon when she lingered in Ghent to present me with our second son, Prince John. I know she would be most happy if our daughter visited one of your convents or abbeys."

"The Princely Beguinage," was the instant reply, and the Flemings, as one man, turned and pointed to the very end of the farthest reach of the Minnewater. It was, they assured the King and the Princess, a delightful little retreat where young maids, without taking any vows, divided their time between prayer and the peaceful task of preparing wool for the weavers of Bruges. "They come from all walks of life," one of the burghers said. "And they are quite free to come and go."

A questioning glance from her father brought a quick response from Isabel.

"If my presence among them will not be a burden," she said smiling at the waiting Flemings, "I would consider it a privilege."

So it was arranged, and, shortly before the bells of Bruges tolled for Evensong, Isabel and two of her ladies climbed down into a small barge. The oarsmen pulled it easily away from the side of the ship and over the smooth surface of the harbor, leaving the crowded quays behind them. The landscape changed; lacy willow trees now edged the shores, swans led their families majestically here and there, and the only sounds that broke the stillness were the soft plashings of their oars and the occasional call of a nightbird. A few minutes later they reached the end of the wide waterway and rowed into a narrow canal; they turned again. In the deepening dusk, Isabel saw a low building on her right, and, blocking their way, an iron portcullis that stretched across the little stream of water.

A hail from their oarsmen brought a dim face to one of the windows. The grill was unlocked and raised, and the

Princess and her ladies helped ashore. There they found the Grande Dame, the head of the establishment, awaiting them. Word of their visit had been sent on ahead, she said, and they were more than welcome at the Beguinage.

"You will find our way of life extremely plain," she warned Isabel. "Even austere. But we will be happy to do what we can to make you comfortable."

The air had turned chill; the Princess was travel-weary, and the one thing she craved with all her heart was a bed that didn't sway, roll or pitch. The Grande Dame took them to a tiny, barely furnished house and left them alone.

Waking out of a dreamless sleep the following morning, Isabel heard her attendants rustling around in the adjoining room, talking very softly together. Unmistakable clinkings and rattlings made her realize how hungry she was, and, disregarding the ceremonious rules that were always part of her rising, she crammed her arms into a robe, shoved her feet into a pair of soft velvet shoes, and hurried in to join her companions.

Sunshine was streaming in the one window, gleaming on a pitcher of fresh milk; a crisp loaf, a bowl of butter, and a comb of amber honey were set out on a small table. There was no meat, cheese, ale, or wine.

Lady Norris waved a deprecating hand at it all. "One of the little Beguines brought everything you see here, Your Grace. There will be meat at dinner, she said."

Isabel twinkled, tossed back her uncombed hair, and reached for a hunk of the crusty bread. "It's the most delicious-looking meal I've seen in many a day," she said. "Come, ladies. Sit down with me—I'm almost starved."

When the Princess, an hour or so later, strolled out into the little enclosure, having left her ladies to pass the time as best they could, she took a deep breath of sheer joy. Never in her life, she decided, had she been in such a peaceful place. A ring of small, whitewashed buildings encircled a spread of tree-shaded lawn, broken only by a few narrow paths. The houses, and she was to learn that each Beguine had her own dwelling, had been built at different times during the preceding hundred years, and varied a little in style although they were all more or less the same size. Each one contained everything necessary for the simple life the women led and there was no dining hall or gathering place except the church on the left side of the close.

On this warm and sunny morning the pretty green square was deserted; its inhabitants were, apparently, busy elsewhere. After wandering for a little while under the trees, Isabel walked to the spot on the end of the canal where her barge had tied up the night before. The Grande Dame's house stood on the far side, lapped by almost motionless water; a web of crimson creeper veiled the worn bricks, dropping a flaming leaf from time to time on the surface of the canal, and a pair of regal swans, followed by four almost fully grown cygnets, drifted contentedly on the other side of the lacy iron portcullis.

Without realizing what she was doing, Isabel sighed deeply and buried her face in her hands. The sight of the swans brought back with a most irritating vividness those weak moments in Enguerrand's arms and his insulting remark that followed them. Was she never to put humiliation behind her? And had she so little control over her woman's body that a swan floating on a moat could still set her quivering?

"Is anything wrong, Your Highness?"

Startled by the soft voice behind her, Isabel dropped her hands and whirled around to find the Grande Dame standing nearby and regarding her with an anxious countenance.

Isabel tried to laugh. "No, no, Madame. Nothing. Something reminded me suddenly of an afternoon some time ago when I behaved in a stupid and most unbecoming fashion. I thought I had forgotten...."

Her companion nodded understandingly. "It's odd how the small awkward things we do come back to plague us more often than the memories of more serious misdeeds. My confessor tells me that when this happens I am thinking too much of myself and must pray for true humility." Then, seeing the Princess flush and drop her eyes, she suggested that it might interest her to watch the Beguines at their work.

"Most of them are off on the bank of Minnewater," she said, "but a few prefer to wash the wool just outside our own gates." She talked of other things as they passed through the deep stone arch, out of the great doors, standing open this morning, and paused on the small stone bridge that spanned the canal, flowing under their feet like a moat.

It widened here and several large and lacy trees, just beginning to shed their leaves, shaded the far bank. There, clustered like a flock of black birds on the still vividly green grass, sat seven or eight young Beguines, chattering together as they rinsed the matted wool in the water.

"They seem so happy, so contented," murmured Isabel, turning to smile at their superior.

'And so they are," was her reply. "Oh, we have our small upsets and differences, but for the most part our days follow each other in peace and tranquility. What order will you join, Your Grace?"

Isabel looked astonished. "What order? But I have no thought of such a thing, Madame. Why do you ask? Had you heard that I would?"

Now it was the Grande Dame's turn to flush. "No, I have heard nothing. Forgive me, Your Highness. I merely assumed that it was your intention. A Princess, in good health and unwed. . . ."

"Of course," Isabel hastened to set her at her ease again. "I forget, you see, how unusual my situation must seem to others. I shan't bother you with my history, but there were some deep hurts in it that were only in part my fault; and my father, who is unusually kind and understanding, gave me permission long ago to arrange my own future." She paused, and looked down into the deep water swirling under the bridge. Then, sighing a little, she went on. "I chose to remain single, as you see. But as I have no vocation, no true desire to retreat, I shall continue to live in the world."

"If that is really so," said the Grande Dame slowly, "I wonder if His Majesty is being truly kind in letting you have your way? To live out your life alone and barren, my dear child, is a denial of God's great purpose—and a very foolish waste. Whatever your past holds in wounded feelings—and I do know some of your story. Your Grace—you gain nothing by keeping those feelings alive. A child in your arms would erase all that."

"I must confess that I have longed for children," Isabel answered. "You are right in much of what you say, Madame. But to have the children would mean a husband, too, and although I have thought sincerely about changing my mind, I shudder away from the prospect of being at the mercy of some vicious foreign prince."

"Can you not trust your father to find you a husband who would be as kind and understanding as he is?"

Isabel laughed grimly. "A king is not as free in these matters as most fathers," she said. "Many considerations enter into what should be a simple business. And how can anyone guess at the true nature of a prince? The husband he chose for my sister Joanna killed his wife, I have heard, and strangled his baseborn brothers with his own hand; he is now known in Castile as Pedro the Cruel.

"And," she continued, "as for *my* first betrothed, your own Count Louis of Flanders, who refused to marry me because he considered himself bound by 'affection and a previous contract' to Margaret of Brabant! I am sure I need not tell you that he threw her into a cold, windowless dungeon and allowed her nothing but bread and water until she died."

The woman beside her bowed her head and made the sign of the Cross. "I know. I know," she admitted. "But he had reasons, Your Grace. Her Highness behaved with unbelievable cruelty to a young peasant girl whom her husband had seduced. Rose Burchard was her name. A lovely maid who had no idea of her lover's high rank. She was about to bear his child when the Lady Margaret discovered what had happened; after giving orders that the girl's nose and lips were to be cut off, she threw her into an unhealthy cell in which, a few days later, poor Rose died."

Isabel had heard this before. It made her sick and only confirmed her horror of the sort of marriage that she had escaped.

"I must say, Madame, that such a story makes me more determined than ever to live and die alone."

The older woman agreed, though with obvious reluctance. "I was thinking only of you, Your Highness," she said, "and of your arid life. I have always thought it wrong that princes should be above the law. . . ."

Calais was the scene of much festivity, and from the moment King Edward's ship anchored in the harbor and he and his daughter joined the Prince of Wales, the Duke of Lancaster, Lionel and the two Johns—John of Gaunt and King John of France—and little Philip, who would return to England but had been allowed by King Edward to accompany his father, there was not a day without its banquet, pageant, or tournament. It was, in fact, such a pleasant interval that everyone was almost sorry when they heard, several weeks later, that the four French princes known in France as the Lords of the Fleur de Lys would, after months of procrastination, reach Calais by the end of October. Many of the other hostages had already joined their sovereign and his captors, and although the list was by no means complete, it began to be a certainty at last that before too long King John would be free and the English party able to return home with their new prisoners.

A day or so after this news reached Calais, Prince Edward sought out his sister in her apartments in the Castle. "Tell your ladies to pack their loveliest gowns," he said, cheerfully. "A letter has just come from Coucy inviting us to visit our friend Enguerrand there."

"Well," said Isabel, her hackles rising, "you may leave me here in Calais. I haven't the faintest desire to go to Coucy— ever—or to see that arrogant young man again. And I don't know why you call him a friend, Ned. Truce or no truce, peace or no peace, he is still our enemy."

"What nonsense!" was Ned's immediate and annoyed retort. "He's always conducted himself as a knight should, and I for one consider his invitation a very natural response to the kindness and courtesy he was shown at our court. And I shall be extremely happy to visit his château, certainly, for I hear it is larger and more beautiful than Windsor Castle."

To Isabel's distress, she discovered that her father agreed. The King refused to listen to her vague reasons for not wanting to go to Coucy, telling her firmly that he had already accepted for her. "De Coucy made it very clear," he said, "that he wished you to accompany me, and as your cousin Lancaster will remain here to see to King John and the others, I shall be happy to have you and my sons at my side."

There being nothing else to do, Isabel gave in with poor grace, riding across the French countryside in what was almost a surly mood. It was impossible, of course, to voice her real objections to the visit; her own behavior had placed her in a position from which she could hardly complain of Enguerrand's. And the stories they had all been hearing about his grave and successful attempts to wipe out the scourge of the Jacquerie had, she knew, made him a hero in everyone's

eyes. Even she had to respect him for the part he had played
at Meaux.

Her first glimpse of his château, a massive fortress with
ten ramparts and four bastions, built out on an eminence at
the western end of the large Coucy holdings, did nothing to
soothe her temper. In fact, as they clattered through the entrance to the principal tower and she saw an angry lion
sculptured in stone over her head, she felt that she might spit
too.

And when Lord de Coucy's High Constable appeared to
help her down from her palfrey and his Chamberlain and
Grand Master of the Household greeted her and King Edward and the princes, leading them to young Enguerrand,
who was waiting for his royal guests in the Salle de Preux,
her resentment deepened. There he stood, smiling cordially at
them all, quite as if he were the king and her father the lord.
Behind him rose a magnificent staircase, more massive and
handsome in its proportions than any she had ever seen at
home, and Isabel, glancing coldly over his head, followed it
with her eyes to several beautiful galleries, broken by a dozen
or more exquisitely carved arches. Again the de Coucy motto
ran through her head: *Je ne suis roi, ne duc, prince, ne comte
aussi. Je suis le Sire de Coucy.*

But her host was greeting her and she forced herself to
smile politely. Her eyes met his, and to her surprise she realized that he was regarding her with what seemed genuine
friendliness. And his voice, when he told her what a privilege
and honor it was to have her at Coucy, sounded truly warm
and welcoming. Isabel, however, who could still hear the con-
descending, mocking tones of his dismissal at the Manor of
the Rose, froze, lifted her lips slightly at their corners, and
stepped back to her father's side.

She was still nurturing her indignation when the Chamberlain led her up the great sweep of stairs, through one of the
lovely arches, and into a sunny, beautifully furnished solar.
There, grouped around a wide carved and gilded bedstead,
curtained in cloth-of-gold and spread with crimson velvet,
were her ladies and chamberwomen, chattering admiringly
about the comforts provided them. Leaping wood fires, piled
high under a pair of white marble chimneypieces, added to
the warmth of the sun, streaming in through the long casement on this fine October day; tall looking glasses gleamed

here and there on the walls, and the stone floor was almost entirely covered with soft fur rugs.

The Princess took little part in the excited talk, but she made no protest over their choice of that evening's costume for her. It was the golden brocade kirtle and côte-hardie she had worn when she and the other members of the royal family had posed for the wall paintings in St. Stephen's Chapel at Westminster, and it was, as she was aware, extremely becoming. A fur-lined mantle, for the evening was already growing chilly enough to make it welcome, waited for her shoulders, and one of her tiring women hunted through her jewel casket for the glittering hair ornaments that matched her delicate, foliated crown, and for the floral buttons to fasten the côte. Her hair, to display the little jeweled ornaments to best advantage, must be looped beside her face in glossy braids instead of being tucked, as usual, into a comfortable caul; it was a tiresome business and, considering her fretful state of mind, one she bore with amazing patience.

Ready at last, she descended to the dining hall. It was evident from the moment she crossed the threshold that she was being conspiciously honored by their young host. King Edward, as was his right, sat in the center of the high table, his chair and canopy fittingly regal, flanked on one side by the Prince of Wales and on the left by Enguerrand de Coucy. Isabel was not surprised to find that she was sitting on de Coucy's other side. Yet when she saw that her chair was almost as tall and gorgeously carved as her father's and that there was a beautiful canopy over it entirely covered with late-blooming sweetly fragrant roses, she recognized it as a pretty and most unusual tribute. Thanking him, her voice cool and her manner distant, she asked herself how he could have the effrontery to behave as if that almost unbelievable incident at the Manor of the Rose had never happened. The slight stiffness in their conversation was brought about by her own short answers to every topic he introduced. His attitude, she could see, was that of one who considered himself an old friend.

Their steps, as they opened the dancing, matched so beautifully that a ripple of admiration ran around the spectators waiting to join them, and Enguerrand, while he moved gracefully around her, making a perfect frame and background for her dainty paces and posturings, continued to smile at her in the warmest, most open fashion.

When the music stopped, he gave her an odd, almost pleading look, and asked her if he might not take her for a short stroll in the long corridor where the air was fresher.

"Thank you, my lord," replied Isabel, her eyes darkening and a deeper rose coloring her cheeks, "but I think not tonight. Just take me back to my father, if you please. I find I have no use for any more of your very helpful lessons in lovemaking."

Although Lord de Coucy tried on more than one occasion after that to have a private word with Isabel, she disregarded all his hints and avoided every trap he set to catch her alone. And she was, in fact, annoyed when, as she and her party were bidding him farewell at the end of their stay, the others moved away, for some reason, and left her by his side.

"You have given us an extremely pleasant visit here at Coucy," she said hurriedly, determined not to remain with him a moment longer than necessary, "and I am very grateful. Thank you for your courtesy and hospitality."

"Please!" Before she could step toward the other ladies, he took her hand and held her. "You must allow me one word, Your Grace. I have been wanting, ever since you arrived, to ask your forgiveness for my unchivalrous and inexcusable behavior when we last met. I can only say that I labored under a misapprehension. . . ."

"A misapprehension?"

"Yes," he went on, speaking as swiftly as he could. "But that does not excuse me. I was a fool . . . a stupid . . . oh, Mother of God, here come your ladies, and I've not yet explained! Let me be your friend. Forgive me. . . ."

There was not time for another word, and his flurried little speech left Isabel completely astonished and honestly puzzled. What did he mean? He had labored under a misapprehension? They were, however, part of a chattering, laughing group from that moment until the time, a few minutes later, that the English party mounted their horses and began to trot out of the square courtyard; but then, as they rode away, Isabel turned in her saddle and looked back.

Enguerrand, who had been watching her intently, gave her

a delighted smile and raised his hand in a little private farewell salute. She found herself wanting to answer it; he looked
so handsome and gay; he had certainly made much of her.
He had, after all, tried to make amends. But the memory of
that moment when ·she had returned his kisses so ardently
and he had rebuffed her—that memory returned in all its
chilling vividness. She swung around again, touching her
palfrey lightly, and moved swiftly after the others, keeping her
head high and her shoulders erect.

Chapter 20

England's trees had lost all their leaves and the countryside was bleak and chill under a late-October sky before King Edward and his daughter sailed from France. They carried with them, however, the memories of many golden days in and around Calais, the most vivid of which was the stirring scene that marked the end of King John's captivity. There had seemed, at first, no end to the delays, the excuses, the procrastinations that held them all in wait; John's brother, the Duke of Orléans, was most reluctant to leave his wife and home, and the two princes, Louis d'Anjou and Jean de Berri, were enjoying life too much at their brother's court to hasten willingly on the errand that would take them to England.

The Dauphin himself was, after all, just a boy of nineteen; Louis and Jean were younger, and Philip, who would return with them as one of the four royal hostages, the youngest of the whole family. They were, of course, the highest-ranking of the twenty-five French noblemen who, with forty-two of France's richest citizens, were to stand security while their king attempted to raise his own ransom money. Many of the older noblemen and burghers were dilatory, making one excuse after another, and it was not too surprising that the young princes followed suit.

When, however, the Lords of the Fleur-de-Lys and most of the others had, at long last, ridden into Calais and submitted themselves to King Edward, he announced that King John need not wait for his freedom until the list was complete. King John answered immediately that he was quite ready to leave the city, and every Englishman who was present at Calais hurried to the Castle to speed him on his way.

The ceremony that followed was very moving. Isabel, standing with the ladies, found her eyes filling with tears as she saw King John enter the Great Hall and make his way to the dais where her father was waiting. John was dressed in the simple woolen robes of a humble pilgrim, a startling contrast to the rich silk and velvet garments worn by the four French princes who followed him up the long aisle; his feet were bare, his head uncovered, and he carried a wooden staff in his hand.

When he reached the platform, he and his kin halted. The trumpets sounded again and now the spectators saw three more pilgrims march into the room, three tall, broad-shouldered, golden-haired young men, also barefoot and carrying staves that matched King John's. They smiled as they strode to the dais, knelt for a moment, then mounted the steps. King Edward smiled back and made room for them at his side.

It was a sight to remember. The two groups faced each other—a king in a pilgrim garb, accompanied by his sons in the handsome robes that befitted their royal rank—and a king in the handsome robes that befitted *his* royal rank, accompanied by his three sons in the woolen habit worn by pilgrims.

King Edward stepped forward and embraced King John, then turned and announced to the assembly that from that moment on King John was free to come and go as he willed.

"Thank you, Cousin," was King John's answer, "if that is so, I will now bid you and my friends farewell. I go on foot to Boulogne, where I shall meet the Dauphin, give thanks at the Cathedral, and then set out for Paris."

The two Kings kissed again, John embraced his brother and three sons and prepared to leave the dais. As he stepped forward, Prince Edward, Prince John and Prince Lionel moved in unison, meeting him face to face. "With your permission, Sire," said the Prince of Wales, "my brothers and I will join you in this pilgrimage and see you safely to Boulogne."

The room had been hushed until this moment, but when the four men descended from the platform, their bare feet visible under their gray mantles, the one dark head leading the three blond ones out of the hall, a great cheer rang out, mounting in waves until the little group reached the open arch at the far end and disappeared from sight. Isabel was crying openly and she was not the only one; the ladies around her were weeping and many of the noblemen near her had wet cheeks.

Isabel's last kiss, before going on board the ship that was to take her and her father home, was for the favorite uncle, Henry, Duke of Lancaster. His task, as usual, was a thankless one; he must remain in Calais until every last hostage had submitted himself and then he would accompany them all on their voyage to England. He looked very tired, and older than ever before; so tired, in fact, that Isabel asked him if he were ill.

"No, no," he replied, smiling at her. "A little weary, perhaps. But I must confess that I find this added delay here at Calais most galling. I promised my little Blanche that both John and I would be with her for Christmas and I'm beginning to wonder if I will be able to keep my pledge. Not that she will care too much if I am absent. When a lass is heavy with her first child, it is her husband she wants at her side, not her father! I urged John to remember this and not to be drawn into any knight-errantry after he and Ned and Lionel leave King John at Boulogne. I just wish I could be sure he won't. . . ."

"He told me that he can't wait to be home with Blanche," Isabel assured her uncle. "It was Ned's idea to make this pilgrimage with King John, and our John said he would have begged off and returned with me if it had been possible. Unfortunately, our father was most enthusiastic and insisted that all three must take part in the—well," Isabel laughed and dropped her voice, "I won't call it *mummery*, Uncle, because it was most stirring, and a pilgrimage is a sacred and beautiful thing. It made me weep at the time, but I couldn't help thinking afterwards that it was probably a most enjoyable chore for our lads. . . ."

"They are all young enough to like any form of disguise," said Henry. "And it is just that spirit that worries me. The three of them together may fall into gallant adventures and never come home!"

"Nonsense! John meant every word he said. And he's no weakling, Uncle. Ned can't sway him an inch when he's made up his mind about something. Lionel, yes; anyone can persuade Lionel into anything. But not John. However . . . just in case something unforeseen does delay you and John, *I* could spend Christmas with Blanche. Would that ease your mind a little, dear lord? I am not Blanche's father or husband, but I could comfort her for your absence and try to keep her amused. ..."

"Bless you!" Henry kissed his niece again. "Do, my child, and, with any luck at all, John and I will join you there and have a merry Yuletide at Leicester!"

The old castle at Leicester, built soon after 1066, had been the favorite home of Simon de Montfort; now, almost three hundred years later, it was loved also by the Lady Blanche and her father, to whom it belonged. Blanche had been born there, and although she had spent little of her childhood in the great rambling house, she had always insisted that it was the perfect place to celebrate Christmas.

Before many days had passed everyone in the party was more than willing to agree with her, and the young chatelaine listened contentedly to their words of praise. She had worked hard to win them, having spent long hours in planning the pretty decorations and delicious food, the games, the music for the dancing. ...

Mass on Christmas Eve was, by her particular request, to be celebrated in the Chapel of the Church of the Newarke, added to the castle by her father some years before to house a thorn from Christ's crown which he had, himself, brought back from the Crusades in 1331. They gathered there shortly before midnight, and although they were in a very giddy mood after some hours spent in romping country games, the quiet of the dim candlelit chapel had its inevitable sobering effect. The wind, which had whined around the castle earlier, had dropped; it was beginning to snow, and as they waited for the bells to peal out midnight, they could hear it flicking softly against the high windows.

Isabel, between her brother Ned and the elderly duke, saw that John was holding Blanche's hand in his and was smiling fondly down into her small, serene face. A little apart from the others were Jack and the Princess Mary, their shoulders touching and their hands, too, clasped together.

A wave of loneliness swept over her. There were moments for her like this every Christmas, but somehow she had never before felt quite so alone as she did now—cold, sad, shut out of the natural warmth of being one of a pair, as God meant man and woman to be. The thought of Enguerrand de Coucy disturbed her suddenly, as it occasionally still did, and she remembered to her annoyance that last warm smile he had given her as she rode away from his château. Rejecting the memory was of no use for the words of the Grande Dame of Bruges followed it—"to live and die barren and unwed is a denial of God's great purpose; a foolish waste!"

Her eyes strayed to Blanche's swollen body. "A child in your arms would erase your hurts. . . ." She could hear it all again; the gentle lady's arguments, she admitted to herself, had been in the background of her thoughts ever since the day they had been uttered. She had loved Bernard d'Albret. He was dead. Had all love died with him?

Edward suddenly interrupted her musing. He, apparently, was watching the happy faces around them and must be feeling lonely, too. But instead of pitying him, Isabel was exasperated. If she had had her way, she would now be wed to Bernard and raising a family; Ned, on the other hand, was single by his own insistence. After that great victory at Poitiers, their parents would, Isabel was sure, have allowed him the widest possible choice in selecting a bride; in fact, his popularity with their people was such that even a love match with some young English noblewoman would have been hailed by all, perhaps actually preferred to a union with a foreign princess.

However, when the bells rang out and the priest moved to the altar to begin the Mass, their eyes met and Isabel's indignation faded. The brother and sister smiled at each other, and as Ned bent down to whisper "Merry Christmas!" in her ear, she kissed him swiftly on the cheek. Who was she, with a heart full of secret memories, to question his actions?

As always in England, the week following Christmas was filled with delightful revelry, and the young members of the household were in the midst of their preparations for that gayest of all the holiday nights when a second royal messenger rode into the castle courtyard and asked to be taken to Prince Edward. He was, as it happened, in the princesses' solar, where, between gusts of laughter, Isabel and Mary were doing their best to disguise him as a woman for a part he had promised to play that evening. It was not easy, no garment in any of their boxes would stretch across his wide shoulders or come within many inches of the ground, and the tiring

women, who had just brought in a roll of uncut silk, hoping
to fashion something in the short time before the feast would
begin, looked impatiently at the messenger as the Prince
freed his hands to break his father's seal.

"It's a summons to court," he told his sisters, having un-
rolled the piece of parchment and scanned the first few sen-
tences. "Parliament will meet to ratify the peace with France
within the next se'e'night and His Grace wishes his sons, the
Princess Royal, and the Duke of Lancaster to be present at a
special ceremony in Westminster Abbey. So," he looked
around, smiling, "tonight will, indeed, mark the end of our
good times here."

"What about me?" asked Princess Mary. "Need I break
my promise to remain here with Blanche until the baby is
born?"

"No," replied Ned, reading a little further, "not if Blanche
still wants your company."

"I shan't even ask her," was Mary's immediate response.
"With John and her father gone—for some weeks, I presume—I know she will feel happier with one of us at her
side. I'd rather stay, anyway."

While she was speaking, her brother finishing the last bit of
the letter, uttered a sudden, startled oath and a strange expression spread over his face.

"What is it, Ned?" Isabel's voice was sharp. She had never
seen the Prince look quite like that before.

"It's poor Tom Holland," he said, avoiding her eyes.
"Word has come from Normandy that he fell seriously ill in
Rouen and died just before the New Year. Little Jeanette
and the children are on their way home now."

Chapter 21

"Well," said the Queen irritably, "I can only hope that my Lady Joan will take her mourning serious enough to remain in seclusion for a reasonable period of time. Not that I expect it. Knowing her as we do, I would not be surprised to see her here at court any day now."

"Then she and the children are safely home . . . back in Kent?"

Philippa nodded. "We had a letter just yesterday, Isabel. Read it, if you want to. It's full of references to her 'poor fatherless infants.' A hint to Ned, I suppose, to rush down there and play the attentive godfather." Sighing again, for about the tenth time, Isabel thought, her mother stared into space and tapped the arm of her chair with restless fingers. "I have always regretted that we didn't *make* Ned marry long ago! I knew then it was a mistake, but my lord is too soft-hearted, too willing to allow you children to have your own way. I argued and argued, but it made no difference; and now here you are, you and Ned, both single still—and for what? Can you tell me, Bel, in all honesty, that you are truly content?"

Rather uneasily, the Princess Royal tried to reassure her. Of course she was content. What more could she ask than the privilege of spending the rest of her life in England, having her own household to retire to when she wished, coming to court at other times and being with her parents and the other members of the family?

"If you had forced me to wed some foreign prince," she went on, "I would be far away now and might never see you again in this life. I could actually go from the altar to the grave without having even one glimpse of you and my father! Would that make me happy? Especially if my husband had treated me as Louis de Mâle treated his Princess Margaret—the lady he insisted on wedding! Or poisoned me, as

Pedro of Castile might well have poisoned Joanna, had she lived to marry him."

"Nonsense!" Philippa's fingers drummed faster and her face was drawn into an annoyed frown. "Margaret was greatly responsible for her own fate—and Pedro's wife may have driven him to dispose of her. If he did. Everyone whispers poison when a king or queen dies suddenly."

She was quiet for a moment or two and Isabel, who was never at ease when her unmarried state was under discussion, tried to think of some way to change the subject. To her great relief, Queen Philippa did it herself.

"What I really summoned you for this morning," she said, her face resuming its usually placid expression, "was to discuss our robes for the ceremony at the Abbey. As you will be in close attendance on me, and I believe the plan is that you will walk directly behind me in the procession and sit beside me when we reach the Sacrarium, I have been thinking that we might wear similar costumes."

"I believe I brought home the very thing we need," replied Isabel immediately. "Let me send for it, dear lady. Two rolls of brocade that a merchant sold me when I was still in Calais. They came from Lyons, he said, where they weave the most beautiful fabrics in France. One is gold with silver flowers and the other is the same pattern reversed; I see you in the gold, and myself in the silver. . . ."

The great Abbey was crowded. England's peers, in their richest robes, were already in their places, their jewels glinting in the candlelight. Although a few brave rays of January sun strove to penetrate the high windows, it was a feeble effort at best and fell far short of the vast center aisle. Cold and damp even on the hottest day of summer, Westminster Abbey was, on this particular morning, miserably chill; the stone floor was icy under the nobles' pointed shoes, and the brightly embroidered standards and altar cloths were stirring noticeably in the drafts that crept in from all sides.

Isabel, following her mother slowly between the rows of lords, and ladies, saw that most of their noses, under their gleaming coronets, were red, and she caught herself, once or twice, almost crossing her eyes in an attempt to see if her nose too was red. She was desperately cold, but not, perhaps, as cold as they were, for she had a sable plastron hanging from her shoulders and a matching sable-lined mantle that spread out almost to the floor. Nor had she been sitting in this tomblike place for hours, as they had been, waiting for the ceremony to begin.

King Edward, his sons, the Lords of the Fleur de Lys, and the highest-ranking noblemen in the band of the French hostages were walking ahead of them, and by the time the ladies neared the Sacrarium the men were all standing in their places on the right side of the enclosure. At the High Altar, facing the congregation, waited the Archbishop of Canterbury, a handsome sight in amice, chasuble, maniple, stole, and alb, all embroidered in glittering gold and silver.

Queen Philippa moved to the left and paused in front of her chair. A moment later the Lady Royal was at her side; the other ladies took their allotted positions and a hush fell over the Abbey. Isabel, glancing across the wide aisle, caught her brother Ned's eye and had to guard her expression as she saw him wink at her. Then, as the trumpets pealed, he and his father moved forward, leading the four Princes of France to the Altar.

When the solemn Mass was over, the six men returned to their former positions; John and Lionel joined them, and, for a long silent moment King Edward and his sons turned and faced the band of hostages. Again the trumpets blared. There was another short hush. Then, with a great shout, the English peers surged toward the Sacrarium.

Before they reached the Altar, twelve bishops intercepted them at a designated point and led them the rest of the way. Six of the holy men were carrying large golden crosses, the others bore aloft brightly burning flares; these they held high over the Eucharist and missal as the nobles fell to their knees.

"On the Sacred Body of our Lord," chanted the peers as one man, "we swear to keep the peace and concord sworn this day by the King of England and the King of France!"

The solemn ceremony was over at last, and Isabel, aware that she and the Queen must step from their places at just the right time, kept a careful eye on the King and her brothers as they led the French princes down the aisle; then she watched the rest of the hostages as they marched past her, walking two by two. Many of their faces were known to her; most of them had reached Calais before she and her father had set out for home, but there were also strangers in the long procession, the noblemen who had been more reluctant to answer their ruler's call.

Each, in turn, made a careful obeisance to England's Queen and Lady Royal, and Isabel, as she acknowledged a particularly graceful bow, found herself suddenly face to face with Enguerrand de Coucy. He smiled at her, and she realized that she was flushing deeply. He was gone a second later, and she took a deep, startled breath. What was my Lord de Coucy doing here in England with the French hostages? His name had never been mentioned as one of those who were to stand security for King John; he had certainly said nothing himself when they were at Coucy, he was not on the list sent for her father's final approval. She knew. She had looked at that list herself.

For some reason, and her ladies thought her mad to travel at this time of year, Isabel now decided that she had been neglecting her duties as chatelaine and must visit each and every one of her manors and castles. This she proceeded to do, moving from one to another as swiftly as the winter weather and bad roads allowed, remaining only long enough to see that all was in good order. She was weary when she reached Carisbrooke Castle, her final destination, and so were her lords and ladies, so weary, in fact, that they hoped she would settle down and spend the rest of the winter there in peace and quiet.

To their disgust she announced, after a few comfortable days, that the sight of the bare hills and gray Solent was depressing. "Pack our boxes," she told the chamberwomen. "I shall return to court."

But if she thought to find the King and Queen in the midst of a continuous round of gay festivities, she was very much mistaken. Nor were they in the cheerful spirits that almost always made their court a pleasant place to be. The root of the trouble, she soon discovered, was that they were having an extremely difficult time with the Lords of the Fleur de Lys; the four French princes were by no means such polite guests as King John and James de Bourbon had been.

John, after his first somber mood had passed, had proved easy to entertain and simple to please, enjoying his life in England so much that he was able to curb his impatience over the length of his captivity. His brother and his three sons, however, now were a different matter, and both King Edward and Queen Philippa soon began to curse the day that they had made the exchange.

Nothing was right, it seemed. One French nobleman after another was sent from the Palace of the Savoy, where they were quartered, to air complaints and make demands. Of these messengers, only Enguerrand de Coucy, already familiar with English ways and on friendly terms with the King, was able to discuss the problem at Westminster without annoying everyone there. Several acrimonious interviews with other members of the French party, in which they presented their grievances so arrogantly that King Edward completely lost his temper, led him to the decision that he would, in the future, listen to the Lord de Coucy and no one else.

This eased the situation but did not cure it. Nothing could do that, for the basic difficulty lay in the differing temperaments of the four French princes and the constant friction between them. They had always quarreled and as they were, for the first time in years, now thrown constantly together, that friction grew worse and worse. At home they had separate establishments; here they must dine, hunt, find all their amusements in each other's company.

King John's brother, the Duke of Orléans, with the Dauphin, had escaped capture at Poitiers (or, as some of his countrymen said, had run away) and had later been frightened into seeking sanctuary at Meaux where de Coucy, Foix, and the Captal de Buch rescued him from the Jacquerie. He was a small, delicate man, more interested in the fit of his elaborately embroidered tunics and jupons and in the length of the points of his shoes than in the rough sports that took most of the other hostages into the tilt yard and adjacent countryside. His nephew Jean, the young Duke de Berri, was cast in the same mold, and the two of them passed most of their days in the Duke of Lancaster's quiet book room, criticizing (adversely) the books, manuscripts, and paintings they found there.

Louis d'Anjou and little Philippe, on the other hand, jeered at their uncle and brother Jean for what they considered their effeminate tastes, and stressed their own masculinity by complaining about the quality of the hunting and hawking provided for them. The truth of the matter, of course, was that all four wanted to go home. Orléans missed his family, Jean his long hours alone; Louis was miserable because he resented his position as hostage and Philippe, his father's favorite, longed to be back at his side.

There was little, in these circumstances, that King Edward could do to satisfy them all. With de Coucy's help, however, he tried. He allowed Louis and Philippe to ride to Windsor whenever they wished, knowing that they would find superb country for hawking and more deer than they could kill; he arranged tournaments for them, at Westminster and at Windsor, and he urged his own sons to help amuse these aggravating royal prisoners.

At de Coucy's suggestion, Queen Philippa sent Jean Froissart, her new secretary, over to the Savoy with her most interesting books, and she also offered his services to the two studious French princes.

Young Froissart, deep in writing a detailed history of the times, had already completed a careful account of the battle of Poitiers, but when he found himself with the Duke of Orléans he could not resist asking the Prince a few embarrassing questions about his part in that disastrous route; as a result the Queen's secretary was promptly returned to her with a curt, almost rude, note of dismissal. Froissart did not, however, reveal the reason and the Queen, shocked and annoyed, told him he need never return to the Savoy.

"Keep those disagreeable creatures out of my sight as much as possible," she said to her husband. "I want nothing to do with them. I have never before allowed myself to hate the French, not even when you and our sons faced them in battle. But now I do, my lord, and the sooner we are quit of them the happier I will be."

"I confess I feel very much as you do," replied the King. "Although I think we must at least try to remember that all Frenchmen are not so irritating. John was a delightful guest, and so are many of his other hostages."

"If they are," she replied grimly, "we have little opportunity to find it out. The princes make everything so unpleasant that I can't enjoy any banquet or festivity when they are present."

Isabel, listening, had to admit that her mother was right. She, too, had found the interchange of visits with the French prisoners extremely disappointing. Only Enguerrand de

Coucy had shown her any particular attention, and although she knew that her father considered him very helpful, Isabel was still wary of him.

She danced with him, when he asked her, and met his conversational sallies exactly halfway, keeping her response to his overtures carefully friendly. But on the few occasions when she thought he might be trying to step over the line she drew between them, her instant chill was quite enough to discourage him, and, not wanting any further complications between them, she never allowed him to catch her alone.

"Well, de Coucy," said King Edward, looking up from the papers in front of him, "what now, my lord?"

Enguerrand, seeing the expression on his face, burst out laughing. "Something so ridiculous, Sire, that I hasten to tell you that it is *not* my real reason for coming to you today. Our newest problem, if you can believe me, is to find a satisfactory barber for their Highnesses! Their own man is ill, and no one else, they say, is skillful enough to shave their royal faces."

"Mother of God!" said His Majesty. "I would certainly hope, de Coucy, that you would *not* waste my time with such nonsense."

"I won't, Sire. I mentioned it only because I thought it would amuse you—my own manservant had promised me to devote himself to their needs, patiently, humbly!" Again he laughed, and smoothed his own clean chin with his long fingers. "I suppose I shall learn to handle a razor myself, or grow a beard. But seriously, Sire, I am not here now to have talk about their foolish little demands, but to see if we may not find a way to spare you any further annoyance."

"Do that, my lord, and I will be grateful to you all the rest of my life."

"There is no doubt," Enguerrand began a little hesitantly, "that all our efforts have completely failed to please their Highnesses. They grow more quarrelsome and discontented every day; I see how they try your temper, Sire, and I watch them stirring up turmoil all around them. If King John were here, he, and he alone, might be able to keep them in order. I confess to you that no one else can. I'm afraid they enjoy making trouble, that it has become their favorite way of passing the time here in England."

"You speak very frankly about your princes, sir."

"Only because I think I should, Your Majesty. And because I have a suggestion to make, a drastic but possible way out of this increasingly distasteful situation."

"Tell me then." Edward was curt but interested.

"Send them to Calais and let them live in the castle there. They will still be England's prisoners but you will not be bothered any longer by their ill tempers and bad manners. Then those of us who remain here can, with your permission, restore the harmony that used to be between us."

"It's a most tempting thought, de Coucy," admitted the King, "but could I trust them so near home? The peace between our countries is a delicate thing, you know, and it would be disastrous to endanger it in any way.

De Coucy stiffened. "Because I have dared to criticize their Graces' behavior, Sire, you must not think that I will not challenge anyone who suggests that a Prince of France would break his royal word!"

"Then I certainly will *not* suggest it, de Coucy. Believe me!" The King laughed and put a friendly hand on the young Frenchman's shoulder. "But I do promise to discuss this idea of yours with my Council, sir. I like it. I like it very much indeed."

Later, when the King was closeted with his wife and the Princess Royal, he revealed to them what de Coucy had said. "I summoned the Council," he went on, "and they agree, but with certain conditions. Each one of the four princes must give me his personal word of honor not to leave Calais, and before they sail for France, we must be provided with a fresh group of hostages to substitute for them here in England. Orléans and de Coucy are drawing up a list now. De Coucy, by the way, has been invaluable to me over all this business, absolutely invaluable."

Queen Philippa sniffed. "If any Frenchman *can* be invaluable!"

"Perhaps he's been useful to me because he is partly English, my dear. Don't forget that his grandmother was Christina de Baliol. Why not comfort yourself with the thought that it's his English blood coming out? As a matter of fact," he added thoughtfully, "I'm thinking of proving my gratitude by restoring the Baliol estates to him, the properties that he would have inherited had we not been at war all these years. Those manors in Cumberland, Yorkshire, Lancashire and Westmoreland—it's a very tidy holding and might ensure his future friendship. He and his family were our fierce enemies before we took King John, as you know, but his visits here seem to have softened his attitude and, between you and me, Philippa, I would do almost anything to ensure his continuing friendship."

"Are you certain, de Coucy," asked the King, "that Guy de Blois and the Comte de St. Pol would be willing to act as hostages?"

"I'm almost sure they would, Sire. Theirs were the first names that His Grace and I put on the list."

"Then, my lords," His Majesty handed the parchment across the table to his advisers, "I believe we have no more questions. If you are satisfied, I am. A good day's work, and I thank you for all your help."

The Council began to bow their way out but as Enguerrand moved to follow them the King put out his hand and asked him to remain for a moment. The Prince of Wales, who had taken part in the discussion, lingered too, and chatted with the young Frenchman until the chamber was empty. Then he fell silent and listened while his father expressed his gratitude and informed de Coucy that he was, as of that day, restoring to him his English inheritance.

After Enguerrand had thanked the King the Prince had a last word with his father, then followed de Coucy into the corridor. He linked arms with him, and they strolled away together.

"Why not leave these troublesome compatriots of yours," Edward suggested, "and visit me for a few days? My house is a poor thing compared with your château at Coucy, my lord, but we pass the time pleasantly there. I am doubly in your debt, you know—both for our hospitality last year and for helping us all out of this difficult situation."

"You have no need to thank me, Your Highness!" Enguerrand's eyes laughed into Edward's as he spoke. "Life is so unpleasant for me at the Savoy Palace that I had my own peace of mind to consider, too, you know. In any case, I will be delighted to join you and your friends, Delighted!"

"Good. Come when you wish and stay as long as you find

us amusing. And tell me, is there any particular way in which I may serve you?"

Enguerrand hesitated, looked warily at the Prince, hesitated a moment longer, then nodded.

"There is something, Your Highness. . . . But you may think me presumptuous. I might lose your friendship by asking for such a thing. . . ."

"Nonsense, de Coucy! Try me!"

After glancing around to see that no one was within hearing distance, Enguerrand, still a little dubious of the wisdom of what he was about to do, moved closer to the Prince and spoke softly.

"My problem, Your Grace, is this. . . ."

Chapter 22

"Your Highness!"

Isabel, strolling alone through the quiet corridor at her brother Edward's new house on Fish Street, paused and glanced back over her shoulder. Had someone called her? As she hesitated, she heard the mysterious voice, a little louder this time.

"If you please, Your Highness!"

It seemed to come from a doorway on the far side of the long passageway, a doorway that led, Isabel knew, into a small anteroom rarely used by the Prince or his guests. But who could be in there today? Ned and all the other gentlemen were, despite the raw February wind, galloping around the countryside—and, in any case, who would be so rude as to hail her in this odd manner? Had someone been taken ill, or needed help?

Seeing no lackey to send into the small chamber, Isabel, after another moment's hesitation, moved closer to the doorway and peered inside. A hand reached out and drew her over the threshold, then closed the door firmly behind her.

"At last!" said Enguerrand de Coucy, still holding her fingers in his. "I finally catch you alone! But how difficult you have made it for me—to what lengths I was driven to arrange this meeting, and the hours I have spent lurking here and there in the shadows!"

Startled and angered at being trapped in such a fashion into another awkward encounter with this young man whose behavior was so inexplicable, whose attitude was so changeable and indefensible, Isabel's one thought was to extricate herself immediately. Drawing herself up with all the dignity she could muster, she jerked her hand free, turned toward the door and gave him a quelling frown.

"As you know only too well, my lord," she said coldly, reaching out to open it, "I have no desire to see you alone. You have, I'm afraid, wasted all those hours of lurking. What

possible business could you have with me that made such
trouble necessary?"

Enguerrand laughed, and before she could make another
move or say another word he was beside her, encircling her
firmly in one arm and tipping up her chin with his free hand.
When she tried to pull away, he held her even tighter and
forced her head back until she met his dark eyes.

"What business have I with you?" he asked her softly,
watching the color come and go in her face. "Why, our
lessons in lovemaking, of course! You have not forgotten, *ma
petite?*"

Her cheeks a deep scarlet, and her heart pounding with anger and—yet—excitement, Isabel, struggling violently,
opened her mouth to scream for help. At that moment, he
bent his head and his lips closed over hers, stifling the scream
at birth. His arm turned to steel, drawing her so close that
she could feel the pounding of his heart, as he kissed her over
and over again. In an unbelievably short time Isabel succumbed, as she had before. Caught by her own swiftly ardent
response, she was hardly aware of the moment when she
ceased fighting him and began to cling to him, answering his
kisses with a mounting hunger.

"Ah!" The sound, deep in Enguerrand's throat, was almost
a growl.

His hold slackened and his lips gentled. Then, with a long,
trembling sigh, he raised his head, smiled down into her
dazed eyes, and led her slowly to a wide, window seat.

"And so," he said softly, "we begin once more. But with a
difference, *m'amie*, but with such a difference! See?" He held
out his hand and let her watch it shake. "This time I kneel at
your feet. This time I am your slave."

Isabel, her head whirling, heard little of what he was
saying. As she began to regain her composure she knew only
that her senses had betrayed her again and that she had,
despite all her resolutions, for a second time acted the wanton with this man. Shame flooded her and she buried her flaming face in her hands.

"No, no—you still do not see!" Enguerrand pulled her
hands gently away and drew her back into his arms. *"Je vous
aime,"* he whispered, resting his cheek tenderly on hers. *"Je
vous aime!"*

For a rapturous moment Isabel believed him. Then, with

chilling suddenness, the shadow of all her old hurts fell over her and she knew that she must, somehow, protect herself from a fresh rebuff.

She rose. "A m-most instructive lesson," she said, in a voice that sounded odd even to her own ears. "I—thank you, my lord!"

"No!" He rose, too, as if bewildered. "Please. . . ."

It was too late. Without another word she swept him a deep curtsey and was gone.

Disturbed and shaken, she ran to her brother's bedchamber and dismissed his bodyservant, telling him that she wanted to see the Prince privately on his return. Then she waited, pacing the floor, until Ned hurried in, his face burned by the wind and his clothes spotted with mud.

He paused, startled, when he saw her there.

"What is it, Bel?" he asked, looking frightened. "Bad news from Westminster? Our lady mother. . . ."

"No," she replied immediately, "of course not, Ned. Nothing like that. I've come to ask your protection, that's all—to tell you that either Enguerrand de Coucy leaves this house immediately or I will! Twice he's forced himself on me under the shelter of your hospitality—once at the Manor of the Rose, and now, today, while you were out with our friends. Be—because I am unwed, he makes me the victim of his light lovemaking—I suppose a Frenchwoman of my age would welcome it—but I do not, Ned, and I will not be exposed to his vile advances again!"

"Phew!" The Prince whistled softly and shook his head. "How could de Coucy bungle matters so? I would have guessed him a skillful lover, not an awkward one. Am I supposed to do his wooing for him, I wonder?"

"What *do* you mean, Ned?"

"Here, come and sit down. I can't talk to you while you pace around like a restless cat. You have everything wrong, Bel! De Coucy is in love with you and wants to wed you.

"I know the whole story, you see," Ned went on. "That unfortunate business at the Manor of the Rose came about because he thought Bernard d'Albret had died for love of you, that you'd jilted the poor lad. He thought to even the score a little, although he tells me he was actually a bit in love with you himself at the time; and, when he discovered his mistake, he asked us all to Coucy so that he could make his peace and begin his courtship. That failing dismally, he changed places with one of the French hostages and came to England to try again. You, my girl, are his only reason for being here; you, and nothing else. But didn't he tell you all this himself? He said that was why he wanted to see you alone."

Isabel flushed. "I—we—I ran away before he could say very much to me. I thought he was bent on insulting me." Then, as a new idea occurred to her, she raised her head and gave the Prince a look of surprise. "But why did you help him, Ned? Even if I were willing to wed Enguerrand, which I am not, our father would never agree."

"Why not? De Coucy's holdings make him one of France's most powerful noblemen, Bel, and he has quite a bit of royal blood in his veins, as well. His grandmother was the granddaughter of the Emperor of Austria, you know, and a Mary de Coucy was the mother of King Alexander III of Scotland. Then there's the de Baliol kinship—that ties him into the royal family of Scotland again; if our father was willing to let you wed d'Albret, I don't see how he could object to de Coucy!" He chuckled, "as a matter of fact," he went on, "I had to remind Enguerrand of all this, too. *He* was afraid that his suit would not be acceptable to our father, even though he knows England wants his friendship. I couldn't promise him, of course, but I think I was a bit reassuring."

Isabel was silent for a moment. "Well," she said, finally, "perhaps I should have listened to his explanation. Then I could have made it clear that I have no intention of marrying anyone and asked him not to bother me again. Perhaps you would tell him, Ned? I'm rather awkwardly placed in the matter now, and you seem to be his confidante. Tell him I made up my mind years ago to remain single and that nothing will make me change it."

"I will do nothing of the kind. Tell him yourself, Bel, if you're determined to be such a fool."

Isabel returned to her apartments at Westminster without discussing the matter any further and took her usual place at court. But her ladies, before long, began watching her with puzzled eyes and, when she was not within earshot, discussing what they considered her very odd behavior. She was moody, a rare state for Isabel—gentle one moment and sharp the next—but it was her forgetfulness that caused most comment. One day, to everyone's, bewilderment, she suggested that they all go riding and then wandered off alone while they awaited her in the palace courtyard, muffled up in their warmest garments and perched on their restless horses. And although she was embarrassed and shamefaced when they gave her up at last, sent their mounts back to the stables, and found her in her own chamber, dreaming over the fire, she had little to offer in explanation.

At first they thought she might be ill and hiding it from everyone, but they soon decided that that was impossible. Her Grace had never looked more blooming or more lovely.

"If she were ill," said one of them wisely, "she wouldn't spend so much time deciding which gown to wear. I saw her tiring woman carrying in seven or eight yesterday before she finally chose one for the banquet at the Savoy Palace. No, it must be love, ladies. Everything points to it."

But who was the man? The only one who could have shed any light on that question was the Prince of Wales and he, having received a call from an old friend at about this time, a call that sent him into Kent to see his "little Jeannette," was suddenly so involved in a problem of his own that he had no interest in anything else.

His errand, and Edward had ridden South extremely reluctantly, was chiefly to urge his favorite cousin to accept the hand of one of his good friends, Sir Bernard de Brocas; and although this was not, perhaps, the man the Prince would have chosen for Joan, and her future been his to settle, de Brocas was a loyal Gascon. Since he had risked his life and fortune to fight beside Edward at Poitiers, the Prince could not say no when he was asked to intercede on his behalf.

Joan, however, had no hesitation in saying no. She said it not once, but several times, and finally told Ned that she had no intention of ever marrying again. "Your friend from Gascony is not the only one I have refused since I came home," she informed him, dropping her eyes. "I mean it, Ned. I shall never wed again."

"Of course you will, Jeannette! You are much too lovely to live your life as a widow. Why do you say such a foolish thing?"

Joan raised her head and let him see that her eyes were filled with tears. They slipped, one by one, down the cheeks, leaving small tracks in the heavy pink powder. "Don't press me, Cousin," she whispered, "don't press me. All I may tell you is that you waste your time in coming here on behalf of any friend, however gallant or charming. I—I desire none of them. And I never shall. Do not ask me why!"

Taking her plump hand in his, Edward leaned over her and tried to comfort her. "There, there, Jeannette. There, there! Don't cry, please don't cry!"

But the tears fell faster. He drew her a little closer and she sobbed, sighed and lifted her drenched blue eyes to his for a long minute, before she dropped them again and turned away. "It's all so hopeless," she whispered, as if to herself. "So hopeless. I must live and die—alone!"

"Why?" asked the Prince, suddenly and sharply. "Why, Jeanette?"

"Because," she answered slowly, "because I have given my heart to the most gallant, chivalrous knight in the whole world. I cannot marry him, but I shall love him forever. Forever!"

Her words and the tone of her voice brought the hot blood to Edward's face. What was she trying to say?

"Jeannette!" he said, hoarsely, "tell me! You *must* tell me. Who is it? Who is it?"

She gave a half sob, shook her gilt head, looked through her lashes and said nothing.

"Who is the man?" It was a demand, not a question.

There was a caught breath—then, finally, the reply.

"You, my lord, you. Are you blind, Ned? Who else could it be? Who else has it ever been?"

"Ah!" The Prince of Wales caught her in his arms. "At last! I never dared to hope!" He kissed her over and over, then he released her and stood up, his face serious.

"From this moment," he said, raising his right hand in the air, "you belong to me. I swear to God, my lady, that as long as I live no other woman but you shall be my wife!"

But as the Prince was soon to discover, it was much easier to make vows than to carry them out. King Edward, almost too loving and easy-going in the past, turned surprisingly stubborn; he was in fact, so angered by Prince Edward's announcement of his betrothal to the Lady Joan that he refused even to consider it.

"I should have listened to your mother," he said grimly, controlling his temper with obvious difficulty. "She warned me of this, often. But, to tell you the truth, my son, I did not believe you could be such a fool!"

"My lord!" Stung, Ned tried to protest. His father, really angry, bade him be silent.

"No, Ned, I mean it. A fool! For who but a fool would pledge himself to a woman older than himself, a woman who had known two men at least, and is his own cousin to boot! And have you forgotten that you are godfather to two of her children? If the Pope is willing to grant a dispensation to free you of the most important impediment, he may well say that there is also a spiritual tie between you that the Church cannot overlook."

"I'm sorry to displease you, Your Grace," replied Ned stiffly, "but I tell you again that I shall wed Joan or no one. I made a solemn vow in her presence."

"And you are the Prince of Wales—the heir to my throne and crown! Your wife, someday, will sit in your mother's place. Is that woman fit to be Queen of England?"

That was not the end of a stormy interview, but nothing that the King found to say moved his son from his determination to have his cousin. Too angry at last to argue any more, his Majesty dismissed him, ordering him to return when he was in a reasonable frame of mind. Prince Edward did return, but the second discussion proved both of them as stubborn as before.

Queen Philippa added her voice, pleading with her son to reconsider.

"I regret giving you pain, my lady," he replied, "but I have vowed that I will marry the Lady Joan and marry her I shall."

"His Holiness will never grant the necessary dispensations."

"I'm confident he will. Try him, try him!"

Although Isabel was secretly as distressed as were her parents when she first learned of her brother's betrothal, his buoyant step, and the new note of deep content in his voice soon persuaded her that she should at least try to forget her own objections to his bride. She succeeded so well that by the

time he came to tell her that a courier was on his way to
Rome with letters to the Pope, she was able to kiss him
warmly and wish him happiness.

"Happy?" His blue eyes were shining. "I never knew the
meaning of happiness, Bel, until now. Just imagine, after all
these years of loving and wanting Jeanette and thinking she
could never be mine! And now I know that she was miserable, too—lonely, unhappy—wanting *me!*"

Isabel found herself doubting his last statement but she
kept her thoughts to herself. "I suppose," she said, "that ex-
cessively important business will take you into Kent from
now on and keep you there?"

Edward laughed. "It would," he replied, "if my lady were
not planning to come up to town. Not to court," he added
swiftly. "That would be most unwise, as I'm sure you'll agree.
No, she will move into a house near Charing Cross that she
inherited from her father and live quietly there until we are
free to marry. It's in bad repair, I'm afraid, but she doesn't
care about that."

"When she is settled," said Isabel, "you must take me to
her, Ned. We will be sisters now, you know, not just
cousins."

Edward looked so grateful that Isabel was almost ashamed
of her secret reluctance. She resolved to meet Joan at least
half way.

"You will be her first guest, Bel," he promised her, delightedly, then proceeded to describe his love's charms in detail
and at tedious length. His sister bore the ordeal with remark-
able patience. When he finished at last, he startled her by demanding to know what she had done about Enguerrand de
Coucy.

"Nothing," she replied, flushing. "We haven't met since
that day at your home, Ned."

"I suppose he's been occupied with this complicated business of sending the princes back to Calais," Edward said. "I
haven't seen him myself, now that I think of it. Of course,"
he smiled contentedly, "I've been busy, too."

Joan was waiting for Isabel and Ned in a small, comfortable chamber that overlooked a stretch of wintry garden.
There was a bright fire burning on the hearth, and after the
two women had kissed each other Joan turned to her be-

trothed, asked him to draw two chairs closer to it for her and
Isabel, then suggested that he seek out his godsons. "They
miss the country," she said "and we are hard put to it to
keep them amused."

"I wanted to see you alone for a few minutes," Joan said
as the door closed behind him. "Ned tells me that you are
our friend in this difficult matter of our betrothal and I want
to thank you, Isabel. You have no idea how much this means
to us both."

Their eyes met, and Isabel saw that Joan was apparently
quite sincere. She saw, too, that her cousin looked much
younger; her face was softer, and the bitter lines around her
mouth had eased.

"Make Ned happy," Isabel responded impulsively. "Make
him happy and everyone who loves him will stand your
friend!"

"I hope so." Joan's voice dragged a little. "I hope so.
Surely Her Grace will make me welcome when she sees that
we do love each other and that we would be miserable apart?
She must know, you must all know that I've adored Ned
since we were children and that I thought it quite hopeless. I
never dared dream that we could wed, Bel, and that's why I
made such a mess of everything! Tom—Will—I didn't care
which one I married, and I let them both make love to me
because I thought it might help me forget Ned. Well, it did,
for a while; then it just made it all worse."

Seeing Isabel flinch, she hastened to explain further. "That
sounds horrible, doesn't it? But when you can't have the man
you love, Bel, it is much too easy, believe me, to do horrible
things!"

As she talked, she led Isabel to the chairs waiting by the
fire. "Be comfortable," she said, when they were seated, "because I have something to tell you. Its—another horrible
thing I did, and I'm bitterly ashamed of it now. So ashamed
that I haven't even confessed it to Ned. But I *must* tell you,
Isabel, and then . . . but first. . . ."

She hesitated and the Princess, feeling nothing but distaste
at the prospect of listening to some further romantic adventure that was weighing on her cousin's conscience, tried to
protest.

"No, no," Joan went on hurriedly. "This *is* your business,
Isabel. It concerns you and I won't feel easy until I've told

you about it. Ned says Lord de Coucy is courting you and
. . . and so I think you should know that I was the one who
told him about you and Bernard d'Albret. I thought you had
jilted him—after all, everybody thought so—and I was angry
and jealous and miserable that night and I hated everyone. It
was the evening after the great tournament—St. George's
Day—the day Ned wore my favor, if you remember. Tom
was jealous and had just been giving me a great scold; I
wanted to hurt him and show him. . . . Oh, I don't know
now! Everything was horrible, and when I watched you dancing with Enguerrand, and saw him eating you up with his
eyes, I began to hate you, too, for being free to enjoy yourself. I wanted to spoil it. . . ."

And now, Isabel said to herself, controlling her anger with
difficulty, you think it wise to confess this to me before I
hear it from Enguerrand and, in turn, tell it all to Ned. "Forget about it, Joan," curtly she added aloud. "My Lord de
Coucy knows the true story now and, in any case, it makes
no difference. I have no desire to marry him or anyone else."

"I hope you don't really mean that. Ned wants you to
change your mind, certainly, and I agree with him. He likes
Enguerrand very much and thinks he would make you happy.
However, I thank you for listening to me, Isabel, and for letting me set things right. I hated myself afterwards."

She rose and moved to the door. "Sit there, if you will,
while I see what Ned is doing with the boys."

The moment she was gone Isabel left her chair, too, and
walked over to the window. As she stared down into the garden, a bleak sight in late March, she struggled to regain her
composure. Of course everyone assumed that she had jilted
Bernard; she had wanted them to think so. But she could
imagine only too vividly the way Joan told the story to Enguerrand, whispering and insinuating and exaggerating,
smiling maliciously while she painted the picture of the cruel
princess breaking the heart of the lowly lord. And she could
see Enguerrand listening, deciding perhaps at that very moment to humble her. Had he then told Joan what he was
going to do, and did they gloat over the scheme together? Or
was it Joan's suggestion, and my Lord de Coucy merely her
willing tool?

The more she thought of it the angrier Isabel grew; angry
and a little ill. It was so demeaning, so unpleasant, so disgust-

ing, Joan and Enguerrand. Joan, that other night so long ago, swaying drunkenly on Enguerrand's arm, and Euguerrand smiling, his face stained with her lip-rouge!

The door behind her opened and Isabel swung around, expecting Joan and the Prince. But it was Enguerrand.

Realizing that her brother had, once again, placed her in an impossible situation, Isabel, too shaken to speak, simply froze; her one coherent thought was that she must conceal her agitation, behave in a fitting manner, and dismiss this smiling young man at the first possible moment.

If he had come to propose marriage, he should. This time, she told herself, as the young Frenchman bent over her hand, she would hear him out. Then, when he had finished, she would put an end to this persecution, this futile, disturbing pursuit.

Enguerrand, his face showing nothing but concern, raised his head and looked at her. "Your fingers are like ice, Your Highness," he said, "and you are shaking. Why are you standing here, in this vile draft? See, the hangings are blowing far out into the room. Come to the fire, *m'amie,* come to the fire this instant!" And keeping her hand firmly in his, he drew her back to the two chairs and pressed her into one.

"May I?" He indicated the other.

Isabel, only too glad to be sitting down, nodded assent. He poked at the fire, first, smiling over his shoulder at her when it burst into a bright blaze. "Ah," he said, "that's better! And now, may I, at last, tell you all that is in my heart? Will you try to forget the unforgivable part I played in the Prince's garden and believe me when I assure you that I came here to England again for love of you and for no other reason? That my home seemed suddenly empty after you left it, so empty that I wanted to ride after you and bring you back? And that I felt all this even though you never let me see you smile when you visited me at Coucy—even though you were punishing me?

"It was not an easy business to arrange," he continued, "this second journey to your country; nor has it been easy to seek you out. And I find it difficult now to find the right words—I have never asked a lady to marry me and it does not come smoothly to my tongue . . ."

Enguerrand glanced from Isabel's downcast eyes to the blazing fire and sighed. "You still make it difficult for me," he said, ruefully. "Especially as I am not a patient man. I think I must love you very much indeed, to allow the days to turn into months without a word of encouragement, to suffer one rebuff after another and yet not lose hope of winning you. Yes, my lady, I must love you very much indeed! And I think that I must also know, deep in my heart, that you love me too."

"Then you know something, my lord, that I do not." Isabel spoke at last, but she kept her head lowered and her hands folded in her lap. "And I assure you that I have no desire to wed you or any other man. Nor do I wish to prolong what can only be a painful interview for us both. You do me great honor, my lord, but spare me, please; I would rather hear nothing more on this—subject."

She struggled to appear composed, to answer Enguerrand's plea as calmly and civily as possible. But she refused to meet his eyes. In the silence that fell between them he studied first the bent head, then the hands; her lips, he could see, were trembling. And so were her fingers, although she was holding them so tightly that her knuckles showed white.

Smiling to himself he waited, saying nothing. She rose to her feet and indicated the door. "You will understand, I am sure, if I ask you to leave me. I think that we have nothing further to say to each other."

"Oh? Do you honestly think that, my lady?" Enguerrand laughed and snatched her into his arms; but as he bent down to kiss her Isabel tore herself free and slapped him across the face.

"How dare you!" she cried, her cheeks flaming with the anger that had been simmering ever since her talk with Joan. "How dare you?"

"Bon!" he said, reaching for her again. "Bon! You come alive at last, *m'amie*. Those stiff, cold words meant nothing. *Nothing!* When I hold you in my arms we both know the truth. We love each other. Come, let me show you again . . ."

But she eluded him and ran to the door. She threw it open and stood beside it. "Go, my lord," she said. "Go, before I summon one of the lackeys."

King Edward tossed the last of the letters from France down on the table and gave de Coucy an exasperated smile. "Well, my lord," he said, "I suppose we will be rid of their

Highnesses some day. I forget, always, how long and tedious a task it is to arrange for hostages."

Enguerrand shrugged. "Does it matter so much now, Sire? The very fact that they will leave England sometime in the near future has made them much more content. Their complaints are nothing these days and life is almost pleasant for the rest of us."

"That, certainly, is something to be thankful for," replied the King, rising. He looked around the Council chamber and saw that the little group of nobleman who were awaiting their turn to bring him their problems were deep in conversation. "Follow me into my Privy Chamber, if you will," he said to Enguerrand. "I would like a few minutes alone with you."

Once inside he turned and told Enguerrand to close the door behind him.

"I brought you here, my lord," he began immediately, "to ask you a few questions."

"Anything, Sire. I will be happy to answer anything you ask me, at any time."

"I hope you meant that, de Coucy, because I want the truth from you. No evasions, please, or half truths."

"On my honor, Your Majesty."

The two men stood facing each other, the King watching the young Frenchman intently. Enguerrand was calm, his eyes tranquil. If he had any reason to dread the King's questions there was no hint of it in his face.

"Then I shall waste no time, sir; my day is a busy one. But His Highness, the Prince of Wales, told me something a few hours ago that has distressed me and I will not be easy until I have discussed it with you. He said, my lord, that you wish to wed the Princess Royal and that you have been courting her behind my back, without my permission. He confessed to me, also, that he has meddled in your behalf, making it possible for you to see my daughter alone."

"Prince Edward's story is quite true, Sire. I love the Lady Isabel with all my heart and my one hope of happiness is to win her for my wife."

"And, after the kindness and favor I have shown you, you considered it honorable to woo her secretly? I'm afraid I do not, de Coucy."

"Please, Your Majesty," replied Enguerrand earnestly, "let

me explain. It was Her Grace's unusual situation that prevented me from coming to you long ago. Nothing else, I assure
you! Knowing that she has remained single by choice, and
with your permission, I thought it only sensible to be quite
sure that the lady wished to marry me before approaching
you. If I was mistaken, Sire, forgive me. I had no desire, believe me, to conduct my courtship in such a surreptitious
manner. You can have no idea of the problems and difficulties! One word from her and I would have been on my knees
to you."

"Then that word has not been spoken?"

"No," replied Enguerrand through tightly clenched teeth.
"It has not!"

"I thought not. In fact, de Coucy, my son tells me that the
Lady Royal rejected your suit and that you have refused to
accept her answer. Surely you must realize that when her
Grace says no she means no."

Enguerrand shook his head. "Many a lady says no with every intention of saying yes later, and I must confess that the
Princess Isabel has her own reasons for strewing my path
with obstacles. I angered her once, some time ago, and I suspect she is still punishing me. And I need not tell you, Sire,
that the lady is stubborn and used to having her way. My
wooing, in the circumstances, has not been easy."

"As I can well imagine. But despite all this, sir, you
haven't given up hope of winning her heart?"

"I still hope to win her *hand*. I have her heart! She loves
me," Enguerrand said violently. "I *know* she loves me! It's
forcing her to admit it that has me almost at my wits' end."

His voice was so savage that King Edward laughed. "If
this is true, de Coucy, you're an odd pair of lovers. But if it
is not, my lord, I tell you now that I will not have Her Highness harassed by your pursuit; much as I would like to see
her wed, and—yes—wed to you. . . ." Pausing, he met Enguerrand's suddenly startled glance. "Yes," he repeated.
"Even though I would be happy to welcome you as a son, de
Coucy, I will not have my daughter's peace of mind broken
again."

"Believe me, Sire," said Enguerrand swiftly, his face alight,
"Her Grace's happiness is as dear to me as it is to you. Trust
me, please, if you will, and allow me to win her in my own
way."

Suddenly kneeling, he took Edward's hand and raised it to his lips.

"Thank you, Sire," he said, "for saying you would welcome me as a son. I pray God that I will someday have that great honor and privilege."

The Duke of Lancaster hurried into the Queen's Presence Chamber, smiling broadly. Most of the Royal family was gathered there on this particular evening, for Her Majesty was not feeling very well; a recurring internal disorder due, no doubt, to her long years of childbearing, had begun to sap her strength, and there were times now when she was miserable to remain in the crowded, noisy Dining Hall. Her discomfort, however, did not prevent her from enjoying a few hours with her husband, children, and good friends, and she answered Lancaster's smile with one of her own.

"You have news, Cousin," she said. "Come here and share it with us."

"It's my little Blanche," he replied. "Delivered safely of a fine healthy daughter! The Prince is overjoyed. I had a letter from him an hour ago. He sends his greetings to you all and says he will return to court when his lady is stronger and can spare him."

After the first burst of delighted chatter had died, the Duke announced, "I shall set out for Leicester at once, and I'm hoping that I need not go alone." Smiling at Isabel, he handed her a letter. "Both Blanche and your brother John, my lady, are eager to have you accompany me, as you may read for yourself."

While Isabel was hastily scanning the letter, her father watched her face. It occured to him that her decision might be an indication of whether or not she was genuinely interested in Enguerrand de Coucy; to leave the court now and remain away from some weeks, would be the obvious way to prove to her suitor that she had meant her rejection. It would only be an indication, of course, nothing more, and he wondered, as he had wondered so often recently, whether he should not take a hand in the matter himself and insist on knowing what was in Isabel's mind.

"I should like nothing better than to go with you, dear Uncle," he heard the Princess say, as she returned the letter to the Duke, "but not while my lady mother is ailing. A little later, perhaps."

"Don't remain here on my account," Queen Philippa protested. "I shall be myself again soon, daughter."

But Isabel continued to refuse, despite her mother's reassurance and Duke Henry's urging. The King, still watching her, said nothing.

A few minutes later he took his cousin aside and asked him, quietly, whether he had heard the rumor that a few cases of the plague had been reported here and there around the countryside. "I heard it myself," the King continued, "only today. I've told no one but you, Henry; perhaps I should move the court to Windsor."

"No word of it has reached me," Lancaster replied. "These rumors spring up every year at this time, of course, but it could very well be true. God help us if it is. Keep me informed, Cousin, if you will; I should reach Leicester in a few days and we will all want to know where you are."

In his eagerness to hold his daughter and new grandchild in his arms, the Duke rose at daylight and set out for Leicester Castle, covering many miles before he halted for the night. He was weary, and his night's selep had left him still tired, but he thought nothing of that and continued on his way. Even when he was assailed, late that afternoon, with a burning thirst and a high fever, he did not remember King Edward's words about the plague nor realize that these might be the first symptoms of the dread disease. He did settle into an inn, however, and sent a messenger back to the Savoy to fetch his private physician. It was too late. By the time the doctor reached his master's side, the Duke was far gone; the black spots had appeared and there was nothing to be done.

The court, still at Westminster, were enjoying an hour or two of dancing. Queen Philippa, her indisposition in abeyance, had opened the evening's pleasure by treading a measure with the King and was now on her throne watching the others. Her husband, she saw, was in a far corner, chatting with a group of visitors from across the Channel; when he joined her, a few minutes later, it was apparent that he had something to tell her.

He had. "You will not be happy about this," he said, in her

ear, "but the word around the Vatican is that His Holiness is disposed to grant Ned his dispensation. Not for a few months, probably, as Tom Holland has only been dead since last December, but just as soon as the Pope thinks it fitting."

"Oh, dear!" Philippa sighed. "Well, we've done all we can, Edward. We must accept it, I suppose. Shall you tell Ned?"

"If we don't he'll hear it from others," answered the King gloomily. "My only reason for hesitating is my doubt about Joan's discretion. I don't want her considering herself the Princess of Wales until the papers are signed."

Philippa agreed and, turning to the Lady Royal, who had just returned to her seat, she told her what had happened.

"Ned will be happy," was Isabel's only comment.

The thought of Joan took her back to her last distressing interview with Enguerrand. She had been trying to put it out of her mind, but every word that he had said kept returning to her, every inflection of his voice, the touch of his hand. . . . Why couldn't she forget? She heard her own stiff rejection of his suit; no wonder Enguerrand had laughed at her. She must have sounded like a child repeating her lesson. If she had only answered him as she intended, easily, lightly, in a manner that would have made him aware, at last, that he and his pleas had left her untouched.

The worst of it was that her anger had begun to ebb soon after she left Joan's house, and in retrospect it was difficult to justify it. Those infuriating pictures of Joan and Enguerrand sniggering together, planning to wound her, seemed unlikely. Joan might be guilty of such behavior, but would Enguerrand? Was it not the thought of them together that had roused her fury? Plain jealousy, and the knowledge that Joan still considered my Lord de Coucy one of her conquests and she, Isabel, his second choice? And that resounding slap—hadn't it really been meant for Joan?

The Queen, leaning over to ask Isabel why she was so quiet, saw a courier in Lancaster livery approach the dais with a letter in his hand.

A moment later she heard her husband give an anguished groan.

"Not my good Henry," he said. "Anyone but Henry!"

Isabel leaned forward to discover what was wrong, but he was already on his feet, signalling the musicians to stop playing. The ladies and gentlemen, halted in the midst of a lively measure, turned startled faces to the royal dais. Philippa, frightened, rose too and stood beside her King.

"The saddest possible news has just reached me, my lords and ladies." His Majesty spoke in a sober voice, but it was loud enough to reach to the farthest corner of the hall. "The best friend that England and I have ever had, His Grace the Duke of Lancaster, died a few hours ago of the plague. I know you will all wish to retire, as do the Queen and I, to mourn in private and to pray for our dear cousin's soul."

The room, after a hushed moment, began to empty, and Isabel, so stunned by her father's announcement that she hardly knew what she was doing, hurried through the quiet crowds, ran down the hall, and turned toward the staircase to her own apartments.

But she was blinded by tears and found herself stumbling as she began to climb. The shock of her uncle's death brought back all the agony of those days in Loremo. She was alone. Alone. Bernard was dead. How many more of those dear to her heart would die *this* time?

A steadying hand, clasping her elbow, slowed her wild plunge up the winding staircase. A familiar voice warned her to watch her footing.

"Allow me to guide you, *ma petite*," his voice said, "or you will surely fall."

Too distraught to ask herself why she found his presence so comforting, Isabel disregarded the astonished faces of the guards standing against the corridor walls and let Enguerrand lead her into her privy chamber.

It was empty. Her ladies were apparently still below and her chamber women, not expecting their mistress here for some hours yet, were having their own late meal in the Palace kitchens.

Without a word Isabel turned and melted into Enguerrand's arms, sobbing uncontrollably. He held her a moment, murmuring gentle, understanding things into her dark hair. Then, when at last she began to speak, pouring out all her terrifying memories, describing the horrible scenes she had witnessed, her fears, her dread of more such nightmares to come, he held her even closer and told her something she had not known. He had suffered as she had; his young widowed mother had died of the plague too, during that ghastly year, and he had watched her go.

"From that moment," Enguerrand said, "I felt alone—deserted. My uncle tried to take my father's place, but he was much older and spent most of his time at Court. Ours had been—an unusually warm and loving family. My mother and father were more than husband and wife, or even lovers. They were good companions, such good companions that I have spent the long years without them hoping to find someone who would make me as happy as my father was." He dropped his arms and looked down at her ruefully. "I need not tell you that I thought, for a while, I had discovered that 'good companion.' But you made it all too clear, when we last met, how wrong I was. And a woman, of course, always means what she says. A woman does not change her mind."

For once in her life Isabel could find nothing to say. Neither could she pull her eyes away from his, until she saw in them the familiar mocking glint, the look that had so often enraged her.

Instead of anger, however, a delicious warmth melted her stubborn doubts and fears. With Enguerrand, life would be exciting. Strangely enough, her life would also be safe, for never would she be able to dominate him or twist him around her finger; he knew her too well! And that was as it should be. They would walk together, man and wife, my lord and my lady. Not, thank God, 'the Lady Royal and her husband.'

She tossed her head and laughed. "*This* woman can change her mind, Enguerrand," she said softly. "But remember I may not always mean *exactly* what I say. . . ."

More SIGNET Historical Romances
You'll Want to Read

☐ **FAR FLIES THE EAGLE by Evelyn Anthony.** Against the rich, sweeping tapestry of czarist Russia under Alexander I, a turbulent novel of lust, intrigue and forbidden love. . . . (#Y5751—$1.25)

☐ **VICTORIA AND ALBERT by Evelyn Anthony.** From the bestselling author of **The Poellenberg Inheritance** comes the passionate novel of a queen in love. The intimate love story of Queen Victoria and her German cousin, Albert of Saxe-Coburg, the sensitive, talented, much resented man who held the only key to the heart of England's great queen. (#Y5738—$1.25)

☐ **WITH ALL MY HEART by Margaret Campbell Barnes.** The tender love story of Catherine of Braganza and Charles II during England's radiant Restoration. "All the makings of a bang-up historical novel."—The New York Times (#Y5387—$1.25)

☐ **REBEL PRINCESS by Evelyn Anthony.** Set against the glittering background of eighteenth century czarist Russia, this is the enthralling story of Catherine the Great in her fight to power; with her loves and intrigues, and her final dramatic defeat of the power-crazed and deadly Romanovs. (#Y5801—$1.25)

☐ **MARY OF CARISBROOKE by Margaret Campbell Barnes.** When Cavalier King Charles fled from Oliver Cromwell to the lovely Isle of Wight, Mary of Carisbrooke Castle found herself caught up in all the intrigues, dangers, and passions, which surrounded this king whom she longed to serve. . . . (#Y5658—$1.25)